Z1N1: The Zombie Pandemic

2012 Was Just the Beginning

MITCHELL LAYNE COOK

Outskirts Press, Inc.
Denver, Colorado

ZINI: The Zombie Pandemic
2012 Was Just the Beginning
All Rights Reserved.
Copyright © 2010 Mitchell Layne Cook
v2.0

Outskirts Press, Inc.
http://www.outskirtspress.com

ISBN: 978-1-4327-5923-0

Outskirts Press and the "OP" logo are trademarks belonging to Outskirts Press, Inc.

PRINTED IN THE UNITED STATES OF AMERICA

For my Dad, the Chief – your boys miss you so very much…

Chapter 1

• *November 28, 2013: Thursday, 1:30 AM - an old barn five miles south of Hot Springs, Arkansas...*

Earlier in the evening, Kara Mayer had positioned herself in the hayloft on the second floor of the cranky old barn. She hid just out of sight from any unwanted onlookers; however, she had a clear view of the entire field below her. For more than an hour, she had sat in the same uncomfortable position watching for trouble. As she stood up to stretch her complaining legs, she saw the first sign of movement on the edges of the old man's property. What she saw wasn't new to her; she quickly knelt down behind the bales of hay for cover as she steadied her weapon.

"We've got incoming!" Kara yelled as the sound of her high-caliber rifle fire fractured the nighttime silence.

An obese, lustrous moon hovered silently in the starless sky. With its theater-like spotlight, the celestial body illuminated the somber world below. The frigid November night reluctantly shared its morbid secret; ten shambling horrors marched erratically towards the barn. Their moans and scraping feet in the leaves sent a chill down Kara's spine. The creatures moved in awkward unison and soon clawed their way through the old wooden fence on the very edges of the farm. She knew it was only a matter of moments before the undead reached her position.

Kara's battle cry from the loft above was all Nikki's subconscious mind needed to rouse her from her restless slumber and set her into motion. She was accustomed to limited and sporadic sleep cycles with her fourteen-month old baby. Eyes wide open and adrenaline pumping, she knew this situation would play itself out like it had done many times before during the past few months. Soon their hiding spot would be infested with zombies.

Had anyone told her at the beginning of the year that she would be trapped in some violent, bloody video game or that she would be fighting against the undead in some tacky, B-movie horror show - she would have laughed at the mere ludicrous suggestion. Now, the thought wasn't so funny. Not only was she surviving the worst human disaster since biblical times, she was also trying to raise a baby! Nikki prayed silently for the strength and wisdom to make it safely through another night.

"James, grab what you can!" Corbin yelled. "We've got to get out of here!"

Megan began crying, startled by Corbin's gruff voice. Nikki tightly wrapped the frightened baby in her favorite pink blanket as she comforted the child; the thundering gunfire from above only exacerbated the situation. The small, rag-tag group of survivors had been found by a ravenous mob of the living dead and time was quickly running out.

"Nikki, will you please shut that damn kid up?!" James snarled menacingly.

Nikki ignored the old war vet's callousness; she had to focus on preparing for the escape. She securely fastened Megan into the baby carrier ensuring the warm, pink blanket completely covered her child.

After the baby was situated, Nikki focused on her gear. The young mother struggled momentarily, but eventually coerced the zipper of her leather jacket to its midway point. She slung her cumbersome backpack over her shoulders fastening the clasps for additional support. She dragged the ill-fitting cap down over her ears; the dark blue hat was as ugly as sin, but it kept her head quite warm.

She double-checked that her 9mm pistol was tucked into the back of her waistband. The cold steel pressed into the small of her back felt *"normal"*, whatever that word meant these days. Most of her life she had shied away from guns of any sort, even more so recently since her mom's suicide at the onset of the zombie infestation. Now it seemed that the firearm was almost as necessary to her survival as food and oxygen. She had quickly overcome her lifelong disdain for weapons, doing whatever was necessary to keep her and her family safe.

The not-so-agile interlopers persistently closed the distance between the felled fence behind them and the old barn in front of them. The creatures wobbled from side-to-side in their now familiar jerky fashion. The parcel of land between the living dead and the barn was short and flat; an almost empty canvass. In one Picasso-esque brushstroke, the moon once again lit the murky landscape, strange and grotesque shadows danced ominously about the farmland. With the use of her rifle's scope, Kara could easily make out the tattered clothes and warped expressions on the creature's faces.

The sniper fired three more times; most of her initial barrage did only minor damage to the wave of oncoming creatures steadily approaching the barn. Her aim was a bit off due to the fact that the cold night air had numbed her fingers. She lay the rifle down momentarily on top of a bale of hay next to her as she briskly rubbed her hands together. Once feeling returned to her hands, she raised the rifle again to her shoulder. The undead were now within two hundred feet of the barn.

Kara adjusted her scope for closer range shooting. The first and nearest zombie she targeted, Kara imagined that when the creature was human, it must have been a doctor or maybe a scientist based on the dingy, blood-stained white coat it was wearing. While she could not make out the first name, she could easily read the white stenciled letters of the last name on the dark blue nametag: "*Clark*".

She fired her rifle again.

The creature's head exploded violently spraying gory bits of flesh and bone in every conceivable direction. The malignant monster's nametag simultaneously somersaulted off of its chest high into the air. In slow motion, the zombie's body collapsed to the ground almost at the exact moment that the nametag made its perfect-ten landing. The oblivious monsters lumbered ever forward towards the barn unaware or uncaring that one of theirs was now truly dead.

Another shot from the high-powered rifle violently kneecapped a second creature. It fell on its stomach and Kara could see that this zombie was wearing a dark blue biker's jacket and a red, glossy helmet. She watched momentarily as the one-legged zombie biker began pulling itself towards the barn in hopes of its next meal. The irony was not lost on her.

"Stupid ass zombie," she muttered under her breath as she aimed her rifle. "You can't eat us with that helmet on." She steadied the rifle taking her final shot. She watched as a kaleidoscopic explosion of safety plastic and rotten face erupted into the early winter sky - the high-velocity round had entered the visor and exited out a softball-sized hole in the back of the creature's skull.

The sniper stood up from her concealed, crouched position behind the bales of hay; she slung the rifle strap over her shoulder and headed towards the small opening at the center of the floor. Kara began climbing down the rope leading to the lower level where the rest of the group waited. As she neared the ground, the moldy rope snapped giving way under her weight. She landed awkwardly on the side of her left foot, cursing and letting out a loud scream, but managed to maintain her upright position. "I'm OK," she yelled regaining her balance, "but I think my ankle is sprained. We have to get out of here. There are too many of them!"

James' past military training and experience in the US Marine Corp made all of his movements fluid and exact. He was a highly decorated war hero from two tours of duty in both Iraq and Afghanistan. More importantly, at least recently, he had killed more than two hundred zombies over the past six months – at least by his *"unofficial"* count. He was ready for this. He was always prepared. James slung the bandolier of shotgun shells over his shoulder and across his chest. Not even his sister's scream broke his routine. Some killing needed to be done – he was just the man for the job.

James finished making final adjustments to his recently acquired 12-gauge shotgun; the powerful weapon had served him well since liberating it from the dead hands of a half-eaten county sheriff a few weeks ago. "Where the hell is Kevin?" James asked in a disgusted tone, barely taking his eyes off his gun.

The old farmer had left the barn over twenty minutes ago to check his house for additional supplies. James had argued with Corbin that no one should be allowed to leave the barn; the old man should stay put with everyone else. However, Corbin did not feel comfortable restricting the old man's movements – they were, after all, in his barn on his family property.

As the group prepared for battle, Nikki thought back to the day's earlier events when they had first met Kevin Greenwood.

Kevin was on his way back home from the city, driving his seasoned muscle car down the dirt road to his house as Nikki and her friends were walking up the same unpaved road. The group was bound for Maine where rumors had it that a safe haven existed, free of zombies. They were on foot since their vehicle had broken down a few miles back. The elderly farmer offered them a ride and invited them to his home. They accepted his generous offer - a place to rest and possibly food to eat was something they could not pass up. The group climbed into the cantankerous gas-guzzler and rode silently the rest of the way to the man's home.

The Greenwood's small farm, located approximately five miles from the city limits, came into view as the car neared the end of the dirt road. The farm consisted of a one story white traditional house probably built in the 1930s, a large two-story rust colored barn, a few small stables and two plots of land that appeared to have once yielded corn as the main staple crop. A large wooden fence separated the farm from the nearby woods.

Modest at best in its heyday, this farm might have boasted a few livestock and some hearty crops that the farmer would have sold at market to make a living and to provide for his daily needs. The farm had recently fell into disrepair since the *"end of days"* – an overused phrase uttered by modern day evangelists to describe the last eight months as the men of God preached the gospel from their pulpits on local radio broadcasts.

Kevin pulled the old green car into the tiny carport, shut off the ignition and exited the vehicle. The group followed his lead.

Mr. Greenwood appeared to be in his mid-to-late sixties, long gray hair hanging out from under his faded blue Mets baseball cap and outfitted in tattered gray overalls. He walked with a minor limp, but the group could see that he was still quite strong from years of working on the farm. He reached back into the vehicle and grabbed a few items that he had gathered from town. He clutched closely to his side what appeared to be an old, leather bound journal with an illegible, worn-off inscription on the front cover.

For most of the morning, Kevin milled around the house doing busy work - dusting lamp shades, tidying couch cushions and washing dishes. While performing those tasks, the old man rarely put down the old journal. He invited his guests to make themselves at home and to dig around in the cabinets for food. During lunchtime the group moved outside to the porch. After formal introductions, Kevin told them his story of how his wife was killed a few months ago during a small zombie attack in the city.

"I still haven't come to terms with it yet," he painfully reminisced as his calloused fingers gently caressed his wife's old journal. "It's been almost three months since her passing. We had heard all of the warnings from the government on the local news when this mess first started. We took all of the precautions. Did what all the experts told us we should do. Mabel and I thought we could wait this mess out and live off our land. Folks were calling them 'zombies' and 'undead' and 'living this or that'...but we didn't believe that hogwash. I thought that maybe these people were sick or something but my old lady...she thought they were escaped government test subjects – Mabel liked to read all of them sci-fi works, you know the ones? She loved to tell me stories. She wrote down tons of ideas and thoughts in this here journal of hers. She had all of these conspiracy theories about JFK and Area-51..."

Kevin rambled on about some of Mabel's ideas as he flipped through her journal pointing out conspiracy theories. Nikki delicately nudged the old farmer back to the present for him to finish his tale. "What happened? If you don't mind me asking...you two seemed to have all you needed right here on the farm."

The old man refocused as he wiped a few tears from his cheek, pushing through the painful memory. "I'm sorry for the tears...we were married for forty plus years." He cleared his throat and continued. "Well, yeah, our farm did have plenty of stuff – don't let how she looks now fool you. We had food and water and a generator to keep all of the electrics running." He glanced around as they sat on his front porch seemingly surveying how terribly rundown the place was now. "Sure, it looks like shit now but I've not had the energy to maintain the place...plus everything reminds me of Mabel..." overcome with emotions - the old farmer buried his face in his palms, sobbing violently for a few moments.

Corbin Sinclair ate his lunch of canned beets and ham while he waited for Kevin to recover and continue with his story. While not a five star meal by any means, the food was a welcome relief to his complaining stomach - plus that's all Kevin seemed to have on hand at the time. He ate in silence lost in thought of years past...

How devastated would he be if he lost Nikki? Corbin had met Nikki Clarkson a little over two years ago in a bar in downtown Dallas and had worked up enough courage to ask her out. By their third date, Corbin knew he was madly in love. They were sitting outside a small restaurant basking in the warm May sun; Corbin watched as Nikki ran her slender fingers through her short red hair. The gentle breeze wafted her light scent in his direction. *Was that her perfume? Maybe it was her shampoo?* He gazed into her light green eyes and studied the small patches of freckles on her pale skin. The couple dated many times over the following year and the romance blossomed. Nikki had gotten pregnant and they had decided to have a summer wedding this year, but those plans were cut short when the *"living dead"* began to canvass the earth.

"I'm sorry," the old farmer sobbed, bringing Corbin back from his thoughts to the conversation at hand. The old farmer seemed to regain his strength and he continued with his story.

"It's OK," Kara said as she placed a caring hand on the old man's knee. "We understand. Take your time."

Perturbed by the crying farmer, the old marine ate quickly; when finished he pulled out the creased atlas from his rucksack. He focused on highlighting different routes to Maine using an orange highlighter and multi-colored pen. He had been the group's navigator the entire time. His field training with the military honed his sense of direction. While they were unsure of the exact location of Mount Hope in Maine, he knew it was in the city of Bangor. He had traced at least four viable routes to the eastern city.

"Mabel and I went into town after our generator broke down. The local news had reported only *'minor activity'* within city limits, nothing to worry about they said. We were assured by the authorities that the city was safe and that we should continue with our daily routines. We made a shopping list for some minor odds and ends and then she and I headed into town in the old Impala." A fleeting look of past good times fluttered across his face; apparently, many fond memories were tied to the old '71 Impala.

Wild dogs howled in the distance startling the group and a cold northerly breeze whispered of a miserable winter to come. Megan stirred but quickly succumbed to sleep's warm embrace. Everyone refocused on Kevin as he finished up his sorrowful tale.

"It was a short trip to town. We went to the hardware store and got the pieces we needed for the generator and then stopped by the local country store to buy a few items. I waited in the car because Mabel said she could do it quicker without me. She went in the store and never came back out..." Tears rolling down his face, unable to finish the story, the old farmer sobbed uncontrollably, clutching the journal tightly to his chest. The group sat mostly in silence, drawing the same conclusion as to her final fate. They too had lost love ones during this dire time in history.

"I'm so very sorry for your loss, Mr. Greenwood," Nikki said, tears slowly falling down her cheek.

The old farmer whispered, "Call me *Kevin*. I've not been able to stop crying myself to sleep over the last month, but it's been a lot less than when it first happened. I'm much better during the day-light hours. I think actually telling the story out loud to you folks dredged up more of the pain than I was ready to deal with."

As the sun began to set, Corbin suggested that they barricade themselves in the barn for the evening. Even though the barn would be less hospitable than the house, it had a higher vantage point and it was surrounded by a solid oak privacy fence. Kevin grabbed his old radio and more canned goods for dinner and joined the group in the barn around 9:00 PM. He had even found a few cans of peaches for dessert and some powdered milk for the baby.

The group hunkered down close to each other on the ground-level floor in order to keep warm. While the thought of building a fire seemed like a good idea, the bright light could attract unwanted attention or worse, it could burn down the barn. The group sat mostly in silence; they ate tasteless canned goods and prepared for the long, cold night ahead.

"Pretty shitty Thanksgiving, huh Kara?" James asked as he tossed an empty can of beans in the corner.

"We've had better," she replied.

"I'm sorry I didn't have more grub," Kevin said apologetically.

"No! We didn't mean it like that, Kevin," Kara assured the old man. "It's just that holidays have royally sucked since…well you know…"

The group finished eating and Nikki and the baby fell asleep around midnight. Corbin paced back and forth on the ground level while Kara climbed up into the loft. She was a medium-sized woman, strong, athletic, and attractive. She had shoulder-length blonde hair and large brown eyes. Over the many months the group had spent together on the run, she had become their resident sniper. Apparently, James had taught her from an early age how to handle a rifle. She seemed to be a natural. She had a perfect spot picked out in the loft above to keep an eye out for unwanted guests.

Around 1:00 AM, Kevin excused himself to head back to the house over the curse-filled protests of James. Corbin OK'd the quick jaunt back into the house but asked that no more than fifteen minutes tops should be spent alone.

At 1:30 AM, the echo of the first shots from Kara's high-powered rifle reverberated across the farmland. In unison, the group readied themselves for battle. Kevin was nowhere to be found. Nikki surveyed her current surroundings as she shook the cobwebs from her head. *When was the last time she had a decent night's sleep?* She couldn't remember…that wasn't important now. What was important was the safety of the group and her baby.

"Where is that old bastard?!" James exclaimed again - regarding the whereabouts of Kevin - as he tended to his sister's sprained left ankle. "You should never have let him go alone, Corbin!"

Kara tried to calm her brother but as usual it was no use. The old marine was simply way too set in his ways. It had become obvious over the last few weeks that James was not pleased with the way Corbin led the group.

"Kara, how many zombies did you see?" Nikki questioned as she double-checked her ammo clips.

"I counted ten but I was able to take out two of them before heading back down here. They are closing in. We only have a few moments before they..." She didn't have time to finish her sentence. Eight stinking, reanimated corpses broke down the barricaded double-door. With outstretched arms and twisted, moonlit facial expressions, the undead ambled into the barn - their unnatural urges pushing them ever forward towards a possible brain buffet.

James stopped bandaging his sister's ankle, pulled out his shotgun and began pumping round after round into the undead group. Bowling ball sized chunks of flesh and intestines exited the backs of the undead creatures but still they lurched forward. Kara hopped back away from the attackers towards the back of the barn, her injured ankle shooting pain up her leg. Corbin had instinctively grabbed the baby carrier and headed towards Kara's new position. Nikki reached around her waist and pulled out the 9mm and began shooting. The sickening sound of lead piercing wet, rotten skin was something that she had never gotten used to. She was even less used to the smell of their rotting flesh….the smell reminded her of three-day-old road kill.

In the commotion, two of the undead creatures had cornered Nikki between an empty grain bin and an old plow; the beasts were within arm's reach of her, their mangled fingers writhing in antici-pation. They grabbed for her as she instinctively rolled out of the way, doing a half (albeit unintended) somersault, bashing her head on a nearby piece of farm equipment. Blood spewed from the three inch long gash behind her left ear; she fought to maintain con-sciousness as she collapsed to the ground. The creatures continued towards her and she thought only of Megan as she fired her pistol. The rounds pierced various parts of their rotting, gray torsos, but the 9mm lacked sufficient stopping power; the zombies moved in for the feast, as the young mother fought for her life.

As the zombies knelt down on either side of Nikki, James could not get a clear shot for fear of spraying Nikki with buckshot. Megan cried at the top of her tiny lungs and the zombies hesitated and stood up – trying to pinpoint the sound of the crying infant. Kara had never seen the zombies hesitate and their moment of indecision al-lowed her to act. As the creatures contemplated the new food source, a piercing rifle shot rang out cutting through one of two thick rusty chains suspending a broken tractor engine from the rafters.

The two-ton engine swung like a pendulum and crashed through the zombies en route to Megan, completely destroying everything above their waists. Two pairs of legs moved around in circles for a few seconds, as if lost, and fell to the ground motionless. The huge engine swung back to its original starting position and the support rafter snapped in half crushing two more zombies and nar-rowly missing Nikki. The young mother laid motionless watching the battle unfold as if in a hazy dream. She reached out towards the sound of her crying baby but blacked out from the agonizing head wound.

The four surviving zombies lurched towards the direction of the baby. Corbin had placed Megan in a very safe spot behind some old whiskey barrels where he also found a half-empty kerosene lamp. He threw the lamp towards the clumped up mass of rotting flesh and the glass shattered covering the zombies with oil. James reacted quickly following Corbin's lead. The old vet pulled out his silver, skull emblazoned Zippo lighter, flicked it once and a white, hot flame danced from the mouth of the small metal lighter.

"Die again, you dirty bastards!" James yelled as he tossed the lighter. A large *FWOOMP* sound filled the barn as the zombies burst into flames. A smile at his handiwork and a few more shotgun rounds disabled the zombies for eternity.

Megan's strong, steady crying told Corbin that she was scared but unharmed. He raced towards Nikki's unconscious body as James walked around the smoldering, stinking pile of zombie flesh towards his sister. "Nice shot, sis! I'm proud of you," he beamed. Kara loved the rare compliments from her battle-hardened older brother. She draped her arm over his shoulder and they moved slowly towards Nikki's limp body.

"Did they bite her?" the old marine inquired. "If she got bit - you know what needs to happen, Corbin. It would be easier to off her now than wait for her to regain consciousness and watch her slowly degrade into one of those freaks."

Corbin looked up from his kneeling position above Nikki, shocked at how callous the older man was. *Did he not have a heart? Why was he so matter-of-fact? This woman was the mother of his child!* "I'm looking now," the former firefighter replied, "but all I see is a head wound behind her ear. I don't see any other marks."

Nikki slowly opened her eyes and saw the frantic look on Corbin's face. "They…didn't bite me. That rafter knocked them away from me before they could do any worse. My head…is killing me and I'm sure I have a concussion." The young mother sat up too quickly, feeling horribly dizzy. "Where's Megan?! Is she OK? Where's our baby?" Nikki tried to move but couldn't. Corbin restrained her and assured her repeatedly that the baby was more than fine.

After a few moments, Nikki got up slowly and reunited with Megan. The injured, but relieved mother cradled her baby tightly next to her breasts, soothingly rocking back and forth. Each and every day, Nikki realized that her baby was exposed to unimaginable dangers. This was no way to live. She feared their luck would soon run out.

"It's OK, baby – it's your momma. I've got you now. You're safe, baby girl," Nikki said, consoling her frightened child –wrapping the infant tightly in the pink blanket for warmth.

Corbin and James did a quick recon around the barn; they found no additional signs of zombie activity anywhere. They walked to the edge of the property where pieces of the devastated fence lay in ruins. Beyond the fence, the two men could make out random, zigzagging zombie footprints from various directions all converging to one final staging area prior to busting through the weak, old fence. After about ten minutes, the two men returned to the barn where Nikki and Kara sat huddled together with baby Megan.

"James and I are going to check the house," Corbin said. "We saw a light on in the back part of the house. You ladies stay here. We've surveyed the area and see no signs of danger." The two men left quickly with only their weapons and flashlights and jogged to the house. Corbin was surprised by how in-shape the old military veteran was. This guy had to be at least twelve to fifteen years his senior.

A heavy, wet snow began falling.

The front porch squeaked in painful protest under their heavy footsteps as the two men entered the house. They heard no commotion, no sounds. They slowly made their way to the illuminated back room. There was no power to the house so the light source must have been a candle or a lantern, probably similar to the one they had just used in the barn fight. James opened the door and moved into the room like a well-trained SWAT team member; Corbin followed close behind.

The two men entered the house's only bathroom. There in a tub filled with water and blood, Kevin's lifeless body silently floated. His eyes stared aimlessly upwards. The oak handled butcher knife - the only witness to Kevin's last minutes on Earth - lay in a pool of blood on the white-tiled floor next to a leather-bound book. The old farmer had finally allowed Mabel's journal to rest.

Corbin closed the bathroom door and the two men solemnly walked back to the barn, their bloody footprints disturbing the newly fallen November snow.

Chapter 2

- *October 21, 2011: Friday 2:30 PM – Illumination Pharmaceuticals - a lab twenty miles south of Boise, Idaho – approximately two years ago, a pair of research scientists whittle away at the remainder of the work week…*

"What do you mean it's only two thirty?" Craig Masters asked, glaring angrily at his watch. "I swear to God this day will never end!" Craig was thirty-eight, slender and he had a well-groomed brown goatee with sideburns that had begun to gray prematurely.

"It's only been fifteen minutes since you asked the last time, Craig. Would you please just focus on the lab tests?" Julie pleaded. "It's Friday and if we don't get these last two reports to Mr. Timmons then you and I will be stuck here this weekend!" Julie Smith was in her mid-fifties, tall with shoulder length black hair (well, black after several color treatments, that is) tied into a ponytail and she had a tendency to wear a bit too much of her favorite perfume.

The two lab techs had worked together since 2008 and recently began working on various reports and calculations for the pharmaceutical giant on flu-related research. Many of the reports related to new vaccines that they had created which were only slight variations of the H1N1 vaccines developed during mid-2009 and early-2010.

There had been an abrupt decrease in flu-related deaths and a leveling off of new cases in mid-2010 due to the availability of quick-to-market, mass produced medications and the general populous following stricter guidelines regarding hygiene. As dumb as it seemed at the time to sneeze into your elbow instead of your hands, apparently this technique along with other common sense precautions seemed to retard the spread of the virus. Many countries had declared victory against the pandemic by July of that same year. Minor reports of the illness, in less industrialized countries, continued to be reported, but for the most part were isolated and well-contained.

The United States, Canada and Mexico continued to develop additional safety precautions, guidelines and vaccines to avoid future problems in North America like the initial *"swine flu"* that surprised the world in early-2009. Britain, Germany and France instituted similar protocols for Europe. China, Russia and Japan developed joint task forces to combat the spread of the flu. OPEC countries funded similar ventures throughout the Middle East and Africa. Additionally, major committees were formed on each continent to coordinate the free flow of information and policies regarding the containment, treatment and control of the H1N1 virus and other possible future pandemics.

"I'm sorry to be so bitchy today," Craig chimed in after a few moments of silence. "It's Mandy's birthday tomorrow and I don't have a gift. She's going to kill me. She's been a bit depressed lately since she lost her job last month and I'm sure me screwing up her birthday would push her over the edge!"

Julie typed quickly and accurately at her computer as she tabled up various test results into the computer program. Multiple graphs and concentration samples were merged together as she patiently listened to her friend. She had been with Illumination Pharmaceuticals for going on twenty years now. Julie had grown accustomed to hearing about Craig and Amanda's plight over the last few years, at least Craig's version of the story. Julie had first met Amanda at a company luncheon about a year ago.

"Craig, I'm sure you will find her something before tomorrow evening," the senior technician assured her partner. "I know you two are going through some tough times, but all young marriages do."

Julie remembered back to her first marriage that had lasted just shy of one year. She had married at seventeen to the dismay of her parents back in the '70s to a man named Cicero Jamison, a young corporal destined for one of the last tours of duty in Vietnam. She was head-over-heels in love with a soon-to-be war hero and dreamed of building a family with him on his return. However, Corporal Jamison was tragically killed by friendly fire the week before he was due back home. His death devastated Julie and she swore off any future relationships for fear of losing another loved one.

However, as she reached her early-thirties and her maternal clock began to tick ever louder, compounded by the fact that her other friends were well ahead of her in raising their own families - she abandoned her commitment phobia. She fell in love with her closest friend, Alexander Smith - an Egyptian sociologist that she had befriended many years earlier in college.

Alexander had left Boston soon after he had finished his degrees to pursue excavation sites just outside of Giza. He urged Julie to follow him but she could not. Even though she had strong feelings for him, she chose to focus her attention on her career. Alexander eventually returned to the States to lecture about his amazing finds many years later.

Julie had attended all of his lectures and they eventually began to date. The couple married and had fraternal twins, a boy named Zack and a daughter named Samantha. Both children were prominently displayed at the office in multiple digital frames on their mother's desk.

Craig was franticly pacing back and forth between the lab station and his computer. He eventually plopped down heavily in his squeaky chair. The younger tech was obviously frustrated at the time consuming tests in conjunction with fretting over the perfect gift for his wife.

His frantic and disheveled appearance matched his desk. It was the complete opposite of Julie's. While her desk was neat and compartmentalized, almost clinical – his desk looked as if an angry, rabid beaver lived there, possibly in one of the desk drawers – coming out nightly after everyone left the office to leave a wake of destruction in its path, the epicenter being Craig's desk.

"Julie, I don't know how you've worked here for the last twenty years. I've been with the company for about three years now and spent nearly the last six months on these flu tests. I'm tired of seeing all of the charts, all of the graphs and especially having Mr. Timmons breathing down my neck the entire time!" he exclaimed as he rubbed his forehead.

"This job has been good to me, Craig," she said. "I've been able to put my kids through college and the house is almost completely paid off. I'm not too far from retiring and getting a great pension. So it's easy for me to focus on the job. Plus, the day goes by much faster when I imagine Amanda choking you with her tiny hands when you give her some lame gift tomorrow evening!"

"That's not funny, Julie!" he yelled but quickly began laughing. He had grown very close to Julie in the three years that they had worked together. He considered her to be the older sister that he never had. She always calmed him down and had often given him great advice saving him from the brunt of Amanda's *"wrath"* when he had done something stupid or forgotten some special date.

"Yeah, maybe I'm blowing this out of proportion as usual," he continued, "but I really must find her a great gift or I might as well just permanently move into the garage!"

The two bantered back and forth as they tried to tidy up the results and finish off the outstanding reports. Over two hours had passed and the 5:00 PM deadline loomed ever larger. At 4:45 PM the phone rang in their office. Each glanced up from their computer screens at each other. As she saved her work, Julie thought to herself how Craig looked like a frightened deer caught in the headlights of an oncoming car.

"It's your turn to answer the phone," Craig said timidly. "I got chewed out by Mr. Timmons last week. Plus I know he hates me. Maybe you will be able to smooth over the fact that we are not done by his precious timeline!"

The phone rang again seemingly louder and angrier than the first ring; Julie pressed the speaker phone button. She simultaneously held one finger up to her lips to signal Craig to keep quiet. Mr. Timmons' tired and cranky voice came over the raspy speaker phone.

"So, Julie – how are the tests coming? Are you finished?"

"The results are within accepted tolerances for this last batch of vaccines, Mr. Timmons. Craig and I have been running the final reports for the last few hours and we are close…"

"Close?!" the manager yelled. "You know those results have to be delivered to our executives by eight AM Monday morning, right? Craig promised me last month that the tests would be in my inbox with all the supporting documentation by five this afternoon and it is five now. I have NO results!"

Julie could just imagine her boss in his luxurious corner office, his fat face turning red with anger, running his right hand through his thinning red hair and the knuckles on his left hand turning white from gripping the phone receiver way too hard. She had worked with Karl Timmons for ten years before he was promoted to regional manager. He had a tendency to underestimate timelines, overestimate his self-worth and promise deliverables to higher-ups under unrealistic schedules.

"Karl, listen," Julie said in a soothing tone, "we will have those results in your inbox before Monday morning." She paused briefly. "Actually, we'll try to have them to you no later than Saturday afternoon. That will allow you ample time to go over '*our*' work and adjust and recheck things and make sure we've done everything correctly."

She had hoped that this approach would allow Karl's ego to overtake his anger. This would give him the opportunity to put his stamp of approval on things and to make it look like he was more involved in the process than he actually was. He'd most assuredly inflate his own involvement - letting his superiors know of his "*intimacy*" with the tests and the "*crucial*" role he played in getting the job finished.

After a moment of silence, Karl Timmons spoke, "Fine. Have all the results to me by four tomorrow afternoon…and Julie?"

"Yes, Karl?" she replied.

"It's Mister Timmons!!" he said, slamming the phone down, abruptly ending the conversation.

"That went well," Craig said as he peeked over a stack of papers at Julie. "What an idiot! You'd think that the first heart attack would have taught him to relax…"

"Let's just focus on finishing up what we can this evening. While Karl was busy blowing a gasket, I was going over test batch 2011_10_20 and it appears our batch from Thursday evening has a few anomalies. I don't think it will cause that much rework but we need to redo that test. It should only take three or so hours. Let's do that tomorrow," she said as she busied herself rechecking the figures.

"Shit!!" Craig exclaimed. "That's probably my fault. I think Amanda might have called while I was running those tests. I was distracted. I'm sorry."

"No worries. We just have to fix it. Let's finish up today's tests - get all of that data entered into the computer. Then let's close down the lab and you and I go get a drink or two from Stubby's then hit the Mall to find Amanda the perfect gift. We need to get that off of your mind so you and I can finish up these tests for Karl," Julie said, as both began laughing, knowing how irritated Mr. Timmons got when any *"subordinate"* called him by his first name.

"Wait…" Craig said. "I thought you hated shopping during this time of year?"

"I do, but this is an emergency. I'd rather take my chances out there in the crowds than listening to your complaints for hours on end!"

The two shut down the lab around 7:15 PM and walked through the deserted parking lot to Julie's Jeep Grand Cherokee. "I'll drive," she said as she unlocked the doors, "but you're buying the drinks!"

Both entered the aging SUV; they left the almost empty parking lot of Illumination Pharmaceuticals merging effortlessly onto the idle freeway. Julie took the third exit and both of them could easily see the glowing neon lights of Stubby's Bar and Grill. The bar was built in the late '80s and continued to be a local hotspot almost since the opening day. The manager of the bar would often say it was the drinks and the food that made the place so popular. However, if you asked the local patrons, the real star of the place was the dancing neon cowboy perched atop of the building.

"I feel better already," Craig joked, "but that cowboy freaks me out every time I see it."

Julie smiled as she pulled the gold SUV into Stubby's crowded parking lot and took the first available spot. Stubby's had become a regular routine for her and Craig. Usually they would stop by after work on Fridays for an hour or so, have a few drinks and be back to their respective homes no later than 7:00 PM - today's late arrival being an obvious exception due to the extra workload.

"Wow! It's crowded in here," he exclaimed, peering inside, as he held the door open for Julie.

"Yeah it is. I guess it's closer to happy hour than we are used to."

"Hey look, our table is empty," Craig said, motioning towards a table in the corner next to the empty stage.

They sat at their normal table and ordered a few drinks. The band returned to the stage and began playing soft jazz music as the lights dimmed. The two made small talk about work but the conversation quickly turned to Amanda's upcoming birthday and Craig's total lack of a meaningful gift.

"What am I going to do, Julie? Why did I have to put this off so long? I'm an idiot. I knew better but still waited to the last possible minute."

Julie's purse began to buzz loudly before she could respond. She reached into her purse and pulled out a large, antiquated cell phone. Craig began to giggle but Julie shushed him. He loved teasing her about the size of the phone. It was ancient. Even though the device was less than five years old, it was more than twice the size of current models.

"Do you need help holding that up to your ear?"

"Hush, Craig!" she playfully scolded him. "Hello?"

Craig knew it was Alexander checking in on his wife. There was never any mistrust from either spouse about the weekly rendezvous at Stubby's – often times, both Alexander and Amanda had joined them. Craig and Julie were very close friends, nothing more. Craig took the opportunity to call Amanda as well to let her know that he had been working late and had a few errands to run after he and Julie finished their drinks at Stubby's. The lab partners filled their significant others in on their current whereabouts and most of the day's events (minus the lack of a birthday gift) and promised to drive safely home when they were done. Both ended their phone conversations simultaneously with *"I love you."*

"Craig, finish up your drink. I just had a great gift idea. You know that little store in the Mall? The one in between Victoria's Secret and that little place that sells all the reproduced Incan artifacts?"

"You mean Mayan artifacts?" Craig corrected.

"Yes, Mayan…I knew that. Alexander corrects me every time I mix up the two," she frowned, trying to make yet another mental note to keep the two civilizations separate in her mind.

"That store between Victoria's Secret and the Mayan store…I think the store you are thinking of is…Colleen's Collectibles."

"Yes! That's the one. Amanda would love one of those keepsake bracelets that you put a new gemstone in every year, right?" Julie inquired.

"That is an excellent idea!" Craig became very excited. Those bracelets were pricey but he felt that he could splurge on such an item even though the Masters' family was now a one-income family.

Once again, Julie had come to his rescue saving him from Amanda's ire and a cold night sleeping in the garage.

Craig paid the bill and left a pretty decent tip. He was usually fairly frugal (although others considered him *"cheap"*) regarding his tipping policies, but tonight he was in a great mood. The two friends exited the bar into the frosty October night and drove to the Mall.

The Mall was full of shoppers taking advantage of early pre-Christmas sales. While Craig enjoyed the holiday season, he felt that each year the giant corporations moved their sales up earlier and earlier into the year to get extra money for their bottom line. Soon people would be shopping for Christmas gifts and fireworks simultaneously. However, he couldn't let his inner Scrooge out just yet…because he could still get a great deal on some jewelry for his wife. After his purchase, he could go back to being angry at the overzealous shoppers and the greedy, faceless corporate giants.

The two friends made their way through a tidal wave of shopping drones as they meandered towards Colleen's Collectibles. As they browsed merchandise on display in a small rack outside of the main store, they could hear a TV from next door in the Mayan shop reporting how the Mayans predicted a possible Doomsday event on the winter solstice, December 21, 2012.

"What do you think about that, Julie?" Craig asked, referring to the program on the TV next door.

"I've talked to Alexander briefly about it. He says some folks think it's going to be a worldwide calamity to end civilization. Other people think it's just the end of an era. I don't really think much of it. People have been predicting the end of days forever and none of them have been right so far. Right?"

"Well what if this is the big one - the end of life as we know it? You know, an E-L-E…an extinction level event?"

"It's going to be an E-O-C," she enunciated each letter with a pseudo-concerned look on her face.

"What the hell is that?" Craig inquired, confused, trying to piece together the acronym.

"End-of-Craig," she said giggling at her own joke. "Some call it *Death by Amanda*' and it will happen very soon if you don't focus on finding her a gift and stop listening to that mumbo jumbo."

Both laughed loudly. They moved into the store and found a perfect gift for Amanda. A polished chrome bracelet with an emerald gemstone embedded in the first link. While a bit more expensive than Craig had originally intended to pay, it was the last one in the display case and would surely keep him on his wife's good side.

They left the Mall and returned to the desolate parking lot at Illumination Pharmaceuticals. Only two security guards were there - one working the front gate and one patrolling the grounds in a golf cart. The gate opened and the gold SUV was waved through. Julie dropped Craig off at his truck.

"See you tomorrow," Craig said, waving and starting up his truck, allowing it to warm up. His perfect gift was placed gently on the passenger side seat.

"I hope to see you too," Julie replied, winking and waving as she drove home.

Chapter 3

• *October 22, 2011: Saturday 6:15 AM - the home of Craig and Amanda Masters …*

*W*HAA!! WHAA!! WHAA!!
The alarm clock screamed promptly at 6:15 AM, but Craig did not move. The work from yesterday coupled with the stress of dealing with his boss had exhausted his mind and body. He teetered on the edge of a narcoleptic coma; his senses immune to pretty much all forms of external stimuli.

"Would you shut that thing off?" Amanda pleaded, unable to reach the alarm herself, more than a bit confused as to why the alarm was even set to go off so early on a Saturday morning.

WHAA!! WHAA!! WHAA!!

The emboldened alarm clock taunted the couple once again. Each morning this same scene played out. *Maybe this time the clock would finally win?* The alarm would continue to shout for hours…announcing its victory to all who came within earshot. It had felt the stinging hand of defeat every morning for years. *Maybe today would be different?*

WHAA!! WHAA!! WHAA!!

"Craig, turn it off, please!" his wife begged as she elbowed him softly in the side.

"Ouch!" Craig screamed, trying to swat the alarm clock, but his right arm was immobilized. "Oh my GOD - I'm paralyzed!"

"Don't be dumb," Amanda joked as she rolled to her side, freeing his arm. "Why the hell is the alarm even set?"

Feeling quickly returned to his right arm and Craig delivered a devastating hook directly into the face of the annoying alarm clock, knocking it off the nightstand and silencing it for at least another day. The alarm clock sulked quietly under the dresser, waiting for its next chance to interrupt someone's dreams. The battle was lost; however, the war was far from over.

"I have to go into the office today. We have a few tests that need to be redone before this afternoon. You know how Karl gets."

Heavy scrambling feet glided across the wooden floor in the hallway and the bedroom door burst open. The couple tried to react but it was too late! A streak of black lightning shot through their door and darted under the covers at the foot of the bed; the intruder quickly wiggled its way to an opening near the headboard. It was as if the bed itself had given birth. A slobbering furry head popped out from under the blankets, its body wedged snuggly between husband and wife!

"No! Bad, Buster! You're a bad dog!" Amanda scolded their ten year old Doberman Pincher. Buster rolled over on his back almost knocking Craig out of the bed. "Bad, dog!" Amanda tried to feign anger but couldn't contain herself; she started to giggle uncontrollably as Buster licked her ear.

Craig sat up and rolled out of the bed cringing slightly as his bare feet touched the cold floor. "I have to get ready for work. I'm going to take a quick shower."

"No worries," Amanda said. "I have to let this beast out anyway before he pees in our bed." Buster's nub tail wiggled excitedly as

Amanda looked at him. Buster understood the keyword *"pee"* and he jumped from the bed taking the comforter hostage in his mouth as he darted downstairs towards the door.

Buster took his sweet time to finish his *"business"* as Amanda patiently waited on the doorstep. Craig showered and dressed in the time it took for the duo to return to the kitchen. Amanda entered the house and sat at the table with the morning paper - flipping page by page, not really reading but searching for something. Most turns of the page were followed by a heavy, almost disgusted sigh.

"Is there anything good in there, Mandy?"

"Is there ever?" she said rolling her eyes, her disdain for reading about recessions, murders, sociopaths and reality show idiots was quite obvious. *Why is there never any good news?* She knew the answer. Good feeling stories with happy outcomes don't sell papers. She felt the majority of world like to read about other people's suffering and misfortune…that allowed the reader to feel better - realizing that others were worse off.

"No, baby doll – I guess not. You know me – ever the optimist." Craig said, smiling at his beautiful wife.

Craig had busied himself with all the ingredients necessary to make breakfast. The coffee was brewing, the toast was warming and the smell of bacon wafted throughout the entire house. Buster sat at attention just between the kitchen and the formal dining room – his nub tail wiggling with joyful anticipation. The sun beamed through the French doors glistening off the light brown highlights in Amanda's hair. Craig absolutely adored his wife.

Amanda was the total package. She was thirty-four years old, quick witted, charming and absolutely gorgeous, even without make-up on or wearing fancy clothes. She had curly auburn hair, insightful and caring hazel green eyes, and kissable pouty lips. She was pleasantly plump and Craig loved that. She was curvaceous with a sexy waist-to-hip ratio; she was not some skin-and-bones anorexia victim – which the media promoted as *"beautiful"* and *"healthy."* Craig had absolutely no interest in those wafer-thin models, the ones where it appeared that their collar bones were mere millimeters from escaping from their torso. Of course, he couldn't forget about the twins. Craig often referred to his wife's breasts as *"Mount Mandy,"* much to her chagrin.

"Hey, dork! You're burning the toast! You'll set off the smoke alarm." Amanda said, snapping her fingers to get her husband's attention and covering her nose with the front of her t-shirt.

"Damn!"

Ten minutes later, the couple enjoyed a hearty breakfast of eggs and bacon sans toast. Even Buster got a few strips of the pork goodness, his early massacre of the comforter apparently forgiven, if not entirely forgotten.

After breakfast, Craig went into the garage and started up his tan colored F-150. He sat in the cab and opened the gift box, proud of the fine piece of jewelry – imagining Amanda's reaction to his gift.

"What are you doing in there?" Amanda asked, tapping on the passenger side window and peeking inside the truck - startling her husband.

"Damn! You scared me, Mandy - don't sneak up on me like that!" Craig replied, clumsily trying to hide the gift but it was too late. Amanda's innate jewelry sensor had been activated.

"Give me!!" Amanda yelled joyously as she slid into the passenger side seat.

Craig put the bracelet on his wife's hand. "Happy birthday, baby."

Amanda fully extended her arm watching the bracelet glitter in the morning sunlight. She grabbed Craig's head, forcefully planting a giant, wet kiss on his lips.

"I love you honey, but we can't afford this...can we?"

"Anything for you, Mandy."

"Let's go back inside...so I can thank you appropriately!" She flirtatiously winked, rubbed his inner thigh and motioned towards the door leading into the house.

"I can't. I have to get into the office to finish up some tests. But I'll be back by four at the latest. I have some dinner reservations for this evening. After all that is done, then you and I can do it like monkeys!"

"You're a dork," she said, lovingly gazing into her husband's eyes.

Amanda kissed him some more and eventually, under protest, slid out of the truck. Craig backed out of the garage and stopped at the end of the driveway. He watched Amanda as she happily inspected the bracelet.

"I love you!" she yelled.

"I love you too, baby doll," Craig replied as he backed out of the driveway and headed to the lab.

The start of Julie's Saturday morning was much more in line with her normal weekday routine. She took a nice, hot bath to relax before work. She dozed slightly but was awakened by her husband's voice from downstairs.

"Julie, don't fall asleep in that tub," he warned.

"I'm not asleep, Alex!" she yelled back. "You worry too much about me!"

"It's only because I love you. Oh and maybe because you make more money than me!" he retorted, giggling slightly.

"That's it – you are *'so'* out of my will, mister!" she playfully teased.

"Well while you are up there *'not'* sleeping in the bathtub, Sam, Zack and I are off to get our last bit of Christmas shopping done. We'll see you later."

"I love you guys, be safe – you know how crazy shoppers are this time of year," she warned as she heard the front door close.

She had finished all of her Christmas shopping over two months earlier. She no longer waited till the last minute to shop. For many years, she would wait till *"Black Friday"* to even start buying gifts. That changed about two years ago.

She had waited patiently outside for one of the *"door buster"* specials at the local electronics store. She was third or fourth in line. She had braved the freezing weather for over two hours just to get a new GPS for Alexander. As the doors opened, the crowd surged forward and she was trampled.

She suffered a broken elbow and a twisted ankle and was rushed to the hospital. The highlight of the whole experience was being interviewed by a local news show for a program called, *"When Shoppers Go Bad"* plus she received a ten-thousand dollar gift card from the responsible store and a free top-of-the line GPS for Alexander's car.

Julie enjoyed an additional fifteen minutes in the hot, soapy water – Christmas shopping was the farthest thing from her mind. Grudgingly she forced herself out of the tub, dried off and wrapped a green wool towel around her chest. She went to her side of the dual sink in the master bathroom and put on her make-up. She sprayed two extra squirts of her perfume on her neck for good measure. She dressed and grabbed a bagel and cream cheese for breakfast as she left the house.

Twenty minutes later Julie pulled into the employee parking lot as Craig was clumsily backing into a spot way too small for his truck. The lot was a ghost town; these *"weekend warriors"* took parking spots as close to the front door as they could.

Julie cracked her window slightly and spoke to Craig. "You drive like a woman," she said pulling in next to him.

"BAH!" Craig replied as he exited his truck.

The two friends went up the stairs into the office building taking the elevator to the fourth floor. They had work to get done. The building was all but empty. The cleaning crew milled about doing their work. Vacuum cleaners and floor buffers whirred in the background. Security guards patrolled the hallways. Most of the building was dark. Craig and Julie prepared for the task at hand. They had to get the final retests done before 4:00 PM.

"Let's do this, old girl," Craig said.

"Well, I'm glad to see Amanda didn't choke you last night. I take it she loved the gift?"

"Yeah, I'll say! I think I have some sweet *'nookie'* waiting for me when I get home!"

"You keep talking like that, PIG - and I'll file a sexual harassment suit against you!"

Both laughed as they turned on the lab equipment and fired up the old computers. A total retest of batch 2011_10_20 would take about three hours. This batch was a cell-based approach to producing a vaccine instead of the old egg-based method. Craig started the bio reactor convinced it was similar in design to that of the large vats used in beer breweries.

Almost as if on cue, Julie spoke, "No matter how hard you wish - that reactor will never make a single drop of beer!"

"That's what I was just thinking!"

"We obviously spend way too much time together, young man," she joked.

Hours passed by as complex calculations were performed by the antiquated desktops. It was an interesting, if not ironic, contradiction. The software programs were state-of-the-art but the computers appeared to be old dummy terminals from mainframe shops of years past. This wasn't exactly the case but the thought around the office was that *"Tightwad Timmons"* should spend more money on upgrading the personal workstations and less time worrying about the bottom line.

"It is way too quiet in here." Julie said, standing up and stretching out her back. "Turn on the TV, would you?"

Craig searched his desk for the TV remote. However, this morning it appeared that the imaginary rabid beaver that lived in Craig's desk had a bit of a kleptomaniac streak in addition to its regular distaste of all things orderly – the beaver had obviously absconded with the remote!

"Never mind, I need to walk around a bit." Julie left her desk and went over to the TV that was perched on a metal swinging arm just to the left side of the large window that resided on the backside of the lab. She flipped the TV on manually.

"That's how we used to do it all the time before you lazy whippersnappers came up with all those fancy doo-dads to do everything for you without having to move," Julie said in an overly-exaggerated senior citizen's voice. She then left the lab to *"powder her nose."*

Craig eventually found the remote, hidden underneath a stack of sports magazines by the side of his desk. He began randomly flipping through the channels. He stopped his aimless channel surfing on one of the many 24-hour news channels. It appeared that the local news was interviewing a NASA scientist about solar activity. Craig turned up the volume and listened intently as the conference started.

"Professor O'Malley," began an elderly gentleman, "I appreciate you taking time out of your busy schedule to answer our questions."

"No problem whatsoever, Mr. Kenning. That's what I'm here for, to educate the public, to separate myth from fiction, if you will. Do you have a question, sir?" the Professor inquired.

"I do indeed. My understanding from interviewing multiple sources is that there is a possibility of solar storms and solar flares next year that could lead to the collapse of electrical power grids, satellites and unprotected communication infrastructures. Is that true?"

Professor O'Malley adjusted the microphone to make sure everyone could hear him. While he'd never admit it out loud, he loved the attention these press conferences garnered him. Such public limelight would go a long way to advancing his career and getting more grant money for his department.

"Yes, I believe that is true for some countries. Our analysis indicates that some internal infrastructure is not shielded sufficiently in many third-world nations. This could lead to catastrophic failure at some point and destabilize those regions. I feel this situation will be more prevalent in less industrialized nations due to lack of preparedness and lack of resources. I've been in contact with the US military and other reliable government sources - they assure me that precautions are in place to safeguard the American way of life in the event such a disaster should occur."

"Do you honestly think our government would tell you differently? If they were not prepared for something like this – do you think they would tell you so?" Leon Kenning drank a sip of water and continued.

"While it may be true that some integral process are protected, there is no way that our entire power grid in every state is protected. There are thousands of satellites orbiting the Earth – I can't believe they've all been upgraded. As for communication systems, these cell phones and WI-FI hot spots barely work on rainy days – how could 'WE' be prepared for a large scale event of this magnitude should it happen?"

"I've answered your question, Mr. Kenning. Next question, please." Professor O'Malley had no intention of debating with a renowned conspiracy theorist. Plus, in his mind - Kenning wasn't even a *"real"* reporter – just some gossip rag columnist.

A plump female reporter named Jenny Cranston stood up from her third row seat. "So, Professor, in your educated opinion - what else does our Sun have in store for us in the upcoming year?"

"Well, Ms. Cranston, as you know, my team has been researching solar activity and documenting its effects for the last decade. We've devised very accurate tests to track changes to the amount of radiation the Sun emits. Our tests indicate that next year, the Sun will give off higher levels of gamma radiation than we've seen in more than a decade."

"Should we be alarmed?" Ms. Cranston asked.

"According to our calculations, there will be a spike of gamma activity around the winter solstice next year," O'Malley said. "I would take appropriate precautions. I always advise limiting Sun exposure due to the hole in the ozone layer. Maybe wear extra sunscreen and avoid the hottest part of the day. Just use common sense."

"By winter solstice, do you mean around December 21, 2012?" Mr. Kenning interrupted. "Isn't that what the Mayans predicted? Didn't their calendar stop tracking time on that date? They predicted an apocalypse or something, right?"

Professor O'Malley sighed in disgust. *Why was Kenning even allowed here in the first place?* The professor had fielded one too many hypothetical situations regarding the long since defunct Mesoamerican society. And Kenning was grating on the Professor's last nerve.

"Look," the professor began, "I don't believe all of that shit and you shouldn't either, Leon." The professor paused realizing he just swore on live TV. "Sorry about that," he said apologetically into the camera.

"All that Mayan Doomsday stuff is nothing but some fanciful story telling. I'm not here to discuss fairy tales or conspiracy theories. If you are interested in the scientific data that my team and I have documented regarding solar activity occurring next year, then I will send it to your respective news outlets. However, I will not waste my valuable time discussing science fiction." With that, Professor O'Malley removed his microphone and stormed off stage.

"What was that about?" Julie inquired, catching the last bit of the professor's tirade as she sat back down at her desk.

"That professor was talking about solar flares or something and got pissed off because some reporter mentioned the Mayan stuff we talked about the other night at the Mall."

"That crap again? That Mayan stuff is going to be all over the news for the next year. There will be countdowns and doomsayers and cultists everywhere! All of them will be predicting the end of time as we know it. Just like they did back in '99 with the Y2K bug...we all know how that played out. This will be the same."

"That's probably quite accurate, Julie. People like to panic and blow things way out of proportion."

The two coordinated their efforts and completed all remaining tests and documentation regarding batch 2011_10_20. All work was now finished ahead of schedule. Then as if some malevolent presence had willed him into existence at that exact moment, Karl Timmons walked through the lab door.

"Don't get up," Karl said as he walked into the room. "I'm only going to be a few minutes."

Julie and Craig glanced at each other, both thinking the exact same things: *Why was Karl in the office today? Was he here to reprimand them? Was he here to lend a 'helping' hand?* Both technicians watched their boss walk to the active bio vat, his back turned to them as he spoke.

"While we have had our differences in the past, I just wanted to come in today to thank you for your extra efforts."

"No problem, Kar...I mean Mr. Timmons," Craig stuttered as he realized he almost dropped the *"K-bomb"* (as it was known).

Julie shook her head.

"As I was saying," Karl continued, "your extra efforts will ensure that we are at the top of the list of qualified companies competing for the IPPC grant." Karl abruptly turned from the vat and left the room without uttering another word.

The International Pandemic Prevention Council was the governing body set up in Stockholm, Sweden to oversee and coordinate international efforts to confront virulent diseases and pandemics. The council was formed in late-2010 and was comprised of representatives from around the world. The multi-national group had extensive powers and rights granted to it by its member countries in order to allow for quick, decisive actions to combat worldwide illness.

Julie waited a few minutes before she spoke. She got up from her desk and went to the doorway, sticking her head outside the lab to double-check that Karl was nowhere to be seen.

"What was that whole *'thank you'* garbage about, Julie?"

Julie sat back down. "I'm not sure. I can't remember the last time he uttered those words to anyone but his superiors."

"Let's just send off our reports and documentation before he comes back. We may have just encountered an alien doppelganger!" Craig joked as they both sent off their final reports.

Both shutdown their computers and hurried to the elevator – riding it down to the ground floor. Once in the parking lot, the two hugged and said their goodbyes, heading for their respective homes to enjoy the rest of the weekend.

For the last two months of 2011 and the first two months of 2012, the Illumination Pharmaceuticals group continued to work diligently towards the IPPC grant. Karl Timmons let his team do their work. Most of his time was spent in closed-door meetings with the financial backers of the firm and his superiors during this four month period.

Chapter 4

March 7, 2012: Wednesday, 8:30 AM - An emergency all-staff meeting at Illumination Pharmaceuticals...

"I'm glad everyone could make it on such short notice this fine morning," Karl Timmons began as he eyed each member of the team. "We've come a long way together in a relatively short time."

The ten person team sat around a U-shape oak table on the third floor of the building. Karl was at the open end of the table pacing back and forth in anticipation. The group was quite unaccustomed to seeing this side of their boss...he appeared, dare they think it, *"happy?"*

"We've done it!" Karl blurted out unable to control his excitement. "All the hard work we did at the end of last year has finally paid off!"

Julie and Craig winced in unison every time Karl would say *"We've"*...most of the team felt the same way. Karl's use of the inclusive *"we"* implied that he actually had something to do with all of the hard work the team did over the past year. This was not the case.

"What did we do?" Michael asked.

Michael Clark was Karl's *"go to"* guy – the teacher's pet. He had worked with Karl for about seven years now. The group tolerated Michael but they always watched their backs with what they said while he was around. He had a tendency to *"inform"* Karl of office gossip. Julie and Craig would often joke that Michael had his nose so far up Karl's ass that at times it appeared the two were conjoined twins.

"I'm glad you asked, Michael my boy!!" Karl beamed like a proud father. "We won the IPPC grant! That's the big one! They've chosen our pandemic vaccine. It will be used around the world to combat the most virulent strains of the H1N1 virus. Not only will it help thousands of people, but the grant is worth fifty-million dollars to our company!"

The room exploded in clapping and cheering. The team had worked long, hard hours during the past two years. Many weekends were spent diagnosing failed batch trials. They forced themselves to continue the arduous schedule because they knew their vaccine was being considered for the grant. However, the thought of beating the larger, more world-renowned drug companies for the grant money was a huge stretch, but they had done it!

Michael, with arms wide open, jumped up from his seat, knocked over his chair and practically skipped over to Karl Timmons. Michael enthusiastically embraced his boss. Craig glanced at Julie as she covered her mouth to keep from laughing at the most awkwardly over-affectionate man hug they had ever seen.

"That's the kind of enthusiasm I want to see, Michael!" Karl said as he embraced his number one fan. "The rest of you could learn a thing or two from old Mikey here about showing some real excitement! Now get back out there and make me proud!"

The scientists began to leave the table, picking up their pens, notepads and bottled water. Craig and Julie were the first out of their seats and almost out the door when Karl spoke again.

"Oh, by the way," Karl said coyly, "there will be bonuses this year!"

The mere mention of the word *"bonus"* elicited more cheering and clapping from the over-worked team but also seemed to confuse them as well. Some of the group double-checked with other colleagues as they left the room to make sure they had not misheard their boss. The consensus was that *"Tightwad Timmons"* had indeed actually uttered that magical word.

Julie left the meeting room and stood at the elevator. She had jogged down the short hallway to catch the doors while they were still open. "Hurry up, Craig," she said, "the elevator is here!" Craig looked over his shoulder one last time as he exited the room for the elevator. Michael had once again embraced Karl, like a kid hugging his father at Christmas time. Craig wanted to yell: *"Get a room!"* But he knew better…however, he made a mental note of the image and knew he would definitely share with Julie once they made it to the safety of their lab.

"Michael and Karl sitting in a tree, K-I-S-S-I-N-G," Craig sang as he plopped down in his chair, "first comes love, then comes marriage, then comes Karl with a baby carriage!"

"You're so bad!" Julie said, shaking her head at her friend. "I'm guessing *'old Mikey boy'* was expressing his gratitude again?"

"Yeah," Craig answered as he logged into his computer, "I think they were getting all naked and stuff…"

"Ewwww! Shut up!" Julie shrieked, covering her eyes – trying to block the horrid sight from her mind, but the damage was done.

The rest of the day would be spent trying to get the image of a naked Karl Timmons out of her head.

The rest of the week and month flew by. Spring came early to the West Coast and with her she brought fresh flowers and plenty of rain to the area. July ushered in the start of summer and a sweltering heat wave. Temperatures were well above one-hundred degrees for more than two weeks straight. Brown-outs were common during that stretch of time since the power company was ill-equipped to deal with the large demand for power; the area was not used to such temperatures and folks that had air conditioners cranked them on full blast for the duration of the oppressive hot spell.

Julie and Craig both used their bonuses and took their vacations during July. Julie spent three weeks on a Mediterranean cruise with Alexander. Craig and Amanda spent two weeks with her parents in Maine, where it was at least fifteen degrees cooler than in Idaho.

- *August 6, 2012: Monday, 8:15 AM – at the main elevator, third floor, Illumination Pharmaceuticals…*

Craig returned to the office a week earlier than Julie since he had accrued less vacation time than her. Julie was due back in the office today and Craig looked forward to his partner-in-crime returning. During her extended vacation, Theo covered her lab duties.

Theodore Ellis was a decent man, but Craig didn't know him very well, at least not outside the office. Theo was an exceptionally bright young man with a great future ahead of himself. He was short and stocky, maybe 5' 9" with a beard and a shaved head. Craig never knew why Theo shaved off his afro, but more than likely, the bald spot on the back of his head had led to his *"preventative"* measure last spring.

The only real problem Craig had with the younger man was that Theo was way too arrogant – he liked for people to know how smart he was. He would tell people often of his one-fifty plus IQ. Theo had a tendency to mention his own name in the same breath with that of Einstein and Da Vinci and would often tell of his Mensa application – which was denied due to *"clerical issues."*

Today, none of that mattered. Theo was back to his part of the building – doing whatever it was Theo did - and Julie was coming back to the lab. Craig wanted to get her a welcome *"home"* gift, but he was strapped for cash, so a gift from the snack machine would have to suffice.

Craig stopped by the break room on the third floor since the machines on the fourth floor were out-of-order again. He fished out some loose change from his pocket. He purchased two sodas and two small bags of chips to share with his returning comrade. Craig left the break room and stood awkwardly at the elevator. With his hands now full, he had to use his elbow to press the UP elevator button. This was more difficult than he anticipated. As he made a third attempt, the elevator doors opened up.

Five men in dark suits hastily exited the elevator. Craig moved aside quickly to avoid a collision - dropping his chips and sodas in the process. The men walked by offering no assistance and no apologies for the mess they caused. Craig bent down and picked up the snacks and watched the men go into Karl's office at the opposite end of the hallway. Two of the men appeared to be from the same group of individuals that Karl had been having meetings with during the last few months of the previous year. Craig did not recognize the other three men. They reminded him of Secret Service agents.

Craig entered the elevator and pressed the fourth floor button. The elevator reeked of cheap cologne, most likely from the recent occupants. The elevator announced its arrival and the doors opened after a musical chime sounded. Craig went to his office and sat down at his desk and began daydreaming about Karl getting chewed out. Obviously Craig had no idea what was going on in the office below, but he often thought about people yelling at Karl. It made his day go by faster.

"What are you thinking about, handsome?" Julie asked with a puzzled look on her face. She had walked in and sat down without Craig even noticing her arrival.

"Hi, Julie, how was the vacation?" He jumped up, happy like a puppy hearing its master pull up in the driveway after a long workday, and hugged his friend. "Welcome, back!"

"Thanks! The vacation was fantastic!" She tightly reciprocated his hug.

"That cruise liner was humongous!" she said after the embrace. "I thought I would get sea-sick but it never happened. I barely felt the boat move." Julie had come back well-tanned, refreshed and as usual - a bit over-perfumed. "There was so much food. They had a mini-golf course and an Olympic-sized pool on the upper deck. It was like a floating city! How was your vacation? Did you get along with the in-laws?"

"BAH!" Craig uttered. "Mandy's parents hate me. I know they do. They want grandkids and well they blame me for the obvious lack thereof…I walked in on them one morning in the kitchen and I heard her dad say something along the lines of *'that boy's swimmers are all retarded from working around lab equipment all day'*…I wanted to leave so badly, but I didn't."

Julie laughed.

Craig deftly changed the subject. "Julie, do you remember those *'suits'* from last year – the ones that were having the closed-door meetings with Karl?"

"Yes, vaguely."

"They're back."

"Well," said Julie, "I think they are IPPC officials. Maybe they've come to ensure that the vaccine is ready. They've invested millions of dollars in our company. They want to make sure we've got the goods."

"Yeah, that makes sense."

"Craig – is it Friday yet?" Julie joked, smiling, as she thought about being back on vacation. "Here we are again…another long week at our home away from home."

"Hey, these are for you." Craig handed her a soda and chips. "I know it's a bit early for a snack but you should probably wait a few minutes anyway. I don't want that soda to explode all over your blouse."

Julie looked confused. "Did you shake them up?"

"No, I was trying to get on the elevator and my hands were full and when the door opened, those men rushed out and I dropped the snacks trying to avoid a collision," Craig said as he explained the strange yet brief encounter with the men.

The two friends then began running their daily tests. Work had piled up for both of them during their vacations. Both hoped that the week would fly by. No one liked the first few days back in the office after a nice, long vacation. Taking a vacation, at times, didn't seem worth it; often times on your return from an extended vacation – you'd most likely have to work longer hours just to get caught back up.

꘡❖꘡

• *August 6, 2012: Monday, 10:30 AM –Karl Timmons' office, third
  floor, the tail end of a lengthy meeting with IPPC officials …*

Karl's office was unnecessarily large, but most of the space was
used very well. Plush beige carpet lined the floors. A large, maroon
leather couch sat parallel to the south wall. A sturdy, handcrafted
oak desk squatted in front of a large plate glass window on the
east side of the building. Two leather chairs were on the opposite
side of the desk. The non-windowed walls proudly displayed expensive reproductions of Picasso and Warhol. Karl often looked
out his window to the busy street below, at what he liked to call
"the little people," but not this morning. Today, Karl was one of
those little people. He was the one taking orders.

Karl's cavernous office felt entirely too small today; he felt
smothered, barely able to breathe. Usually, he was the only one in
his office; however, five additional men occupied his office today.
Karl was the sixth man. Not like the basketball term, Karl was not
the unseen teammate urging his team on to victory. Karl was not
part of this team…he was more of an obstacle. At the start of the
meeting, the three armed agents moved into position. One agent
stayed inside the office while the other two exited the room and
stood guard outside the closed office door.

"So, Karl – do we understand each other?" the gentleman sitting in Karl's chair asked.

"Yes, sir, Mr. Hastings – I am fully aware of who is in charge of
this operation," Karl replied as he sat in one of the leather chairs on
the opposite side of his desk.

Gaylord Hastings was the Chief Financial Officer of the IPPC. His financial backing in conjunction with his clout within the US government made him a formidable and persuasive business man. Karl Timmons was very rarely in awe of any man other than himself…however, sitting across from Mr. Hastings made Karl feel infinitesimally small.

Donovan Bryant was the Vice President of the Deployment and Logistics Division for IPPC. He was responsible for the coordination and distribution of new vaccines to various areas of the globe that were in need of assistance. Donovan had been offered the job with the IPPC about thirteen months ago; he resigned from his former position as the Director of the World Health Organization to take up his new post.

Karl had met with these two men on multiple occasions last year prior to winning the IPPC grant. Those previous meetings were nothing like the current meeting. Last year's meetings involved the firm's senior management, Karl and IPPC officials. Those meetings were cordial and professional.

Now Karl was alone, isolated from the herd – two predators in Armani suits flanked him. Illumination Pharmaceuticals was now a subsidiary of the IPPC. Once the grant was accepted by his corporation's senior officers, Karl Timmons managerial stature plummeted. He was no longer involved with any high-level decision making. He was responsible only for the laboratories in Idaho and New York.

Karl spoke softly, for fear of angering his new bosses. "I am sorry to reiterate this, but I'm not sure I fully understand. I thought the vaccine would be equally distributed to those nations in need?" Karl was by no means a lawyer, but his initial understanding of the guidelines set forth in the IPPC charter clearly indicated that products under the control of the IPPC would be distributed on an as-needed basis.

"I don't think we understand each other, Karl," Donovan said. "How would it look to the company if you lost the grant money?"

"Um, I uh..." Karl fumbled for the words.

Mr. Hastings interjected, "What Donovan is trying to say, in a less-than diplomatic way, is this - do you consider yourself a patriot? Do you love this country?"

"Yeah...of course I do." Karl felt as if he was being interrogated by the KGB. *Why would they question his love for his country?* Sweat dripped down the back of his neck. He reached back with the already damp handkerchief and wiped off the perspiration.

"Of course you are, Karl" Mr. Hastings replied in a condescending tone. "What we are *asking* you to do is in the best interest of your country. You should be proud to be doing your part to protect the United States."

Donovan spoke again, "As I said at the onset of this meeting - you will store fifteen percent of the new vaccine in our warehouse in Florida. We don't want anyone else at the headquarters back in Sweden to get too inquisitive. You'll have to come up with a way to 'massage' the amounts of vaccine produced and 'misplace' shipping destination documentation."

"I'm not sure that is possible – there are very stringent guidelines in place..." Karl said.

Donovan became visibly frustrated. "Gaylord, are you sure this guy can do the job? He's asking way too many questions. Maybe someone else should handle this for us?"

"No wait, I'm sorry. I think I can make this happen." Karl said as he pictured himself jobless - no more opulent office furniture, no more fancy sports cars and no more three-thousand square foot home on the golf course.

"You think?!" Donovan stood up, wagged his index finger from side-to-side in Karl's face, talking down to Karl like a teacher scolding a misbehaving student.

"Sit down, Donovan," Mr. Hastings said in a low-pitched, monotone voice. "There is no need for threats – right, Karl? We do understand each other, right?"

"Yes, sir – I'm crystal clear. I will make the necessary adjustments to store the fifteen percent in the warehouse – no one will know. All of it will be taken care of as soon as possible. You have my word on that." Karl looked up for approval.

"Very good, Karl," Mr. Hastings replied. "You are keeping our country safe. Those 'secret' stockpiles will aid the United States should a shortage occur during a future crisis. We must protect ourselves. You agree with me, right?"

"Yes, sir – I guess. What happens if there is a shortage and our official stockpiles cannot meet the needs of other charter members? What if those members find out that surplus vaccines were stored in our warehouses and not distributed to countries that needed it?" Karl asked.

"Let us do the thinking, Karl," Donovan said. "You be a good boy and just follow orders."

Karl nodded his head in defeated acknowledgement. He stared down at his shoes. This meeting was adjourned.

Mr. Hastings nodded slightly in the direction of the agent. Karl had all but forgotten about the wraith-like armed man that was standing guard. Like a well-oiled machine, the muscular agent pivoted one-hundred eighty degrees and walked to the door.

"We are coming out," the guard instructed as he opened the door. The two agents outside the office nodded at their compatriot. Gaylord Hastings and Donovan Bryant followed behind the lead agent and the two other men flanked the IPPC executives as they walked to the elevator.

Karl stood up and moved to the window trying to decipher what had just happened and what he had gotten himself into. As he looked out over the streets below, he formulated a plan and thought of the resources required to fulfill his boss's orders. A few moments passed and a dark blue Chevy Tahoe exited from the building's lower level at a high-rate of speed. A jet black limousine immediately followed the SUV and finally a dark maroon Ford Expedition tailed the first two vehicles. Karl knew he was way out of his league – not even a pawn in this high-stakes game.

Chapter 5

- *November 14, 2012: Wednesday, 1:08 PM – IPPC Emergency Call Center, Stockholm, Sweden …*

The International Pandemic Prevention Council consisted of five multiple level, steel and brick buildings located in mid-town Stockholm; the buildings were set up similar to a compass. The three-story main building, referred to as the *"HUB,"* sat at the center of the compass; its main function was the communication nerve center of the complex. The other four buildings were equidistant from the center; all were connected to the main building via one-hundred yard glass corridors. These walk ways to the North, South, East and West buildings (as they were called) were connected to the main building from exits on the second floor of the HUB.

The North building functioned similarly to a mini-United Nations - all of the delegates that comprised the charter members of the IPPC worked and conducted business from this facility. The East building served as research and lab facility for the onsite scientists and doctors. The West building was the main storage facility – vaccines and other medicines were stored on all three floors. The South building housed the security division of the corporation and all of the employees of the firm.

The Call Center on the second floor of the HUB, which measured approximately one-thousand square feet, had been quiet most of the morning. The main floor was dominated by three rows of four tables – each table had two chairs. All twenty-four charter countries had a dedicated call support team that manned each workstation in twelve-hour rotations. On top of each table stood two flat screen monitors and keyboards, used by the call staff to monitor and report disease activities around the world. The employees in this room were the first line of defense that nation's health officials would contact in the event of an outbreak.

Three phones rang within a one hour window. The Call Center operators would definitely earn their money today.

"IPPC Call Center, this is Operator-Seventeen, go ahead please."

"Yes, this is Doctor Mikhail Goranski from Nukus, Uzbekistan in Russia."

"Go ahead, Doctor," Operator-Seventeen replied.

"We have a possible situation developing. Five of our local hospitals have reported treating at least three-hundred and thirty-two suspect cases within the last three days. Symptoms are similar to the H1N1 flu strain. I'm requesting Uzbekistan's Health Status to be elevated to Orange Alert."

"Uzbekistan is now at Orange Alert status," Operator-Seventeen replied as he entered relevant information into his computer. "We are now tracking the cases you referenced. Please keep us advised of any more activity. Operator-Seventeen, out."

Eighteen minutes after the Uzbekistan call...

"IPPC Call Center, this is Operator-Nine, go ahead please."

"This is Melvin Dorchester from the New York State Department of Health."

"Go ahead, Mr. Dorchester," Operator-Nine replied.

"This is the first time that I've called one of these in, except for the times during our training sessions. I think we have an issue in up-state New York."

"Can you be more specific?" Operator-Nine inquired.

"Yes, of course. One of our local college campuses has had to shut down due to illness. Over one-hundred students were complaining of flu-like symptoms and were sent home. Some students and teachers still tarry on campus."

"Are you requesting an upgrade to your state's Health Status, sir?"

"Yes, Yellow Alert," Melvin said.

"Thank you, Mr. Dorchester. Yellow Alert status has been activated. Please keep us apprised of any changes. Send additional information as the situation develops. Operator-Nine, out."

Thirty-two minutes after the Uzbekistan call...

"IPPC Call Center, this is Operator-One, go ahead please."

"Hello, this is Colonel Benito Chavez of the Colombian National Defense located in San Juan de Pasto. Can you hear me?"

"Yes, go ahead please," Operator-One replied.

"Excellent. We've tried since last week to contact you, but our communication systems have been less than cooperative. We sent emails – did you receive them?" Colonel Chavez inquired.

Operator-One checked the log records from the previous week. "No, Colonel – there are no records of any contact from Colombia."

"Damned technology..." Colonel Chavez said, slamming his fist down on his desk.

"Sir, can I be of assistance today?"

"Yes. Last week approximately forty of our soldiers became ill. The initial prognosis was food poisoning but that diagnosis proved incorrect. Those men should have been better after two days but none of them improved. Subsequent testing revealed they were all sick with the flu. They were quarantined Wednesday of last week. We tried to report this as we were required to do by our IPPC charter agreement, but as I mentioned, our communication backbone was overly stressed."

"What Health Status are you requesting upgrade to?" Operator-One asked.

"Last week it would have been Orange, but now we must request Red Alert status. Twenty-six of the quarantined soldiers have died from complications."

"Red Alert status has been applied. All information will be summarily redirected to Deputy Director Pamela Bristow," Operator-One said as she emailed all the data to Dr. Bristow.

As protocol dictated, any reports of deaths related to possible epidemic or pandemic related causes were immediately routed to Deputy Director Dr. Pamela Bristow. Her team's main duties involved root cause diagnosis and the coordination of supplies to compromised areas. Dr. Bristow was second in command of the Deployment and Logistics Division.

Dr. Bristow had just returned to her office from a high-calorie BBQ lunch that was sweetly punctuated with a large portion of chocolate ice cream. Pamela Bristow was forty-one years old and morbidly obese. In her mid-thirties, she was diagnosed with a thyroid condition that she constantly blamed for her over eating. She wedged herself into her chair and began reading over her emails. The high-priority email from Operator-One caught her attention immediately. She phoned Karl Timmons after reviewing all three status changes.

The phone rang loudly startling Karl, even though he was already awake. He stared at his phone's caller id and recognized the first few digits of the international prefix and knew it was someone calling from the Deployment and Logistics Division of the IPPC. Flashbacks from his previous meeting during the end of summer caused him to hesitate. *Was Donovan calling to berate him again?* For the three months following the August meeting, Karl had done as instructed. While he was unable to get the full fifteen percent of the vaccine stored at the Florida facility, he felt that he had procured enough of the vaccine without raising suspicions. After seven rings, Karl reluctantly pressed the talk button on his Blackberry.

"This is Karl."

"Karl – this is Dr. Pamela Bristow. Sorry for disturbing you, I know it's early back there in the States."

"Oh, hey Pamela – don't worry about it, I was already awake. Sorry I didn't pick up sooner, the ringer volume must have been turned down for some reason." Karl was relieved to be speaking to Pamela instead of Donovan. "How can I help you?"

"I'm forwarding to you information regarding three new hot spots. Disburse one-thousand units to San Juan de Pasto, Colombia and five-hundred units to both Uzbekistan and New York. The location and contact information is in the last email I just sent to your Blackberry. Our teams in those areas have already been notified. They are expecting shipments ASAP. Priority one is the deaths in Colombia. We are sending a specialist team in from Sweden to assist there."

"I am approving those shipments now." Karl opened a secure application on his Blackberry and entered his password. He began accessing the facilities of the New York office to begin transfer of supplies. "By the close of business tomorrow," he continued, "those vaccines will be airborne and should arrive ready for distribution by the IPPC teams in those two distant locations. The New York shipment should only take a few hours tops." Karl submitted the request and the automated process began.

Advanced assembly line robots in the New York warehouse began pulling the required amounts of the 2011_10_20 vaccine and packing them into shipping containers. Within hours of the automation order, all shipments had been pulled and loaded for transport. Two C130 supply planes departed from the private Illumination Pharmaceutical's airstrip outside of Rochester, New York for Russia and Colombia.

Three hours after the initial request, two trucks filled with vaccines and additional supplies arrived at the local community college campus located just outside Syracuse. The health facility at the college was quickly overrun with the remaining students and faculty that had not already left for an early winter break. While the situation was peaceful, there were a few frantic individuals that had to be forcibly removed from the premises by campus security. After the commotion calmed down, the members of the college still on campus were vaccinated in an orderly fashion.

IPPC officials arrived shortly after the majority of the vaccine had been distributed; they were delayed by almost two hours due to rush hour traffic. To their dismay, as they assessed the situation and spoke to the onsite clinic staff, the IPPC team was informed that many sick but treated individuals were already sent home to start an early winter break. While the officials would have preferred more time to interview the sick, they were at least somewhat pleased that enough supplies were available to treat everyone at the college. However, the IPPC specialists were concerned that the treated individuals had left the campus potentially spreading the flu-like symptoms elsewhere.

- *November 16, 2012: Friday, mid-afternoon Pacific Standard Time –
distribution centers in Russia and Colombia …*

In Russia, the vaccines arrived earlier in the day at the Nukus Airport and were transported to two major distribution centers, one in the eastern and one in the southern part of the town. Teams of doctors, nurses and volunteers staffed the local clinics to distribute the medication to those in need. The first rounds of medication were given only to those already exhibiting flu-like symptoms. Preventive shots would come at a later date. The directive was clear – treat those in need first. Russian Special Forces and the police kept order while working directly with the IPPC officials on scene.

The vaccine shipment bound for Colombia was sent directly to the National Defense headquarters in San Juan de Pasto. The specialist team from Sweden, led by Dr. Christina Finch, arrived a few hours after the medication. Colonel Chavez briefed the team on the deaths of the soldiers. After the short meeting, Colonel Chavez had to attend to other pressing matters, but the specialist team was escorted to the restricted zone by a military entourage. About two-hundred yards from where the soldiers died, Dr. Finch motioned for the driver to stop the vehicle. The area was poorly quarantined. Four soldiers moved throughout the contaminated area without proper hazmat gear.

"Get those stupid fools out of here!" Dr. Finch yelled. "This area should have been quarantined with absolutely no access without prior authorization from me!"

The driver of the jeep abruptly stopped the vehicle and the communications officer in the backseat contacted the base. The call was quickly routed to Colonel Chavez's personal cell phone. The driver handed the cell phone to Dr. Finch. "The Colonel, he would talk at you, doctor," the driver said in broken English.

Dr. Finch took the phone. "Yes?"

"Dr. Finch – sorry for the confusion," Colonel Chavez said. "Instructions are being relayed as we speak. No one was supposed to enter the area directly. They were instructed to only seal off the area. Apparently their curiosity got the better of them, no?"

"With all due respect sir, those four men are now most likely infected with whatever killed your other soldiers. They will not be able to leave the area. My men are now suiting up and we will make a proper safe zone around the area and seal off the danger zone."

"That is fine, good doctor," the Colonel said. "My second lieutenant has been instructed to follow your orders. My men will follow his. Keep this phone. You have a direct line to me...assuming the communication satellites continue to cooperate."

"Thank you, Colonel. By the way, as my team works to contain this area, will the vaccines be distributed?"

"Yes, Dr. Finch. My soldiers have already split the supplies and delivered them to three nearby clinics. The staff there is already treating our people. Soldiers are posted there to maintain order. No need for panic, right?"

"I wish I could honestly answer that, sir," Dr. Finch said as she surveyed the site in front of her. "I'm just not sure right now."

Dr. Finch had seen this situation before and was well trained at her job. Her crew was top-of-the line professionals. Within four hours, the experienced bio-hazard team had the offending two-hundred square yard area completely quarantined. Military guards were positioned about fifty feet from the perimeter of the danger zone, each guard about thirty feet apart from one another.

"Dr. Finch?" Eduardo Castillo, the second lieutenant, stood at attention as he waited for the doctor to acknowledge him.

"Yes, Eduardo?"

"Everything and everyone has been positioned as you requested. The zone is secure and all four soldiers have been moved to the low-risk location. The sick soldiers from the initial platoon have been moved to the designated high-risk area."

"Very good, Eduardo," Dr. Finch said. "Now the real work can begin."

• *November 19, 2012: Monday, 9:18 AM – Illumination Pharmaceuticals, a conference call taking place in the office of Karl Timmons…*

"Excellent work, Karl," Dr. Bristow said. "All shipments arrived as anticipated."

"Karl, with the increase in H1N1 activity," Donovan Bryant began, "we feel it necessary that within the next two to three weeks, you should have your employees vaccinated. Keeping them healthy will ensure an uninterrupted workforce to continue producing the vaccine. We've set aside a small amount of the product to distribute to your people."

"Thank you," Karl responded. "I will get that taken care of as quickly as possible."

"We will contact you later if we need your services." Donovan shut off the phone, abruptly ending the meeting.

Julie and Theo sat in the large leather chairs; Craig and Michael were comfortably reclined on the leather couch. All four employees had been involved with various stages of coordinating resources. Their main objective had been to find ways to increase production rates and decrease the time to market. The research tasks were in addition to their normal daily activities.

"Craig, you and Julie will lead the effort to get the Idaho employees vaccinated within two weeks," Karl stated. "I will make sure the New York office is handled."

"Sure," Craig responded. "We'll add that to the rest of the work on our plates…"

Julie glanced sidewise at her partner in an effort to reel in his smart mouth.

"Excellent. I like your enthusiasm." Karl stood up and walked to his favorite window. "Julie, you and Craig may go. Theo and Michael, please stay behind, we need to discuss the logistics and storage issues that were brought to my attention last week."

Julie and Craig left the conference room.

• *December 13, 2012: Thursday, 11:18 AM – Illumination Pharmaceuticals, the fourth floor lab…*

During the past few weeks, Craig and Julie had organized the vaccinations of the Idaho facility employees as Karl had requested. They were both tired and frustrated by the increased workload but were very happy to see the last person standing in line. As the final shot was delivered, Craig crossed off the last name on his list; they were done! They cleaned up the meeting room that had been used as a makeshift clinic returning it to its original layout then went upstairs to their lab on the fourth floor.

For the last thirty minutes, Craig had indulged in what he called *"relaxation time"* - flipping through infomercials and various midday news events. He unconsciously stopped channel surfing on one station interviewing *"experts"* on the upcoming Mayan Event set to occur next week.

Julie stood up quickly throwing her hands up in the air and thrusting her chair backwards into the wall behind her desk. "Turn that crap off, Craig!" She walked over to the window and opened it slightly – she needed some fresh air.

"What do you mean? This stuff is hilarious," Craig said, referring to the program on the TV.

"I can't take anymore of this doomsday shit. I'm so tired of hearing about the Mayan shit, so tired of hearing about death cults and new religions that have sprung up…some of which have declared Nostradamus their own personal savior…this shit is driving me bonkers." Julie paced back and forth in front of the window. Both she and Craig had been under tremendous stress with the extra work.

Craig muted the TV. He knew Julie was a bit frazzled. He also knew that she was seriously angry about all the news coverage and events focusing on the Mayan Doomsday prophecies. Craig had rarely heard Julie swear so much.

"I'm sorry, J-"

"It's not you, just please promise me not to watch anymore of that crap for the rest of the week," Julie pleaded.

"It's a deal," Craig said as he turned off the TV. "Let's go get some lunch, then we can come back and finish up these reports for Karl. I think he'll be impressed that we've come up with a way to decrease production time by eight percent."

"I highly doubt it," Julie said shaking her head. "That man is impossible to please."

- *December 21, 2012: Friday, 12:18 PM the beginning of the Winter Solstice…*

The mighty Sun rotated angrily in his ancient orbit burning tremendous reserves of hydrogen and helium that had built up in his unimaginably dense core over the past one-hundred thousand years; this magnificent combustion emitted increased levels of gamma radiation in an epic temper tantrum. Solar flares and storms danced across the face of the Sun. Mercury and Venus were punished like disobedient children, absorbing tremendous levels of radiation. The Sky King would punish all of his children in the Milky Way galaxy, but first – he fixated his glare on his favorite offspring…the Earth.

The Sun stood still as if deep in thought, he surveyed his Earthly kingdom below knowing there was very little time to act this day – the shortest day of the year. The clouds dispersed seemingly in fear as the winds cowered and ceased their whispering – it was as if the world was holding its breath waiting for a sign from the magnificent yellowish-orange sphere as to what would happen next.

Cults from every nation around the world stood outside; their leaders espousing *"New Age Prophecies"* regarding the end of days. Men and women around the world cowered in bunkers, surrounded by supplies of canned goods, bottled water and short-wave radios. Sporadic reports of riots and mass suicides began to clog the news outlets.

The scientists of Earth watched as the Sun soared to its highest position in the sky. Most astronomers and scientists tended to focus on facts; they recorded the massive energy levels emanating from the Sun and reported their findings to their superiors. These men of science had no faith in the antics of the mainstream population. They cared only for data, not for the hysteria that seemed to grip popular culture. The majority of these intellectuals frowned on the lay men and women that hid in their bunkers. The world would not end, at least not this day.

Government agencies monitored their power grids and precious communication infrastructures. Some nations had been able to protect a small percentage of their highest security facilities at the urging of scientists. Armed forces prepared for any eventualities.

The majority of the world went about their everyday routines. Most felt that the world would not end. Of course, many of the more tech-savvy folks constantly monitored their Face Book pages, blogged on their Twitter accounts and watched their favorite 24-hour news stations...just in case a real-time update came across informing the world of its own demise...

The Earth seemed to collectively sigh in unison as it awakened on the following Saturday morning. The end of days did not happen. There was no cataclysmic earthquakes, no reversal of the magnetic poles and the Earth was not sucked into a black hole at the center of the Milky Way galaxy. Nostradamus and the Mayans must have miscalculated. The world was still here, minus of course a few thousand idiots that died in riots and mass suicides. Governments, businesses and citizens spent the last two weeks of the year cleaning up human-caused messes. Life would go on; many folks prepared to watch the giant crystal ball drop in Times Square – signaling the start of a new year.

During January of 2013, the world continued about its way as it had done prior to the supposed end of time. Doomsday predictors and Armageddon experts were chastised in all forms of media. New Age Religious zealots began to focus on other doomsday timelines such as the 2060 date that Isaac Newton purportedly predicted in some of his lost papers. Rioters were prosecuted and jailed. Governments dispatched repair teams to reinforce and repair non-protected infrastructures. The Sun continued to emit massive levels of radiation and solar flares wreaking havoc on power grids and satellites. A few countries experienced short, sporadic nation-wide brownouts.

All-in-all, the general consensus around the world was that everything was going to be OK. The people of Earth had just survived the most documented end-of-time periods ever foretold or predicted. Besides the relatively small amount of collateral damage and loss of life from the recent events, life quickly began to return to normal.

People joked often that they would be able to look back on this event ten years from now and laugh at how silly they had been...

Chapter 6

- *February 2, 2013: Saturday, 9:41 AM – the HUB, Stockholm, Sweden…*

"Dr. Pamela Bristow, go ahead please," the deputy director said after pushing the dull, red speaker phone button. She leaned back in her chair, rotating her head in a clockwise motion trying to get the kinks out of her sore neck – a migraine wasn't too far away. She had been hunched over her computer for the better part of two days; her team had been tracking multiple reports of H1N1 infections from the Middle East and the Korean Peninsula for the past forty-four hours.

"Pamela, this is Donovan. I need a situation report now. I just landed at the Stockholm-Arlanda Airport about ten minutes ago and I'm in a cab en route to the Hub now. I'm probably a good twenty-five minutes out."

"I hope you had a decent flight. I'm sorry for contacting you so late, sir – I didn't consider the time zone differences when I called. This situation is spiraling out of control and I was just following protocol…"

"Fuck!" Donovan yelped into the phone as he bumped his head on the passenger side window of the cab. Pamela could hear the cabbie apologizing to his passenger for the rough ride.

"Don't waste my time apologizing," Donovan said in frustration as he rubbed his throbbing temple.

"...but it was an accident, sir," the cabbie said with a thick Swedish accent.

"Not you, dumbass," Donovan said to the cab driver. "I'm talking on the phone here – mind your own damn business! Just get me to the IPPC home office...and learn to fucking drive while you're at it!"

Pamela never liked Donovan; she sincerely doubted that anyone liked this man. He treated her and everyone else like scum of the earth. Like he was better than everyone – that people should be grateful that a man like him even looked in their general direction, let alone doing them a tremendous service by actually speaking to them. While she loved her job and she felt like she was actually making a difference in the world, any time she had to deal with her boss...it made her sick to her stomach. However, hearing her boss's immense discomfort on the other end of the phone made her smile...just a little.

Pamela spoke after a few brief moments. "Two new H1N1 hot spots have emerged. The first is in Labboune, Lebanon – reported by our sources close to the Israeli border. These are unconfirmed reports since Lebanon has no charter with our agency and their government fails to respond to our official requests for information. Needless to say, the Israelis are watching the situation very closely. According to preliminary reports, about eight- to ten-thousand possible cases have been diagnosed. Again, we don't have official numbers. Plus some of our satellites are out of commission in that area due to the solar activity. We are literally flying blind in that region of the world."

"Figures," Donovan said. "What's the other area?"

"Well, we do have an official report from our affiliates in Seoul, South Korea. Our doctors at the Asian Medical Center, located in the Songpa-gu district, have reported estimates of twenty-thousand cases with more cases streaming in every hour. We've been in constant contact with the facility for the past two hours. They are becoming overwhelmed and requesting immediate disbursal of aid…" Pamela paused mid-sentence; a priority email flashed in her inbox.

"What?" Donovan inquired. "What's going on?"

"We have just received an additional unconfirmed report out of Pyongyang that the North Koreans are also suffering from an extreme outbreak," she said. "Some reports, according to this email, estimate upwards of forty-five thousand cases in that city alone."

"We don't have enough units on hand to deal with non-charter nations at this time. Get Karl up-to-speed on the situation. Tell him to expect a call from me on the secure conference line – he'll know the one. He and I will deal with Lebanon and North Korea. Tell him to ship out thirty-thousand units to Seoul. I'll be in the office shortly."

She knew it was very late evening or early morning in Idaho, but as soon as Pamela finished with Donovan, she immediately contacted Karl Timmons filling him in on the events of the last two days. She informed him of the H1N1 hot spots and the surreal number of cases plaguing the Korean Peninsula.

Karl was a night owl and normally wasn't in bed till two or three AM on most nights, so the phone call didn't bother him. He ran a few instant queries from his Blackberry. The report showed a combined warehouse inventory in Idaho and New York of just under forty-thousand units. He punched in a few codes on his hand-held device and the automated shipping facilities began boxing and loading the vaccines.

In less than eight hours, four military cargo planes would be heading to Seoul, South Korea.

Dr. Bristow thanked Karl for his quick response time. She then ended their conversation with even more *"happy"* news for Karl – that he should be expecting a call from Donovan within the next few hours. She heard Karl groan as he hung up the phone. No one liked an early morning conference call with Donovan. Hell, she was pretty sure that no one really even liked the man no matter what time of day it was.

• *February 2, 2013: Saturday, 3:45 AM – Boise, Idaho, A secure teleconference line between the HUB and Illumination Pharmaceuticals...*

Michael Clark patiently waited in Karl's office. Karl was standing in his usual spot staring out the window looking down on the empty street below. They both listened to the instrumental music blaring over the speakerphone as they waited for Donovan to dial in to the urgent conference call. Michael drummed his fingers on the desk and rocked back-and-forth in his own rhythmically challenged way. Apparently, all the years of choir practice in junior-high and all of the time spent as a male cheerleader in college never improved his coordination.

Theodore Ellis rushed into the room. He was late, which was highly unusual. Theo prided himself in not only being brilliant, but also being reliably prompt. He liked to show up early for meetings and for other functions. He believed sincerely that *"being on time"* should be considered *"almost being late."* He often argued that if one showed up exactly on time, then by definition, they were just mere moments from being late. Theo really liked to argue – he felt it was a great way to impress upon people how smart he was… many were often overwhelmed by his quick wit and encyclopedic knowledge.

"Sorry, boss – I fell back to sleep after you paged me," Theo said, stretching and rubbing his eyes. "I stayed up late working on a paper for my third master's degree."

The brilliant young man sat down next to Michael. He watched as his co-worker gyrated to the beat of his own drummer. Theo thought silently to himself how it appeared that *"ol' Mikey boy's"* dancing mimicked someone having a seizure. Theo imagined Michael going into convulsions and collapsing out of his chair to the floor below - the only way to save him would be for Theo to ram his wallet or a dirty sock deep into Michael's foaming mouth…

"Donovan Bryant has joined the session," the computerized female voice indicated. The music stopped and Michael ceased fidgeting a few seconds later. Theo's daydream about *"saving"* his co-worker would have to wait for another day. Karl quickly walked from the window to his desk and sat down in his plush chair.

"Is everyone there, Karl?" Donovan asked.

"Yes, sir – we are all here and waiting for instructions. I've already mobilized the last remaining units to Seoul."

"What do our stockpiles in the Florida location look like?" Donovan inquired.

"Let me check," Karl said as he accessed one of the many apps on his Blackberry. He loved all forms of technology, but he loved this hand-held device the most. If he ever had kids, he promised himself that his first born would be named *"Blackberry."*

"What Florida facility?" Theo asked with a confused look on his face. "I thought we only had the two facilities? The one at home base here in Idaho and the other one located in Rochester…"

"We have a fail-safe in place, Theo," Donovan said calmly as he lied to the young man. "This is a top-secret government facility used to store additional vaccine supplies in case of a pandemic striking the continental United States. It's a precautionary measure, but a necessary measure nonetheless to keep our country safe." Karl knew that Donovan wouldn't reveal the fact that the Florida facility was a personal warehouse owned by a dummy corporation linked to an offshore subsidiary created by Donovan and Gaylord Hastings for personal gain.

"I'm pretty sure our charter agreement states that all H1N1 supplies will be stored in official IPPC approved facilities." Theo wasn't buying Donovan's explanation.

"Theo," Karl interjected, "all of the required documentation, transportation and storage information pertaining to the vaccines in the Florida facility were approved by the IPPC commission. Don't worry about the details right now. Just know that everything is on the up-and-up and has been approved by your superiors." Karl had become quite adept over the past few months lying about shipments and documentation to cover up the secret facility, but he knew Theo was way too smart just to accept some random answers without valid proof.

"That's correct, Theo," Donovan replied. "Your primary objective over the next few days is to pick two or three of your most advanced coworkers to follow you to the Rochester office. That place is falling behind and I feel that with your strong leadership skills and the help of a few other dedicated resources - that we can get that facility up-to-speed. This is not a permanent transfer, I figure maybe a three- to six month gig tops…so you don't have to relocate. Go there, get the job done – and come home. It's that easy."

"I'm still not sure that I under…"

"You're dismissed," Donovan said cutting off Theo in mid-sentence. Theo looked at Karl and Michael. Karl nodded towards the door.

"Theo, I'll contact you sometime Monday regarding the temporary transfers," Karl said as Theo exited the office and closed the door behind himself.

Theo walked to the elevator trying to assess what had just happened. He wasn't the least bit fond of the cloak and dagger routine that just occurred. He knew something was awry…he just couldn't put his finger on it. He exited the elevator on the basement floor and walked to his 2009 Harley-Davidson. He straddled the touring bike and started up the bright green machine, revving the engine a few times. This was his baby – his gift to himself for being so awesome. Theo shifted into gear, squealed his tires and sped off into the empty streets of the pre-dawn morning.

As he rode home, he methodically went through each resource available to him. By the time he reached his house, he had narrowed his list to five potential candidates. While the Florida facility explanations failed to alleviate his concerns, he still had a job to do. This would be a perfect opportunity to demonstrate his leadership abilities on a high profile assignment. Doing well on this job could easily earn him a much deserved promotion.

Back in Karl's office, Karl and Michael listened as Donovan instructed them on his plan to distribute the vaccines from the Florida warehouse to the new H1N1 hot spots. Of course, he only shared the barest of information with his subordinates – no need for them to know the entirety of the plan. Donovan explained that he had already contacted the Premier of North Korea and the Prime Minister of Lebanon earlier in the day to set up meetings to discuss disbursement and payment. Karl and Michael were instructed to fly to Florida early Monday morning to facilitate the transfer of the merchandise. The promised delivery date would be one week from today. The end of the conversation was punctuated by Donovan offering both men large bonuses should the transactions run smoothly with expedited deliveries. Karl and Michael left the office to enjoy the remainder of their weekend. Donovan left the conference room and made his way to the HUB to see Dr. Bristow to go over documentation from the previous two days.

- *February 4, 2013: Monday, 7:45 AM – Boise, Idaho, The airport at Gowen Field...*

Karl and Michael boarded the large passenger plane bound for Florida. The two men moved to their comfortable seats and relaxed. Michael had quickly fallen asleep as soon as the Boeing 737 had exited Idaho airspace. Karl spent the entire flight organizing information on his always present Blackberry.

Michael awoke as the plane touched down at Ocala OCF Airport five hours later. Karl and Michael were the last passengers off. As they exited, a large, black Chevy Suburban with limo tint on all windows pulled up to the outermost gates. Three men exited the vehicle, arms crossed, each wearing white earpieces. Karl walked quickly towards the SUV with Michael close behind - they knew the ride was for them. The secret warehouse was located in Silver Springs – less than ten miles from the airport – that's all the info Karl had about the facility. Obviously these men were here to take them to Donovan's warehouse and to ensure the location remained secret.

Karl and Michael sat nervously in the middle section of the Suburban. Two of the three men sat in the back row behind them while the third man rode shotgun. The driver, a fourth man, wore dark sunglasses, had a shaved head and sported a dark brown beard. This man never spoke nor did he even acknowledge his new passengers. The short ride felt like an eternity. Michael felt like a prisoner… he kept his head low and never even looked at the surrounding area – he didn't want to remember where or how they got to their destination. Karl had the inescapable feeling that these men could make him disappear and never be found or heard from again…

The SUV entered a very unassuming alleyway that led to a small gated checkpoint. The driver came to a stop and lowered his window. The young man stationed at the gate waved the vehicle through. The small lot consisted of four non-descript brick buildings. The fourth building, the farthest back on the lot, had a small garage door that opened as the Suburban closed to within two-hundred feet. The driver skillfully navigated the small opening and pulled the SUV to the side of the room. The driver nodded his head and the three men exited the vehicle in unison.

Karl reached for the handle but the door swung open before he could grasp it. The largest of the three men motioned for their *"guests"* to exit. Karl and Michael did as instructed and followed the lead agent to a small elevator. The elevator descended two floors to the bottom level. As the doors slid open, Karl was shocked to see the expansive lower level. No one would ever have guessed that such a facility existed. That was the point, he assumed. The lower level must have run the entire length of the above lot that they had entered a few moments earlier.

"You two are to go to that office," the largest of the three men pointed to a small door on the east end of the facility. "Wait there for further instructions. Mr. Bryant gave specific orders that you are not allowed to contact anyone while inside this warehouse. All communications to and from this facility are strictly monitored. It is imperative that you adhere to these conditions."

Michael glanced nervously at Karl but his boss nudged him towards the office. The two men walked briskly. The scale of the facility dwarfed the warehouse facilities in Boise and Rochester… Karl figured that this facility would be close to the same size as both of those added together.

As they walked, Karl recognized the pre-packaged shipping crates that housed the H1N1 vaccines. Each crate was the standard three-by-three-by-four baby blue colored crate with a large dark blue *"IP"* logo on each side. A whole section of the southeast quadrant was filled with Illumination Pharmaceutical's products. Eight HUMVEEs were parked against the north wall. Karl briefly glanced towards the west wall where two objects were hidden under a large gray tarp. He wasn't one-hundred percent sure, but the outlines of the objects appeared to be military grade helicopters.

The two men covered the rest of the distance very quickly and made their way to the small office. A conference phone sat perched on top of an oval shaped table in the middle of the room. The east side of the room had a small cloth loveseat against the wall. A water cooler was positioned on the north wall. A few out-of-date magazines rested on a small bookshelf on the south wall. Karl picked up a random magazine and sat at the table. Michael did likewise but sat on the couch. Both men felt like they were in an interrogation room - being monitored from the other side of a one-way mirror.

They spent what seemed like an eternity in the small office. Karl had lost track of time. He knew they had been there for a good while because he had already finished reading two magazines from cover-to-cover. Some of his reading was interrupted sporadically as Michael snoozed on the couch.

Chapter 7

- *February 4, 2013: Monday, 5:18 PM – Silver Springs, Florida, A small office in a highly guarded, secret warehouse…*

Michael gasped almost rolling off of the couch as the phone in the center of the room buzzed loudly. He had been napping for over an hour. He tried to regain his composure in front of his boss. Karl pointed to his mouth with his index finger indicating to Michael that he had something on his own face. Drool. Michael nonchalantly wiped it off and moved over to the oval table. Karl pressed the intercom button.

"Karl, there has been a slight change of plans since we last spoke," Donovan said.

"What happened?" Karl inquired.

"We only have one buyer at this time. Apparently the North Koreans feel that our price is too exorbitant. They have chosen not to use our product."

"But all of those people could die!" Michael exclaimed. "Maybe we could lower our price or maybe just send them some of the supplies. It would be a shame…"

"Yeah, it's a shame," Donovan said sarcastically. "I have informed Gerald Tarkanian, our warehouse manager, to work closely with you and Michael. Take about eighty-five percent of our on-hand stock and load up the helicopters. We don't have the fancy automated system like in Rochester, but that's OK – two strong men like you shouldn't have any issue loading up a few crates. It's good to get your hands dirty every once in awhile - right, Karl?"

"Yes, sir," Karl said almost embarrassed.

"Sir?" Michael spoke.

"Yes?"

"Why not ship all of the vaccines to Lebanon then?"

"Because, young man," Donovan said, "I think the North Koreans will come to their senses as soon as throngs of their people start dying. They will want to buy our product, but a little economics lesson will unfold right before their eyes – less supply and more demand equals a higher price. Now get to work. Your plane leaves for Idaho tomorrow at 6:00 AM. Don't be late…it's a long walk home."

Karl and Michael stared across the table at each other in disbelief. Hundreds, maybe thousands of people would die and Donovan only cared about making money. *What kind of monster would do something like that?* Both men realized that they too would be responsible for the deaths, but saw no way out of the catch-22. *Do as their boss says now and withhold needed supplies from North Korea or stand up to Donovan?* If they stood up to their boss, surely they would be fired and the IPPC would more than likely take control of their facilities back in the States. They were indeed stuck between a rock and hard place.

Both men left the office contemplating the gravity of their current situation. As they opened the door, they were accosted by two of the original four men that had been in the SUV with them earlier. Karl and Michael followed the agents to the far end of the warehouse to the west wall. Karl was correct in his earlier assumption regarding the covered objects. Two helicopters were now fully exposed. An older gentleman skillfully guided his overloaded forklift to the side of the first helicopter.

"Don't just stand there," Gerald said, "these crates won't unload themselves!"

The two agents left the area and Karl and Michael began unloading the heavy crates from the forklift to the belly of the helicopter. Gerald Tarkanian hopped down from the forklift and lit up a cheap cigar. He leaned against the helicopter and watched. He knew that these cubicle cadets, accustomed to an easy, non-physically demanding office schedule, would soon run out of steam. There was no way that they could unload all of the crates.

"Pathetic," Gerald said through gritted teeth as he puffed on his cigar. "I've seen one-armed women work faster than that." Michael and Karl heard the comment but continued to move as fast as they could – both ready to leave this facility as soon as possible. After about two hours, Gerald mercifully radioed in some additional help. A little before eleven that evening, all the crates bound for Labboune, Lebanon were loaded.

Karl and Michael were escorted out of the facility and driven to a local motel close to the airport. They were exhausted but glad to be away from the warehouse. They checked-in with the front desk and were given a key. They entered a small, poorly lit room and prepared for sleep. The room smelled like old people's feet but the tired men didn't care. Two twin beds were separated by a small nightstand with a lamp and a Bible placed neatly in the middle. Both men plopped down into their respective beds, kicked off their shoes and within minutes were sound asleep. Karl's phone rang around 12:17 AM.

Karl fumbled around in the darkness to find his Blackberry. "Hello?" Karl said half asleep.

"I've been trying to reach you all day, Mr. Timmons."

"Who is this?" Karl said angrily as his exhausted body demanded sleep.

"It's Theo. You told me that you would contact me on Monday and it's now Tuesday. Like I said, I've been unable to contact you all day. Did you have your phone off?"

"Get to the point, Theo."

"It's regarding the resource allocation to the Rochester office. I have it ready and can discuss my reasoning for my choices with you now," Theo said.

"Just do it. You have my authorization. Good night." Karl angrily slammed down his Blackberry and buried his head in his pillows. He would of course apologize to his *"baby"* later…there was no need to take his anger out on his favorite toy.

Theo was a bit perplexed by the conversation, but spent the next few hours finalizing the paperwork for the trip to the Rochester office. He was ready to lead the small group and more importantly, he was ready to show off to upper management his ability to get the job done. As he finished up his tasks, he hoped that his new *"subordinates"* would be as happy about the temporary relocation as he was at this point. If he didn't know himself better, he would almost guess that he was *"giddy"* with anticipation. It was his time to shine.

Karl and Michael slept soundly – too soundly in fact. The alarm clock failed to wake them and they missed three wake-up calls. Michael awoke around 7:00 AM and woke his boss. Both men hurried to check out and then hailed a cab to the airport, but it was too late. Frustrated and tired, Karl booked a flight for them back to

Idaho. The earliest flight to Boise was at 10:00 AM. They went to their terminal and waited. Both rested but never fully slept – they didn't want to miss a second flight.

- *February 5, 2013: Tuesday, 8:22 AM – Boise, Idaho, -Conference Room 307A, Illumination Pharmaceuticals...*

"So how long are we going to be stuck there?" Craig asked.

"I don't think *'stuck'* is the right word," Theo responded. "Look at it as more of an opportunity to impress the corporation and to get our sister facility back on track. We've estimated this process will take about six months."

"Six months?!" Craig exclaimed.

"So why did you pick the two of us? Unlike you, we have family to consider. What about them?" Julie asked. "They can't just pick up and go with us. They have responsibilities here."

"Arrangements have been made that you will be allowed to travel back home every second weekend if you choose to do so. In addition, the company is offering to pay three months of your expenses at home and your pay will be doubled during this period." Theo felt his presentation was spot on...*It was a great plan and opportunity. What was the hold up?*

"Can we discuss this with our families first?" Craig asked as he took a long drink of his hot coffee.

"Sure but we need your answer by noon on Thursday. Should you choose not to partake in this career growth opportunity, we would have to contact our second choices and they would need ample time to make arrangements as well. Our plan is to be in the Rochester office no later than one week from today." Again, Theo was unsure where the resistance was coming from. Craig and Julie were two of the top researchers/technicians in the company. He had done all his research and chose very carefully. The young man began to second guess himself. His *"Plan B"* was to choose less experienced but more readily available employees without immediate family to hinder their decisions. Theo genuinely wanted the top tier talent from the Idaho facility on his team…that's why he had chosen these two.

Julie and Craig left the conference room and went to their lab on the fourth floor. Both technicians knew the Rochester gig would be a huge boon to their career. However, neither one really wanted to spend that much time away from their loved ones.

"So?" Julie inquired.

Craig pressed random buttons on his computer to appear busy. He shuffled around one messy pile on the corner of his desk to another less messy spot. He opened and closed his desk drawers as if searching for a lost treasure.

"I know you heard me, dummy!" Julie joked.

"Hmm? Did you say something?"

"What do you think Amanda will say about Rochester trip?"

Craig already knew Amanda would be fine with the trip. More appropriately, she would be ecstatic about the double pay and the house expenses being covered for three months. They needed the extra cash. The lack of a second job had caused them to have to dip into savings recently.

"She's going to be OK with it," Craig answered. "We need the funds. We've had too much month left at the end of our money…"

"I told you that if you needed some extra money…"

"I'm not taking your money!" Craig snapped at his friend.

Julie looked hurt but she knew her friend was quite stubborn. She didn't let his multiple refusals hurt her feelings. She loved this man like a brother and Amanda like a sister. She only wanted to help and she knew that Craig understood that.

"I mean thanks. Sorry for yelling," Craig said. He looked over to his friend and smiled. "I know you are only trying to make sure that I don't end up in a cardboard box under an overpass."

The two friends laughed at the imagery. They began working on the day's assignments but the six month Rochester relocation played heavily in their heads. Lunchtime came quickly and so did the end of the day. They had accomplished very little but it was time to go home. They hugged each other in the parking lot and drove to their respective homes to explain the deal to their significant others.

By the deadline on Thursday, both Craig and Julie reported back to Theo that they had accepted the six month relocation offer. Thursday was also the first day that Karl had been back in the office. Theo discussed all the pertinent info with his boss. The plans were finalized and on Saturday – Theo, Craig and Julie arrived at Rochester. Monday morning would come quickly and the team had a lot of work ahead of them.

Living arrangements were made ahead of schedule; personal belongings from both employees were transported on separate flights. Everything went very smoothly, a testament to his great leadership abilities – well at least that is how Theo viewed it. The three member team would coordinate with onsite Rochester division leaders to lay out the framework for improving the warehouse facility in New York.

By the end of the second full week of February, vaccines were delivered to Seoul, South Korea through official IPPC means. Thousands of infected citizens were treated each day. The sickest were treated first. The distribution method was less than adequate to deal with the influx of those in need. Military personnel had been dispatched earlier to ensure the safety of the patients and of the medical professionals. No one wanted a riot. An orderly method was the only logical choice for the country to distribute the cure to those in need.

The people of Labboune, Lebanon received their vaccines through not-so-official means, but the reaction and distribution of the product almost mirrored that of the Koreans. People were sick and needed help. They heard of the vaccine and rushed to the hospitals. Donovan Bryant and the Prime Minister had correctly gauged the riot-like response and skillfully deployed the vaccines to six different hospitals around the country to lessen the burden on each facility. Still, the sick flocked to every clinic and hospital looking for the vaccine.

Unruly citizens were arrested and some even killed by the military during more intense encounters. However, calm soon overtook the citizens. They too realized that a more orderly approach would ensure that the vaccine would be distributed more quickly.

By the end of the third week of February both countries had distributed every vaccine in their inventory. Unfortunately, more new cases of H1N1 began to trickle in at first, then a deluge of infected once again clogged the hospitals. Both countries put in additional requests for the vaccines. Donovan Bryant gave orders to both the Idaho and New York facilities to move to a twenty-four hour production schedule. He also made sure that Karl and Michael were siphoning off appropriate amounts of the vaccine to the Florida facility.

The last week of February 2013 saw a ten percent increase in the number of reported H1N1 cases compared to the previous month's totals. IPPC officials worked diligently with the World Health Organization, NATO and individual charter countries to stem the tide of increasing cases. Charter and non-charter countries alike watched the reports of the increasing cases. Governments enacted policies and procedures to limit the interaction of those infected with severe cases of the flu. Minor quarantines were set up as needed in heavily infected areas. Some travel restrictions were enacted to keep people from traveling to and from at risk nations.

A bit of good news spread quickly through the twenty-four hour news outlets. Top scientists from Britain, the United States and France reported that the solar activity of the Sun had returned to normal levels. Apparently the recent outburst of gamma radiation and solar flares was over.

Unfortunately the damage had already been done to much of the communication and power infrastructures throughout the world. These things could be repaired but it would take time. Certain less industrialized nations had been almost completely cut off from communication with the outside world. Even the highly advanced nations suffered structural issues. Spotty communication, loss of cell phone signals, lost emails and even loss of radio transmissions were not uncommon. The world governments assured their citizens through less fickle communication sources that these issues would soon be corrected.

There was no need to panic.

Chapter 8

- *March 14, 2013: Thursday, 11:27 AM – Rochester, New York – Secondary production site of Illumination Pharmaceuticals …*

"Can you believe that we've already been here for close to a month now?" Julie asked her friend as she finished off her status report entry for the day.

Craig busied himself watching the news. The lab partners had ordered roast beef sandwiches and fries from a local BBQ joint. Most lunches for the past month had been eaten on campus. There was very little time to do anything else due to Theo's strict work schedule. The team had made significant strides in productivity, but the stress had begun to affect everyone. The company barely met the throughput demands of the IPPC officials, but they were keeping up. The hectic schedule had drained the entire staff mentally, physically and emotionally.

"A month? Already?" Craig haphazardly answered.

"You're not even listening to me," Julie continued. She picked up the largest fry from her plate and hurled at Craig's head, hitting him directly in the left ear.

"Hey! Don't waste those fries!" Craig picked up the fry from its final resting place on his desk and ate it.

"Yuck!" Julie stuck out her tongue and shook her head in disbelief. "You know those germs will kill you, right?

"Maybe I'll create a vaccine to inject into fries to ward of all types of germs. Then there would be no *five-second* rule to worry about. You could pick up fries from anywhere and eat them!"

"Why don't you focus on some meaningful tasks instead?" Theo stood at the doorway holding his ever present clipboard. "Don't you have enough work to keep you busy today?"

"No need for an attitude, *Theodore*," Craig snapped. "I'm on a break anyway. Besides, *Theodore*, you are not really our boss so stop pretending like you are. It got old the first week. It's not any better now."

"Guys, please – this is not necessary," Julie pleaded.

Julie had tried since the end of the first week to keep the men civil to one another. Theo had indeed overstepped his boundaries and Craig had been downright snotty to Theo. They were not getting along – not even close. Like oil and water.

"Do I need to call Mr. Timmons again?" Theo asked in a threatening tone.

"No, *Michael*... I mean Theo." Craig started to giggle and Julie almost did the same, but she held her composure. Theo stormed off out of the lab down the hallway to his office.

"You know he's only trying to get the job done, right Craig?"

"Take his side why don't you..."

"Don't make me hit you in the face with this whole plate of fries. I'll do it, mister!"

A special news bulletin flashed on the TV screen. "This just in to our news headquarters in New York," the TV anchorman said. "We have confirmed reports that North Korea has amassed a large number of its military regime on the southern border of its country. Let's send it to our on-the-scene reporter, Trish Maloney in the capital city of Seoul, South Korea for more details."

"Turn it up, Craig," Julie said.

"Thank you, Jonathan," Trish began. "I can confirm at this time that the report you received is indeed accurate. As of forty-five minutes ago, the North Korean military made hostile movements to the edge of its country. The reason given, or at least what we've been able to uncover, is that the North Koreans have demanded the potent H1N1 vaccine for its own citizens. If their demands are not met, North Korea will cross the DMZ and invade South Korea, taking the medications by force."

"Trish - why don't they just get the vaccines like the other countries?" Jonathan asked.

"Well, we contacted IPPC officials who refused to comment. However, we were able to obtain a copy of the charter between the nations that make up the official IPPC conglomerate. North Korea is not one of those members."

"So what does that mean, if you don't mind explaining it to our viewers?"

"Certainly, Jonathan," Trish said. "The IPPC was created, sort of like a League of Nations, to combat epidemic and pandemic outbreaks. Twenty-four original members came together, mostly supplying funds and medical knowledge, to create the vast corporation. Each charter member would in turn receive specific, rapid deployment and help should the need arise in the future dealing with mass sicknesses."

"Like the recent and still continuing H1N1 outbreaks?" Jonathan asked.

"Precisely, Jonathan. By our own reports, although not verified, estimates have about twenty percent of the North Korean population suffering from some version of the flu, whether it's the seasonal flu or the more potent H1N1 virus has yet to be determined. We'll keep you updated as the story progresses. This has been Trish Maloney reporting for Action News Eight."

"Please keep the channel right here," Jonathan said, "well be right back after these important announcements."

Craig turned the volume down and looked at Julie. Her face most likely mirrored his. Neither one of them had any idea that the situation had become so volatile. They finished their lunch in silence.

- *March 14, 2013: Thursday, 9:45 AM – Boise, Idaho – Office of Karl Timmons …*

Karl already knew what was coming. He had just finished watching a local newscast that was covering the aggressive actions of North Korea. He called Michael into his office and dialed into a secure IPPC conference line. The meeting was already in session.

"Well, it's nice of you to finally join us, Karl."

Karl really hated the sound of Donovan's voice, especially when Donovan was being his normal asshole self…which was just about any time the douche bag was conscious.

"Sorry, Donovan, we are here now," Karl said.

"Oh good, now we can get started," Donovan continued. "As I was saying, due to the actions of North Korea, we feel it's appropriate to enact Security Measure 7A. I've contacted my sources in the US military. The plan is already in motion."

"This is crazy," Pamela said. "We could be teetering on the brink of World War Three if things don't cool down."

"That is a possibility," Gaylord Hastings said.

Karl knew this was a big deal. All of the *big* players were on the same conference call. He had previously studied the procedures when the IPPC officials granted the money to his firm. He had no idea that something like this could actually happen. Luckily, he thought to himself, somebody or a group of very smart *"somebodies"* had already conceived of this possibility. Karl had never imagined that he would ever be involved in anything that could lead to conflict, especially a possible world war.

"Karl how are the production facilities taking the news?" Pamela inquired.

"I've had a few reports come in from the Rochester office from my man in charge there. As you know, we just learned about this. We probably didn't have the same advance warning that the IPPC had. I will send out the high-priority email regarding Security Measure 7A and both facilities will be put into heightened alert."

"Very good, Karl," Gaylord said. "Well it looks like you folks have this covered. I've got a few other meetings to attend. I'm trying to secure more funding for additional production facilities. Keep me apprised of the situation." Gaylord exited the conference call.

Donovan took control of the meeting as soon as Gaylord exited the room. He always had to be in charge, but played second string when Gaylord was present. Karl imagined that there might be friction between Donovan and Gaylord. When the two were together, Gaylord was the man in charge. He held all the purse strings. He made the decisions. Donovan was always quick to spring to the forefront once Gaylord had exited any situation. The man was driven by pure ego.

"Pamela, get the Stockholm teams up-to-speed," Donovan began. "Karl, the US government will be sending two platoons, about forty soldiers to each facility. According to my source in the government, those troops should arrive by Monday."

"Yes, sir."

"Oh and Karl?"

"Yes?"

"The special IPPC teams will be sent as well. They are in charge. Be a good boy and do as you're told," Donovan said in an overly condescending tone.

Karl imagined the delight spreading across Donovan's face. *Why was this man such a dick? What drove a man to become like this?* Karl sat back in his chair and offered up the only response he could muster: "Yes, sir – I understand." With that the emergency meeting came to an abrupt end. All parties moved into action.

"He doesn't like you, does he?" Michael inquired after being quiet throughout the entire meeting.

"He doesn't like anyone. Hell, I doubt he even likes himself."

Karl pulled up the IPPC Charter information on his Blackberry. He read over the pertinent information about how to relay Security Measure 7A to the appropriate teams. Karl composed an email and sent it to both the Boise and Rochester facilities.

"Michael, let's go ahead and get things started around here," Karl said after sending his email from the portable device. "The Rochester office will be doing the same."

"Sure thing, boss."

- *March 14, 2013: Thursday, 12:10 PM – Rochester, New York – Secondary production site of Illumination Pharmaceuticals …*

"I think this place is driving me nuts," Craig said, breaking the awkward post-lunchtime silence.

"More so than normal?"

"Yes. We've been cramped up in here for a month now. I feel more like a prisoner than an employee."

"Just hang in there," Julie said, reassuring her distressed co-worker. "Besides, in about two weeks, Alexander and Mandy will be here. They would have been here sooner, but Alexander couldn't clear his schedule."

"Yeah, and I know he and Amanda wanted to travel together. She never has liked to fly alone. I'm glad the company is flying them in, but it's too bad we'll probably be working most of the time and never get to see them."

"Well, they will be here for quite some time. We'll be able to spend plenty of time with them and show them the town." Don't worry about the details..." Julie stopped mid-sentence as she stared at her computer screen.

"What is it?" Craig inquired.

"Check your inbox. It's a high-priority message from Karl."

"Oh, let me rush right over and do that. You know I can't call my day complete unless I read some of his inane dribble...he loves to type crap out on the Blackberry of his. Sometimes I think he loves..."

"Stop it," Julie quipped, interrupting her friend. While she too often felt irritated by the amounts of *"spam"* email from the company, this message appeared to be very important. "This looks serious. Go check it out."

Craig quickly tabbed through his applications to his email. Nothing. He clicked the *"send/receive"* button over and over, still nothing. His computer began making loud churning noises in the background as the overworked hard drive struggled to keep up.

"I hate this sorry ass computer," Craig fumed as he slapped the side of the computer case repeatedly. His computer, apparently not too fond of the abuse, abruptly issued the *"blue screen of death"*.

"Damn it! I'm going to chunk this piece of shit computer out the window, I swear to God above." Craig said through gritted teeth.

"Calm down, Craig. Gosh, kids these days...so impatient. Come over here and I'll let you read it, but you must promise me that you'll be a good boy!"

Craig smiled at Julie. She always had a way to make him laugh. However, before shoving himself over to her desk, he delivered one last kick to the side of the computer and spoke softly to the unresponsive hunk of failure: "I'll be back for you. This isn't over." Craig leaned back in his wheeled office chair and pushed off from the side of his desk, gliding over the well-waxed floors to Julie's desk.

While neither partner was usually overly interested in reading emails from Karl, this email had been sent with the highest priority. As Craig got into position, Julie adjusted the monitor so both of them could read the email:

March 14, 2013
12:17 PM EST

From: Karl Timmons
To: Rochester Facility, Boise Facility
CC: Donovan Bryant, VP DLD IPPC

RE: Security Measure 7A

Our company must act quickly to protect our facilities and associates in times of possible national unrest. Based on the aggressive actions exhibited by North Korea, we as a company must take appropriate precautions.

While there is no reason to believe foreign invasion a possibility, our main concern is that unruly and frightened citizens might take action into their own hands. Mass hysteria and mob rule often incite otherwise law abiding citizens to make poor choices.

As we all know, fear of the unknown is a powerful motivator that can and sometimes does cause individuals and groups of people to act irrationally. Based on this, our IPPC counterparts have enacted Security Measure 7A.

This measure is an agreement entered into by the US Government military forces and the IPPC. By mid-day, Monday, March 18 – 1 platoon (about 40 soldiers) will be sent to both the Boise and Rochester facilities to ensure the safety of our associates and to ensure that production of the much needed vaccines continue uninterrupted.

In addition to the US military soldiers, IPPC science teams will be dispatched and should arrive no later than mid-week. These IPPC teams will take control over the production facilities during this time.

More details will follow as the situation progresses.

"Wow…this is serious," Craig said after finishing the email.

"Military guard at both facilities?" Julie looked very concerned.

"It's for our protection, Julie," Craig said as he put his hand on her shoulder. "They are only trying to protect us from people that might try to force their way into our buildings to steal the vaccines. Folks are terrified."

"This is just crazy." Julie sat staring at the email.

"Well at least one good thing is coming out of this mess."

"Oh yeah, what's that?" Julie inquired.

"At least we don't have to watch Theo pretend like he's in charge anymore!"

Chapter 9

- *March 16, 2013: Saturday, 12:44 PM – a small village two miles east of San Juan de Pasto, Colombia…*

"Look at this, father!" Alejandro yelled in Spanish. The young boy stood up and dusted the dirt from his jeans. His father watched closely as the boy wrestled with the large fruit. Alejandro squealed in delight as he fell backwards onto the seat of his pants. Victory! He had finally managed to lift the large pumpkin from the fertile soil.

"Yes! It is spectacular," Sebastian replied. "Your mother will be very proud. Speaking of your mother, she should have lunch just about ready for us." The old man estimated the weight of the pumpkin to be around ten kilograms. "That magnificent pumpkin should make for an excellent dessert after dinner."

Sebastian and his eleven-year old son had been working in the garden since sunrise. Normally, Alejandro did only minor work on the farm, but since his grandfather had taken ill late last year, the boy had been trying to help his father more with the everyday chores. The heat of the day had begun to take its toll on the pair. Now was as good of a time as any to take a break for a refreshing meal. They could finish the gardening chores later in the evening when the temperatures would be slightly less brutal.

"Should I put the pumpkin into the wheelbarrow with the other crops, father?" Alejandro inquired still clutching the large orange fruit firmly in his arms.

"No, son – *that* is your prize. Carry it with you and surprise your mother." Sebastian watched his son's eyes grow in anticipation. The young boy struggled against the hefty weight of the fruit, but he could barely contain himself. No matter how heavy his burden, Alejandro held firmly to the pumpkin, refusing to let it drop. His mother would be so proud.

Though the family was poor, even by Colombian standards, they never wanted for food. Each and every day, the family worked the earth. They cared for and respected nature and for the last ten years, the earth had provided for them. More than half of the years during the past decade, the farm produced enough surplus crops that the family was able to sell the extra produce at a market in San Juan de Pasto. This year, even though early in the growing season, Sebastian had predicted that the garden's bounty could potentially be the largest of the decade.

Alejandro walked beside his father who was pushing the full wheelbarrow. Even though the boy wanted to rush inside and share his great find with his mother, he still helped his father return all the tools to their rightful spots. He wasn't much help with the chores since he was whimsically distracted; the large pumpkin required both arms and all his concentration.

For many evenings over the past few months, Sebastian had often expressed his joy to his wife, Paola, of how well his son had handled additional chores allotted to him. His son had done an excellent job in place of his ailing grandfather. Sebastian pushed the wheelbarrow under the shed and covered it with a tarp. He nodded for his son that they were finished with the chores for now.

Alejandro turned toward the house, visualizing his mother's happy face as he presented her with the large pumpkin. To speed up the cooking process, he would even offer his help in readying the fruit. *Maybe this year his mother would allow him to prepare the fruit by himself?* Last year, his mother had cut open the large fruit while he removed the seeds. Now that he was a year older, Alejandro hoped that his mother would trust him to make the whole dessert from start to finish. He could already taste the sweet pumpkin pie on his lips.

"Go now, son – show your mother," Sebastian said. "Be quiet though. Be respectful. Your grandfather may not yet be awake. You know he's been ill. The medication he received a few months ago seemed to have helped him, but recently I fear he is getting worse."

The young boy sprinted awkwardly towards the front porch. Each and every step the young boy took, the fruit seemed to be trying to free itself from its captor, but no such luck. Tonight, the family would dine on sweet pumpkin pie.

Sebastian meandered towards the house at a slower pace than his son; the years of hard labor had not been kind to his body. However, minor aches and pains would not stop him from providing for his family. He began to laugh as he watched his son struggle to open the screen door while balancing the behemoth pumpkin on his hip. Moments like this, Sebastian could never remember being happier or more proud of his son.

Alejandro braced the pumpkin between his right thigh and the side of the wall next to the doorframe. He reached for the handle with his left hand and swung open the door. His young eyes viewed something that would haunt him for the remainder of his short days. He yelled at the top of his lungs simultaneously dropping the large pumpkin; it smashed to the ground, erupting in a geyser of sticky juice and seeds. The boy stood motionless – white as a sheet hanging out to dry.

Sebastian's body instinctively reacted to the horrific screams of his son before his mind could even process what was happening. He sprinted the agonizing few meters to the house and hopped up onto the porch. He grasped his son by the shoulders, looking down directly into his son's vacant, tear-filled brown eyes.

"Alejandro! Alejandro! What is it?"

The boy collapsed to his knees and could barely muster the strength to point into the house. Sebastian looked through the door into the kitchen. There on the floor was Sebastian's own father, Santiago, straddling his wife, Paola. Her broken body pointed away from the door and lay awkwardly beneath the weight of her father-in-law. Her neck abruptly twisted so that her head faced the door in opposition to the positioning of her body. Her frantic, fear-etched face forever frozen in time stared blankly into nothingness. Dark blood seeped into the stone floor from a large wound on her neck just below her left ear. Santiago was chewing on her severed right arm.

"Father! Paola! Oh my God!" Instinctively, Sebastian picked up a nearby chair and smashed it over the back of his father's head. The old man tumbled off of Paola and rolled across the ground. Santiago looked up and grunted while continuing to rip flesh from the woman's arm. Sebastian made eye contact with his father. The man that had raised him, taught him to till the earth, taught him to be a family man no longer resided within those blood-filled, soul-less eyes.

Sebastian paused momentarily, taking his eyes off of his father. *What was going on?* Sebastian kneeled down and tried to stop the bleeding from his wife's neck. Santiago leapt from his crouched position and tackled Sebastian. Alejandro watched in horror as his grandfather gnawed out a mouthful of flesh from Sebastian's upper thigh.

"Run, Alejandro! Get to town! Bring help!" Sebastian yelled as he fought with his father.

Santiago stood up in an unnatural, lumbering way as he hobbled toward the front door in the direction of Alejandro. Sebastian grabbed his father's leg to slow his momentum. "Run, son!" Sebastian pleaded.

The young boy stood up and jumped off the small dirt-covered porch. He ran towards town as fast as his pre-pubescent legs could take him. He never looked back. Not once. He had to get help. He ran as fast as he could; his lungs began to burn but he pushed on. He would save his mother and father. He would bring help.

Alejandro entered the village square. He hunched over, placing his hands on his knees trying to catch his breath. Instead vomit spewed from his mouth. The physical exertion combined with unbelievable fear and lack of anything of substance in his stomach was too much for his digestive system. He stood up and wiped his mouth off with the back of his hand. He vomited again.

His young mind could not decipher what had just transpired. The thoughts of his mother and father being eaten by his grandfather came close to shutting down his fragile mind; his tenuous connection with the real world almost faded. *What had just happened? Why was his grandfather attacking his parents?* None of it made any sense. One centralized thought kept him going: He had to find help. Surely someone in town would be able to help him. Maybe one of his father's favorite trading partners or maybe even someone from the church. Alejandro looked around for a familiar face.

As the young boy fought off the urge to vomit, he scanned the town centre. He saw no one at the vegetable stand, no one near the tavern. Movement or a reflection off of the barbershop window caught his attention. Alejandro looked in the direction of the town fountain and fell to his knees. His body seized, refusing to move. Unable to close his eyes, the young boy glimpsed malefic atrocities that smothered any remaining vestiges of the once sane world that he had lived in less than an hour ago. The town he had visited so often had turned into a slaughterhouse. Everything unfolded in front of him in a vivid slideshow of pain and gore...

To Alejandro's left, he could see Ms. Rodriguez, the school librarian, thrashing around in the fountain. Her face strangely contorted, her mouth filled with blood. She grunted and groaned as screams for help came in between gasps of air from her elderly victim that struggled to remain above water. Ms. Rodriguez viciously pounded and kicked the now limp body, ending her victim's panicked screams for help; the final blow - a vicious bite to the throat – severing the jugular vein. Blood spewed all over the stone statue in the center of the fountain and soon red water poured over the sides of the fountain wall as the former librarian feasted on the mangled flesh of her victim.

To his right, the young boy saw three men, men who Alejandro knew as *"fair"* trading partners with his father, on their knees in the opening of the alleyway between the local tavern and the barbershop. They wailed and thrashed on a middle-aged man's broken corpse. Alejandro recognized the victim by his dark wardrobe...it was Father Juan Carlos. All three men chewed on various appendages of the Catholic priest.

A primal scream from deep within his lungs echoed out of his mouth. Alejandro had finally been pushed over the edge; his young mind began to shut down. He could no longer process the horrific stimuli all around him. His body and mind went numb, which in the end, served him well. His scream garnered the attention of two sickly women nearby. The women moved awkwardly towards the helpless young boy. Wobbling from side to side, moaning and groaning, almost falling down with each step, the two women bumped violently into one another as they closed to within arm's reach of the boy.

BLAM!! BLAM!! BLAM!!

Three large caliber gunshots rang out from behind Alejandro. The two would-be attackers fell to the ground motionless. Alejandro did not react. He squatted motionless in the same spot, his chin resting on his chest. The dark grasping fingers of unconsciousness tickled his mind; his eyes closed as he blacked out momentarily.

"Little boy? Little boy?" A women's voice cried out in broken Spanish. "Are you injured? Did they bite you?"

Alejandro struggled to open his eyes straining to turn his tired head in the direction of the woman's voice. Within moments, a woman knelt down in front of him. She put her gun into her holster and gently put her hands onto the boy's shoulders. Tears began to flow from his eyes as he looked up at the stranger who had saved his life. He tried to speak but only his lips moved, no sounds – no words.

"It's OK. My name is Dr. Finch. We're going to be fine. Just fine."

Dr. Finch lifted the boy to his feet. He was filthy and reeked of vomit. She pressed him against her hip and felt his body shake violently almost to the point that he would fall back to the ground if not steadied. He clasped his arms around her leg and squeezed tightly. The scientist looked around the village square; she saw total unimaginable mayhem. She easily spotted ten different attacks in various stages of assault. Whatever caused the soldiers at her quarantined site to seemingly die and come back to life...appeared to have spread to the townsfolk. Many of the local inhabitants now exhibited the same unrestrained berserker rage that she saw befall her compatriots just less than twelve hours earlier.

"Dr. Finch, come in. Come in Dr. Finch." A Spanish speaking male voice came over the short-wave walkie-talkie at her side. "Dr. Finch, are you there?"

She pulled the walkie-talkie from her belt and responded in English: "Yes, Colonel Chavez. I'm here. I've found a small boy. He's alive but barely. Please respond in English. No need to frighten him any further. We are making our way to the east edge of town."

"Damn communications are still down," the Colonel responded in English. "I have not been able to contact headquarters nor have I been able to contact the IPPC on the frequency you gave me."

"Meet us behind the old tourist shop, Colonel. Dr. Finch out."

Dr. Finch looked down at the young boy. "We have to move," she said in Spanish. "We are not safe here. Do you understand me?"

Alejandro stared blankly at her but nodded that he understood her. He turned to take a step and fell to the ground; his body too exhausted to do anything. Dr. Finch picked up the boy and put him over her shoulder. She almost lost her balance due to the extra weight but she knew this was the only way. She moved as quickly as she could and hoped that none of the infected villagers would notice her attempt to escape. No such luck.

Almost as if she was fresh meat and someone had just rung the dinner bell, the lumbering undead focused their unnatural gaze on her and the young boy. Each seemed to stop devouring their victims and tossed them to the side – like a dog that has lost interest in its play toy. By quick glance, Dr. Finch counted at least eight separate sick townsfolk moving towards the old tourist shop, blocking off her escape route. She panicked and placed the young boy on the ground next to her feet. He lay on the dusty street balled up in the fetal position. Had she been a mother herself, she would have attributed her protective nature of the boy to mother's instinct. She unlatched the strap on her holster keeping her gun in its place. She only had three shots left. The addled townsfolk formed a semi-circle around her and the boy.

BRRAPPT!! BRRAPPT!! BRRAPPT!!

The sound of machine gun fire and squealing tires from behind her brought a smile to her face. She knew that Colonel Chavez had entered the fray. She saw the jeep come to a sliding sideways stop about ten meters from her. More gunfire erupted from the driver's side seat. She dropped to the ground, covering her head and providing shelter for the boy. Bodies began to drop all around her. She looked up after a few moments and there stood Colonel Chavez extending his hand towards her.

As the Colonel lifted the boy into the back seat he asked: "How was that for an entrance?"

Dr. Finch slid into the passenger side and strapped on her seatbelt. She looked into the back seat to make sure the boy was secure. She covered him with a blanket. The trio sped off out of the center of town towards a nearby hill that overlooked the town. The Colonel pulled the jeep off to the side of the rocky road and exited the vehicle.

"Well this spot will have to do," the Colonel said in disgust as he kicked the driver's side tire.

"What's wrong?"

"Well, my good doctor, it appears that my erratic driving has busted two of our tires." Colonel Chavez paced back and forth as he surveyed the area. "There," he said as he pointed east, "there is a building we can make camp in and figure out what to do next."

Dr. Finch spent the next two hours trying to contact IPPC officials. During the same time, Colonel Chavez attempted to contact his base and even tried to contact one of his sources in the government. Neither was successful. It appeared as if all communication had been permanently severed.

Chapter 10

- *March 17, 2013: Sunday, 9:30 AM – Stockholm, Sweden – IPPC Emergency Call Center…*

Rick Simmons, the call shift supervisor, made his way down to the first row of the call center. He had already had a busy day and it was only an hour-and-a-half into his shift. Communication issues from around the world seemed to be the topic of conversation. The call center's main responsibilities were neutered if they couldn't maintain contact with their member nations. Multiple failed transmissions, both sending and receiving, had kept him very engaged this morning.

"What's going on?" Rick inquired as he made his way to the lower level of the floor.

"Sir," Operator-One explained, "we seem to have lost contact with our specialist team in Colombia. They missed their scheduled status report this morning."

"Did they call in and get interrupted?" Rick asked.

"No, sir. They missed the call altogether."

"Did you try to contact them?"

"Yes, sir – I've tried multiple times. I know the procedures."

"Sorry…didn't mean to imply you were not doing your job," Rick apologized. "It's going to be a long week. Keep me updated."

"Yes, sir," Operator-One replied.

Rick hid the fact that his previous tone with the call center operator had deeper implications. He had been in love with Christina Finch all through college. He had followed her around the campus like a puppy in love, but she never returned his affection. After they both graduated, he even followed her to the jobs they currently had with the IPPC. He never considered himself a stalker…but often thought to himself over the past few years that Christina took the international jobs to be far away from him…

Rick walked up a small set of stairs to his office, which was perched on a slightly raised platform in the back of the spacious room. The positioning of the office allowed the shift supervisor to oversee the entire floor, like a shepherd watching over his flock. He called Pamela and informed her of the plethora of issues plaguing operations so early in the morning.

• *March 18, 2013: Monday, 08:14 AM – Boise, Idaho – Illumination Pharmaceuticals outside the main entry area of the research facility…*

Michael looked down from Karl's office window; he could see US Special Forces arriving at the Boise facility. In the military convoy, he counted two armored personnel carriers, three jeeps, two motorcycles and two non-military supply trucks. The vehicles came to a simultaneous stop about two-hundred yards from the front door of the facility. In an orderly single file fashion, ten soldiers exited each of the troop transport vehicles; they stood at attention waiting for orders from their superior officer. Michael counted about forty military personnel down below.

Michael didn't know his military ranks, but as soon as the foot soldiers began saluting a balding, older gentleman, *"ol' Mikey"* knew who was running the show. The soldiers were apparently directed to remove eight saw-horse shaped barricades from the supply trucks. Then the soldiers formed a line from the back of one truck to the west side of the entry lane. They began unloading sandbags, passing each bag from one to another with the final solider placing the bags flanking the road. Michael lost count of the number of sandbags after he had counted approximately two hundred. The soldiers began setting up the rest of their gear around the main entrance of the facility.

"They're here, Mr. Timmons," Michael said as he turned towards Karl's desk.

"Yeah, I figured they'd be fairly prompt. The last communication that I received put their arrival time here around eight fifteen." Karl leaned back in his comfortable chair, clasping his hands around the back of his head. Secretly, Karl resented the fact that Donovan had once again usurped his power. Now Karl feared that he would be subjected to some dumbass, loud-mouthed jarhead ordering him around for the next who-knows-how-many months…

"Are you going to go down there and see if they need any help? I think that bald guy is in charge. He seems to be giving all of the orders down there."

"No, Michael – I have a business to run," Karl snidely remarked. "Plus, I'm waiting for the IPPC group to show up. My direct orders from Donovan were to assist them in any way possible. I was also instructed *not* to interfere with the military operation…"

Michael sensed his boss's frustration and he quickly turned to look out the window, once again marveling at the precision below. Within the fifteen minutes that he had been standing idle at the window, the small platoon had isolated the main entrance. Each side of the road was flanked by large barricades. Sandbags were piled up at least waist high, restricting access to the building.

"Don't you have some work to do, Michael?"

"Yeah, boss - sorry about that," Michael said as he hastily exited the room. He knew Karl was in a pissed off mood and Michael figured the safe bet was to get out of Karl's office as quickly as possible.

Karl stood up and walked over to the window and scrutinized the activity below. He never liked the military. He felt, and rightfully so, that the *"Corp"* had stolen his father from him. Karl never really got to know his father. His dad wasn't killed by snipers in 'Nam, wasn't killed by landmines in Iraq, hell – his father died of lung cancer fifteen years ago in a retirement home on the outskirts of Philly from asbestos poisoning.

The thing that pissed Karl off the most was that his father devoted his entire life to the military instead of spending time with his family; his father was all too happy to volunteer for extra tours of duty or stepping up to lead the next super secret mission. Karl wholeheartedly resented that man. Since his father died, with no real resolution between the two, Karl tended to project his deep, inner anger onto the military…and it wasn't necessarily just the armed forces. That anger was usually directed at any authority figure.

As Karl stood at the window contemplating his father's past transgressions and failures, a loud knock echoed throughout his office. Startled, Karl turned towards the door. A small entourage of lightly armed officers entered the room followed by the bald guy. Karl gritted his teeth and tried to prepare himself for some well-rehearsed military bravado.

"You must be Karl," the balding man said, reaching his hand out to shake Karl's. "I'm Lieutenant Dwight Samson." Karl grudgingly shook the man's outstretched hand. A slight battle for superiority lingered in the handshake as both men tried to *"tactfully"* out squeeze the other.

"Now, to me," the lieutenant continued after breaking off the handshake, "you look like a man used to running the show." Lt. Samson lit up a large, sweet smelling cigar, clinching it between his teeth. Karl felt as if the military man was staring through him, as if he wasn't even there.

"I'm going to be honest with you - this is still your show. I'm just here to keep this place safe. My men will make a few adjustments inside the building to protect your employees and your assets. However, for the most part, we will stay out of your way. Kindly stay the hell out of ours." With that, the lieutenant and his entourage exited the office.

"Asshole," Karl said softly as he briskly rubbed his aching hand.

• *March 18, 2013: Monday, 11:22 PM – Rochester, New York – Secondary production site of Illumination Pharmaceuticals outside the main entrance…*

"Yes, that's fine, officer," Theo said as he signed off on some paperwork presented to him by the soldier.

"Thank you, sir," First Sergeant Tolliver replied as he ensured that all the documentation was in correct order. "Captain Massey will return shortly to detail his plans for the next few months. He apologized in advance for his tardiness but took a squad with him to survey the surrounding area."

"No problem at all," Theo said. "I look forward to meeting with him."

First Sergeant Tolliver nodded and rejoined the rest of the platoon to finish securing the border around the secondary research facility. The soldiers had been working for a bit more than an hour to erect barricades and sandbags around the front of the building. The soldiers built a small guard tower with a manual gated arm. Most of the fabricated tower reminded Theo of giant Lincoln Logs. There was no bolting, drilling or other method to secure the walls together. The soldiers followed a basic plan and attached each section of the wall by connecting the slotted out portions of each piece, one on top of the next.

"Look at him down there," Craig said as he looked out the lab window to the ground below.

"Craig, it's too early to start with that crap."

"Come on, Julie – you know Theo's ego is about level with this third floor window." Craig reached up with both hands trying to touch the top edge of the window. "If he stands out there any longer pretending to be in charge, his head might explode."

Julie stood up from her desk and walked over to the window. She playfully punched Craig in the shoulder. "Can't you two just get along? He's really not that bad of a guy. I think you're just being stubborn."

Craig rubbed his arm. "I don't know which hurts worse, you punching me or the fact that you think he's 'not really that bad of a guy'."

"Oh someone is calling him," Craig said as he watched Theo flip open his cell phone.

"Get to work, dummy. I'm not doing all the work today."

"Please. You know I'm the lynchpin holding this operation together." Craig grudgingly left the window and sat down at his computer. This desk was a bit tidier than the one back in Idaho, but that wasn't really saying much. Craig tapped on a few keys while staring at the picture of his wife on the corner of his desk. He really missed her but the bright spot was that she would be in Rochester in a little over two weeks.

- *March 18, 2013: Monday, 9:45 AM – Boise, Idaho – Illumination Pharmaceuticals, office of Karl Timmons...*

"That sounds better than what I had to put up with here, Theo," Karl said into the speaker phone. "This dumbass lieutenant here was running around like a bulldog in heat pissing all over his new territory."

"I'm sorry to hear that, sir," Theo replied. "By the way, I tried to contact you last Thursday with a status report update, but all the lines seemed to be down. Couldn't get any bars on the cell phone and it seemed like every office phone I tried I got a busy signal."

"No worries, Theo. I got your email update on Friday morning. I was reading the paper and there have been other reports of sporadic communication problems. Most experts blame the solar flares from the beginning of the year."

"So far, the crew here at the Rochester facility has been putting in a lot of overtime to meet the demands for the vaccine. We're a little behind for last week, but a few of the group have volunteered to put in some extra hours."

"Very good, Theo – keep me informed."

- *March 19, 2013: Tuesday, 11:30 AM – Rochester, New York – Secondary production facility...*

A group of IPPC officials had arrived earlier in the day. Theo did a convincing impersonation of someone in charge as he showed the group around the production facility. A thorough inspection took about two hours of Theo's time, but he was glad to be involved in the "decision making" portion of the process. *What better way to make a name for himself?* Around lunchtime, the leader of the IPPC Special Task force pulled Theo aside to a small conference room and closed the door.

"Theo, you've done a tremendous job here," Sully Howard began.

"Thank you, Mr. Howard. It's been tough…and I know we've been behind on a few weeks of totals, but…"

"Let's not dwell on the past, Theo. Let's be more forward thinking. There are a lot of sick people out there that need our treatment. Besides, some folks are not cut out for management anyway."

"That's very true," Theo replied blissfully unaware that Mr. Howard was referring to him.

"I'm glad you understand, Theo. Let the professionals take care of this. We'll get you and the rest of this place back on track." Sully left the conference room after delivering the verbal dagger to Theo's chest.

Theo felt like he had just taken an uppercut directly to the family jewels; he felt as if all the wind had been sucked out of his body. He sat down on one of the conference chairs to collect his thoughts, but soon, he began to feel ill to his stomach. Theo played the last few weeks over and over in his mind trying to see where he failed. *Where did he screw things up?* He had planned things so well, driven the others at the facility to work harder, longer hours and even invested tons of overtime himself to meet the demands for the vaccine. None of it made any sense. Theo prided himself on his work ethic, but maybe he had deluded himself… maybe he really wasn't cut out to be a leader.

Theo sulked for a bit longer and then left the conference room. He walked downstairs to one of the break rooms thinking that maybe some food would ease up the gnawing pain in his belly. The words of Sully Howard bounced around in the back of his head. As he walked to the back of the room, he grabbed a cup of coffee and didn't even notice that Craig and Julie were in the room enjoying an early lunch.

"Hi, Theo," Julie said.

Theo just walked by and sat at a table in the far back corner.

"What's up with him," Craig inquired.

"Not sure, but he seems really down. I'm going to invite him over to our table. Be nice, OK?"

"I'm always nice." Craig feigned a look of innocence.

"I mean it." Julie stood up and walked over to Theo's table. With some determination, she convinced the younger man to join her and Craig. Both walked over to Julie's original table and sat down.

"Hey," Craig said.

"Hey," Theo replied. "Am I a bad boss?"

"Yes," Craig answered and was swiftly rewarded with a severe shin kick from underneath the table. "Ow!"

"What Craig meant to say," Julie began, "is that you could use a bit more people skills, but for the most part, you got things up and running quite smoothly here in very little time."

"Yeah, that's what I was trying to say," Craig grimaced as he rubbed his shin.

"The lead IPPC guy told me I wasn't cut out for management. It's just that I've invested so much time in this job trying to please others and I mean, I really wanted to do a good job." Theo took a drink of his hot coffee.

"Theo, don't worry about those guys," Julie said after a few moments. "You've worked very hard to make a name for yourself and to make this company a better place."

"Thanks," Theo said after taking another sip of his drink. "It's just that I've never second guessed myself like this. With as smart as I am, everything comes so easy for me."

Julie quickly shot a glance at Craig that yelled for him to keep quiet. Craig acquiesced, but it took all of his strength not to let his inner smartass escape. Theo's arrogance irritated Craig. And while he kept quiet, for Julie's sake, he had to be honest with himself. Seeing Theo knocked down a few pegs made him feel all warm and fuzzy on the inside.

Chapter 11

• *March 22, 2013: Friday, 11:53 PM – Stockholm, Sweden, the Hub, the office of Pamela Bristow …*

"D r. Bristow – there is a Code One priority message coming in for you from one of our agents in Colombia," the young supervisor reported, out of breath after running full speed to his boss's office. "Oh, sorry Mr. Bryant…I didn't mean to interrupt."

"Put the call on the secure line, Rick and return to your desk," Pamela said. Within moments the phone began to buzz loudly. Donovan nodded for his two guards to exit the room and to close the door behind them. Pamela pressed the intercom button.

"Come in Hub Operations," a panicked, garbled female voice pleaded. "Can you read us? Please respond!"

"This is Pamela Bristow, who am I speaking with?"

"Oh thank God. We've been trying *KRZZT* you for almost *KRZZT*. This is Dr. *KRZZT* Finch."

"You are breaking up, Dr. Finch. We are having a hard time understanding you," Donovan stated.

"I don't *KRZZT* time. The vaccine *KRZZT*… kind of mutation. People *KRZZT* died and come back somehow… *KRZZT*…infected attacking villagers… *KRZZT*…"

"Where are you, Dr. Finch?" Donovan inquired.

"Two miles *KRZZT* of the city. *KRZZT*...repeat, two miles east of San Juan de Pasto. *KRZZT*..."

"Christina!" Pamela yelled as she impatiently waited for her friend to respond; there was no answer. Pamela angrily pressed the button over and over again but only static returned. "Donovan, we've got to get people down there. Something is wrong in Colombia. Our specialist group is in trouble - seems like something went wrong with the vaccine."

"Whoa, calm down there, Dr. Bristow. I don't know how you jumped to that conclusion. There is nothing *wrong* with our vaccine. More than half of that message was jumbled up static and..."

"Donovan, you heard what Christina said. She was reporting that something was terribly wrong with the vaccine. We have to put a hold on production until we get this worked out. If there's been a mutation, then we need to research why the H1N1 vaccine has changed. I'm calling for a full stop on the current runs until we get more information."

"I think you are overreacting, but you're right. Just calm down and listen. You've had a hard week and it's late. Go home. I will get Gaylord on the phone immediately and we will halt production until we figure out what is going on. Just go home and relax. I'll call you in the morning with details."

"She sounded so afraid," Pamela said as she stood up and gathered her stuff, fearful that her old college roommate was in terrible danger.

"Don't worry, Pamela. I will get this fixed. You have my word on it. Will you be OK driving home? I can send one of my guards home with you if you want."

"No. I'm fine." Pamela grabbed her briefcase and jacket and opened the office door, heading toward the elevator. Donovan's two guards entered the room as she exited. Pamela pushed the basement floor button of the elevator and soon arrived in the parking deck below.

"Agent Templeton," Donovan said, waving the man in closer, like a child about to spill a precious secret.

"Yes, sir?"

"You and Roberts follow her home. Don't let her out of your sight."

"Yes, sir."

Both agents rushed out of the small office and quickly made their way to the garage area below. They entered a large, dark blue Chevy Suburban and squealed the tires on the smooth pavement. The vehicle shot up a small exit ramp out of the building and for the briefest of moments, the vehicle was airborne before gravity once again made its presence known.

Donovan closed the door and walked over to Pamela's desk and sat in her comfortable leather chair. He lifted up the phone receiver and dialed a secure line to Gaylord Hastings. After a few rings, Gaylord answered.

"What?"

"Gaylord we have two problems," Donovan began.

"Stop right there, *Donnie*. *We* don't have any problems. *You* get paid tremendous amounts of *my* money so that *we* don't have problems. *You* have problems. Fix them."

Donovan could visualize Gaylord emphasizing each word, maybe even using "finger quotes" to further clarify his message. "It's about the vaccine…"

"Fix them." Gaylord hung up the phone.

"Mother fucker…" Donovan said in disgust as he slammed down the phone receiver. "Oh I'll fix it all right."

Donovan hurriedly left the Hub's main office and entered the parking deck below. He raced over to his GMC Yukon, where two of his other guards were waiting. Donovan entered the vehicle through the back passenger side door. Once inside, he dialed Agent Templeton.

"Yes, Mr. Bryant?"

"You know that problem that you are following up on for me? The one we just discussed in the office? Take care of it, now. It's in the best interest for our business that the issue is taken care of promptly."

"Understood, sir," Agent Templeton replied. As he slid his cell phone cover closed, he turned towards Agent Roberts who was driving the large SUV a comfortable distance behind Pamela Bristow's Honda Accord.

"What's up?" Roberts inquired.

"Run her off the road. Make it look like an accident."

Agent Roberts thrust his right foot on the gas pedal. The large SUV sprung to life with an angry roar of the V8 engine. The metal beast soon closed the distance with the small family car ahead of it. Roberts flipped on the high beams and the fog lights simultaneously; Pamela instinctively slowed down, unable to see.

The SUV shot around the beige colored family sedan and raced ahead at speeds approaching one hundred miles per hour. Within moments, Pamela couldn't even see the taillights of the maniac driver that had just passed her. She regained her composure and continued on her way home. The voice of her frightened friend echoed throughout her mind as she continued home. She slowed down as a dangerous curve was coming up; she never liked driving this road, even with a clear mind, but many long nights at the office forced her to do so. The last stretch of the road prior to getting on the expressway was a narrow two-lane concrete bridge.

As her front tires touched the bridge, the large SUV shot out from a side road, clipping the rear end of her car in a modified PIT maneuver. Pamela fought to control the vehicle but over compensated. The rear end fishtailed and the sedan flipped over twice, finally coming to a stop right side up. Pamela could feel blood oozing down the side of her neck where her laptop computer had catapulted out of the passenger side seat, gouging into her forehead above her right eye. She breathed a sigh of relief. While her body screamed in tremendous amounts of pain, she was still alive; the seatbelt had done its job and held her in place.

Pamela unclasped the seatbelt and grabbed the door handle. It was stuck. She wrestled with the mechanism for a few moments and the door partially opened. Her only thought was to get out of the car. She didn't smell smoke or gas, but she knew the vehicle couldn't be safe to stay in much longer. Pamela leaned into the door with her left shoulder and pressed her feet firmly against the floorboard shoving her body outward. The door opened about half way.

She grabbed the door frame, careful not to cut her hands on the broken glass. Then she heard the roar of the V8 engine. She turned her head towards the end of the bridge where the growling motor waited. The RPMs revved and the bright lights were suddenly flipped on. Pamela covered her eyes, recoiling back into the confines of the car. The SUV raced towards her at more than fifty miles per hour. The deafening impact slung the tiny sedan off the bridge to the darkness below.

Bright red brake lights illuminated the night sky for a brief moment, soon followed by the screeching of tires on the dew covered road as the SUV came to a sliding stop mere feet from the edge of the bridge. Templeton and Roberts exited their SUV and rushed to the side of the bridge. They peered over the edge; Pamela's car had burst into a plume of fire as soon as it reached the bottom of the eighty foot deep ravine. Both men looked around for signs of witnesses and found none. They hurried back to their SUV and sped off in the opposite direction.

• *March 23, 2013: Saturday, 1:45 AM – Stockholm, Sweden, an undisclosed location on an almost empty expressway …*

As his first problem was being taken care of by his agents, Donovan Bryant tried multiple times to contact his well paid resource in the Colombian military. Almost thirty minutes passed before he actually reached his contact. Even the secure line that was specially installed for private communication between Donovan and his associates in Colombia suffered from minor communication lapses.

"Diego, can you hear me?" Donovan asked.

"Yes, but I am surprised you made contact," Diego said with a thick Spanish accent. "Our communications are shit recently."

"We have bigger issues than your antiquated technology."

"Do tell, Mr. Bryant."

"How secure is this line, Diego?"

"The most secure in Colombia, sir."

"That's not saying much…" Donovan said callously but continued. "We have two issues occurring outside the city limits of San Juan de Pasto. The first is that there is some kind of situation; I don't know the full details. Engage the *'dragons'* and see what's going on."

At the beginning of the year, specially designed modifications were made to two Colombian attack helicopters to deal with possible crises situations, all paid for by a dummy corporation owned by Gaylord Hastings. The main upgrades and the reason for the nickname were the napalm launching mechanisms located on either side of the helicopters. The gunships maintained enough raw firepower to level a small town.

"Do we have the green light to cleanse the area if necessary?"

"Yes, but I need you to get as much info from the village as you can – then you have the green light to burn that place down."

"And the second issue?" Diego inquired.

"According to the phone call I had earlier, a doctor from our special ops team is reporting some kind of mutation that's adversely affecting the villagers. Find her and contact me."

"And after I get the info you need from her?"

"After that point, Diego, I don't care what happens."

"I understand, Mr. Bryant. Can I assume this will be double pay?"

"You will be compensated, but don't screw this up," Donovan said. "This could unhinge our whole operation. If the operation goes down, there will be no money for anyone."

Donovan turned off his phone and leaned back against the soft leather seat of the speeding SUV. For the rest of the ride home, he rested his aching head on the side of the window. He watched countless streetlights overhead whiz by as his SUV sped through the empty expressway.

Chapter 12

- *March 22, 2013: Friday, 8:45 PM – a small adobe structure, two miles east of the village square, Colombia…*

"We just have to sit here a bit longer, Alejandro," Dr. Finch said in Spanish. "I've finally contacted my friends. They should be sending help soon. We'll be able to leave this place."

Alejandro had barely spoken more than his name in the time the group had been together. The young boy was in a semi-perpetual catatonic state after witnessing the death of his mother and father at the hands of his deranged grandfather. The boy had to be force fed what little food his liberators could find. He spent most of his time wrapped up in a scratchy wool blanket, lying underneath a small table in the corner of the room.

"It's been over two hours since you made contact," Colonel Chavez said in English. Both adults had previously agreed to keep the bad news or any negative updates of their situation in English. They didn't want to upset the fragile boy if they could help it.

"Give them time. The IPPC may have had trouble contacting your military. Something is seriously wrong with communications. Every day since this all started, we've both made multiple attempts to contact anyone and this was the first time we got through…we have to be patient just a little bit longer."

After their escape from the village square about a week ago, the group had found an abandoned adobe structure that they used as a hideout; most of their time had been spent in the lowest level of the structure. The building was strong and provided a relatively good amount of safety from the sick villagers. Since the structure was perched on a hillside, it was the perfect vantage point to try and get a communication signal out. Each day the adults had taken turns to make trips to the village square to return with water and food, careful to avoid any of the infected.

Colonel Chavez and Dr. Finch had discussed many times over the preceding week whether to stay hunkered down in the building or to make a break for San Juan de Pasto to find help. If it had just been the two of them, they would have surely chosen the latter option. They opted to remain in their secluded hideout to wait for help to arrive. Had they known it would be over a week before the first contact got through, they may have opted for the escape. None of that really mattered at this point; help was now on the way.

During the week, Dr. Finch tried to figure out what had transpired to cause the horrific chain of events that she had witnessed. Her initial hypothesis seemed to hold true. The first cases of the living dead occurred with the soldiers that had the earliest H1N1 vaccine treatment – the same soldiers that her group initially had arrived in Colombia to quarantine. Many other townsfolk had also been treated during the similar time frame. They too made the transformation after becoming violently ill and dying. She couldn't narrow down the window of time, but there were some folks that had been vaccinated that did not turn, but most of them had been vaccinated at a later time. *What did the different vaccination times, almost three months apart have to do with this?* She couldn't figure out that piece of the puzzle.

Colonel Chavez spent much of his time wondering how many of the townsfolk had escaped from this hellhole. If he hadn't seen it with his own eyes, he would never have believed that the dead could rise again. But that's exactly what he had witnessed. People were feasting on and attacking each other. It made no sense, but he had witnessed it firsthand on a small scale. *What if the infection spread to the bigger city of San Juan de Pasto? What if it made it all the way to the capital city?*

Both had witnessed the infected Colombians attacking their neighbors. They saw the victims, in turn, transform into the mindless, rage-filled creatures after a period of a few hours. This info had to be relayed to the IPPC and the world governments. Dr. Finch knew that if other nations fell victim to this same process, the world would be plunged into catastrophe. Her information would be vital to stemming the tide of the apparent new pandemic.

Diego carefully maneuvered his jeep over the rough, unpaved road as he approached the western edge of the small village. He didn't even know this small town existed. He had been born in Bogotá but was actually raised in San Juan de Pasto. All the years that he had lived in the large city, he never once had made it to this small satellite village. *Did this place even have a name?*

"Where are we?" Sergio asked in Spanish.

"No idea," Carlos mumbled. "I bet we are lost."

"That's a shame that Diego can get lost even with a GPS right under his nose!"

"Would you two shut up?"

Diego and the two other men had been friends for about ten years. None of them were ever able to hold down steady jobs as they grew up. Fortunately for them, they were good with guns and explosives and found their way into a mercenary group that functioned as a security team for one of the many local drug cartels. Their stint in the drug business ended abruptly about eight years ago when a joint raid team consisting of the Colombian military, US ATF and DEA agents raided their main base of operations. Most of the cartel was wiped out but these three surrendered. To reduce their time in the Colombian prison system, they accepted an offer to work with the military to expose other drug cartels.

"What are we looking for, Diego," Sergio inquired. "You've kept us in the dark the whole ride here."

Diego pointed towards the small unnamed town. "Over there, our US financers want us to investigate that village." He parked the jeep about one hundred yards from the town and the three soldiers exited the vehicle.

"That's just some old farming village," Carlos matter-of-factly pointed out. "Why did we bring all of this gear? Are they going to attack us with shovels?" Both Sergio and Carlos laughed heartily at the comment.

"Yeah…this doesn't make sense," Sergio said, rubbing his bald head as if deep in thought. "And on top of this you have one of the dragons on standby? You are not telling us something…and I still don't know why you call them 'dragons' – I just don't understand."

"All I know," Diego began as he holstered his sidearm, "is that our US boss said there could be rioting or some breach of quarantine that could require cleansing."

"Cleansing, eh? I love the smell of napalm in…"

"Shut up, Carlos," Diego barked. "Let's move out."

Sergio nudged Carlos in the side as they followed Diego to the edge of the town. "That's a good movie," he said just loud enough for Carlos to hear.

The three soldiers made their way to the north end of the tiny farming village. There were no lights coming from any of the buildings; a thick darkness enveloped the town. The three men kept low to the ground darting from building to building until they reached a small Catholic church. All three men crouched down with their backs against the adobe wall. Sergio opened up his backpack and handed Carlos and Diego night vision goggles.

"Here take these," Sergio instructed.

All three men pulled back the elastic straps and fitted the small infrared goggles to their faces. The town square lit up in an eerie green glow. Each man slowly surveyed one portion of the town, like they had done many times before in other situations. They were cocky but actually quite good at their jobs. As the three men surveyed different sections of the town square, movement from outside a small store caught their attention.

A teenage girl cowered next to the side of the small building. The men could see her quickly looking over each shoulder. She was breathing heavily. The young girl placed her hands on the wall… she couldn't see anything. She began feeling her way across the wall until she reached the very edge. As she rounded the edge she tripped over a small display of gardening tools. The loud metal items clanged against each other as they fell to the ground. The girl lay still as if paralyzed.

Sergio stood up and began to move in her direction to help the young girl. He had only taken two steps when Diego grabbed his backpack pulling him back to the church wall.

"What the hell, Diego?"

Diego put his index finger to his lips and then pointed towards an alley next to where the girl had fallen. Three lumbering men meandered out of the alleyway. Their heads were crooked at impossible angles as they reached out a total four arms amongst them as they moved in the direction of the prostrate girl.

"What the hell?" Carlos whispered. "Two of those men are missing arms…"

"We have to help that girl," Sergio insisted.

"Stop." Diego said firmly. "Look around."

Sergio and Carlos surveyed the town square once again. Packs of disfigured and contorted townsfolk began coming out of every corner of the small village. Within moments, there were at least thirty former villagers homing in on the girl's location. Each gruesome disfigurement of the townsfolk was enhanced in the eyes of the men wearing the night vision goggles.

"Those people look like shit," Carlos said. "What's that smell?"

"I don't get it," Sergio mused, "those injuries should have been fatal. Some of those people are missing parts of their necks and heads…not to mention missing legs and arms."

"What the fuck, Diego?" Carlos asked as he grabbed Diego by the shoulders.

Before Diego could answer, Sergio un-holstered both of his .45 caliber handguns and began spraying bullets into the villagers. The lack of depth perception of the night vision goggles caused him to miss many of his shots, but a sufficient number of the rounds found their intended targets. Bodies began to drop to the ground. The mass of sick villagers turned their attention from the young girl in the direction of the church.

"Idiot!" Diego yelled as he pulled the shotgun from his back. The leader of the group ran towards Sergio's new position behind the town's decorative fountain. Carlos hurried close behind with his sub-machine gun at the ready.

"Are you out of your fucking mind?" Diego yelled, berating his long-time friend. "I didn't give the order to attack. We don't have any clue as to what's going on here, you stupid son of a bitch!"

Carlos looked over the base of the fountain. It was too late for the girl. In the small amount of time that had passed as the three men had tried to assess the situation, two groups of villagers had grabbed the girl, fighting for control of her body. A bloodcurdling scream erupted from her that echoed off of the walls. The creatures proceeded to grope her, battling for control of her body. The end result was that they had ripped her almost in half...each side seemingly pleased with their portion.

"She's dead, guys!" Carlos yelled. "And we are in deep shit. You two need to focus."

Diego and Sergio looked around. The entire courtyard was now filled with deformed villagers. More than two hundred infected had swarmed the tiny area drawn to the gun fire and screaming. The men were surrounded by a sea of reanimated corpses. The first wave began to close the distance to the fountain. The men instinctively opened fire but for each villager that they downed, two more seemed to take their place.

"Now!" Diego screamed into his shoulder-mounted walkie-talkie. He reached into his hip pack and pulled out a small flare and tossed it behind the mass of villagers about fifty yards from their current position; the fluorescent green glow illuminated the entire courtyard.

On cue, the medium-sized helicopter ascended from behind the small hillside and launched a barrage of gunfire and small explosive ordinance into the town square very close to where Diego's flare had landed. The concussive blasts of the explosions knocked the men to the ground. Soon fire engulfed a small portion of the rickety townsfolk that had clumped up around the dead girl's half-consumed body.

Sergio looked up into the sky from his back. A wry smile crept across his face as he watched the helicopter breathe fire on the earth below, like a dragon defending its lair. Now, he was quite clear as the why the machine had been given its nickname.

"We've got to move, the napalm is coming in," Diego yelled. All three men sprinted out of the village, past the church and behind their jeep. A loud whistling noise filled the air above their heads... the dragon rained down hot sticky liquid death on the diseased townsfolk below.

After an extensive barrage of napalm, the pilot radioed down to Diego. "You need any help?"

"Yes," Diego replied. "Drop down and pick us up."

The helicopter pilot made one more full circle around the village dispensing the rest of his fiery liquid around the town walls, hopefully securing the area momentarily. As he made his final turn he lowered the aircraft down to about three feet from the ground next to the group's jeep. All three men jumped aboard.

"Let's get the hell out of here," Carlos yelled as he strapped himself into the cargo bay.

"Not yet. We have one more thing to do." Diego instructed the pilot to move east towards the small hilltop. He hoped that the people Donovan instructed him to intercept were still there. Maybe they would have the info on what the hell had happened in this town.

WHUP!! WHUP!! WHUP!!

Dr. Finch stood and rushed up the stairs. "Come up here, Colonel. Hurry!"

"What?"

"Do you hear that?"

Colonel Chavez listened but could hear nothing. "What are you talking about? I don't hear anything."

WHUP!! WHUP!! WHUP!!

"That! Do you hear that noise? It sounds like a helicopter! My team must have contacted your government."

"I definitely hear something," Colonel Chavez said as he strained to listen into the night sky.

A high-pitched squealing noise echoed from the center of the village towards the area where they were hiding. Colonel Chavez looked towards the town and shook his head; he knew all-too-well what that sound was. "That is not a rescue helicopter, it's an attack helicopter! They must be *cleansing* the area to keep the sickness from spreading from this village into San Juan de Pasto."

According to statistics that Colonel Chavez had provided to her, San Juan de Pasto's population was around four-hundred thousand inhabitants. The tiny village that they were currently trapped in only had about four hundred people. Dr. Finch feared the worst should any of the infected make it from the village to the heavily populated city due west. The carnage that would happen if the sickness spread would be tantamount to a biblical disaster.

Loud sonic booms filled the air and bright plumes of red and orange fire could be seen coming from the town. The helicopter was outlined against the black night sky by the bright fires erupting from the village below. Dr. Finch hoped that anyone still not affected by the sickness had escaped from the small village…but she had her doubts. Anyone that was going to make it out had already done so. *Maybe some people had made it into the big city to warn others? Maybe more help was on the way?*

The smell of napalm, smoke and the sickly sweet smell of burning flesh began to inundate the small building where the group hid out. Dr. Finch tore off part of her blouse and doused it with water. She ran downstairs and covered Alejandro's nose and mouth. She tore another piece off and did the same for herself. The smell almost made her vomit. She helped Alejandro to his feet and they both moved up the stairs.

Eight to ten minutes of constant explosions finally came to a stop. The trio left the confines of the small adobe structure and moved closer to the edge of town. Colonel Chavez had picked up the boy so that they could move faster. If they were going to be rescued, they needed to get to within eyesight of the helicopter. As they moved closer to the town, they saw the helicopter maneuver towards the ground and hover momentarily then lift back into the air and move in their direction.

The helicopter landed about fifty yards from them. Both Colonel Chavez and Dr. Finch shielded their eyes as the blades kicked up massive amounts of dirt and debris. When they were finally able to see again, a man was standing about ten yards from them. The trio began moving towards the person and the lightly armed soldier pulled out his small caliber handgun and pointed it at them.

"Halt! Identify yourselves," the man commanded.

"I'm Colonel Chavez and this is my friend Dr. Christina Finch. The boy is Alejandro. We are glad to see you. Apparently our call to the IPPC finally got your attention. You can put your weapon down...we are not infected."

Another man exited the helicopter and hurried to the side of the original soldier standing in front of them. Dr. Finch heard the new arrival refer to the first man as Diego. From what else she could tell, the second man named Carlos, seemed quite anxious to leave the area. Dr. Finch knew why. They had witnessed firsthand the effects of the sickness.

"You know he's right," Colonel Chavez yelled. "We really should get out of here. All of us. You have plenty of capacity to take us with you."

Carlos turned his attention towards the trio. "What the hell is going on here?"

"The vaccine," Dr. Finch started, "has somehow mutated within certain people. I'm not sure how or why…but it leads to their death. But they come back. I know it sounds crazy, but you've seen it. Those folks down there were alive a week ago."

Diego silently assessed the situation. He pulled out his cell phone trying multiple times to reach Donovan Bryant. Carlos listened to the explanations of the doctor and the colonel regarding what they saw over the last week. Finally, Diego made contact.

"Yes, sir – we've found them. More importantly we found something terrible here. The doctor believes that the vaccine has mutated causing people to die and then come back to life in some unrestrained and violent reanimated state."

"I don't believe in the boogeyman, Diego," Donovan replied. "Think about this logically. Can someone that dies actually come back to rejoin the living? Bring the doctor and her friends in and we'll discuss what…"

Diego listened as Donovan barked orders from thousands of miles away, safely removed from this unimaginable nightmare. The soldier hurriedly turned around when he heard the disjointed rustling of heavy feet behind him. "You scared the crap out of me, Sergio!" Sergio didn't answer. As the large, bald man approached, Diego saw his longtime friend struggling to walk.

"No!" Diego screamed as he dropped the phone.

"What's going on?" Donovan yelled on the other end of the phone, but Diego was unable to answer his boss.

"They...got...me," Sergio uttered as he dropped to his knees, blood spewing from his neck. "But I got two of them first." Sergio held up his machete in one hand and the severed head of an infected villager in the other. Diego tried to hold the large man up, but he was too heavy and both men slumped to the ground.

Carlos turned away from the doctor and ran towards Sergio, dropping to his knees next to his fallen comrade. "What the hell?" the confused man yelled over the sound of the helicopter's clamorous blades. He saw his friend lying in a pool of his own blood, illuminated by the under carriage lights of the helicopter.

"Run!" Dr. Finch yelled, pointing in the direction of the helicopter. The bright lights of the helicopter illuminated a field of infected. There were too many to count. All of them shook and gyrated as they moved towards the group. Colonel Chavez grabbed Alejandro hoisting him over his shoulder and he grabbed Dr. Finch by the hand; his only thought was to escape to the safety of the adobe structure, but as they turned, they found themselves surrounded by the rest of the undead villagers.

Gun fire rang out behind them as Diego and Carlos engaged the undead. Their heroics were too little, too late – the soldiers were quickly overrun. The trio stopped mid-stride with nowhere to run. Colonel Chavez squeezed Alejandro and held firmly onto Dr. Finch's shaking hand. The undead descended upon them like a plague of locusts.

"Diego! Diego! Answer me now!" Donovan yelled.

A group of infected villagers unable to feast of the fallen humans began to form a small circle around the cell phone. Their heads swiveled slowly from side-to-side looking for their next meal. An unnatural instinct within them directed them to the sounds of human voices. One zombie finally located the source of the voice and picked up the device.

"Hello?" Donovan said. All the man on the other end of the phone could hear was grunting and heavy breathing. "Diego?"

The zombie shook the phone violently, apparently realizing that there was no meal here and angrily bit the phone in half.

Chapter 13

- *March 26, 2013: Tuesday, 3:34 PM – Rochester, New York – Greater Rochester International Airport …*

Julie and Craig waited outside the airport entrance in her rented SUV. They were supposed to be there over an hour ago to pick up Alexander and Amanda, but a few assignments at work were running behind and they had to stay until the tests were finished. They had been waiting over fifteen minutes in the unloading zone, but still no sign of their significant others.

"Do you see them?" Craig asked as he looked around for Amanda.

"No. Maybe we should get out and go find them?"

"There! I see them!" Craig jumped out of the parked vehicle running full speed to intercept his wife. He grabbed her in a forceful hug and kissed her repeatedly on the mouth and neck. She dropped her luggage and lovingly embraced him as well. He knew that he had missed his beautiful wife but hadn't fully realized how much. The smell of her sweet perfume and the feel of her body pressed against his made him reconsider the current work assignment. No amount of money seemed worth it to him to be away from this gorgeous woman.

"I feel a little underappreciated here," Alexander said after putting down his luggage. "Where's my slobbery greeting at?"

"Sorry," Craig said as he momentarily came up for air, "I don't think my wife would understand…"

Julie made her way from her SUV to her husband in a more civilized manner. She embraced him, wrapping both arms tightly around his neck. Alexander kissed his wife and wrapped his arms snuggly around her waist.

Amanda lovingly pushed Craig away. "Save some of that for later!"

All four picked up various bags and luggage and moved towards the SUV. Craig motioned for them to leave the bags at the back of the vehicle and nodded for them to enter the SUV. Craig loaded the luggage in the back storage area. Julie slid into the driver's seat while Alexander grabbed the front passenger seat. Amanda had entered the back driver's side seat and Craig joined them as soon as the final piece of luggage was loaded. Julie pulled out of the unloading zone and they drove out of the airport onto the freeway heading east towards the production facility.

"The company was nice enough to rent vehicles for us and also some very nice apartments close to where we are working," Julie said.

"Bah!" Craig replied. "They got us close enough to the facility so that we would have no excuse not to be able to make it in to the office…no matter the weather."

Julie exited the freeway after about fifteen miles and turned on the main road running parallel to the production facility. As they passed by the entrance, Amanda quickly noticed the amount of military presence guarding the site.

"Wow! It looks like a warzone in there," Amanda said. "What's going on? Why is the military there?"

"They were put in place by the IPPC," Julie said as she drove by slowly. "It was for our protection because of North Korea's posturing along the DMZ demanding the vaccine we produce to be delivered to them."

"Yeah, the US government has units at both facilities," Alexander chimed in. "During the flight, I read about the increased protection in today's paper. If I remember the article correctly, it mentioned something about trying to deter civil unrest and protestors or something like that...."

"I think it's all a conspiracy anyway," Craig said as he reached down to hold his wife's hand. "I think they put all of those soldiers in place to keep us from leaving that damn building! We had to be frisked just to leave the premises to come pick you two up from the airport..."

"Don't listen to him," Julie said, "you know how he gets."

Julie turned right at the third traffic light and entered the Fountain Crest Apartment complex. She pulled the SUV into the covered parking area outside of building seventeen next to Craig's rented family sedan. Craig and Alexander unloaded the heavier luggage while Amanda and Julie grabbed the lighter stuff. They piled up the luggage in the small breezeway that separated the two apartments. Julie stayed in apartment #1701 while Craig was actually in building eighteen, apartment #1801.

"OK," Julie began, "it's a bit after four now. Why don't you two come over here around seven to discuss dinner plans...I figure that will give us plenty of time to...ummm...'catch up' with our significant others."

"One step ahead of you, Julie..." Craig had already hastily distributed the luggage to the appropriate apartments and was standing inside the doorway to his apartment sans shoes and socks and already beginning to unbuckle his belt.

"Good Lord, Craig," Julie said. "You're like a dog in heat." The two women quickly hugged each other. Amanda waved at Alexander and everyone entered their respective apartments.

Amanda entered apartment #1801 closing and locking the door behind her. She knew the game was on. *Was she the prey or the hunter?* She looked around the living room and Craig was nowhere to be found. She checked the kitchen and bathroom – nothing. She was playfully stalling. She already knew where her husband would be…the bedroom. The only question on her mind was whether or not he had started without her. She slowly opened the bedroom door and there was Craig, all naked and hairy, lying on the bed.

"Seems like you started without me," Amanda said, feigning a look of sadness as she began to undress. She slowly removed her shoes, one at a time making Craig wait. She pulled her sweater off and tossed it over Craig's face. He shoved it to the floor. She unbuckled her belt and unbuttoned her pants, sensually sliding the jeans to the floor and kicking them to the side of the room.

Craig could wait no longer. He jumped from the bed, grabbing his wife forcefully by the hips and pressed her against the wall. He gently removed her undershirt and bra, exposing her medium-sized breasts. He grabbed the sides of her panties and ripped them off.

"Hey! Those are expensive," she playfully scolded him.

"Don't worry," Craig said between passionate kisses, "I'm good for it."

Craig picked up his wife and carried her over to the bed, laying her down gently. He briefly stared at the beautiful, naked woman in his bed. *How did he get so lucky?* He loved her so much, but often wondered what she saw in him.

"Are you just going to stand there, dork?" Amanda joked.

Craig made a diving motion and hopped into bed with his wife. The two made passionate love for the next hour. They lay in bed for an additional hour wrapped in each other's arms. Craig playfully ran his fingers through her hair, massaging her scalp. Soon they both fell asleep.

• *March 26, 2013: Tuesday, 7:22 PM – Fountain Crest Apartments Apartment #1801...*

Amanda nudged Craig in the side again. She never understood why he was such a sound sleeper. Alarm clocks were practically useless. She had actually witnessed him sleep through fire and police sirens, not to mention a freak accident where a powerful thunderstorm actually knocked a tree over into the side of their first apartment. She nudged him again.

"What?" Craig asked.

"We overslept. Julie has been knocking on the door for about two minutes now. They called on your cell phone – that's what woke me up. Get up...I'll go and tell them we need a few minutes to get ready for dinner."

"You do that, Mandy," Craig rolled back over on his side and began to snore.

Amanda got out of bed, slid on her sweater and jeans and went to the door. She looked through the peephole - safety first. Just as she thought, Julie was standing at the door. Amanda brushed back her hair trying to be a bit more presentable; she opened the door and smiled at her friend.

"Hey Mandy."

"Hey. Sorry about making you guys wait. We overslept."

"No worries. Alex and I figured that we could all just stay in this evening. We ordered some Chinese food. Why don't you and Craig get showered and come on over. We've got plenty of hot food on the way."

"Oh that sounds wonderful. We'll be over in like thirty minutes."

Craig and Amanda arrived at Julie's apartment twenty minutes later in perfect timing with the Chinese delivery guy. Julie opened the door to greet her friends and stepped back inside to get her purse to pay for the food. Craig insisted that he pay for half. After a few moments of negotiations, Julie paid for this round of food while Craig agreed that tomorrow's dinner would be his treat.

"Well now that's taken care of," Alex began, "what should we do now?"

"How about we watch a scary movie?" Julie suggested.

"No!" Amanda said sternly. "I don't like scary movies."

As the friends enjoyed dinner together, they finally decided on a romantic comedy for the evening's festivities. As the movie ended, Julie turned the channel to the local news station. The main topic of discussion revolved around new outbreaks of H1N1 in various portions of the United States and Britain.

"Looks like more work for us," Craig said as he got off the couch to get another soda from the refrigerator.

"It's job security, right?" Alexander joked.

"It just seems like we never get ahead of the flu, no matter how hard we work." Julie sounded tired and irritated.

"…this just in to our news desks," the anchorman said.

"Turn it up," Mandy requested.

The anchorman held his white earpiece in with one finger, listening to the info being relayed to him from the control room;

he then spoke to the audience. "We have confirmed reports from the police in Stockholm, Sweden that the car of Deputy Director Pamela Bristow of the IPPC has been found at the bottom of a deep ravine a few miles from the IPPC main campus. Apparently she lost control of her car and crashed over the side of the bridge. Our thoughts and prayers are with her family and friends."

Julie turned off the TV.

"That's sad," Mandy said. "Did you guys know her?"

"Not really," Julie answered.

The friends parted ways for the evening; it was getting late. Craig and Julie both knew that they had plenty of work waiting for them in the morning. The whole week they were required to put in extra effort to meet production demands. Alex and Mandy spent time exploring Rochester and spending money on gifts. Julie and Craig spent time with their loved ones when they could, but the work week often kept them into the late evening hours. Luckily, Alexander and Mandy had planned to spend at least two, maybe three weeks in Rochester (if Alexander's schedule allowed) – surely, given the extra time, Julie and Craig's workload would have to ease up some.

For the last week of March, operations at both facilities continued to work around-the-clock in order to meet the almost insatiable demand for the H1N1 flu vaccine. The military presence warded off most unauthorized guests. Small pockets of overly vocal protestors stood on the fringes of each of the properties demanding free vaccines to be given out to those countries in need, even if those countries were not part of the initial twenty four charter member nations that founded the IPPC. The production facilities could barely meet the demands they were contracted for – let alone trying to meet the needs of non-member nations.

IPPC officials met almost daily in special sessions of the United Nations. The hot topic was the aggressive position taken up by North Korea. The communist nation had moved ever closer to fulfilling its promise of invading South Korea should it not receive any medication for its citizens. As the end of March approached, many countries began to take sides. Most notably, China and the former Soviet Union continued to lobby for the North Koreans while the United States, Britain and Japan vehemently defended the sovereignty of South Korea.

After two days of intense deliberations, the North Korean delegation left the UN assembly under protest of favoritism to the South Koreans by the West. A final act of defiance as the North Korean delegation left the building was a lingering warning that the soon-to-be debacle was of the West's own doing. The North assured that the forthcoming massacre could have been averted had the selfish Westerners only shared some of their medicines with those countries in dire need.

- *March 31, 2013: Sunday, 12:00 AM – North Korea, approximately two miles outside of the Demilitarized Zone on the south western edge of the country …*

"It is unfortunate but not unexpected," Commander Cheong began as he addressed all of the divisions under his control by means of shortwave, encrypted field communications. "The South has once again lorded over us its richness aided by the Westerners. They have a potent vaccine that could have prevented many deaths among our families, yet they refuse to aid us."

Over the past two weeks, the North Korean military had amassed approximately forty thousand troops along various portions of the DMZ. Fifty thousand troops were on standby in the capital city of Pyongyang awaiting deployment orders. The troops, currently spread along the length of the DMZ, were broken down into four divisions, each under the leadership of much respected lieutenant commanders, all reporting to Commander Cheong.

"There has been no word out of Pyongyang since my last communications with them three days ago. Our orders are standing orders and we must act. The UN special sessions have failed to convince the Westerners of our need for immediate medical assistance." The commander paused briefly. "We must preserve our way of life. Our peaceful negotiations with the UN have failed. We must now take what we need by force. With heavy hearts then, we must move forward..."

Before Commander Cheong could give the order to attack, he was interrupted by a high-priority communication from the military headquarters in Pyongyang. The Commander entered the communications truck and instructed all of the other personnel to exit the vehicle. He put the earphones on his head and pressed the talk button.

"Commander, hold the attack! You are to leave the DMZ and return to the capital city at once.

"I don't understand."

"The South has redirected its forces back to their capital, away from the DMZ," General Pak said.

"They retreat already?"

"Our spies have informed us that they fire upon their own people! We've been trying to contact you for two days now...but have been unsuccessful until now."

"That makes no sense, General" Commander Cheong stated. "Why would they turn their guns on their own people?"

"Our reports indicate that Seoul has been without communication for over a week now. They have been embroiled in riots, looting and mass hysteria."

"What caused this?"

"Commander this conversation is wasting time; you are ordered to fall back now. Reliable sources have indicated to us that South's infected citizens have died off very rapidly. Apparently the vaccine from the West did not cure them."

"Then what better opportunity to attack now that they are unfocused?"

"Commander, is anyone else listening to this communication?"

"No, sir – this is a scrambled and secured channel."

"Do not interrupt me. Just listen to what I am saying. Their dead have reportedly come back to life. They attack their own people; reports of hordes of contagious citizens attacking and feeding off one another."

"I don't understand, General." Commander Cheong had served under General Pak for more than thirty years. In all of that time, he never once remembered the General to be prone to fits of fantasy. He respected his senior officer, but this story...it seemed too strange to be true.

"We've wasted enough time, Cheong," the General stated. "Leave ten thousand men there to guard the DMZ. You and the rest of the troops and equipment must return to Pyongyang immediately."

Commander Cheong relayed the new orders to his divisions. The remaining forces along the DMZ were consolidated to guard the area just north of Seoul, South Korea. The troops would be the first line of defense should any of the infected try to invade the

North. Of course, Commander Cheong didn't fully relay all info to his soldiers. They did not need to know the true threat looming on the horizon. Like good soldiers, they did what they were told to do and did not question direct orders. Commander Cheong took the rest of his force and began the trip back to Pyongyang.

Chapter 14

- *April 1, 2013: Monday, 8:14 AM – Rochester, New York – Secondary production facility…*

Unconfirmed reports began to circulate about H1N1 infected people dying and subsequently returning to life after just a few hours. Most of these reports indicated that the previously deceased person would somehow reawaken in a fit of rage punctuated by attacks on their friends, neighbors or anyone within close proximity. These stories were originally only carried by a few shady tabloid magazines. Similar stories simultaneously inundated the internet on urban legend web pages. Since the majority of these reports appeared on April's Fools Day, the stories went largely unread by the general public.

"Read this one, Julie – it's crazy!" Craig said as he forwarded yet another email message to his friend. "It says to forward this message to ten of your friends in order to stop the *'undead'* from rising in your neighborhood. Since I don't have ten friends…you may very well get a few more sent your way!"

Julie pressed the delete key as soon as she received the email. She had no desire to waste any of her precious time reading stupid chain emails of any kind. She leaned sideways and looked around her monitor at Craig, making eye contact with him. She had known this man for years, but sometimes, especially on days like this, she felt like Craig was a ten-year old boy trapped in a man's body. "Don't send me any more of those. Why do you read that crap? More importantly, why do you try and make me read it?"

"Oh, come on – it's not that bad. Plus I needed a break. I figured you needed one too!"

"A break? We've only been in the office for a little over an hour." Julie returned to entering data values in her spreadsheet. "If you would focus on getting some work done, maybe we would get out of here at a decent hour and be able to spend more time with Alex and Mandy."

Craig bowed his head in pseudo shame. "Yes, mother..."

Julie playfully tossed a notebook at her friend's desk, knocking over a small stack of papers and spilling his cup of pens and pencils. "Hey!" Craig yelled. "Don't mess up my desk!"

Both laughed as they continued to trudge through some of their daily assignments. Julie had made reservations at a local Indian restaurant for 7:30 that evening. Mandy and Alex would be waiting at the restaurant, so Julie constantly urged Craig to keep focused throughout the day in order for them to be able to leave the office no later than 6:00 PM. They didn't want to keep their loved ones waiting any longer than necessary.

• *April 2, 2013: Tuesday, 10:31 AM – Boise, Idaho – Illumination Pharmaceuticals – main campus ...*

Karl sat in his office going over status reports from last week when he heard one of the large military vehicles below roar to life.

He pushed himself away from the desk and walked over to his favorite window. Like a colony of well-organized ants, the soldiers stood in formation and listened to Lieutenant Dwight Samson bark orders. Karl had no idea what was being said, but the men and women split off into two groups after the lieutenant had finished his speech.

A group of about twenty soldiers led by Lt. Samson left the facility and headed north. The remainder of the platoon stayed behind and focused on their duties. Karl saw Michael speaking to one of the soldiers but the conversation did not appear to be going Michael's way. As Michael turned to enter into the building, he looked up and saw his boss standing at the window. Karl motioned for Michael to come up to his office.

After a few minutes, Michael rushed into Karl's office – apparently he had run up the stairs to deliver the important news to his boss. "You will not believe this!" Michael blurted out. "I didn't hear everything that Lt. Samson said," Michael conceded, "but something big is going on!"

Karl tried to appear disinterested, but his curiosities were definitely piqued.

"There is some kind of riot or something two miles north of here at the mall," Michael continued. "Lt. Samson and his soldiers are going to restore order!"

"A riot here in Idaho?" Karl paused briefly as he looked out the window. "I bet it has something to do with those hippie-ass protestors that have been living outside our facility for the past week…"

Lt. Samson and his small cadre of soldiers arrived at the local strip mall. The first civilian teams on scene had already cordoned off a small section of stores. An ambulance siren blared in the distance. Lt. Samson directed his driver to pull the armored personnel carrier to the side of the U-shaped blockade comprised of police cars and fire trucks. The lieutenant exited the vehicle and maneuvered his way through the yellow tape to find the civilian in charge.

After questioning a few policemen, Lt. Samson was directed to speak with Detective Holcomb. The lieutenant walked over to the backside of a large black SUV where four police officers listened to a man wearing a dark gray suit and navy blue tie. The well-dressed man fit the description of the person the lieutenant was looking for. The detective stood about six feet tall, dark brown hair and sported expensive, coal black sunglasses.

"Detective Holcomb, I presume?" Lt. Samson inquired.

"Yes, sir - that's me," the young detective replied, standing a bit taller as he addressed the military man. He had previously worked with the FBI and DEA on a few of his more difficult cases, but the US military? This was a first for him. *What the hell had he gotten himself into? Apparently he had picked the wrong week to transfer to Idaho…*

Lt. Samson removed a half-smoked cigar from his pocket and clenched it between his teeth. He flicked his lighter a few times and soon, with a few deep puffs, the cigar blazed to life. "What does it look like in there, son?"

"We didn't understand the original call from dispatch," Detective Holcomb said softly. "The nine-one-one call stated that an angry mob of people had entered the jewelry store and began tearing up the place and attacking the customers."

"Go on."

"Well, when we got here…what we saw…well this part didn't make any sense." The young detective began to hyperventilate slightly as he tried to find the words to explain what he had witnessed an hour earlier.

"Calm down, son - take a deep breath."

After a few brief moments, the detective composed himself and continued. "We got here and barricaded the area about an hour ago. We could see inside the store. There appeared to be eight customers and maybe two employees trapped inside with the angry mob. It looked like a hostage situation at first."

"How many rioters are there?" Lt. Samson inquired.

"Six...I think. I saw one of the rioters grab a woman by her face...her head looked like a grapefruit in between his huge hands." Detective Holcomb paused as he realized how apt the analogy was. "That man bit her face repeatedly."

Lt. Samson rubbed his index finger around in his ear as he tried to make sense of the words that had just come out of the detective's mouth. The lieutenant motioned for his soldiers to approach the command area where he and Detective Holcomb were standing. The troops formed a single-file line, waiting for instructions from their leader.

"All right, boys and girls," Lt. Samson began, "this is the real deal. Our detective friend here says that the rioters are some sort of whacked out cannibals...whatever the hell that means. We have at least six hostiles cooped up in that store and maybe ten civilians."

"What do you want my people to do?" Detective Holcomb asked.

"Secure the area – basic crowd control, son. Do not allow anyone past that barricade."

Detective Holcomb and the four police officers left the makeshift command area and moved back to the start of the barricade. Two ambulances and another fire truck had arrived on scene. Detective

Holcomb directed the emergency crews to stay behind the barricade until the area was secured. A Channel 14 News helicopter circled overhead; soon more media would converge on the area once the other news agencies got word of the major story brewing at the small outlet mall.

Lt. Samson split his soldiers into Alpha and Bravo teams; he would lead the former. Alpha team approached the jewelry store from the west and Bravo team closed in from the east. A purple neon "For Sale" sign flickered on and off above a full display case. The sign's downward pointing arrow flashed above some cheap costume jewelry behind the thick glass outer window. The flashing sign indicated that there was still power to the store, but the rest of the interior was jet-black and neither team could see any hostages from their vantage point. Apparently the rioters had moved their prisoners to the back part of the store after knocking out the overhead lights.

Lieutenant Samson kneeled down at the west side corner of the building. He made eye contact with the Bravo team's lead soldier on the east end of the building. Lt. Samson motioned for Bravo team to move to the back of the store. Their job would be to guard the rear just in case the perpetrators decided to make a break for it. Bravo team backed away from the front of the building as they moved into position behind the store. The soldiers sloshed through the muddy, unpaved parking lot and positioned themselves behind dumpsters and parked cars. The protective barriers would provide good cover in case anyone from inside the store had weapons.

Lt. Samson pivoted on his knee as he turned to address his team; his back faced the large glass window that occupied the majority of the store front. As he did so, a thundering crash of expensive glass exploded behind him followed almost immediately by a loud

"THUMP" as a mutilated body hit the sidewalk next to him. The lieutenant instinctively rolled out of the way and pulled his pistol from its holster and scanned the area. He glanced down quickly at the body and then back to the store; he couldn't see anyone inside the building.

Blood quickly began to pool up on the sidewalk around the body. Lt. Samson put his gun back into its holster and motioned for Alpha team to maintain their positions about twenty feet from the body. The lieutenant walked over to the body and gently pushed it over with his boot. The body sluggishly rolled over on its backside. What used to be a young woman was now a mutilated corpse - missing over half of her face and neck and part of her blouse. The lieutenant knelt down to inspect the body; there were bite marks and scratches all up and down her forearms, obviously defensive wounds from her failed attempt to fend off her attacker.

"Look out!" Sergeant Vaughn yelled.

Lt. Samson quickly turned his attention from the corpse to the busted out window behind him. He sized up the large, sickly looking man that had emerged from the cave-like interior. The purple neon sign flashed overhead illuminating the behemoth's awkward features. His pale gray skin looked like old hamburger meat that had been left out too long. The man was hunched over but still easily topped six feet in height and must have weighed in excess of two-hundred and fifty pounds based on Lt. Samson's best estimate. The hulking man's swollen face was twisted and contorted; his eyes were dark and sunken in. Most of his body seemed to twitch sporadically – like a horse does when shaking off flies. He was covered in blood and held the other half of the woman's blouse between his teeth.

With a terrible growl, the large man flung himself through the window lunging for Lt. Samson's throat. A deafening shotgun blast echoed off the buildings knocking the giant man out of the air; he crumpled to the ground, sliding for a few feet before coming to rest on his side. Now two bodies lay side-by-side on the small sidewalk. Lt. Samson glanced back towards Sergeant Vaughn, thanking him with just a look for saving his life. Once again, the lieutenant motioned for Alpha team to hold their positions.

As expected, local news crews began flocking to the scene, but the barricade did its job and allowed Detective Holcomb to better do his. He and his men kept the overanxious reporters some twenty feet to the south of the original barricade. Threats of police brutality bubbled up from the crowd as the police used *"reasonable"* force to restrain some of the media. Detective Holcomb had heard it all before. He'd rather do his job and keep everyone safe. At the end of the day, it was much easier to answer for his *"excessive"* tactics than contacting families to let them know that a loved one had died because he failed to do his job properly.

Lt. Samson knelt down next to the second body and grabbed the man's arm. He tried to roll the large man over to better see his face, but the man was too heavy. Sergeant Vaughn moved away from Alpha team's current position towards the body. He knelt down as he tried to assist the lieutenant. Both men were finally able to roll the mammoth man onto his back. As the body came to rest, a giant hole in the center of his chest was exposed; the two soldiers could see the pavement of the sidewalk through the cavernous wound. Sergeant Vaughn looked away briefly…he had never been so close to a dead body.

The beastly man opened his blood-soaked eyes. In an instant, he sat straight up, reached out and clamped his massive right hand around Sergeant Vaughn's throat. Before Lt. Samson could react, the large man jerked Sergeant Vaughn close to his chest and gnawed a large chunk of flesh and bone out of the soldier's face and tossed him like a ragdoll into the side of the building. The members of Alpha team stood shell shocked at the scene playing out before them. Half of them hesitated while the other half tried to steady their weapons on the monstrosity in front of them. They chose not to shoot for fear of hitting their lieutenant.

Lt. Samson stood up from his kneeling position; he reached down and unclasped his machete from his leg strap. At this particular moment, the grizzled soldier felt vindicated that he had decided to purchase the weapon with his own money since his asshole requisition officer had denied his earlier request. The newly-freed blade glistened in the sunlight as it made its downward arc deep into the large man's left arm, severing it from its body just below the elbow – a feat that a standard issue K-bar could never match. Thick blood spewed all over Lt. Samson's fatigues. The depraved beast-man grunted and groaned as he pushed himself up from a seated position to a kneeling position.

Lt. Samson kicked the large man in the ribcage; the force of the blow knocked the one-armed man off balance causing him to fall face first onto the body of the dead girl. The colossal man recovered and quickly moved to an upright position. Lt. Samson dropped his machete and once again un-holstered his SOCOM 45 caliber pistol. Two shots rang out in quick succession, hitting the large man in the neck and collarbone; un-phased, the large man kept advancing towards the lieutenant. Lt. Samson unloaded the final rounds into the attacker's body, but the target acted as if the gunshot wounds were just a minor inconvenience. In desperation, Lt. Samson threw his empty gun at the seemingly unstoppable man.

Corporal Jackson quickly joined the fray. She picked up the lieutenant's discarded machete, grasping it firmly in both hands and moved behind the bullet-riddled attacker. She raised the blood-soaked blade above her head and began hacking into the large man like a lumberjack chopping wood. The first strike lodged deep in the man's neck midway between his shoulder and spine. She struggled fiercely to remove the blade as the behemoth turned his attention towards her. As he spun around, she was able to free the blade and deliver another gashing strike to his face. The gray-skinned man raked his hand across her chest; she could feel his fingernails rip deep into her flesh; she dropped the machete as she doubled over in pain.

Lt. Samson propelled himself towards Corporal Jackson knocking her away from the angry man. Alpha team now had the opening they needed. A hail of gunfire erupted and the man fell to the ground motionless. The team ran over to assist their leader and Corporal Jackson. One man went to check on Sergeant Vaughn, but one look told the soldier that Sergeant Vaughn was already dead. Lt. Samson picked up the sergeant's shotgun and moved over to the downed gargantuan man. He placed the barrel of the gun directly against the base of enormous man's neck and pulled the trigger; blood, brain, bones and cement erupted from the blast finally ending the confrontation.

Multiple gunshots from Bravo team rang out from behind the building.

"You three come with me," Lt. Samson yelled as he pointed at three of his more veteran soldiers. "Someone get to Detective Holcomb. Tell him to get an ambulance over here ASAP!" Lt. Samson and the three soldiers cautiously ran off to the back of the building as a light misting rain began to fall. Hundreds of shots rang out before the lieutenant and his men entered the back parking lot. An ominous cloud of steam rose from Bravo team's superheated rifle barrels; the spent casings littered the ground like the abandoned playthings of a whimsical child after playtime had ended.

As the smoke cleared, Lt. Samson surveyed the area and called out to Bravo team for them to hold fire. A plethora of corpses lay strewn over the ground. Bravo team came out from behind their barricades when they saw their leader arrive; the soldiers were mortified by what they had just partaken in.

"Sir, they busted out of the building chasing after those people," the leader of Bravo team began. The soldier pointed at three disfigured, almost unrecognizable bodies that lay in a deep puddle of bloody mud. "We ordered them to stop, but they didn't listen."

Another soldier spoke from behind Lt. Samson. "They caught those people and knocked them to the ground. They started clawing and ripping flesh from their bodies...they were chewing on them, sir...we had no choice...we had to fire."

"Don't worry, soldier," Lt. Samson said as he turned and placed a firm hand on the young man's shoulder. "You did the right thing."

"What the hell's going on here?" another member of Bravo team asked.

"I don't know. Call in backup," Lt. Samson ordered. "Get the IPPC team from the lab over here now! We may need to quarantine this area."

"What about the hostages, sir?" A female soldier inquired. "Should we go into the store and see if anyone needs our help?"

Lt. Samson bowed his head. "They're all dead...there are no hostages alive in that store."

Lt. Samson surveyed the carnage in the muddy field. He counted eight bodies lying in the back parking lot of the building. Each body gruesomely displayed in some twisted, mangled final resting position. As Lt. Samson walked out of the kill zone to return to the front of the store to assist Alpha team, he said something that would haunt his men and women for the rest of their days:

"I know this will sound bat shit crazy, but listen closely," Lt. Samson motioned for Bravo team to move closer to him. "If any of these fucking corpses move – use your E-tools and decapitate these sick sons of bitches…"

Chapter 15

- *April 5, 2013: Friday, 4:17 PM – Boise, Idaho – Illumination Pharmaceuticals – main campus …*

For the last three days, Lt. Samson and his soldiers had been quarantined at the mall along with the police, rescue and media agents that had ventured into the danger zone on Tuesday. Medical personnel had been rushed to the scene to treat the injured only after the quarantine was in place. Makeshift hospitals or *"bubble domes"*, as they were called, had been constructed onsite made from lightweight aluminum structures and medical-grade plastic sheets. All of the stores around the mall were under strict IPPC quarantine guidelines. Only officials with proper hazmat gear and authorization could enter or leave the area. The streets of the surrounding area were blocked off; local police authorities stood guard in twelve hour shifts.

During the rest of the work week following the Tuesday incident, the production facility had almost returned to its pre-military involvement atmosphere, even with half of the soldiers still present. Karl was highly pleased at the transition. Those *"grunts"* as he often referred to them as had no inclination to lead any new endeavors or change the status quo. The soldiers basically fulfilled their previously assigned roles and stayed out of Karl's way.

However, that all changed earlier this morning with one phone call. With incidents of riots and attacks becoming more prevalent in the evening news, the US Marine Corp felt it prudent to fortify the Idaho facility. They contacted Karl and informed him that a Major Pavlik, another platoon of soldiers and some additional technical personnel would be dispatched to the Idaho facility by Monday of the upcoming week. This news did not please Karl.

Karl had been in the office since before sunrise; he couldn't sleep last night and figured he might as well come into the office. He had draped his sports coat over the back of his chair like he did every day. He really hadn't accomplished anything during the morning except for becoming increasingly angrier about the news of the soon-to-arrive troops. Sure it would be three more days until they showed up, but it didn't matter to him. He wanted control of his facility back. He was tired of going through the military check-point at least four times every day – when he arrived, when he left for lunch, when he returned from lunch and when he finally left the facility at night. He was tired of showing his credentials to the soldiers on duty and tired of seeing them in and about the facility itself. *How much longer would they be here?*

Karl had just returned to his office from a three hour meeting with the financial backers of his firm. He sat behind his desk and was soon interrupted by what sounded like multiple high-powered firecrackers going off outside. At first the sounds didn't register with him. He sat behind his desk in his comfortable chair trying to figure out if he had actually really heard anything. He listened closely but heard no other sounds.

Karl busied himself downloading the rest of the weekly status reports from both facilities. As the reports printed, he organized an agenda for next week's meeting with the IPPC officials in the

Stockholm office. He made corrections to the agenda but was interrupted as the outside noises began to fire off again in rapid succession. Karl heard yelling from outside his office and more *"POP"* *"POP"* *"POP"* sounds outside his window as Michael rushed into the office.

"Holy shit, Karl...I mean Mr. Timmons – look out your window! We are under attack!" Michael rushed over to the window waving his boss over to him.

"What the hell, Michael? What are you blabbering about?"

Michael stared out the window at the horrifying scene below. At least two hundred *"rioters"* were cresting the small hill leading into the facility. The soldiers below were shouting warnings for the intruders to stay out of the restricted area but the interlopers paid no attention. Wave after wave of rioters were being struck down by light gunfire, mostly handguns and shotguns. The soldiers on scene lacked the initial firepower they once had at the beginning of their stint on the Idaho campus; Lt. Samson and his crew had taken the majority of the heavier caliber arms with them to combat the initial riot at the mall.

Screams of terror from all floors of the building echoed about the complex. Many people were trying to leave work a bit early to start the weekend off the right way, but their plans forever changed today. People dialed nine-one-one to report the vicious attacks going on just outside the walls of their building. Karl's office phone buzzed repeatedly, multiple channels lit up indicating that various heads of departments were trying to get his attention. Karl sat at his desk trying to figure out what was going on...he barely paid any attention as Michael continued to yell.

"I'm going down there to see if I can help in any way." Michael rushed out of the office before Karl could reply.

Karl eventually snapped out of his fugue-like dream state as he saw Michael leaving the room. Karl didn't try to stop the young man. As he began to focus more clearly he pushed himself away from the desk and walked to his favorite window; a warzone had erupted in the parking lot of Illumination Pharmaceuticals. Bodies of non-military personnel lay strewn out all over the street and inside the cordoned off area. Karl watched in horror as the attackers broke through the military line. At least half of the soldiers were dead or dying. The attackers continued to push through the small arms fire as if the bullets were mere bee stings to them. Karl watched as the soldiers began to retreat towards the building. He ran out of his office down the stairs to the first floor of the building.

By the time Karl made it to the reception area, the remaining soldiers had moved inside the building. Karl looked at these young men and women, most of them were barely out of high school. He counted nine soldiers in total. Three of the soldiers had barricaded the front entrance by pushing furniture against the door. Three other soldiers had blocked off the back entrance by wrapping chains around the door handles binding them together. Both sets of doors were predominately glass outlined by thick metal support structures.

Two soldiers lay on the marble floor. The center mosaic design with the dark blue IP logo was splattered with their thick crimson blood. Karl knew the soldiers had been dragged through the front door because two trails of blood led directly from that door to their current location. Karl stepped over the dead soldiers and slipped in their blood but he regained his balance and steadied himself as he moved towards a female soldier standing at the side of the room.

She appeared to be the highest ranking officer left on scene since Lt. Samson had left earlier in the week. Karl saw a look of fear etched deep into her young face but her training had taken over; she robotically barked out orders to her soldiers. To their credit, the young men and women did as instructed. Karl heard her yelling instructions but the words made no sense to him; he was shell-shocked. The gunfire and the screams had overtaxed his nervous system's capacity to cope with all of the extra stimuli; he began to feel dizzy as he sat down on one of the out-of-place sofas.

A small crowd of five or six employees converged around the receptionist's desk. Most had been trying to exit the facility and were forced back inside by the soldiers. As Karl steadied himself, he saw more employees - his accounting team, the accounts payable team and a few scientists were huddled into one of the back corners. What he hadn't noticed earlier was that some of his employees, people he knew and saw every day, lay motionless on the floor around the perimeter of the room. Apparently some of them, Karl counted at least four, had made it outside and were mauled by the rioters. The soldiers had dragged all of the wounded back inside the building before barricading both entrances.

Karl cupped his hands around his ears to drown out the screaming and crying. His world spun around and he felt the overwhelming urge to vomit or pass out – maybe both and not necessarily in that order. He took more deep breaths and heard the faintest sound of a voice calling out his name. It took a few seconds to register but he turned his head to look in the direction of the familiar voice. A fifth downed employee was within arm's reach...it was Michael. Karl fell off the couch to his knees and kneeled next to the downed man.

"Michael?"

"Karl...they got me."

"Don't call me *Karl* – you know I hate that. It will look bad on your yearly review if I have to write you up for insubordination."

Michael could barely muster enough strength to smile at his boss's attempt to downplay the gravity of the situation. "I'm not sure…if I'll need that raise…"

"What happened?" Karl asked as he inspected the man's wounds. Michael had bite marks on his neck and bone-deep gashes in both forearms from what appeared to be vicious fingernail scratches. The young man's lab coat was torn and bloody, the remaining white areas of the coat stood in stark contrast to the maroon stained arm and neck areas.

"I was trying to see what was going on…" Michael coughed out syrupy thick blood that ran down his chin and neck. The young man struggled to speak. "Those things out there…not…human…"

Michael's eyes rolled backwards as his body began to spasm; Karl didn't know what to do for the young man, but felt holding him was the right thing to do. Soon the spasms stopped and Michael breathed his last breath dying on the cool marble floor next to the company logo. Karl lay the man down gently and rushed in the direction of the female soldier in charge.

A large panel of glass at the front entrance exploded inwards – confetti-like glass shrapnel hovered momentarily in the air before crashing to the ground. Karl glanced over to the door, not paying attention to the blood-slicked flooring, he slipped and fell. He rolled onto his shoulder to absorb some of the impact as he crashed awkwardly to the floor.

As he stopped sliding, he looked over at the back door. A cabal of the attackers had clumped up shoulder-to-shoulder against the glass doors. He could hear them moaning and growling as the mob scratched and pounded on the glass. Karl knew that the thick security glass would only hold for so long. He sat up and faced the front doors. A similar scene played out there as well as the sick minions tried to crawl through the new opening. Karl scooted across the floor to the woman in charge. He used a nearby coffee table to push himself to his feet.

"What the hell is going on? We need to get the hell out of here!"

"Calm down, sir." Sergeant Womack insisted as she continued to give orders to the soldiers. "I need you to get into that corner over there with the rest of the employees."

"This is my facility! I'm tired of all of your people's bullshit. I refuse to take orders from some low-ranking cunt!" Karl put his hands on her shoulders to force her to pay attention to him.

Again, the young female soldier's instincts and training took over. She quickly pressed her palms together, as if praying, and shot both of her hands in an upward motion, inside of Karl's outstretched arms, breaking free from his forceful grip. A quick knee strike to his groin doubled him over in pain. As he turned his head up towards her, she pulled her sidearm from its holster and rammed the cold steel barrel of the weapon deep into the side of his cheek. "Sir, you will do as I say or I will shoot you in the fucking face."

Karl limped away holding his groin area; he moved slowly towards the clumped up group of his fellow coworkers. The group sat on the floor in silence in very close proximity to one another. None of them spoke – they barely even noticed Karl's arrival. Karl sat down next to them. He had known, or more accurately – had supervised most of these people for at least five years, some of them more…yet he could never remember ever being this close to them unless he had been barking orders at them. Now he stared at their blank faces and couldn't remember a single one of their names.

Karl watched as Sergeant Womack gave more orders to her soldiers. She then turned her attention to the group of people that

Karl sat with. She walked quickly towards them and knelt down on one knee next to a young woman on Karl's right side. Sergeant Womack addressed the entire group in a calm, orderly fashion:

"I need all of you to get up and go back to your offices. Find a place to hide upstairs. Stay off the elevators. Lock the doors. Do not come out for any reason. We will hold off those…things…as long as we can. Help should be here soon. Go hide and don't come out until we come and get you. GO!"

Karl took off up the stairs. He didn't consider himself to be a selfish or bad man, but he wasn't going to wait for everyone else to get up the stairs before he made his move. Even the painful groin strike from moments earlier didn't slow him down. Karl made it to the top of the third floor staircase. His heart was pounding, sweat streamed down his forehead and neck and he could literally hear his heart pounding in his ears. He sat down on third floor landing breathing deeply – he feared he might have pushed himself too hard. Karl fumbled around in his shirt pocket for his nitroglycerin tablets. He placed one white pill under his tongue and closed his eyes. *"Just breathe"* he thought silently to himself as the brief bout of angina slowly began to subside.

Gunfire erupted from the first floor. Karl knew that the rioters had breached the interior of the building. He gingerly pushed himself up to his feet and walked briskly past the cubicles to the end of the aisle to his office door. He grabbed the cool, metal handle and gently turned the knob. Karl peeked inside his well-lit office; nothing was out of place and more importantly, no one was inside. He slipped inside the room, closed the door behind him and locked the door.

Karl walked over to his window. Looking down, he saw more faceless waves of the rioters or whatever they were, canvassing the entire parking lot. Karl knew there was something horribly wrong with those people below...*Were they even people?* It didn't make any sense to him. Karl had seen some of those *"people"* up close and personal as he had looked out the back entry doors on the first floor. Many of them suffered from horrific injuries...life threatening injuries, but they still moved around. Their faces, etched in Karl's mind, were distorted and somewhat vacant. While he didn't have tons of time to analyze the attackers, it seemed to him that they were operating on instinct alone...as if some guttural, innate force guided them to move forward in spite of their damaged bodies.

Karl walked from the window to the closest edge of the maroon leather couch on the south wall of his office. He pressed the mid-part of his thigh against the overstuffed arm of the couch and began to slide the heavy couch towards the door. He didn't realize how heavy the couch actually was. When it was delivered six years ago, after he ordered it from an online retailer, two large men had maneuvered the lumbering piece of furniture to its current resting place. He hadn't moved the sofa since then and had given no particular scrutiny towards its mass over the past half decade.

Slowly but surely, Karl was able to reposition the large couch in front of the inward opening office door. It had taken him at least twenty minutes to slide the couch the fifteen feet from the south wall to the office door, but it was well worth the effort. There were no other entry points into the office. Karl surveyed the deep gouge marks in the expensive beige carpet but that was the least of his concerns now. He had to remain safe until additional help arrived.

Karl sat down in his comfortable leather chair behind his desk and opened the mini-fridge positioned under the desktop on his left hand side. He moved some sodas and sports drinks around. He found a package of chocolate cookies, an unopened single-sized bag of chips and a half-eaten deli sandwich left over from his brief visit to the office the past weekend. He had enough food and drinks to last until help arrived…assuming they showed up soon.

Karl picked up his office phone receiver – all the lights that were flashing earlier were dim now. He put the phone to his ear but there was no dial tone as he pressed the buttons. He slammed down the receiver and frantically patted himself down feeling for his Blackberry. He rummaged around in his desk drawer for the device but it was nowhere to be found. He came to the sad realization that his *"almost always present"* Blackberry must have fallen out of his pocket in his mad dash up the stairs.

Karl glanced at his watch, the time was 4:48 PM - he had already been in the office for well over twelve hours now and had eaten nothing. He opened the mini-fridge again and took out a sports drink and the bag of chips. He ate and drank quickly. His body was exhausted from the long day and all of the surreal activity on the first floor. His recent angina attack at the top of the stairs had also sapped precious energy from his body. He was exhausted. Karl stood up from his desk and walked over to his newly positioned couch. The old man sat down and swung his legs up onto the cushions; he stretched out his tired body the full length of the couch.

No one or nothing could get into the office except through the door. With the large couch now blocking the only entrance, Karl allowed himself to relax. If anything tried to get through the door, it would surely wake him. He would just lie here until help arrived. It would soon be night – surely help would arrive before the sun went down…

"I'll just rest my eyes," Karl said softly, to no one in particular, as he soon drifted off to sleep.

Karl awoke to the sounds of a woman's desperate screams. Gunfire and loud echoing knocks accompanied the terror-stricken voice. He sat up glancing around the dimly lit room; darkness lovingly caressed the thick glass of his favorite window. Gunfire erupted just beyond the thick oak door; empty shell casings danced loudly on the cold marble floor. Karl rubbed his eyes and glanced down at his watch - the time was now 9:33 PM! *How the hell had he slept for nearly five hours?!*

"Let me in," a muffled female voice pleaded from the other side of the door. "They are coming up the stairs!"

More gunfire echoed around Karl's office; he could smell the gunpowder seeping under the door. Now that he was fully awake, he began to panic. *Where was the additional help? Why hadn't someone come to their rescue?* A brief moment of silence passed then a few more rounds went off. Karl heard the female voice yell in pain. It was Sergeant Womack for sure.

"Please help me," Sergeant Womack pleaded. "For the love of God – I know you're in there! I'm out of ammo...more of those things will be coming up the stairs soon. Please..."

Karl hesitated, not because he hated that bitch for kicking him in the nuts, but because he truly feared for his life. If he moved the couch and those things got into his office, he would surely die. Karl sat on the couch and said nothing. He only listened. Soon, Sergeant Womack's screams of pain stopped. He looked down on the floor as her blood began to spill into the office. Loud groans and growls replaced her screams; soon deep, penetrating scratches began to tear into the outside part of the door.

Karl leapt off of the couch avoiding the slick pool of blood that began to form at the base of the couch. He ran towards his desk and crouched underneath. His legs began to cramp but he didn't move. *Maybe the creatures would just leave if they couldn't get into his office?*

The sturdy wooden legs of the couch began to rip through the carpet as the large piece of furniture was pushed out of its place. Karl sat silently, tucked away out of sight. Within moments, the door swung open and the heavy couch tumbled over landing on its backside. Karl heard one set of awkward footsteps scuffle across the carpet as something entered the room. The heavy steps moved towards the desk and stopped. A terrible stench invaded his olfactory senses; a pungent odor so vile and thick that he could taste it. Karl remained stationary as he listened to the creature moan – seemingly lamenting the fact that room was empty...

BRNNNG!! BRNNNG!! BRNNNG!!

Karl knew the sound instantly. It was his Blackberry. He now remembered where he had placed his precious piece of technology. It was in his left-hand coat pocket of his sports jacket – draped over the back of his office chair! The creature erupted into a fit of anger and sped towards the source of the sound. The chair guarding the entrance to Karl's secret lair was ripped away and tossed through the window to the ground three stories below. The desk became airborne and Karl was fully exposed.

Karl uncovered his head and slowly looked up from the creature's feet to his face. It was Michael! Karl stood up slowly and held out his hands in a sign of peace towards his former employee. Michael's face had turned gray and his eyes a dull, bloody red. Drool and fleshy particles hung from the side of his mouth.

"It's me, Mikey...remember? It's Karl, your old buddy!"

Michael tilted his head slightly as if he recognized Karl - at least that was what Karl thought. *Maybe if he could get through to his old colleague...then everything would be OK?* Karl moved towards

Michael in a slow, soothing manner. Michael moaned deeply as his body twitched, he raised his arms and moved arduously towards Karl.

Karl moved away from the vacuous eyed being in front of him towards his favorite window. He backed cautiously away from the thing standing in front of him. Karl could feel the breeze blowing through the broken window against his sweat-covered head. Karl weighed his escape options, he saw two bodies piled up at the edge of the door, one was the disfigured body of Sergeant Womack and the other appeared to be one of the rioters that the former sergeant had killed. Karl looked deep into the man's eyes standing in front of him; Michael was gone – a twisted, deformed creature was all that was left of his favorite employee.

Karl sprinted for the door but he was too old, too slow. *"Michael"* intercepted his former boss wrapping his hands around Karl's fat, fleshy throat. Karl tried to fight off the creature as he backed closer and closer to the office window, but the creature's grip was too strong. Man and creature both ran out of office space simultaneously and plummeted three stories to the ground below. Karl landed on his head; the impact snapped his neck and crushed his skull killing him instantly. The creature lay motionless on his former boss…his body twitched as he sat up.

"Michael" straddled Karl's disfigured body and began chewing and ripping out large chunks of flesh like an overzealous kid opening presents on Christmas Day…

Chapter 16

- *April 6, 2013: Saturday, 2:22 AM – Rochester, New York – Fountain Crest Apartments Apartment #1801…*

"**D**o you hear that, Craig?" Amanda groggily asked.
"Huh? What is it?"

"Craig…wake up, someone is at the door."

A frantic repetition of knocks, like a woodpecker drilling into a tree, echoed through the small apartment. The short burst of knocks were not loud enough to wake anyone in the adjacent apartments, but irritating enough that no one within the intended apartment would be able to sleep.

"Maybe they'll go away." Craig rolled over and tried desperately to fall back to sleep. This was the first weekend he had off in over two months. He had promised himself that he would not get out of bed before noon. Whatever or whoever was at the door could wait till lunchtime.

A few moments passed and the knocking subsided. Craig's cell phone buzzed angrily on the nightstand. Mandy reached over her husband and grabbed the cell phone. She flipped open the cover and the caller id showed one missed call. She scrolled through the menu and the last caller's name was Theo. The knocking at the door began again; the cell phone buzzed in unison with the knocking.

"Hello?" Amanda said as she pressed the talk button.

"Is Craig there?"

"Where else would he be?"

"Who are you talking to, Mandy?" Craig asked as he pulled the pillow from underneath his head and covered his ears.

"It's Theo."

"Of course it's me," Theo said.

"I'm not talking to you, Theo."

"Tell him it's my weekend off. I'm not coming into the office."

"Tell him to open the door, please Amanda." Theo continued to knock on the door as he tried to convince her to wake her husband.

Craig reached back his arm holding open his hand. Mandy handed the cell phone over to him. He bitterly flipped the cell phone cover closed and tossed the phone into a pile of dirty clothes in the closet. He uncovered his head and rolled towards his wife putting his arm around her waist. He kissed her gently on the forehead and neck. Craig looked at his gorgeous wife as the moonlight danced into the room highlighting her delicate features. She almost glowed.

KNOCK!! KNOCK!! KNOCK!!

"Holy shit!" Craig indignantly yelled as he sat up. He slid his feet into a pair of flip flops beside the bed and put on a gray t-shirt that matched the cotton sweatpants he had worn to bed earlier. He rubbed his eyes and forced himself to a standing position. He walked quickly out of the bedroom to the living room area. Craig looked through the peephole and sure enough, there was Theo standing at the door. Craig swung open the door.

"The world had better be ending for you to show up here at two thirty in the morning on my only weekend off in two months!"

Craig glared irately at his unwelcomed coworker, but his expression softened when he saw the look of fear on Theo's face.

"Can I come in?" Theo softly asked.

"Yeah, sure, I guess. Come on inside. You look terrible."

Theo slowly walked over to the couch and sat down. He nervously checked his watch and rubbed his hands together as he sat staring out the window. Craig had never seen Theo so…disorganized. Craig walked into the kitchen while he continued to watch the man sitting on his sofa. He pulled two sodas out of the refrigerator. As he was closing the door, he saw his wife enter the room so he grabbed a third drink. Craig walked into the living room where Mandy sat on the couch next to Theo. Craig handed each of them a bottle of soda and he sat on the recliner facing them.

"Theo," Craig began calmly, "what is so freaking important that you had to show up here at two thirty in the morning?" Craig twisted open his soda and took a long drink.

"I don't know any other way to tell you this," Theo nervously attempted to open his drink but his hands shook horribly. Amanda reached over and twisted off the top. "There is something terrible going on in the lower level of the facility. The IPPC group and the US Army are involved in something bad…"

"Have you been drinking?" Craig asked as his patience began to run out.

"Craig, hear him out. Look at him. He's obviously upset." Amanda put her hand on Theo's back. "Calm down, Theo. What did you see?"

Theo sipped his beverage and continued. "I've been watching them for about a week now. A small group of the soldiers have been going out in the very early hours of the morning. I don't know where they've been going…but when they come back…they have prisoners or hostages with them."

"What?" Both Craig and Mandy said in unison.

"These hostages look like old bums and vagrants - street people that won't be missed should something happen to them…"

"What are they doing in there?" Amanda asked.

"I don't know…"

"Then how do you know they are doing something bad?" Craig shifted in his chair trying to remain calm. He was tired and all he wanted to do was go back to lie down in his warm, comfortable bed.

"I saw them take another group into the facility about two hours ago. The soldiers had at least four people with them. Please, I need someone to go with me to find out what they are doing. If nothing is going on, then fine – I'll walk away and chalk it up to my imagination, but I know something is wrong."

Craig looked at the man sitting in front of him. While he would never admit it out loud, Theo was probably the smartest person that Craig knew. Theo had an analytical mind to rival some of the most respected scientists that Craig had ever worked with. Craig also knew that the man sitting in front of him lacked any type of creative imagination…so he was almost positive that Theo had not *"imagined"* anything happening that wasn't truly taking place.

"Fine. I'll go with you, but I want a comp day off on Monday…" Craig left the living room area and went to the bedroom to dress. He returned a few minutes later and kissed Mandy on the forehead.

"Be careful, Craig." Mandy hugged her husband tightly. She stood up from the couch and closed the door behind the two men and locked the deadbolt.

Theo and Craig walked through the apartment's parking lot and entered Theo's car. Craig watched as Theo fumbled around with the keys having troubles starting the engine. Theo steadied his hand, started the vehicle and backed out of the parking spot. The small car entered the main highway running parallel with the secondary production facility, but Theo drove past their office building.

Four buildings comprised the entire layout of the secondary production facility. Building-1, on the west side of the lot, functioned as the main office building where accounting and finance type activities took place. Building-2, on the north end of the lot, acted as the main storage facility for the entire campus. The H1N1 vaccines were stored here on the ground level floor for pickup and distribution. Building-3, on the east end of the lot, was rented out to a different company at the current time. Building-4, on the south end of the lot, housed the main production facility where all the vaccines were produced. This building also contained the automated packaging facility used to load the H1N1 vaccine onto conveyor belts. The large retractable conveyor belts were attached to Building-2 during business hours. This allowed the automated facility to move product from the origination point to the storage facility.

A large stone sign displaying the company name stood about fifty feet cattycornered from the Building-4, easily viewable from the main street. In the center, between the four buildings, a large fountain spewed water into the air. At night, lights below the water line turned the water display into a small light show that could be seen at just the right angle by passing motorists.

Theo finally pulled the car into the parking deck of a neighboring business. He drove up a small incline to the second floor and parked the car behind a large stone pillar that almost hid the car completely from view. Theo shut off the engine; he opened the glove box and took out a small flashlight. Both men exited the car. Theo popped open the trunk and took a tire iron out from underneath the large swath of carpet covering the spare tire. He put the flashlight and tire iron into a small backpack then slung the backpack's straps over his shoulder.

"Just in case," he said. "Follow me."

Theo cautiously jogged down the incline to the first floor of the parking deck. He stood at the corner and checked from side-to-side. Everything looked OK. He glanced around one more time to be sure; he made a dash across the open field between the two businesses. Craig struggled to keep up but eventually caught up with Theo behind the large stone monument with their company's name displayed on it.

"Is all of this running and sneaking around really necessary?"

"Those men have guns," Theo said matter-of-factly, "and from what I've seen, they do not want anyone to know what they are doing."

"Then what the hell are we doing snooping around? I can't believe I've followed you this far..."

"Hush!" Theo knelt down and pulled Craig closer to the ground with him. Theo pointed towards the front entrance of Building-2. In the dim overhead light, both men could see three armed soldiers escorting a group of men inside. A large, non-descript packaging truck blocked most of the entrance. The back door of the vehicle opened up and two IPPC members dressed in low-level hazmat suits exited the truck. They reached back into the truck and pulled out what appeared to be a thick chain but whatever was on the other end of the chain struggled to linger within.

Another IPPC official exited Building-2 and rushed over to the back of the truck. He wrapped the end of the chain around his waist and the three men played tug o' war with something inside. After a brief struggle, a large man was dragged out and his body hit the ground with a tremendous thud. The three IPPC officials spread out. What Craig and Theo thought was one chain was actually three separate chains.

The IPPC crew moved apart and began to drag the man into the building. Their prisoner stood up and jerked one of the chains to him, knocking an IPPC person to the ground. The captive man began to drag the downed IPPC member towards him. The fallen man quickly made it to his feet. The garage door used for package deliveries on the west side of the building opened up. A small forklift sauntered out and the three IPPC officials attached the end of each of their chains to the chassis. The driver of the forklift backed into the garage pulling the captive man behind the vehicle. The three IPPC members jogged inside and the garage door began to close behind them, but it didn't close all the way – a dim light from inside could be seen from underneath the garage door.

"What the…?" Craig exclaimed. "Why was that man chained up?"

"See? I told you. And look – that garage door is still open. I bet we could slide underneath."

"I'm pretty confident now that this is not a good idea at all. Let's just get out of here. We could end up arrested or worse." Craig stood up and began walking back to the parking deck.

"How are you going to get back to your apartment? I have the keys."

"I'll walk."

"Please, Craig – I can't do this alone. I need to know if our company is involved in some illegal activities. Those people were taken into that building against their will. You saw it for yourself… some were taken in at gunpoint while that last man was dragged in by chains. How can you just let this go?"

"For a man as smart as you are, Theo – you are one stupid son of a bitch. Why would I screw around with anyone willing or able to snatch people off the streets at gunpoint? I see this kind of crap all the times in the movies…just let it go. These people will make you disappear."

But Theo had already made up his mind. He had come this far and he had to know what was going in the basement level of Building-2, he couldn't turn back now. Theo surveyed the area and took off running to a grove of trees just to the east of the Building-3. The tree line provided ample cover from prying eyes. Craig hesitated momentarily but decided to chase after the impetuous young man. Theo waited next to the building to give Craig time to catch up with him.

"I knew you would come," Theo said.

"I hate you."

The two men stealthily crept along the edge of the tree line to the back of Building-3. There were no lights on the east side of that building but enough light from the moon and passing cars allowed them to see where they were going. Theo ran to the edge of the building and waved Craig over. The two men pressed their backs against the cool brick exterior as they caught their breath.

"Now what do we do?" Craig inquired.

"Wait a few minutes. Watch the edge of the garage door. I haven't seen any shadows moving across. Give them a few minutes…if we don't see any movement then we go in."

Chapter 17

- *April 6, 2013: Saturday, 3:58 AM – Rochester, New York – Secondary production facility of Illumination Pharmaceuticals …*

The two men waited by the side of Building-3 for about five minutes in the chilly early morning air. They saw no shadows from inside and no one moved around on the outside. Theo had previously watched the machinations unfold earlier in the week. He knew it was a very small group of individuals involved in whatever was going on. After three previous days of reconnaissance, he knew there were at most three IPPC folks and maybe four soldiers. He had memorized their movements and schedules over the past three days in preparation for this evening.

"Go." Theo said.

Both men rushed to Building-2 and knelt down on opposite sides of the garage door. Theo quickly peeked under and saw nothing. The young man flattened out on the ground and pulled himself under the door. Craig shook his head but followed suit. Both men lay motionless on the ground as they entered the first floor of the building. Theo quickly got onto his knees and looked around. Craig did likewise while he checked the other side of the room for any signs of activity.

While there wasn't much light, it was enough for the two men to be able to see if anyone was in the room with them. So far, so good – no one was standing guard. Theo felt that those individuals in charge of this secret operation had been very clumsy not to have guards stationed at every point within the building. Or maybe more accurately those leaders craftily limited the number of those involved to keep things under the radar from prying eyes. Either way, Theo and Craig easily worked their way from the garage door to staircase leading to the basement level without revealing their presence.

"I haven't been past this point before," Theo admitted in a whispered tone.

"What do you mean?"

"On two of my previous stakeouts, I've come this far, but was never able to convince myself to go down the stairs."

Craig looked around the room and down the short staircase. "We still have time to turn back. We don't have to go any farther."

Theo shook his head and walked down the stairs. He listened after every step he took; carefully balancing his steps as he descended the stairs - he did not want to alert anyone to their position. Theo crept down to the last step and peeked around the corner to his right; the coast was clear. He turned to his left looking down the long hallway where he heard a group of men talking. Both men followed the hallway to its end and the only way to go once they got there was to the right. As they crested the final corner, they found themselves on a small balcony overlooking a makeshift iron cage below them, about thirty feet from their location. Theo estimated the cage was about twenty feet by twenty feet and the sides were maybe eight feet tall. The only entry point into the cage was through a wide, heavily chained and locked door.

Around the outside of the cage, one US military soldier and three IPPC officials were present. Two of the IPPC officials were seated behind desks typing furiously into their laptops. Craig and Theo looked over the balcony's edge into the center of the cage. Inside the cage, scraps of clothing were piled up in a corner; bloody scratch marks painted the floor.

At the opposite end of the room a door opened up. Craig and Theo ducked down as far as they could but still be able to see what was going on below them. The hobo captives that they had seen earlier in the evening were being marched at gunpoint towards the cage by two heavily armed soldiers. The prisoners wobbled side-to-side down the small path leading to the cage. Theo assumed they were either drunk or drugged…either way, they were not putting up much of a fight.

The soldier standing closest to the iron cage unlocked two thick professional-grade locks and untwined the chain. The two armed gunmen walked their inebriated captives into the cage. The hobos looked around the cage as if they were lost in a foggy haze. They offered little to no resistance against their captors. Two of the bums sat down in the center of the cage while the third walked around the perimeter calling out a name, but neither Craig nor Theo could hear what or who the bum was asking for. The hobos were clearly under the influence of heavy narcotics or other mind-altering drugs.

"What are they doing down there?" Craig asked.

"I have no idea."

A loud, angry growl erupted from a different room than where the hobos originally entered from. The two IPPC men stood up from behind their desks and joined the third member of their team that was standing near a large collection of metal file cabinets; they walked around to the other side of the cabinets just out of view of Craig and Theo. More angry screams and growls from the second room echoed around the basement. Within moments, all three IPPC officials emerged in their bright yellow hazmat suits…each man carried a large chain with a giant question mark-shaped hook on the end. They checked each other's suits one final time to ensure complete closures of all the seals and gaskets. The IPPC team cautiously walked to the room where the growls emanated from.

Craig and Theo could not see the scientists anymore. The two men also noticed that the soldiers had quickly moved a good distance away from the cage in preparation for whatever was coming out of the second room. The three IPPC members backed out of that room, struggling to pull the large man out…Theo and Craig knew it was the same man that was yanked out of the back of the truck as the night started.

Two of the three soldiers rejoined the IPPC team. Each soldier also carried a chain. They were no longer in their military fatigues; they now wore a US military version of the same hazmat suits worn by the IPPC. The chained man's hands were somehow tied in place behind his back. The captive man sported a thick leather collar around his neck; five shiny metal o-rings were embedded in the collar. The IPPC members had attached their chains to three of the five o-rings. The two soldiers carefully put their chain hooks into the final two spots and helped drag the beastly man the rest of the way to the cage door.

"Cut his hands loose," one of the IPPC members said. The third soldier, the one originally guarding the locked door appeared; he also wore a hazmat suit. In his hands were large hedge clippers. He positioned himself behind the captive man and with a bit of effort cut through the tough leather bindings.

Craig and Theo watched in stunned silence and the large man swung his arms wildly at his captors. With five men controlling his neck and head, the prisoner was unable to reach any of his intended targets. Craig glanced into the center of the cage; all three hobos looked out the cage door but their stoic faces showed no fear, no recognition of the events playing out before them.

The chained man reached up clasping both of his powerful hands around the leather collar. As he focused his attention on freeing himself, his captors took advantage of the opportunity and slung him into the cage using the chains like a giant slingshot. The man with the hedge clippers quickly moved into position and slammed the iron door shut. He began wrapping the chains around the door as the beastly man finally snatched the collar from around his neck.

The overhead light shined down on the once chained man now standing in the cage with the street people; Craig gasped as he saw the deformed man clearly for the first time. His face was pale gray with oddly sagging skin around the ears and chin, the left side of his head seeped with a thick, greenish puss from a devastating head wound and the femur of his right leg protruded violently through his pants – the chalky white color stood out in amazing contrast to the otherwise dingy garb of the man. Theo didn't notice the life-threatening wounds that Craig had focused on; the younger man could not look away from the large man's soulless bloody eyes.

The misshapen man growled angrily beating his newly freed hands against his head. He shuffled his feet as if he was a bull ready to charge. The three hobos simultaneously snapped out of their drug-induced funk. They began to scream and cry – begging to be released from the cage. They all ran to the door, pushing and pulling but the thick metal door stood firm. One hobo climbed on top of the other two men and jumped up to grab the edge of the cage. He began to pull himself over the top, but the original gatekeeper hurried to the edge of the cage and stabbed the bum in the abdomen with the hedge clippers. The obese hobo grabbed his side and fell backwards on top of the other two street people. The sick man in the center of the cage erupted into a fit of blind rage – hurling himself towards the pile of flesh at the base of the door.

All three of the hobos still seemed to have an intact sense of self-preservation no matter how much drugs pumped through their system. As the rage-filled man descended upon them, they split up and ran in three different directions around the enclosed cage. The speed of the attacker seemed rather agile compared to the half-drugged street people, but in reality, his movements were only slightly faster. He cornered the fattest of the three hobos next to the door, the one that had just been stabbed. The hobo turned and raised his arms to protect his face, but his efforts were futile. The crazed man rained blows down upon the injured hobo like a professional fighter would do to a third grader. Each vicious blow to the hobo's head and torso sounded like a wooden baseball bat being slammed against a large, ripe watermelon.

The sick man reared back his scythe-like right arm and struck deep into the bum's chest. The bum's whimpering turned into loud, blood curdling screams of terror. The attacker thrust his balled up left hand deep into the mouth of the bum, silencing his victim's screams forever. The force of the last blow broke the bum's jaw on impact, his head bounced off the iron cage splitting open the back of his head exposing his brain, for the first and last time, to the outside air. The fat bum slumped to the ground as his attacker knelt down gnawing a large pink chunk of flesh from the dead bum's face. The two other hobos ran to the opposite end of the cage and tried to climb up the walls, but it was no use. Their cries of terror reverberated around the basement.

Theo and Craig glanced at each other, unwilling to accept what they had just witnessed. It made no sense. Both men were unable to speak; the look of fear and uncertainty in each other's eyes told the same story – it was time to get the hell out of Dodge. As they backed away from the edge of the balcony, their attention once again was directed towards the center of the cage where the screams from moments ago had abruptly ceased.

As Craig and Theo inched back to the edge of the balcony, the two men looked down into the cage once again. In the brief time they had backed away from their vantage point, the crazed attacker had downed the other two bums like a lion would do to an injured gazelle in the open plains of Africa. However, there was no grace or balance in the devastation below. The lion would never kill for sport – only for food, unlike the predator in the cage. This *"man"* killed because he could. This man-creature was an abomination – Craig and Theo now clearly recognized this fact. What transpired below was unnatural and horrifyingly disturbing. What they had once considered to be the *"sick man"* had quickly turned into a mindless beast…

As the creature feasted on human flesh, two of the three IPPC officials sat behind their small desks and continued to type into their laptops; they callously recorded the results like any good scientist should do. The three soldiers bantered back and forth seemingly disinterested in the scene that had just played out in the cage behind them. Obviously they were accustomed to seeing the results. This was not the first test they had performed in the basement of Building-2.

"What the hell?" The third member of the IPPC team that was not recording results turned his attention from the cage and pointed directly to the balcony where Craig and Theo hid. "It looks like we got ourselves some trespassers!"

Two of the soldiers quickly took aim at the balcony area and opened fire with their machine guns. Bullets whizzed and bounced all around Craig and Theo but neither of them was hit. They spun around on their stomachs and crawled away from the edge. As they reached the end of the short hallway, they stood up, turned left and ran down the remainder of the hallway leading to the staircase going up to the first floor. They could hear shouting behind them but neither man looked back. They ascended the staircase two and three stairs at a time until they emerged into the first floor of the building. Less than thirty feet separated them from the garage door and the outside world. No one was guarding the entrance that they had used earlier to enter the building. Theo and Craig could hear at least three men giving chase behind them; they made a dash for the garage door and slid through the slim opening like they were major league baseball players sliding into second base. High powered rounds punctured the metal door above their heads as the two men rolled into the fresh nighttime air.

"I'm sorry, Craig."

"We don't have time for this. Get to the car. We've got to get out of here!"

The garage door began to open behind them. Both men stood up slightly, in a hunched position and ran towards the stone sign. Yelling from behind the two men was punctuated with more gunfire and the rumbling of a large engine starting up. Theo and Craig dove behind the sign and quickly looked back. Two soldiers and one IPPC member had commandeered a small pickup truck that sat on the west side of Building-2. The headlights flipped on, cutting through the darkness, shinning directly on the opposite side of the company sign from the two men.

Craig and Theo sprinted across the open field between the two businesses. The truck behind them sped to life squealing its tires as its driver pushed the vehicle too hard. The small truck fishtailed clipping the fountain with its back wheels and began to zigzag between Building-3 and Building-4. The driver tried to regain control but the truck hit the wet grass leading to the company sign and the truck smashed sideways into the sign. The soldier in the back was flung through the air, over the edge of the truck bed, headfirst into the still erect base of the sign, killing him on impact.

Craig and Theo entered the parking deck and ran up the incline to the second floor where their car was positioned stealthily behind the stone support pillar. Craig held out his hand and Theo, without question, handed over the keys. Both men swung open the doors plopping heavily onto their respective seats. Craig started the car and pulled out of the parking spot. As he backed out he clipped the column but it only did minor damage to the passenger side brake light.

The small car hurtled down the incline to the opening of the parking deck. Bullets crashed through the windshield narrowly missing both men. Craig stomped on the accelerator and cut the wheel sharply to avoid hitting the soldier in front of him. More bullets sprayed through the car destroying the back and passenger side windows. Seat cushioning exploded from the rear of the car, falling throughout the interior like confetti at a birthday party.

Craig raced out into the empty road running parallel to the secondary production facility. He constantly checked the review mirror for signs of anyone following them as he headed back to the Fountain Crest apartment complex. He punished the car's small four cylinder engine by pushing it to its max output, but the small foreign car held up. Craig recklessly drove through the empty streets and pulled the car up on the grass area outside of building eighteen leaving the engine running. He jumped out of the car and ran directly to his apartment. The door was locked and he wasted no time with keys; he stepped back and kicked open the fragile door.

"Mandy! Mandy! Where are you?"

There was no answer. Craig hastily checked each and every room but there was no sign of his wife. Theo had gotten out of the car and was standing idly in the breezeway looking into Craig's apartment. Craig came back to the door, stepped outside and grabbed Theo by the shoulders.

"Where is she?!"

As Craig shook Theo, the door to Julie's apartment opened up. Both Julie and Mandy stood looking out into the breezeway shocked by all the noise Craig was making this early in the morning.

"What's going on, Craig?" Julie asked.

Mandy stepped around Julie and rushed over to her husband. He grabbed her in a mighty bear hug sweeping her off of her feet momentarily. Julie and Alexander came out of the apartment and moved closer to Craig. Everyone stared at Craig waiting for an explanation.

"We have to get out of here. Grab some clothes and that's it… that's all the time we have. We've got to get out of here!"

"I don't understand," Mandy began but Craig cut her off.

"Go put on some shoes and clothes NOW! We're running out of time."

Gunfire erupted from behind the north side of building eighteen. Craig reacted flinging his body on top of his wife knocking her out of the way. A hail of bullets and tracer rounds lit up the small apartment complex. A lone gunman had driven the mangled pickup truck from the production facility after them and now he exacted his judgment on the small group of people standing in the breezeway.

Theo instinctively rolled out of the way of the gunfire. He reached into his backpack and pulled out the tire iron. As the gunmen focused on spraying more rounds into the breezeway, Theo got to his feet and charged the man's blindside. The young man wailed on the gunmen repeatedly bashing the thick piece of iron against the man's arms until the soldier dropped the gun. The high-powered machine gun dropped harmlessly to the ground, but Theo did not stop his violent attack. He raised the tire iron above his head continuing to club the man like a baby seal about the head and neck. The gunman's body twitched sporadically on the ground and then stopped moving. Thick, dark blood dripped off the end of the L-shaped piece of metal; Theo finally stopped swinging the weapon when his arm went numb.

Craig lay completely still on top of his wife until the gunfire stopped. He gently grabbed her face between his shaking hands; his face was mere inches from hers. "Are you OK?" She nodded her head slowly. Craig pushed himself up to a kneeling position and looked back towards the gunman. He saw Theo, with his head bowed, standing above the dead soldier.

Craig stood up and rushed over to Julie's side. She was lying in a small pool of blood face down on the cold concrete of the breeze-way. Craig dropped to his knees and gently rolled her over and held her firmly in his arms.

"Where is Alex?" she asked.

Craig looked over to the doorway leading into apartment #1701. Alexander's body was doubled over, slumped inside the doorframe; Alexander was dead. Craig turned his attention back to Julie. He needed to stay calm – years of training came rushing back to him. *How badly was Julie hurt?*

"He's not in any danger anymore."

"I'm so cold, Craig. I don't understand."

"We've got to get you to a hospital," Craig said as he slid his hands between Julie and the cold pavement; he struggled to lift her shivering body. Her entire backside was sticky and wet, covered in blood from multiple gunshot wounds. Her warm blood soaked through his clothing; he felt her life draining quickly from her body. Craig knew it was too late to save her. He laid her back down as he comforted his dearest friend, holding her in his arms resting his forehead gently on hers. Her fearful eyes darted around momentarily and then focused on Craig's eyes. Julie smiled slightly taking her last breath and dying in his arms. Mandy walked over and placed her hands on her husband's shoulders. Craig pressed his lips against Julie's forehead and kissed her goodbye.

"Let's go, Craig – the rest of those men won't be far behind," Theo said as he dropped the tire iron to the ground.

Craig lovingly lowered Julie's head to the ground and closed her eyes with his fingertips. He kissed her once again and stood up. In a fit of anger, he rushed at Theo and slugged the younger man in the jaw. Theo collapsed to the ground and Craig mounted him and began punching the man in the chest and face. Mandy rushed over screaming at the top of her lungs for Craig to stop. Theo tried to cover up but Craig hit him two more times before stopping and rolling off to the side of his human punching bag. Craig sat cross-legged in the wet grass and glanced over at Theo.

"You fucking killed them, Theo. You've probably killed us all." Craig stood up and looked into Mandy's eyes. "Get some clothes and shoes, we've got to go. I'll explain what I can when we get on the road." Craig grimaced painfully as he saw Julie lying exposed in the night air on the cold concrete. "Mandy, go get as many supplies from our apartment as you can – Theo and I have some things to finish out here. Meet us at Julie's SUV when you are finished."

Craig jogged over to the breezeway and delicately moved Julie's body into her apartment laying her gently on the sofa. Theo moved Alexander inside the apartment placing the dead man's body on the floor within arm's reach of his wife. Both bodies were covered with blankets from the bedroom. Craig stood above Julie's lifeless body, the smell of her perfume wafted gently into his nose; tears began to stream down his face.

Theo respectfully rummaged through the apartment and gathered light supplies that he felt would come in handy. He knew that he was now a fugitive. With no idea of how long he would be on the run nor where he might end up - he gathered what he could carry stuffing his backpack full of snack food and bottled water. He quickly swept through the bathroom area and emptied the medicine cabinet into a duffle bag that he had taken from Alexander's side of the room. The young man piled his items next to the door and looked towards Craig for instructions.

"Take the supplies to the gold SUV outside," Craig said as he tossed a set of keys that he had taken from Julie's purse to Theo.

The young man grabbed the bags and hurried outside to where Mandy was already waiting for him. Craig walked to the door and turned off the lights as he exited the apartment. He jogged quickly to the waiting SUV. Theo had pulled the vehicle out of the covered parking area and drove the vehicle to the grassy area next to his rental car. Mandy sat in the rear seat on the driver's side. The gold SUV rolled slowly towards Craig; Mandy reached across the back-seat and opened the passenger side door. Craig slid in and sat in silence as the SUV slowly exited the parking lot and merged onto the almost empty highway, travelling in the opposite direction of the production facility.

The frightened residents of the Fountain Crest Apartments looked out cautiously from behind partially opened doors. The scene of destruction that had visited them so early this Saturday morning would be forever etched in the minds of those that had witnessed it firsthand. Multiple nine-one-one calls had already been made as sirens wailed in the distance.

The sun had not made itself completely visible in the light gray sky above, but it peeked out ever so cleverly from behind the pre-dawn clouds as if inspecting the carnage below. As if it had decided the time was now right, the magnificent yellow orb ascended into its rightful place in the sky; its bright rays of light illuminated the horrific scene below for the first police and medical professionals that arrived on the scene.

Interlude

- *April 11, 2013: Thursday, 5:48 AM – South of Labboune, Lebanon – A small outpost on the Israeli side of the border…*

During the first two weeks of April, multiple unconfirmed reports circulated amongst Israeli intelligence groups that a number of *"infected"* Lebanese civilians had been spotted crossing the border. Additional intel from Israeli spies located in Lebanon, indicated that a plague of some sort had inundated random villages on the southern tip of Lebanon causing madness and violence in its victims.

With other countries reporting similar sporadic infectious outbreaks, the Israeli government felt compelled to act. They sent a company of soldiers to secure the area to ensure that no one illegally entered their country, especially those posing considerable health risks to the Israeli people. Approximately two kilometers from the main Israeli base camp, Corporal Maya Ferber and Private Joseph Cohen had been tasked by their Captain with patrolling a small patch of land just south of Labboune on the Israeli side of the border.

"It looks like we have movement," Joseph said in broken English. While Joseph preferred to speak his native tongue of Hebrew, he had been practicing his English while on patrol.

"I see something," Maya responded.

The two soldiers promptly crouched behind a small stone wall that bared the craterous scars of bullets and explosions from past encounters between the two countries. Maya peered over the wall and readied her weapon. Both soldiers had been instructed prior to the beginning of their patrol to *"observe and report"* suspicious activity back to the base camp. Joseph tugged at Maya's fatigues and motioned for her to lower her weapon. She sat back against the wall; her face had turned anemic – void of most of its usual color.

"There are so many of them," Maya shakily said in Hebrew.

Joseph had never seen Maya so spooked. She was his superior officer and had years of training with the Mossad prior to joining the military unit that they now both served in. She had been involved in many *"unsubstantiated"* incursions into Lebanon on fact finding missions – that was the main reason she was reassigned to this base camp. Her knowledge of the areas close to the Lebanese border had provided valuable information to her superiors.

Joseph gathered his wits and stood up slightly as he peered over the remnants of a once proud stone edifice. The early morning sun began to crest in the eastern sky; its powerful rays not yet fully realized, minimally highlighted the field in front of the young man. He could see what had frightened his experienced partner. In the distance, maybe two hundred yards from his current position, a surging billowy mass of the infected wandered with no particular destination. A mass of human flesh of untold numbers had entered into Israel.

"Recon Unit to base camp, come in please," Joseph said into his shoulder-mounted radio. "We have visual confirmation of the infirmed intruders." Joseph wanted to call the uninvited guests by the name the internet had labeled them as – *"Zombies"* but he thought better of it.

"We have your location noted by the GPS receiver that you are wearing," a dry, monotone voice replied. "How many are there?"

Joseph glanced over to Maya who only shrugged in response. Neither of them had any way to know the exact numbers. Joseph pressed the talk button on his radio and responded: "Too many to count, I would say well over three hundred."

"Do not engage the hostiles. Track their movements - reinforcements are heading towards your location."

Maya and Joseph tracked the *"invaders"* for nearly twenty minutes when the roaring engines of three dark green and light tan military vehicles arrived on scene. Ten shock troops exited the vehicles outfitted in silvery flame resistant suits. On their backs they supported a backpack comprised of three cylindrical tubes – two tubes of fuel and one tube filled with high-pressured propellant. For balanced support of the heavy gear, a leather strap ran across their waists to securely fasten the backpack in place. From a main valve on the bottom edge of the backpack, the fuel source was connected via a thick rubber hose to a large metal tube with a handle and trigger. Each soldier lowered their silver colored helmet to protect their heads; their faces now covered with a thick black visor. In eerie unison, the fire squad clicked their flamethrowers to life; a small yellow-blue flame danced at the end of each of their barrels.

The Israeli troops surrounded the mass of infected Lebanese rounding them up like cowboys in the old west herding horses to stable. Maya and Joseph watched as streaming flames of liquid engulfed the mindless infected. Thick black smoke covered the area, the smell of burning flesh wafted downwind to the two soldier's current position. They watched in horror as the shock troops did their job; both soldiers knew it was the right thing to do to keep the plague or whatever it was from spreading into Israel.

"News" of the Israeli massacre of hundreds of unarmed Lebanese people quickly spread throughout the Arab dominated Middle East. Lebanon cried out for help from her Middle Eastern neighbors to thwart the aggression of the Jews. The state sponsored news outlets failed to mention even the slightest bit of information regarding the *"condition"* of those citizens that were *"cleansed"*. The propaganda machines maliciously spun and twisted the reports to such a degree that by the time the average Arab citizen had heard the news – Israel was guilty of passing into Lebanese territory and slaughtering close to five hundred innocent civilians including over one hundred school children.

Iran stoked the fires of hatred throughout the region to unite support for their proposed retribution. For years Iran had held mock tests of its rocket capabilities. Western countries had imposed strict sanctions on Iran to force them to cease and desist from their nuclear operations. However, Iran refused to stop developing their technology. *What gave the West the right to tell them how to run their country?* The leaders of Iran used the massacre of the Lebanese citizens at the hands of the Jewish oppressors to justify the use of their recently acquired nuclear capabilities.

Iran responded in anger by launching three tactical nukes at their hated foe during the last week of April. This action was not endorsed by the other Arab nations. Even though the whole region was infuriated by the recent actions of Israel, the Arab nations understood that any use of nuclear weapons would be detrimental to the entire area; they also fully recognized the fact that Israel would vehemently defend herself from any aggressive action. Iran acted alone in its final decision to launch its weapons of mass destruction;

a proverbial spark was tossed into the powder keg of cultural hate and regional instability that had been building for centuries...

The first pair of Iranian missiles was launched obliterating two different cities in Israel killing untold thousands of people instantly. Unfortunately for Iran, their third and final missile malfunctioned; the weapon prematurely detonated above their capital city of Tehran mere seconds after launch. The debacle killed upwards of eighty thousand people during the initial blast. Israel retaliated with extreme prejudice targeting a plethora of *"first strike"* targets throughout the Arab world; the Middle East became hell on Earth.

From the safety of their distant homelands, the rest of the world watched in abject horror as the tragic conclusion to the centuries old hatred of the Jews unfolded before their very eyes. The blackened landscape lay mortally wounded; the Holy Land cried out for forgiveness, but their prayers fell on deaf ears...

During the months following the nuclear attacks in the Middle East, life progressively worsened as other countries were exposed to the *"plague"* of the twenty-first century. As scientist futilely raced to uncover the root cause, governments strived to control the pandemic. Extreme militant measures were used once the general public was able to accept what was happening, but by that time it was far too late – the pandemic had taken an undeniable foothold in almost every country. At first the plague was referred to in hushed silence as the *"zombie pandemic"* but the mainstream populations vehemently refused to accept this nomenclature.

Sure, many people had seen movies or read books about the undead or zombies taking over the world, but these same folks – once presented with the very real face-to-face evidence of such a debacle occurring, refused to piece it all together. In the early months, the denial of such a condition allowed the infected to roam freely and contaminate others. Tens of thousands of people became infected each week. What started as small pockets of infected soon turned into full cities being quarantined by the military to control egress and entrance into those dying cities.

It is now early winter 2013 - almost nine months have passed since the initial zombie attacks that began in Colombia, South America. The world is a horrifyingly different place now. The zombie plague has raced across six of the seven continents like the bubonic plague that paralyzed Europe more than five centuries past. Nothing could have prepared the nations of the world for the speed at which the infection spread throughout the population.

Government containment policies failed to control the zombie pandemic. Contingency plans were never conceived to deal with such a dynamic threat. Martial law and curfews were declared throughout the world. Most citizens did as instructed but the disease followed its own orders. The zombies roamed freely; the laws of man were meaningless to the undead.

Many once powerful governments evacuated their seats of power and moved underground with only minimal support staff. The consensus of the high-ranking political figures and their scientists was that the undead plague would burn itself out eventually. These *"experts"* felt that within six months, the plague would be over and then governments could return to clean up the aftermath and rebuild their nations.

The vestigial governments that did not go underground failed their people miserably. Court systems, organized military, law enforcement and hospitals became almost completely useless without the professionals that once staffed them. Military regiments continued to exist in small pockets, some remaining loyal to their native government, while some went rogue - operating for their own personal self-interests.

Now the vast majority of the world hides in the shadows as chaos reigns around the globe. Industrialized nations have been brought to their knees, now eye-to-eye with third-world countries. These once rich nations no longer protect nor provide for their surviving citizens. Economic epicenters are bankrupt; money has no value; food, medicine and weapons are now the currency of choice.

Familiar cityscapes weep silently, shadows of their former glory. These once bustling metropolitan areas stand idly by - no longer able or willing to greet anyone with their burned out neon signs. Interstate systems that once connected all the major cities of the world are clogged with wrecked and abandoned vehicles, like plaque-hardened arteries from a dead heart.

The once bountiful breadbaskets of the world rot with no one to tend them. Easily accessible food is a luxury of the past. Survivors must move from town to town in search of canned goods and other nutrients to eke out a minimalistic existence. Fully functioning gardens are now guarded like Fort Knox of the past.

For the vast majority of the world, global communication systems no longer function. There are no fancy touch-screen cell phones, no GPS, no internet and no cable TV. Most of the world lives in darkness when the sun goes down – easily available electricity at the flick of a wall switch has almost become a thing of myth. A few government facilities located in only the once richest of industrialized nations still function but way below max capacity. Some forward thinking groups were minimally able to prepare for the collapse of their power and communications systems. This *"preparedness"* has allowed for limited electronic communication between small numbers of partially operational facilities.

The exact ratio of zombies to human survivors is unknown. The best estimate given by experts prior to the collapse of mainstream communication systems was that if the sickness continued to spread at its current rate – within six months, there would be two times as many undead as humans. Their mathematical calculations also stated that if the rate of infection continued unchecked, then within one year there would be no one left to give a damn about the math…

Chapter 18

- *December 2, 2013: Monday, 2:30 PM – the Greenwood farm just outside the city limits of Hot Springs, Arkansas - four days after the zombie attack at the barn…*

The group stayed a few more days at the Greenwood farm. They buried Kevin in the backyard next to the gravesite of what they assumed was his old hunting dog based on a makeshift tombstone that read: *"REX 1992: May he hunt forever in the pastures of Heaven"*. The snow fell heavily and within hours the farmer's new grave was almost completely covered.

During the preceding three days after the initial zombie attack at the barn, the men gathered up supplies from around the house and planned their trip to Maine; the rumored Mount Hope their final objective. Kara rested her foot and Nikki nursed both her baby and her head wound. James found some gas for the old four-door Impala. The car was definitely not *"eco-friendly"* but it was spacious and had a working heater and sure the hell beat walking. The trunk was filled with canned food and various toiletries such as toothpaste, toothbrushes, toilet paper and other necessities taken for granted prior to the zombie plague.

After double checking all the supplies, Corbin closed the trunk and entered the driver side of the car firing up the powerful V8 engine. Nikki gingerly placed Megan next to her in the back seat. Kara hopped around to the other side of the car. The vehicle's interior began to warm up and soon all passengers in the cavernous backseat were asleep. James opened the passenger door and entered the car. Corbin backed the car out from under the carport and drove towards the little town for additional supplies. James watched the farm fade into the distance in the passenger side mirror. The sun shone brightly but the temperature hovered just below freezing.

The drive into the *"big city"* was uneventful. Corbin drove very slowly on the icy roads. They did not need this vehicle to break down; there was no way they could travel on foot in temperatures like this. Both Corbin and James scoured the landscape looking for any signs of human activity or for the undead. Neither presented themselves. Deer bounded to and fro on the sides of the road, blissfully unaware of the peril facing the world.

"What do we need to get?" Corbin inquired.

"I think we have food covered for now," James answered. "We need to find warm clothes and more ammo. I'm sure this hick town was full of red-neck hunters so let's see if we can find a pawn shop or something."

Corbin pulled the car into and old Shell gas station; he spoke to James as he eased the shifter into park. "We'll need to find a few items for Megan as well – maybe some soft canned fruit and linens that can be used as diapers."

James responded only with a heavy sigh. Corbin knew that the vet considered the baby a liability. *Did the old marine think that he and Nikki knew the zombie apocalypse was coming but decided to have a child anyway?*

James reached gingerly into the back seat and nudged Kara. "Hey, sis, we are stopping for a minute. We are going to see if we can find anything of use here from this old gas station." Kara woke and looked around; her ankle was feeling much better but was not completely healed.

"OK," she said. "I'll wake Nikki and we'll keep an eye out for trouble. Corbin – would you leave the car running? The heat feels great!"

"Not a problem," he said turning up the heat a bit. "If you see anything, ANYTHING at all – just yell and James and I will come right back."

Driver and passenger exited the car closing the heavy doors gently. They headed single file past the out-of-order gas pumps. Most of the windows at the station were shattered either from rioting or maybe from bad weather. This gas station appeared to be a mechanics shop as well with the garage on the left side of the building. The garage door was wedged open, an old Ford truck stuck underneath, like prey caught in a giant monster's mouth.

James nodded towards the garage. "I don't like the looks of that. Who knows what might have crawled in there."

Corbin nodded and the two men cautiously approached the opening. Corbin stood on the left edge while James was on the right. Again, Corbin marveled at how well the older man moved. James obviously kept up with most of his training and exercises that the military drilled into him over the years. Too bad he was still a dick.

By hand gestures alone, James informed Corbin of the plan. James would roll under the door and quickly scan the left side of the interior and Corbin was to follow and scan to the right. James quickly dropped to the floor and rolled under the garage door. Corbin did his part. He rolled to the ground less gracefully than the older man but still he fulfilled his part of the plan.

The garage was empty. Well at least empty of things wanting to eat their faces. The two men foraged around. With ample sunlight during the daylight hours, the men quickly searched for supplies. Corbin found an unopened package of batteries, a small tool kit and a guide book outlining shops and attractions to visit.

"What a waste." James said.

"What?" Corbin inquired only half paying attention to the old marine.

"This!" James held up an old nudie magazine riddled with holes. Apparently the mice decided the centerfold made for an excellent snack and had devoured all but the legs of vivacious vixen.

"Let's head back outside, James. There's nothing else we can use in here."

In the distance, prying eyes surveyed the old gas station as three men began formulating an attack plan while hiding behind the old bakery a few blocks away.

"Those two dudes just went into the garage," Rodney said. "They have guns."

Rodney was 34 years old, tall and slender with short brown hair. Before the zombie invasion, he was a door-to-door salesman. He sold knives. However, Rodney's manager was informed on multiple occasions that many customers felt an overwhelming desire to stab Rodney with the products he peddled due to his terrible attitude. Rodney wisely decided that he should try his hand at selling vacuum cleaners instead. It was a lot less likely that a customer would stab him in the spleen with a crevice tool...but *"Rod the Bod"* (as he called himself) was pretty irritating...so that option was never fully dismissed.

Barry surveyed the situation. He was the leader of the group. He had dirty blonde hair and was quite muscular from years of weight lifting to combat the effects of his asthma. "Yeah, we have to act now," he said, "while they are focused at that old gas station. What do you think, Booger?"

Matt was a few years younger than the other two men and had been known as *"Booger"* ever since junior high when he *"affectionately"* referred to his girlfriend's clitoris by the same name. A strong country boy with a shaved head and full beard, he looked like the lead singer of a heavy metal band. In school, the other kids used to make fun of him saying that he had *"retard strength,"* but not anywhere Matt could hear them for fear of getting slapped around. Matt was pretty sensitive about his *"smarts,"* as he called them.

"We got guns too," Booger said with a thick southern accent. "I don't care what we do as long as I get to sniff some panties." He held up his tobacco stained handkerchief, clinched in both hands, and made a rubbing motion under his nose, imitating what he'd do with a fresh pair of female underwear.

"What the hell is wrong with you?" Rodney angrily inquired, shaking his head in disgust.

"Nothing's wrong with me except that I ain't seen a naked woman in almost a year. I'm tired of doin' it with my hand!" Booger yelled.

"Would you two calm down?" Barry pleaded.

These three guys had been friends since junior high, bullying their way through the education system one year at a time (sometimes requiring more than one year per grade). They were assholes then too, but way worse now. Since the plague started, they had been terrorizing anyone unlucky enough to cross their path, like they used to torment the underclassmen at lunchtime. Except now, instead of wedgies and black eyes, they did whatever the hell they wanted, robbing, raping and killing - not to survive…but because they could.

The triumvirate had left a path of destruction from San Antonio all the way to Arkansas. There was no law. No one was around to punish wrongdoers. No one offered to protect the weak from falling victim to the strong. In this new world, might did indeed make right. At least that's how these three men justified their actions.

"I mean, damn Rodney, don't you want to see some big ol' titties?" Booger made a juggling motion around his chest area cupping his own man-boobs. "Nah, probably not…since you been off screwing one of your vacuum cleaner hoses!" Matt, pleased at the vivid image he had created in his mind, laughed loudly, as chew came flying out of his mouth.

Barry was exhausted and tired of the constant bickering. His asthma was acting up on top of everything else. Booger and Rodney argued all the damn time, like an old married couple. Sometimes it was funny, but most of the time it irritated the hell out of him. However, there was strength in numbers; Barry struggled to keep the group focused on small, attainable goals to keep them from killing each other.

"This is what we are going to do," Barry said, raising his voice over Booger's guffawing. "We are going to do kind of like what we did to that Mexican family back in Texarkana a few months back. Remember that?

Rodney just shrugged his shoulders as he remembered back to the incident.

About three months ago, Barry and his cronies were living in a burned out Catholic Church with gray stone walls on the Texas side of Texarkana. The Hernandez family, originally from Austin, was heading to St. Louis, but Fate had a different plan in mind for the displaced siblings. The old maroon van they were driving in broke down roughly two miles south of the same church. Barry had been doing reconnaissance in the area looking for supplies. He approached the van and introduced himself to the occupants, already having a devious plan concocted in the back of his mind. The two brothers introduced themselves as Ivan and Max, who were bankers prior to the zombie infestation, and their younger sister Maria, who was studying to be a corporate copyright lawyer prior to the plague.

Barry led the Hernandez family on foot to the church where they were introduced to Rodney and Booger. Right away Rodney was entranced by Maria. She was olive skinned, had beautiful dark green eyes and short, curly brown hair. She wore a bright orange scarf to hide a small birthmark on the left side of her neck, just below her ear. All of her friends had tried to convince her that it was just a beauty mark, but Maria felt otherwise.

The next day, after a restless but safe night, Booger and Ivan left the church to repair the Hernandez's broken down van. Booger's only redeeming quality revolved around automobiles; the backwards redneck was a savant when it came to repairing cars - he could fix just about anything attached to four wheels. Barry had also left the church telling the others that he was off to find more supplies. In reality, Barry was playing his part in the plan that he and Booger came up with while everyone else was sleeping.

Max, Maria and Rodney stayed behind at the church. After about twenty minutes of awkward silence, Max left the sanctuary to relieve his bladder; he would only be gone for a few seconds and would be just around the corner – those precious few seconds cost him dearly. Rodney immediately seized the opportunity becoming sexually aggressive with Maria. She scratched his face trying to prevent him from molesting her. Rodney recoiled slightly as blood trickled down his right cheek. Max heard his sister's screams and ran back into the sanctuary.

As Max rushed into the room, Rodney quickly scanned the area for a weapon; he grabbed a statue of the Virgin Mary by its head from beneath a church pew. Max hesitated as he looked at his baby sister to make sure she was OK before turning his vitriolic stare towards her attacker. Rodney rushed the man swinging the heavy porcelain figure in a wide arcing motion smashing it against Max's unprotected head; Max fell limply to the ground surrounded by the shattered statue.

Maria rushed over to her critically injured brother diving on top of his body trying to fend off further attacks. Rodney grabbed her by her hair tossing her over an upside down pew. He bent over and sliced Max's throat from ear-to-ear with a jagged piece of porcelain. Maria shrieked in terror as she tried to run around Rodney to get to her brother. Rodney kicked her in the stomach and she crumpled to the ground like a ragdoll. Rodney mounted her tying her up with her orange scarf. Like a madman, he ripped off her clothes as she fought in vain against him; her struggle only excited him. Maria prayed to be saved, but her prayers went unanswered as Rodney savagely raped her.

Around the same time that Rodney's disgustingly vicious actions took place back at the church, Barry had sprinted ahead of Ivan and Matt; he stealthily crept behind a small building a few yards from the van waiting for his opportunity. The two men arrived; Booger moved to the driver's side of the van and popped open the hood. As Ivan began replacing some hoses to the radiator, Booger moved back to the front of the van slamming the hood on Ivan's hands. Ivan's banshee-like screams shattered the morning calm. Barry sprang out from behind the meager structure; he rushed over to the van repeatedly bashing Ivan's head with a crowbar. Booger giggled like a school girl at the display of violence. Ivan slumped halfway to the ground, still held in place, dangling by his wrists from the front of the old van.

Booger and Barry spat on him before they got into the van and drove back to the church – dragging Ivan the entire way. They arrived at the church and exited the van. Booger looked at the front of the vehicle at their new human hood ornament.

"That's fucking awesome," he said, giving a *"thumbs up"* as he followed Barry inside the church.

Barry and Booger were drawn to the sanctuary by Rodney's obscenity laced tirade towards his victim. The three men continued to abuse Maria for two full days, taunting and violating her. Due to internal injuries, she mercifully died during the second night.

Before leaving the church the next morning, Booger stuffed all three bodies into the priest's confessional, just to see if they'd all fit – and with some inventive positioning, Booger accomplished his task.

"Are you even listening to me, Rodney?" Barry asked again, trying to make sure Rodney was focusing on the current situation.

Rodney looked around. "What?"

"Did you hear any of the plan?"

Rodney shook his head. "No, tell me again." He paused for a moment. "That bitch got what she wanted. She was asking for it."

Obviously Rodney had a distorted view of what transpired at the church many months ago.

"OK, Rodney - you will go to Rick's Pharmacy." Barry pointed down the road at a two-story red and white brick building, "You can get a bird's eye view of the area from the second floor. Take the rifle with you but don't shoot unless I give the signal."

"Booger, you go to the hardware store. Use the back door…"

"I'd love to use the back door!" Matt snorted as more chew flew out of his mouth.

"Matt," Barry said, taking his friend by the shoulders, "pay attention to the words coming out of my mouth!"

"Sorry Barry…" Booger bowed his head; he looked like a kid that was just put into the corner for a timeout for being naughty.

Booger never wanted to be on Barry's bad side. About a year before he had graduated high school, Booger was arrested and thrown into jail for touching himself inappropriately while at a local strip club. Barry had bailed him out with money stolen from a local video rental store, so Matt's dad never found out. Booger was saved from the wrath of his abusive, alcoholic father and every day since the *"incident"* (as it was now known), Booger was forever indebted to Barry.

"Now, Booger," Barry continued, "you go to the hardware store and use the back door. Sneak around to the counter where you can see the road. Wait for my signal."

"What are you going to do, Barry?" Rodney asked.

"I'm going to pretend I'm injured from a zombie attack or some shit - like I barely escaped." Barry ripped his shirt and took a knife from his boot and cut himself across the face. Crimson blood flowed out of the gash. Injuries to the head and facial area always appeared traumatic, due to the large amount of capillaries below the skin.

Barry then cut three gashes in his left forearm and two into his right leg. Blood seeped through his pants. All the self-inflicted wounds were superficial but pretty convincing, nonetheless, as telltale signs of a recent struggle.

"You're as crazy as a shithouse rat!" Booger exclaimed, taken aback at Barry's self-mutilation.

"Don't you ever forget it either!" Barry said, smiling as he surveyed his handiwork.

"I don't want any shooting unless we have no other choice. You two are positioned to protect my ass. I think we should fake like we are injured and maybe they will take us with them. Once we gain their confidence, then we will make our move. Are there any questions?"

Rodney pointed at Booger. "I'm sure Einstein over there is going to fuck this all up. Maybe I should draw him some pictures to make sure he understands?" Rodney began drawing stick figures in the dirt with the toe of his shoe.

"Eat me!" Booger snarled as he grabbed his crotch.

"That's enough guys. You know the plan. Now get into position. If everything works out like I think it will – just wait for my signal," Barry said. "If things are hostile, I'll cross my arms in front of my chest. That's the signal to kill shit."

"And what's the…not to kill shit signal?" Booger inquired – honestly already confused by the complexity of the plan.

Barry thought about an easy-to-recognize *"all clear"* signal. "I'll raise both arms in a stretching motion, but for fuck's sake – whatever you do, you big dumb shit – don't shoot me!"

"Shit, I ain't goin' to shoot you, Barry…but I'd sure as fuck shoot Rodney…but not you," Booger said with a big grin on his face.

"I'm pretty sure this should go down without a fight," Barry continued. "Don't rush out of your hiding spots...give me a few minutes. After I get out of the road, go to the van and wait there. I'll lead them to it."

Booger and Barry moved towards the hardware store a few blocks from the gas station and Rodney darted off in the opposite direction positioning himself across the road in the second floor of the pharmacy. As they reached the hardware store, Barry pointed towards the back of the store to remind Booger where he was to hide. The group's leader ran towards the intersection, just out of view of their prey; he lay down in the road as sleet began to fall.

Barry covered his head and waited.

Chapter 19

- *December 2, 2013: Monday, 3:05 PM – an abandoned Shell gas station - Hot Springs, Arkansas …*

Nikki and Kara exited thru the rear passenger side door of the car when they saw James and Corbin slide under the garage door. Megan slept peacefully in the backseat. The wind had picked up and the clouds held the Sun hostage; nightfall was fast approaching.

"Did y'all find anything?" Kara asked.

"Some batteries and tools," James replied. "We need to find warm clothes and shelter – that's what we need." James looked over both shoulders, up and down the road, checking for any signs of trouble. He didn't feel like being ambushed again like back at the barn. James reached inside the car and popped the trunk; he placed the items from the garage inside.

"I also found this," Corbin said, showing the group a wrinkled tour guide. "Maybe there are some clothing stores or something mentioned in here that will help us." He began flipping through the pages looking for any stores within a few blocks of their current location.

"It's cold out here," Nikki said, shivering. "I'm getting back in the car."

The others followed her lead and entered the vehicle. Corbin checked the gas gauge and knew they couldn't afford to waste much more gas keeping the car running for heat. James checked the side and rear view mirrors; his paranoia had saved him before – he trusted his instincts. Something was wrong. Kara readjusted her ankle bandage. There wasn't much pain anymore and soon she would be back to her normal self. Megan began *'cooing'* at her mother.

"That's right, baby – it's your momma," Nikki said, rubbing Megan's cheek with her hand. "Can you say *'momma'* for me?" Nikki had been trying for a few weeks now to get Megan to say her first words, but no real luck – only a few gurgles and extra cooing.

"Here's something that might help us," Corbin said after a few moments of browsing the brochure. "There is an antique store on Central Avenue, a pawn shop on Grand Avenue and a clothing outlet on Spring Street." He dog-eared all the pages and handed the guide to James.

"Ha!" James exclaimed after reading some of the pamphlet. "All of the places mentioned in this guide are favorites of former President Bill Clinton. The captions say he would run by all of those stores while he was out jogging. I bet there is a dry cleaner store listed in here somewhere that *'Cousin Bill'* probably visited once or twice!" James laughed at his little joke.

"Let's get moving," Corbin said, backing the car out of the old Shell gas station. "James, flip to the back of that guide – there is a map of the town in there. Let's go see if there is anything in that store on Spring Street. We really need some clothes."

The temperature had fallen a few more degrees and a light precipitation began to freeze on the windshield and the roads. Slick roads and nighttime visibility issues would soon make any travel too dangerous for the group. Corbin looked down and dropped the car into a lower gear to help with traction.

"Look out!" Kara yelled.

Corbin swerved instinctively and slammed on the brakes - not the wisest choice of actions with sleet on the roads. The car began to slide sideways. "What the hell?" Corbin asked, trying to regain control of the runaway vehicle.

"There's a body in the road!" Nikki said, pointing to a figure lying in the turning lane near the intersection.

Corbin fought for control of the car and narrowly missed running over the man in the street. The car finally came to rest - perpendicular to the turning lane. Corbin breathed a sigh of relief and released his death grip from the steering wheel, putting the car into park and shutting off the engine.

"It's moving," James said.

"Can you tell if it's a zombie?" Nikki inquired, trying to get a better look.

Barry pushed himself up off the ground and limped towards the car. He clutched his right arm and hobbled up to the vehicle. He slipped on the icy road, falling on his back. He rolled over and crawled on his hands and knees the rest of the way to the Impala. Barry reached up and grabbed the passenger side door handle pulling himself up.

"Help me, please!" Barry said. "I'm hurt pretty bad…I barely escaped from those things…my two friends ran off in different directions. I'm not sure if they are still alive. Please you've got to help us…"

"Let go of the door handle!" James yelled, raising his shotgun to the window. "Back the hell up!" James pumped the shotgun and aimed it at the man's head.

"Jim - Don't shoot! Calm down," Kara said. "He doesn't look like a zombie."

"That doesn't matter! He could have been bitten. Look at all of that blood." James became agitated; it took all of his willpower not to squeeze the trigger.

Barry could hear them yelling inside the car. "I'm not a zombie," Barry said, "I didn't get bit...I got away from them..." He thought quickly and dropped to his knees again – at least at that lower height, should the shotgun go off, it would miss him if the man in the passenger seat decided to pull the trigger. Barry had no intentions of getting his brains splattered all over Central Avenue.

"James, keep the gun on him," Corbin instructed. "I'm getting out to check on him."

"Be careful," Nikki said.

Corbin had extensive medical experience from years of working at a Dallas fire station. All of the members of his firehouse were certified EMTs. Many times their group would arrive on scene before the ambulances – his crew had to be prepared for just about anything. He opened the door and stepped out onto the icy road.

Rodney watched from the second floor of the pharmacy. As the driver side door opened, Rodney set his sights on the exiting driver. He imagined pulling the trigger. At this range, the round would have decapitated the man; his brains would have painted the icy roads a festive rouge color. He gently tapped the side of the trigger a few times with his index finger, but opted not to fire.

Booger was in position as well inside the hardware store. He couldn't hear what was going on, but he could clearly see that the passengers inside the car were becoming very agitated. He saw a man exit the vehicle and Booger watched for Barry's signal.

As the simple-minded redneck waited in silence, he made sure his .357 Magnum handgun was ready for action. Booger casually opened the cylinder spinning the chamber around a few times then closing it after counting all six rounds were in place. He inspected the stainless steel eight inch barrel of the Colt King Cobra that he had stolen from his father many years ago. Matt giggled at the nickname scratched into the thumb-side of the barrel; not at the manufacturer's name, but the name he had recently carved himself: *"Mr. Holmes."* The opposite side of the barrel had twenty parallel scratch marks that he had etched in with his survival knife; each scratch corresponding to a kill. Human or zombie – Matt never really distinguished between the two.

Barry persevered in a kneeling position on the passenger side of the car, again not wanting his head to become spaghetti sauce. He watched as the driver moved towards him, but he never fully took his eyes of the man wielding the shotgun. Barry had anticipated this reaction and did his best to remain calm. He had gambled with his life that this group was not a *"shoot first and ask questions later"* type. So far, the situation played out the way he had envisioned it.

"My name is Corbin - what's yours?" Corbin said as he approached the bloody man kneeling against the passenger side of the car.

"I'm…Barry…thank the Merciful Heavenly Father that you found me!" Barry poured it on thick; he had to concentrate, doing what he could to keep from laughing at his own melodramatic response. "I've lost a lot of blood…it's so cold. Please help me!"

"Have you been bitten?"

"No."

"Are you alone?"

"No," Barry said. "I have two friends that were with me during the last attack. They ran just like I did. We were attacked outside of the Burger King earlier today." Barry pointed across the road to the burger joint, the site of the imaginary attack.

As Nikki crawled out of the car on the driver's side, she spoke to James. "James, would you open the trunk?" James reluctantly lowered the gun and popped the trunk. She went around to the back of the car. Digging around, she finally found some clean rags, bandages and alcohol that they had taken from Kevin's home. She walked over to the injured man.

"I'm Nikki, don't be frightened. I just want to help you."

"I'm Barry and I'm not worried about you," he said. "It's that dude with the shotgun that scares the shit out of me!"

"James, put the gun down. It's OK," Corbin said, motioning for the old vet to ease up some.

The old marine lowered the weapon reluctantly and got out of the car. However, his attention was not focused on the injured person in front of him like Corbin and Nikki had so recklessly done. Instead he inspected the surrounding area. He looked into windows on both sides of the streets. All his training told him that being overly exposed in the open made his group easy targets. This setup reeked of an ambush.

"We need to find cover or get moving," James insisted. "I don't like this. It could be a trap. We are way too exposed."

"I'm sorry, mister," Barry said in an effort to distract James. "The only other folks that might be out here are my friends, but I'm not sure where they might have ran off to. After we were attacked, I held off the zombies so that my friends could escape."

"Those wounds look nasty," Nikki said as she bandaged up Barry's arm.

"I've lost a lot of blood but I think I'm going to be OK. I really appreciate your help."

Barry stood up slowly. He faked losing his balance and braced himself on the side of the old muscle car. The ice-cold sheet metal stung his hands and he withdrew them quickly. He steadied himself in an upright position with Nikki's help. The sleet and snow had accumulated over one inch on the road in the last ten minutes. The car's windows had begun to ice over as well.

"I hope my friends are alive." Barry said as he briefly raised both arms in a slight stretching motion as if inspecting the bandaging that was just applied.

"It's not too tight is it?" Corbin asked.

"No, I think it's just fine." Barry smiled.

From his hiding spot perched in the second story window, Rodney saw Barry give the *"all clear"* signal. Booger slowly re-thought through the plan details…and realized that Barry didn't want him to shoot anything and he began making his way to the back of the store. Rodney was actually quite disappointed. He had secretly hoped for a gunfight or something but it appeared, at least for now, that the bloodshed would have to wait. Both men left their positions and headed for their van.

"We need to get out of this weather and out of sight," James said. "Anyway, there's not enough room in the car for another adult."

"Please don't leave me here," Barry pleaded.

"We won't leave you," Nikki said. "I'll put Megan in my lap. That should give us some extra room in the backseat for you, Barry. You can sit in the back with Kara and me."

"No," James said. "He can sit up front in the passenger seat. I'll get in the back so I can watch him."

James walked to the back of the car and opened the passenger side rear door. Kara was already holding baby Megan in her lap. His sister had heard everything that transpired outside the car. She could see that her brother was severely uncomfortable with the new passenger.

"It'll be OK," Kara said.

"Something about this doesn't feel right. Plus we don't have enough supplies to support some random ass drifter," James said as he closely watched Barry enter the car. Nikki got in the back and Kara handed Megan to her mother. Corbin opened the driver side door and dusted off some of the sleet from his head and sat down behind the steering wheel.

"Thank you," Barry said. "You don't know how much this means to me to find humans out here…let alone kind souls such as yourselves." Barry looked in the side mirror and quickly glanced away when he caught sight of James' piercing gaze.

"Do you have any idea where your friends might have gone?" Corbin asked as he started up the car.

"We had made a plan earlier to meet back at our van should we ever get separated. I'm hoping they went back there. I'd hate to think that anything might have happened to them. They're like a family to me." Barry looked down quickly, appearing to be overcome with concern about the well-being of his friends. However, in actuality, Barry was trying to hide the grin that had slowly begun spreading across his face. *"This was almost too easy,"* he thought to himself.

Kara reached up front and placed a caring hand on Barry's shoulder. "Don't worry, dear – we'll find them."

"Where is your van?" Corbin asked.

Barry continued with his act and faked further confusion. He needed to give Booger and Rodney ample time to move from their hiding spots to the van. It would take them some time to get there on foot. Barry stalled.

"I'm not sure…with all of the running around and fighting

off those damn zombies…I've lost my bearings. I don't remember where we parked it."

"Just concentrate, Barry," Nikki said.

"Look. We need to get to some shelter," James said angrily. "The roads are slick as owl shit and it's going to be night soon. We need to find somewhere warm to rest for the evening."

"But what if my friends are injured?" Barry asked. "What if they need help now? Please, we need to find them before nightfall!"

"Give me a general direction, Barry. We'll drive around for as long as we can," Corbin said as he slowly straightened out the car.

"East of here…" Barry replied. "I'm pretty sure it's within a few blocks. We didn't travel far before we were attacked. It's a dark red van. Kind of old and not in very good shape, but it keeps us warm."

Corbin slowly maneuvered the heavy, rear-wheel drive vehicle down Central Avenue and turned east on some unnamed side street. "Calm down, Barry and try to retrace your steps," Corbin tried to comfort his new passenger.

"This is pointless," James interjected. "We are putting ourselves at risk and we don't even know if his friends are even alive…"

"James!" Kara snapped at her brother's insensitive comment.

"He's right," Barry bowed his head again and remained silent for a few moments. He knew the intersection was coming up fast but didn't want to let on. He had to make it look like he suddenly remembered.

"Does any of this look familiar, Barry?" Kara inquired.

"Wait! I remember now. We parked next to one of those barber poles. Turn right at the next intersection." Barry decided enough time had passed. Booger and Rodney should be in place. Plus Barry knew that James was about at his limit. Barry wasn't stupid. He had accurately assessed the situation and knew that he teetered on the edge of pushing the old marine's patience too far.

Chapter 20

- *December 2, 2013: Monday, 4:17 PM – Central Avenue - Hot Springs, Arkansas…*

"There!" Barry said as he pointed towards a trio of stores located in a decent sized parking lot just off the main road.

The sleet and ice continued to fall as the winter sun began its early descent into the horizon. Corbin flicked the windshield wipers on and off quickly as he maneuvered the car off the slick road to the spot that Barry had just pointed out. Corbin pulled into a parking spot in front of the barber pole and turned off the ignition. Barry exited the vehicle walking carefully over the iced blacktop to the van. After a quick glance inside the vehicle, he entered the tobacco shop.

From a precursory inspection, James could tell that all three buildings in the lot had seen better days. Almost every windowpane was busted out. The brick exteriors were blackened from rampant fires most likely started by rioters trying to loot the stores at the onset of the zombie pandemic. The roof of the rightmost building had collapsed inward upon itself to the floor crushing multiple display cases.

"I don't like this one bit," James said as the passenger side door closed behind Barry.

Corbin turned towards the old vet. "I know, James. I know. Kara and I will go with Barry. James, you and Nikki stay here. Watch our backs."

"I should go with you," James said.

"We'll be fine," Kara said as she winked at her brother.

Kara and Corbin exited the car taking a closer look at their surroundings. The first building, on the left end of the lot proudly displayed a white sign with red lettering that read: *"Prime Time Styles."* Corbin glanced over to the middle store but he couldn't read the worn off name on the faded old sign; he assumed it had previously been a tobacco store due to the giant cigar displayed above the doorway. Only those two stores were easily identifiable to him as he inspected the final building. The third store had no signs and no obvious markings as to what its main function was prior to the undead infestation. The large maroon van was parked outside of the tobacco shop.

Kara walked over to the van with her right hand close to the .38 Smith & Wesson tucked into her waistband and in her left hand she held a large black flashlight. James watched his sister's movement every step of the way. He had stepped out of the car propping his shotgun against his shoulder in the ready position just in case. Earlier in the day, he had swapped out the buckshot load for slugs. While the area effect of the buckshot came in handy, he realized from the barn encounter last week that it was too risky to use in close combat if one of his group was in the line of fire. Corbin followed closely behind Kara with his .45 caliber handgun drawn.

Kara peeked into the van as she shined the flashlight's beam through the dark tinted windows; no one was inside. She tucked the flashlight in her right armpit, looking back towards Corbin giving him a quick thumbs up. Corbin moved to the side of the van next to Kara. James continued to watch all three store fronts. The hair on the back of his neck stood up. He didn't much care for the current situation and he had become frustrated, even angry at Corbin for putting his sister in harm's way.

"I can't believe our luck," a loud voice seeping with a Deep Southern inflection bellowed out of the tobacco shop.

Corbin and Kara spun around towards the door with their guns drawn. James moved a few paces away from the Impala and knelt on the ground. He trained his shotgun on the doorway of the tobacco shop. Barry exited the building first along with two other men following closely behind.

Barry raised his hands into the air. "Hang on guys. These are my two friends that I was telling you about." Barry pointed to a large bearded man holding two boxes of cheap cigarettes. "This is Booger and the other guy is Rodney."

Rodney and Booger stood still. Rodney glanced around catching a brief glimpse of the attractive woman next to the van. The woman lowered her gun as did the man directly in front of him. Rodney was transfixed by the woman. He was sure that he would have been able to smell her delicate scent if it wasn't for the fat redneck standing next to him that was smoking two cigarettes simultaneously.

Corbin and Kara lowered their weapons and walked forward introducing themselves. Corbin moved back slightly to the front of the van and pointed at and introduced James and Nikki. James continued to hold his shotgun focused on the three outsiders. Corbin motioned for the old vet to lower his weapon; James did so as he stood up and walked back to lean against the muscle car. He lit up a cigarette of his own never letting his guard down as he watched the men.

"Is that a fuckin' baby in the car?"

"Watch the language, Booger," Barry instructed. "And yes, it is a baby. Her name is Megan, right?"

"Yes," Corbin answered as he began to move back towards the Impala.

"Booger?" Kara inquired with a confused almost amused look on her face. "What kind of nickname is that?"

Barry quickly answered, "It's because he used to pick his nose and eat them in junior high." Barry did not want his backwards-ass friend to tell the true tactless origin of the nickname.

Booger tilted his head towards Barry but didn't argue with the explanation. "My name is Matt," he said, "but yeah folks call me 'Booger'."

"Did you guys find anything useful in the other stores?" Kara asked.

"Nah," Matt responded, "except for these here smokes." He held up the cartons like a proud father would his newborn child.

Rodney kept quiet. Since he was in no imminent danger of being shot, he walked to the passenger side of the van and entered the vehicle. He leaned back in the seat and fastened his seatbelt. He knew the old military man was watching his every move. Rodney adjusted the seat and mirrors to pretend like he was preparing for the drive. As he did so, he would glance quickly back and forth at Kara. Something about her…he couldn't get his mind off of her… dirty thoughts darted around in his perverted mind of what he would do with her if they were ever alone.

James flicked his cigarette butt to the ground using the thick heel of his army boot to crush out the hot embers. The old vet meticulously analyzed the man in the van and his two accomplices; James didn't trust any of them. Something about Barry's story and his *"graphic"* wounds didn't quite add up – the gashes were too neat, too clean. The skinny prick in the van was overly fidgety…always moving around – a grown person unable to sit still made James nervous. As for the fat redneck, whatever his name was, James wasn't overly concerned. Sure he appeared to be a powerful man, but the old marine knew the hillbilly was at least twice as dumb as he was strong.

Barry and Corbin quickly discussed a plan as daylight waned. Corbin mentioned the three stores that he had seen in the tour guide. Barry knew the area well and offered to lead them to the stores, but he quickly informed Corbin that the stores on Central and Grand had been demolished during the riots – only the clothing store on their original list of places to go might still be viable. A decision was made to round up what supplies they could from that store and then make their way to an old hotel to wait out the storm. Barry and his crew entered their van and pulled out of the lot. Corbin, Kara and James entered the Impala.

"We will follow them," Corbin said. "They know the area. I think those guys may have grown up here." Corbin started up the finicky V8 engine and entered the main highway a good distance behind the van, but not too far back; he didn't want to lose them in the limited visibility. After about twenty minutes of driving (which equated to only about two miles), the van pulled off onto Spring Street where a clothing store waited anxiously for the first shoppers it had seen in more than six months.

The maroon van skidded sideways across the parking lot and onto the sidewalk running around the small store. Corbin eased the Impala slowly into the parking area and stopped the vehicle a few yards from the van. Booger jumped out of the driver's side of the van, without shutting off the engine, obviously ecstatic by his driving finesse…

"Holy shit, did y'all just see that?" Booger inspected the gouge marks in the icy snow mixture on the ground. He walked around the front of the van to see how close he was to the wall; the van had stopped mere inches from smashing into the brick structure. Barry glared angrily through the windshield at his friend. He was unable to open the passenger side door, so he quickly climbed across the seats shutting off the engine on his way out of the van.

James, Kara and Corbin exited the Impala. Nikki stayed behind with baby Megan. It was always a delicate balance on how to proceed in the new world with the baby. *Was she safer staying in the car?* That meant splitting up the group whenever it came time to investigate new areas. *Was she safer coming out of the car?* The second choice would keep the whole group together but could potentially endanger the baby. Most of the time over the past few months, the group would choose option one - split up and clear the inside of wherever they were going. When it was determined the area was safe, whoever was watching Megan would bring her out of the car. Usually Nikki would stay behind with her baby. This pleased Corbin for the most part because he felt it kept his loved ones safer.

"This is it," Barry said as the three passengers from the Impala approached the van.

"Let's get this over with," Rodney said.

James heard the man's voice for the first time and knew for sure now that he already hated the man. Rodney's somewhat effeminate voice instantly infuriated James; the skinny man sounded like a snotty bitch. James could tell Rodney was a whiner, a user and most likely a manipulator. James could read people very well. If he had to bet on it, he would have guessed that Rodney was a used car salesman or something very similar.

"Rodney," Barry began. "Stay out here and watch for trouble."

"Why do I have to stay out here? I hate this weather. I'll die of pneumonia or some shit!"

"Good," Booger said as he walked to the front door of the store.

"Ten minutes tops, guys. We are going in to find some clothing and then we are off to the hotel." Barry didn't show it, but he was becoming increasingly nervous that his two imbecile partners would be unable to hold it together long enough to get what they wanted or needed from their new acquaintances. Barry had already devised a plan that in two day's time, he and his partners would have all of the other people's supplies and maybe their women too.

"I'll stay out here with Rodney," Corbin volunteered.

Kara handed out a second flashlight to Barry. James, Kara, Barry and Booger entered the dark store. It reeked of moldy fabrics and wet dog hair. The group moved slowly through the cluttered store surprised that anything was left on the racks after the rioters had bull rushed the place. Each person grabbed a few items here and there and stuffed them into a large duffle bag that Barry had brought with him. They would split up the items later once they reached the hotel and settled in for the evening.

The group worked together as they collected salvageable clothing, but soon Booger's ADHD got the better of him. He meandered slightly away from the group towards the checkout counter. Behind the checkout counter was a closed door with a *"manager"* sign across the wooden lower portion; the upper quarter of the door used to be a glass window but had long since been busted out. He laid his .357 Magnum on the glass counter and began pushing the buttons on the old timey cash register that sat on a small elevated box above the counter top. The old register keys became stuck in the depressed position.

Matt soon became frustrated as he was unable to open the cash drawer. Sure money meant nothing now, but old habits were hard to break. In a mild fit of redneck rage, Booger smashed his fists down on the keys; the machine dinged loudly and the drawer shot open – startling Booger to the point that he fell backwards still holding onto the register. He pulled the machine from its slightly raised pedestal and let go of the heavy device as he fell. The register crashed loudly through the glass counter top and Booger landed hard on his backside.

"Damn it, Booger – what the hell?" Barry was not pleased. He worked his way over to his simple, man-child of a friend and helped him to his feet. "Would you please concentrate, Matt?"

Matt nodded his head and walked over to the counter to retrieve his weapon. Angry clawing footsteps scratched across the stone floor; four gigantic feral dogs shot into the air from out of the manager's office leaping through the door's only opening and over the counter. The smallest of the dogs hit Matt squarely in the chest knocking him back down to the floor. Matt rolled to his side knocking the dog off of him; the beast skidded across the smooth floor winding up next to the rest of the vicious pack.

Kara shined her flashlight onto the feral dogs. Three of the animals appeared to be some combination of German Shepherd and Rottweiler mix; the biggest canine possibly a wolf. The powerful beam of Kara's flashlight highlighted the scowled faces and bared fangs; thick drool streamed from their mouths. Their grayish brown fur was matted down with dirt and blood. Their synched up panting fogged the cool air. But their eyes…the group had all seen before. Each of the dogs stared out angrily at the world through the same soulless, bloody eyes common to all zombies. Two of the dogs on either side of the largest wolf-dog growled angrily; the alpha dog tilted back its head howling at some unseen moon.

"Fuckin' shoot them!" Booger yelled.

Two dogs split off from the pack leaping into the air towards Kara. James pushed his sister out of the way as he pulled the shotgun's trigger; one dog fell limply out of the air, both of its front legs blasted off at the chest. The injured beast fell to the ground and began to push itself towards James using its hind legs only. James aimed the weapon again and fired – the dog's head exploded into a deep red mist like firecrackers lighting up the night sky on Independence Day. The second dog crept around to the backside of James and came at the old vet sideways; the mutt clamped down forcefully on the barrel of the shotgun and James failed to shake off the enraged beast. Kara bashed the end of her flashlight down on its head until the beast fell flaccidly to the ground.

The runt of the pack, the original mongrel that had knocked Matt down just moments ago, rushed across the floor towards him. The redneck felt around for his gun forgetting that it was in the glass shards of the broken counter. He reached down and pulled out his Bowie knife that was tucked snuggly into the side of his boot. The southern hillbilly and the infected bitch circled each other for what seemed like an eternity. The dog lunged but Matt was ready; he delivered a deep, penetrating blow - the thirteen inch steel blade entered the top of the dog's head and exited out its throat.

The dog collapsed to the ground growling angrily; it kept trying to stand back up despite the skewer wedged deep into its skull. Matt smashed his foot down on the dog's muzzle for leverage; through brute force alone, he snatched the knife out of the dog's head like King Arthur removing Excalibur from its famous stone prison. In one final slashing cut, the large redneck separated the canine's head from its neck. "All dogs go to heaven, my ass," Matt said to himself as he moved to retrieve his gun from the glass shards.

Rodney and Corbin both stepped into the store at the first sounds of gunfire. The large wolf-like beast turned its attention towards the new intruders and accelerated towards them. James and Barry fired off one shot each at the last remaining dog but both missed. The dog leapt into the air over Corbin and Rodney – both men dropped to the ground instinctually. The wolf-dog slightly lost traction on the last remaining slick tiles of the floor closest to the door; its body jackknifed like a semi out of control bashing its side on the exit door as it made a dash for freedom.

"What the hell was that?" Corbin asked as he stood up.

"Zombie dogs…" Kara responded a bit unsure as the words left her lips.

"Let's get out of here," James said as he walked over to his sister. They both walked out of the store with the rest of the group close behind. No sign of the dog outside except footprints leading off into the snow-blinded distance.

No one was injured. Somehow Fate had smiled on the small group this day. Barry tossed the duffle bag of clothing into the van as he sat behind the steering wheel. Rodney and Booger entered the van. Barry started the engine and pulled up next to the Impala. He rolled down his window. "Follow us to the hotel."

Kara hopped into the back of the Impala with Megan and Nikki. James and Corbin stood outside the vehicle. The old vet shook his head showing his utter disgust for what had just transpired. Corbin knew they had gotten very lucky. Corbin slid into the passenger side seat and handed the keys over to James when he had entered the car. James started the engine and followed the maroon van to the hotel.

Whining and whimpering could be heard back inside the clothing store. Stuffed behind an old bookshelf in the manager's office lay a spastic litter of puppies. Each of them rolled around on the cold floor - their red eyes swollen with hate. They were hungry and could wait no longer; the puppies made their way to the back corner of the room where they began chewing on the stringy, gray flesh of a zombie's torso...

Chapter 21

- *December 2, 2013: Monday, 5:55 PM – The Historic Gemini Hotel - Hot Springs, Arkansas…*

Barry looked up from behind the van as James pulled into the garage area. Before the plague, valets would have patiently waited side-by-side in this area quickly parking cars for the arriving guests and receiving hefty tips – but not anymore. Bellman carts lay tipped over near the large oak entry doors; orphaned clothes hangers dangled awkwardly from the aluminum carts. Ravished, empty suitcases littered the walkway as sole remnants of their fleeing owners. Horse racing forms fluttered along the ground – the city, a once proud host to a famous horse racing track, no longer had use to advertise such events. No tourists visited this town (or any town for that matter) for leisure – only arrivals to this now barren southern cityscape were those passing through to some other equally ailing destination.

Barry had just finished unloading some items from the van when James pulled up beside him. Rodney and Booger darted from car to car on the other side of the garage searching for supplies; the cars had been left by guests as they checked into the once famous hotel. The zombie plague must have swept through the hotel with violent speed; the guests more than likely never had time to check out – if they made it out at all. Rodney knew the cars belonged to hotel guests because all but three of the cars had square beige tickets hanging from their review mirrors indicating the owner's last name in heavy black marker. The non-tagged cars must have belonged to other survivors stopping by the hotel after the onset of the undead apocalypse. Rodney stopped what he was doing and watched Kara get out of the old muscle car.

"You like that don't you, Rodney?" Booger impudently mentioned as he looked the women up and down as they exited the car. "Yeah," Booger continued in a taunting whispering tone, "you like that a whole bunch don't you? Well this is about as close as you are ever going to get to touching that piece of ass."

Rodney didn't respond, but he knew his redneck companion was right. Rodney tried to focus on the interior of the car he was searching but Kara traipsed whimsically naked through his mind. *Oh the things he imagined doing to her when he was finally alone with her...*

"I'd like to give those girls a cup just to see what they would do with it," Booger chuckled.

"Go screw yourself you sick, fucking hillbilly," Rodney blurted out angrily. "Do like Barry said - finish searching these cars, asshole."

Across the garage area near the front doors, Corbin reached into the back of the car and gently lifted Megan. She cooed excitedly as her daddy hoisted the chubby, freckle-faced little girl to his shoulder. Nikki and Kara, shivering in the cold winter air, stood beside the driver side door. James swung open the car door and stepped out, his bandolier of shells draped across his chest, the leather strap of his shotgun suspending the weapon from his shoulder. As was his routine, James quickly assessed the area for signs of danger. This time, however, he felt the danger had already presented itself to them – the trio of failure that had arrived at the hotel just before them. He felt undeniably confident that these men would be dead before he parted ways with them.

Rodney and Booger returned to the van. They hadn't found many useful items except for an undisturbed package of twenty four plastic bottles of water and some sealed cheese crackers. Finding items of value, especially food or water, bordered on miraculous. As the many months pressed on after the initial outbreak, evacuees and survivors pillaged everything left out in the open as they tried to escape the dying cities. Rioters had burned and looted most businesses and homes as they randomly moved about the crippled cities. With cars boxed in by the congested roadways, people gathered what they could carry in small bags and satchels and made a break for the open countryside hoping to find safety.

The two groups merged at the backside of the van. An uneasy tension pervaded the area as the strangers struggled against their recently acquired fear of people. It was easy to know where the zombies stood when encountered. There was never any second guessing their intent – they would always – ALWAYS – attack you. With people, a whole different duplicitous storyline often presented itself. Most people on the roads were solely interested in self-preservation. Groups of people, whether they were better armed or more in number, had a well-earned reputation of being untrustworthy – most of those groups preyed on the weaker more unassuming travelers.

"Booger hand out some water to our friends," Barry said breaking the awkward silence. Matt did as instructed. Each drank the water quenching their parched throats. Corbin allowed Megan to sip from his bottle as well.

"Let's go inside it is cold out here," Nikki said.

"I'm sure there are some vacancies," Matt snorted pleased tremendously with himself.

James pumped his shotgun and cut his eyes briefly towards Rodney. "He and I will go in first."

"Fuck you – who made you boss?" Rodney spit out the words defiantly.

"OK. OK – calm down," Barry instructed. "I know we are all a bit uneasy here but we need to work together. It's our best chance of making it through this whole ordeal in one piece."

"I agree," Kara said. "Let's try and be civil."

"You're right," Rodney acquiesced as he looked over at his mental play toy. He deeply hated the old military bastard already but would do just about anything to please the man's sister maybe increasing his chances to be with her.

Rodney's rifle slung over his back, he reached into his waistband and pulled out a 9MM pistol. He moved to the right side of the oak doors and James moved to the left side. Barry and Nikki stood at the back of the van, each wielding their firearms in the ready position. Corbin and Kara stood farther back next to the Impala; she readied her rifle and Corbin held his baby closely. Booger stood at the front of the van with his .357 aimed at the door or Rodney – it was hard to tell which his true target was.

Rodney stepped back to kick open the door but James halted him with a condescending look that screamed: *Try the fucking door handle first before you kick open the door alerting anything and anyone to our presence.* Rodney reached down for the handle and pulled the door open with ease. James just shook his head and moved inside the half-opened door. Rodney gritted his teeth to keep from shooting the old bastard in the back of his head as he passed by. Rodney moved inside the foyer as well and stood next to James. Each man quickly checked the corners and sightlines to see if trouble waited for them. The coast was clear. Rodney peeked back through the door and motioned the rest of the group inside.

Matt, like a giant five year old quickly succumbed to the alluring metallic domed ringer sitting on the front desk. It called out to him – even beckoned. He walked over oblivious to the possible consequences of ringing the bell. He reached out his hand, but Barry – who knew Matt's weakness…stupidity – slapped the man's hand away from the metal dome just before he made contact. Barry disapprovingly shook his head as Matt rubbed his stinging hand.

The first floor of the hotel was dimly lit by the sun passing through the many windows and glass doors around the entire building. Chairs and tables were overturned and thick layers of dust blanketed those pieces of furniture that somehow remained upright. A thick, wet scent of decay mixed with sewage and rotting wood drifted through the air. Two large marble staircases ascended the east and west walls leading to a mezzanine area perched above the first floor. Barry pointed towards them and each group cautiously walked up opposite sides.

As they crested the staircases, James stopped at the top of the east staircase and dropped to his knee. Barry did the same on the western side of the mezzanine. The old marine pointed at an overturned couch where two sets of socked feet protruded from underneath. James motioned for Barry to move forward as he did the same. Both men moved to the backside of the couch that covered the victim's feet. Barry flipped over the couch and James swung his shotgun towards the opposite end of the feet where a head should have been. As the couch tipped over, there were two sets of unattached legs with no bodies. James motioned for everyone to move up.

The groups ascended three small steps to the second floor proper. Posted on the corner of the wall was a *"You Are Here"* map of the hotel. Barry wiped the dust off the front glass cover and both groups tried to familiarize themselves with the layout. In front of them was an area marked as *"The Diamond Ballroom."* Management offices were on the west end and guest rooms on the east side of the building. Farther down the same hallway leading to the guest quarters was a large room marked as the *"Exhibition Center."* A small room directly behind the ballroom on the map indicated an area of great interest to everyone - *"Banquets."*

- *December 2, 2013: Monday, 6:28 PM – Second floor of the Historic Gemini Hotel – east side of the building …*

Corbin handed a sleeping baby Megan to her mother. "Let's find us some rooms to put our stuff in and then we can figure out what our next plan is," Corbin said as he moved towards the guest rooms. There were bedrooms on the second floor ranging from rooms 209 to 218. According to the hotel map, the management offices were numbered 200 to 208.

Kara reached into her backpack and handed flashlights out to everyone. Corbin and Barry led the way down the eastern wing of the second floor. The bright beams of light crisscrossed one another racing up and down the stygian hallway. Each dark forest green door proudly displaying large golden embossed numbers set at eyelevel. The doors boasted silvery metallic swipe sensors for the guests to slide their cards through for entry into their rooms. With no power to the building, the electronic locks had operated on reserve battery power for a few hours. However, after the batteries wore down, the locking mechanism on many doors became stuck. Signs of forced entry into most of the rooms on the second floor were quite obvious – broken doorframes and splintered doors littered the hallway.

A flowery blue suitcase wedged between the door and the frame of room #209 appeared like a tongue sticking out from a semi-closed green mouth. Corbin stood outside the room next to the hinged side of the door. Barry stood on the handled side of the door. Rodney and Booger held their flashlights steady. Barry kicked open the green door and Corbin followed him inside. The room was empty except for two coverless queen-sized beds. Corbin moved to the small bathroom and checked inside – it was clear as well. Both men exited the suite and nodded that it was OK.

Kara and Nikki walked into the room. "We'll take this room," Kara said.

Corbin and Barry split off to check the rooms on the left side of the hallway. Rodney and Booger checked the right side. James stood by room #209 and covered their backs. Most of the remaining rooms the men inspected were covered in ankle-deep water from a sewage line that broke at some indeterminate time in the past. They neared the end of the hallway where the last room should have been numbered "218" but the "8" had fallen off.

"Hey, Booger," Rodney began, "it looks like your uncle-dad Jim-Bob numbered this room!" Rodney smiled as he inspected the faded out area of the door where the missing "8" should have been.

Matt paused. He looked at the door then back at Rodney. He was pretty sure that skinny fuck was making fun of him, but he wasn't quite sure how. Numbers had never been his specialty anyway.

The hallway past room #218 bent into an L-shape just past

≈ 240 ≈

the final guest room; the group turned their attention towards a sign with an arrow directing guests to the Exhibition Center. The men rounded the corner working their way down to the Exhibition Center, but the double doors were chained closed. The hallway ended abruptly. On the wall opposite the Exhibition Center, two bathrooms without doors stood silently. Corbin checked the men's bathroom while Booger giggled slightly checking the women's bathroom – both were empty.

Rodney and Barry shined their flashlights around the Exhibition Center's doors but chose not to disturb the locks - just in case someone had chained them for a reason. They could check out the Exhibition Center later – nothing was getting in or out with those thick chains interlaced through the door handles.

"We can check that place out in the morning," Barry said.

"I agree," Corbin responded. "Let's get this last room checked out and get some sleep. What's ever back here can wait."

The group of men returned to the last unchecked room. Rodney jiggled the door handle of room #218, but the door refused to budge. Corbin and Barry highlighted the door with their flash-lights. Booger shouldered his way through the door into the room. He almost immediately stepped back out as he vomited onto the pastel colored carpet. The rotting stench of decayed human bodies flooded the hallway.

All four men covered their mouths and noses with the front of their shirts as they entered the room. A pile of bodies in the final stages of decomposition were clumped up at the foot of the bed; a revolver clinched in the bony hands of the largest skeleton. Three smaller skeletons had their arms wrapped around another adult. The men had all seen similar stories like this played out before – most likely a desperate father had killed his family and finally himself to free them from the incoming horrors to soon be visited upon the Earth – a darkly poetic end to the worst vacation ever...

"We'll take this room," Barry said as he opened the window for a breeze to pass through.

"What the hell?" Rodney complained. "It smells like rotten ass dead people in here."

Barry looked out the window to the street below. The cool, odorless breeze invigorated him slightly as he inhaled deeply through his nostrils. "Well you got two options: this room with dead people or the other rooms flooded with shit. You choose."

"I'll take the first watch tonight," Corbin said. "We can split up in four or five hour shifts. I'll head back to two-oh-nine and let them know the plan."

"Rodney will join you on the first rotation," Barry said. "Then early in the morning after sunrise, we can scout around the place for supplies.

Corbin left the last room on the right side of the hallway and returned to the first room they had checked. He informed Nikki and his friends of the watch duty rotations. Nikki had already snuggled Megan into a warm section of blankets that she had packed in her backpack and Kara had placed her and James' bags on the other bed. James stood like a watchdog outside the room.

"James, come in and get some sleep," Kara said. "You'll need all the rest you can get before going on the second watch." She smiled shyly at her brother for volunteering him for the pre-dawn assignment. He reluctantly walked into the room and sat in a surprisingly comfortable recliner. He placed his shotgun on his lap and rocked back and forth.

Corbin left room #209 and rejoined Rodney at the midway point between the two rooms. Two chairs were placed back to back for them to sit in. The old hotel creaked and moaned as Old Man Winter tugged and pushed on the outside of the building. Drafty, cold breezes raced up and down the hallway; both men covered themselves with blankets to ward off the effects. Their five hour shift ended just around midnight without incident and they each returned their respective rooms.

Nikki, Kara and Megan peacefully slept; none of them stirred as James and Corbin swapped out roles. James exited the room and closed the door softly behind him. Corbin walked to the window pushing the thick curtains to one side as he peered down at the street below. Snow and ice had piled up in two inch high mounds on the window ledge. The moon sat quietly in the sky judging the frozen world below. Corbin closed the curtains and crawled into bed next to Nikki. Megan whimpered slightly but her father's caring hand placed on her chest appeased her and she quickly fell back to sleep.

Chapter 22

- *December 3, 2013: Tuesday, 12:33 AM – Second floor of the Historic Gemini Hotel – room #218…*

Rodney sluggishly walked into his room after his long watch. He kicked the side of Booger's bed multiple times to wake him. Booger tossed and turned but the embrace of comfortable sleep refused to let him go. Rodney bent over and slapped the man on top of his bald head.

"What the hell?" Booger grimaced as he sat up.

"It's your turn, fat boy – get out there and keep me safe."

"I fuckin' hate you, Rodney."

"Would you two shut the hell up? I'm so tired of hearing y'all bitching all the time," Barry said as he too sat up in bed. "I swear to God that if I didn't need you guys I would have allowed you to kill each other. More than likely I would have slit your throats myself while you slept."

"He means he would have killed your skinny ass," Booger said pointing at Rodney.

"Go on, Matt," Barry said. "Get out there on guard duty. Rodney and I have some things to discuss. We'll fill you in on the major details at sunrise."

Booger put on his jacket and grabbed his .357 from the night-stand. He laced up his combat boots and snuggly fit a wool hat over his head. The temperature had dropped tremendously over the past five hours. Matt ruffled around in his backpack and pulled out the pack of smokes from the cartons that he had found earlier. He lit up one cigarette and exited the room closing the door behind him.

"So what's the plan?" Rodney asked.

"We need to get them to split up. Somehow convince them that forming two or three separate groups would increase our chances of finding food, water or clothing."

"I just don't get it, Barry. Why do your plans have to be so complicated? Why can't we just walk down to their room in the morning and shoot those dudes in the face?"

"Be my guest, but I guarantee you that old military prick will see it coming a mile away. You'll be dead before you hit the ground if you pull some gung-ho bullshit like that."

Rodney conceded and listened to Barry go over multiple plans.

• *December 3, 2013: Tuesday, 3:18 AM – Second floor of the Historic Gemini Hotel outside the guest rooms by the doors leading into the Exhibition Center…*

During the second watch, James paced up and down the long, dark hallway. Booger sat in one of the chairs Rodney had brought out during the first watch. Both men were quiet but James could tell that the redneck wanted to talk to him. James kept his distance – he had no real intentions of interacting with any of the three screw-ups that now shared the second floor with him.

"Do you ever get lonely out here?" Booger asked the old marine as the war vet passed close by. James didn't answer; the redneck didn't even seem interested in an answer – he had posed a rhetorical question…not that he understood or knew the meaning of such words. He just continued talking while James watched for any signs of trouble.

"I mean, don't you get lonely out here? All I can think about is getting with one of them – you know what I mean? I've got these urges…"

"What are you talking about?" James replied finally tired of hearing the redneck's inane ramblings. "One of those girls is my sister and the other is a new mother to that baby back there."

"No, I'm not talking about one of those girls with you. I mean one of those zombie bitches. I've seen some of them that still look pretty good if you know what I'm saying. And they are always moaning…it makes me hard sometimes…"

"You're a sick freak, boy – you know that?" James walked to the other end of the hallway completely disinterested in hearing any more of Matt's sick fantasies.

"Oh don't be all offended and shit," Booger yelled as he remained seated. "I'm not talking about anything gross - just dippin' my pecker into one of them zombie chicks. I'm not crazy. I'll wear a rubber!"

James stayed at the opposite end of the hallway while Matt continued to watch the area closest to the Exhibition Center. The next five hours passed by quickly. James had to intermittently walk to the end of the hall closest to the Exhibition Center to wake the fat redneck…but for the most part – Matt did a decent job of being a lookout. The next hour brought out the sunshine and the rest of their group woke from a relatively peaceful night's sleep.

- *December 3, 2013: Tuesday, 7:23 AM – Second floor of the Historic Gemini Hotel – outside room #209…*

Barry and Rodney walked down the hallway away from their room. James and Corbin were already standing outside of room #209; James watched the two men coming towards him. Rodney accidentally made eye contact with James and quickly looked away as the old man's stare penetrated deep into his mind. James knelt down and shoved his survival knife into its sheath on his left boot. He stood up pumped his shotgun and let the weapon dangle idle by his side. He never once broke eye contact with the two men.

The ladies joined them a few moments later; Megan gleefully cooed as she rode in a baby carrier strapped to Nikki's back. The early morning sun shined into the hallway through the doorways sans doors. The chill from last night had lessened slightly but everyone's breaths lingered like cottony clouds in the thin cool air. Delicate patterns of multi-colored carpet, previously obscured by the inky night, now danced from side-to-side the entire length of the hallway.

"I'm hungry," Booger said as he nonchalantly joined the group.

"Well, let's make that our first course of business this morning," Corbin responded. "We should check out that Banquet area we saw on the floor plan."

The group retraced their steps from late yesterday afternoon and arrived back to the corner where the wall map hung. They turned right towards the glass lined ballroom doors. Each person gasped slightly as they saw their own reflections. They appeared tired, dirty and much skinnier than they realized. Months of being on the run had worn down their spirits but also the lack of nourishment had taken a physical toll on their bodies as well. After a slight pause, Barry closed the distance to the ballroom doors.

"If we go through here," he began, "it will lead us to the Banquets area."

"That's not on the map," James said.

"Trust me. I worked here as a high school student. If we go through the ballroom, there will be two doors leading to a staging area; a place where the food service folks would prepare the meals prior to bringing out the entrees to the guests."

"Why didn't you tell us you worked here?" Nikki asked.

"It was fifteen years ago and I didn't see any relevance to it until now."

"Fine, but you three lead," James said as he pointed at Barry, Rodney and Booger. "We'll follow behind you."

"How do we know you won't shoot us in the back?" Rodney asked without making full eye contact with the old vet.

"You don't."

Barry pulled open the double doors and propped them open with the foot stands. Windows from either side of the ballroom had long since been busted out; light and wind passed casually through the expansive room. The ballroom was completely empty except for some knocked over tables and chairs. Dull warped mahogany planks ran lengthwise from the entry door to the opposite end of the room. The elements had wreaked havoc onto the once gorgeous dance floor. The group walked cautiously along the floor to the back of the room where two doors awaited – just as Barry predicted.

The group proceeded to the doors at the opposite end of the room. As promised, the narrow doors did indeed open up to a small staging area; stairs descended in the back right corner to some un-known depths. The light from the ballroom fearfully stopped at the edges of the door as if afraid to step foot into the new area. The group stood still momentarily allowing for their eyes to adjust to the darker room; they pulled out their flashlights and flicked them on.

Banquet trays, silverware, pots and pans cluttered the ground. An old conveyor type dishwasher stood against the main wall. Rats bounded to and fro as the new light sources swept through the room. Old tablecloths and napkin dispensers lined a wooden shelf on the backside of the wall. Two large walk-in freezers occupied the far left corner opposite the staircase.

"We should see what's inside of those," Booger observed.

"I don't know about that," Kara replied. "Anything of use spoiled a long time ago once the power went out."

Booger walked over to the freezers and grabbed the handle of the left door, but it wouldn't budge. It had been locked securely. Booger tried to force open the lock but without the key or using brute firepower the contents of that first freezer would remain a mystery a bit longer. Booger jiggled the handle of the right door and pulled it open. Stale air rushed out but no sounds of movement from within. He shined his flashlight inside.

"Hell yeah!" He exclaimed. "Take a look at this."

Booger walked into the freezer and backed out pulling a service cart. On top of the cart were hundreds of packages of salt, pepper, ketchup, mustard and other varied condiment packets. The group gathered around. On the second shelf, unmolested bags of coffee and tea sat perfectly arranged. The lowest shelf of the cart had two full packages of peppermint candies. For months they had eaten nothing but bland canned food – their mouths began to salivate just thinking about the possibilities.

Corbin grabbed two large tablecloths and placed them on the ground next to the cart. He helped Matt sweep everything into two neat piles. Corbin grabbed the four ends of one table cloth and Matt followed his lead on the other. They tied the cloths into two large bundles securely holding their newfound treasure.

"We're not going down this way," James said from the other side of the room by the staircase. "Standing water about midway down the stairs – that whole area back there is flooded with sewage."

The group went back through the staging area doors. The cool morning air drifted through the ballroom but the temperature held steady. Birds chirped outside the window; Nikki and Kara walked over to the closest window and looked out. Matt stood behind the women looking over their shoulders to the outside world. Rodney leaned nervously up against the wall. James began to right some of the tables and chairs for them to have a decent spot to eat breakfast.

"Let's get some food from the vehicles," Barry suggested. "Corbin come with me. We can bring the food back here." Barry casually looked in Rodney's direction winking giving his partner the sign that their plan from last night was beginning.

"Hold on a second, Corbin," James insisted. "Could you help me with these tables and chairs first?"

Rodney panicked. He had no idea whether or not James had caught the slight signal from Barry. Rodney reached forward and snatched baby Megan from her mother's back. The baby squealed in terror flailing her tiny arms as she reached for her mother. Kara and Nikki spun around simultaneously. Nikki moved forward to grab Megan but Booger violently punched Nikki in the solar plexus; the young mother dropped to her knees gasping for air. Kara moved to help her friend but Booger delivered a devastating uppercut to the left side of her jaw knocking her unconscious to the ground. Rodney held Megan in front of his chest with a blade to her soft throat.

James knocked over the table he had just situated and squatted behind it; he pulled his shotgun into firing position. Corbin began to move towards his baby but Barry cold-cocked him on the back of the head with his bony elbow. Corbin fell to the ground barely conscious. He began strenuously pulling himself along the rotting wood planks towards his family. Barry kicked the man in the side causing him to double up in pain.

"What the fuck, Rodney?" Barry exclaimed. "This wasn't the way we planned it."

"That old bastard saw your signal," Rodney yelled back. "It was now or never!"

"Let's be reasonable about this," James yelled from behind the flipped over table. "You don't want to do this – you don't want to hurt that baby."

"Come out from behind the table, James," Barry said in a cool, calm voice. "Or I'll shoot Corbin in the back of the head right now." Barry reached into his waistband to remove his pistol. He pulled out the shiny metallic gun.

Nikki was much less hurt than she let on; her adrenaline had helped ease the blow to her stomach. Out of the corner of her eye, in slow motion, she watched as Barry pulled out his gun and cocked back the slide of the semi-automatic pistol. Nikki sprang forward grabbing the humongous Bowie knife from Booger's boot; she jammed the thick metal blade deep into Rodney's unguarded crotch. Rodney dropped his knife and Megan in unison as he reached down cupping his severed testicles – blood erupted from his pants like a crimson Niagara Falls. He collapsed to the ground in perfect harmony with the baby and the knife that he had clutched only moments before. Nikki rolled on top of baby Megan to protect her with her own body.

"You bitch…" Rodney muttered. "You dirty bitch…"

James fired off a round grazing Barry's left arm knocking the man backwards and he dropped his gun. James stood up to get a better shot but Booger tackled the old vet from the side. The shotgun strap ripped away from his shoulder and the weapon slid across the floor. Barry dragged himself behind a column to assess the damage to his arm. Corbin grabbed the gun in front of him - he aimed and pulled the trigger. A giant exit wound of brain and flesh splattered the wall; Rodney's eyes went vacant.

"That's for touching my baby girl," Corbin muttered before passing out.

James had the wind momentarily knocked out of him from being blindsided; he lay on his stomach trying to catch his breath. Booger jumped onto his back and began punching the marine in the back of the neck and head. James twisted quickly moving into the guard position – years of Brazilian Jiu-jitsu paid off. Booger's heavy hands rained down but James was able to absorb most of the blows with his forearms and elbows.

Kara slowly opened her eyes as she regained her senses. She saw Nikki lying next to her holding Megan but both seemed to be relatively OK. She grimaced as she saw Rodney's canoed out head splattered against the wall. She glanced back behind her hearing Barry grunting in severe pain. Corbin was unconscious on the ground but still breathing. *Where is James?* She thought to herself. She sat up and saw Booger pummeling her brother. She groggily fumbled with the rifle on her back.

James timed the next blow coming from the larger man. As Booger's fist whistled through the air, James rolled out from underneath his attacker and Matt smashed his left fist into the hard flooring. James stood up as did Booger. The redneck lunged at the old marine but James used the man's rage against him. The old vet sidestepped the vicious blow and as Booger tumbled forward off balance, James wrapped his right forearm beneath the man's throat and his left arm across Booger's face. Booger panicked as his air flow was completely obstructed. He began to spin violently trying to shed the marine from his back but it was no use. Booger dropped to his knees but James continued to squeeze harder and harder. Blood vessels in Matt's eyes began to rupture and he soon blacked out but James gripped the man like a savage pit bull clamped down on a piece of raw meat.

Barry made a mad dash from behind the column for the doors in which they originally entered the ballroom. A loud echoing boom filled the air and Barry somersaulted through the air crashing into the glass outlined doors. He felt blood oozing out of his stomach. He looked back seeing Kara crouched down behind the scope of her rifle. He watched as she pulled back the bolt action; Barry never heard the shot that obliterated his skull.

Nikki sat up quickly inspecting her precious baby feeling and squeezing her arms and legs for broken bones. Megan giggled loudly thinking her mommy was playing the tickle game with her. The baby's only real sign of injury was a large, deep bruise protruding slightly above her right eyebrow.

Kara stood up helping Nikki to her feet. Nikki ran across the ballroom floor to Corbin's side. Kara slung her rifle over her shoulder and sprinted to where James was still choking Matt. Nikki laid Megan softly on the ground next to her father who was beginning to sit up already by himself. Kara squatted down just out of arm's reach from her brother. She had seen him in this type of berserker rage before and knew better than getting too close. She softly spoke to him.

"James. James. Let him go. He's dead."

James stopped squeezing at the sound of his sister's voice. He knew the man was dead; the marine had twisted Matt's head almost to the point where his chin could have rested on his spine. James unclenched his death grip and kicked the redneck's limp body away from him. He stood up, blood flowed from his busted nose and cut cheek…he could taste coppery blood running into his mouth. He wiped off what he could with the back of his arm and walked with his sister to where Nikki and Corbin sat on the ground.

James helped Corbin to his feet. Nikki clutched baby Megan snuggly to her chest. Kara slid under Corbin's arm to assist him as they walked to the front door where Barry's body continued to ooze blood in all directions. James picked up his shotgun and the two tablecloths filled with spices and condiments. He stopped by Rodney's and Matt's body and took their weapons placing them in one of the tablecloths. He hoisted both sacks over his shoulder like a vagabond Santa Claus and he jogged over to his friends waiting at the door.

"Wait one second," Corbin requested as they exited the ballroom. He took his arm from around Kara's neck and walked back to Barry's body. He rummaged around in the man's pockets until he pulled out the van keys.

"Thanks, asshole."

Chapter 23

- *January 3, 2014: Friday, 2:07 AM – Charleston, West Virginia, outside a neglected condo nestled deep within a former retirement community …*

About a month had passed since their run-in with Barry and his group of thugs back in Arkansas. While Corbin and his friends were still bound for Maine, the trip was extremely hazardous and exponentially slower than originally anticipated. The winter had been severe and most pervasive throughout the end of last year and the beginning of this year. Side roads, the main paths that the group travelled, were icy and treacherous. They could not use the vast majority of the interstate system due to the fact that most of it was blocked off by crippled and discarded vehicles.

Luckily for them, the trip to West Virginia was mostly uneventful. Now the group had two vehicles to keep up with, the Impala and the van that they took from Barry's group. The dual vehicles were good for gathering and carrying supplies, but not so good because they had to constantly search for twice as much fuel. Neither vehicle had four-wheel drive, so the snow covered roads mercilessly taunted the drivers as they endeavored to reach their final destination. James and Kara led the way in the van while Corbin, Nikki and Megan followed close behind in the old Chevy.

As they reached Charleston, West Virginia, both vehicles were running on gas fumes alone. James pulled the van into a parking lot between an old bookstore and a children's clothing store around 1:45 AM. The muscle car pulled in beside the van in the next available parking spot. Unfortunately, the group was completely exhausted, they did not survey the area sufficiently; they failed to notice the nearby gas station parking lot full of zombies. The mindless undead focused their attention in the direction of the rumbling V8 engines that had just shut off.

On instinct alone, James quickly rushed the tired group of his friends out of the parking lot heading for a nearby community that they had just driven past. The group ran almost non-stop for a full twenty minutes before they reached their current destination. They entered the gated condo community looking for a place to crash… away from the prying eyes of the living dead.

"Do you see any of them?" Kara asked, trying to catch her breath.

"I can't see anything now. The fog is way too thick," James answered as he deftly climbed up the stairs in the back of the condo. He moved towards the balcony on the second floor - hoping to get a better view of his current surroundings.

"Corbin, do you see anything?" James whispered loudly as he peered over the edge of the balcony.

Corbin was positioned under the front porch with Nikki and Megan. Megan continued to whimper and Nikki gently covered the baby's mouth to muffle the sounds.

"Shush, baby – listen to momma, you have to be quiet," Nikki said softly.

Corbin shook his head in response to James' question as he

made eye contact with the old veteran. The whole group kept completely motionless for the next three minutes, even baby Megan stopped her crying. *Where was the group of zombies? Had they followed them all the way to this retirement community?*

Kara cautiously jogged up the front steps to the decking above Corbin and Nikki. She rammed her shoulder into the front door of the small condo. The door creaked in protest but remained steadfast. Kara looked down, slightly amused by the flowery welcome mat underneath her feet. She stepped back and smashed up against the door again. A small crack formed around the door handle. Kara retreated back to the top of the steps; she thrust forward with all her weight against the solid, oak door and it reluctantly gave way. She tumbled inside, her momentum forcing her awkwardly onto her backside. She slid a good eight feet on the slick, solid wood flooring as she finally came to a stop in the entryway.

"In here," she groaned trying to regain her composure.

Corbin began to roll out from underneath the porch but James let out two distinct whistles and pointed east - Corbin froze. The former firefighter looked around as he scrambled back underneath the deck. Two houses down from their current position, he could see the undead mob that they had encountered just a few minutes earlier. He counted quickly - there were at least thirty zombies meandering around looking for sustenance.

"It's not safe out here and it's freezing," Nikki whispered as she gently rocked Megan. "We need to get somewhere safe and warm."

Like a well-trained ninja, James silently tip-toed down the back stairs leading from the second floor balcony. Once the old vet reached the ground, he laid flat on his stomach and military-crawled his way towards the couple and squeezed under the porch with them.

"James, can we make it back to the vehicles?" Nikki asked.

"No, it's too far away. I think we are cutoff. We should stay here tonight. We need to lead those zombies away from us," James paused to consider all of his available options. "Listen...you two get ready – I'll distract that mob. I've got a plan."

Before Corbin could protest, the old marine crawled out into the open and ran around the opposite side of the house. Corbin and Nikki waited. A few moments later, they saw James at the corner of the red single-story house that stood between the condo and the zombie mob. James was positioned with his back against the corner of the house. He looked back to Corbin and through hand signals alone relayed that the couple and their baby should get inside with Kara when the coast was clear. Corbin nodded and the old vet ran straight for the mob.

"Over here, you dumb shits!" James screamed as he waved his arms. "Come eat some of this you bastards!" James fired his shotgun into the zombie mob. In unison, the creatures turned and pointed their outstretched arms in his direction. He had clearly gotten their attention. The mob, although quite slow, moved with purpose and began to close the distance. James backed farther and farther away unloading round after round. Arms, legs and other various zombie body parts flew into the air as the shotgun rounds randomly ate into undead flesh. The decaying mob continued forward.

"Go!" Corbin said as he gently nudged Nikki out from under the porch. The couple kept low to the ground in a crouched position as they moved up the front steps. Soon they were inside the condo with an agitated Kara who was standing half inside and half outside the doorway.

"What the hell? He's going to get himself killed!" Kara said, pointing at her brother as she began to move outside. "I've got to help him!" Corbin grabbed her by the arms to keep her inside but she struggled fiercely.

"Damn it – let go of me, Corbin!" Kara screamed as she struggled to free herself from Corbin's vice-like grip.

"You can't," Nikki pleaded. "Your brother knows what he is doing. You'd only distract him and you'd both wind up dead. You have to stay here. Trust him."

Kara stopped struggling and fell to the ground. She watched helplessly as the zombies gave chase after her brother. She lost sight of the mob and James two houses farther down the road as the fog enveloped the melee. Kara glanced up each time she heard the gun go off in the distance – every echoing boom of the shotgun told her that James was still alive.

Thirty grueling minutes passed and Kara continued to sit in the doorframe. Nikki, Corbin and Megan had moved into the living room area, where it was warmer and just a few paces from their distraught companion. Outside, there were no signs of any straggler zombies or any sign of James. The last shotgun blast sounded well over fifteen minutes earlier. Tears rolled down Kara's face; she began to sob loudly.

"He's dead, isn't he?" Kara asked as she buried her face in her hands.

"Yeah, he's dead," whispered a voice from the side of the condo, just out of view.

Kara whipped her head around in the direction of the familiar voice. "JAMES! You're alive!" Kara shouted as she stood up and hurdled over the low guard railing to the ground. In one motion she landed on the cold, snowy ground and embraced her older brother in a massive bear hug.

"Of course I'm alive." James said, pushing his sister back at arm's length but still tightly clasping her shoulders. "No dumbass zombie is going to eat this pretty face," he jokingly mocked, pointing to his rugged face with his index finger.

James and his sister walked arm-in-arm into the house and closed what was left of the front door behind them; the door served as a poor barrier but did keep out some of the cold wintry air. The moonlight shined through the windows illuminating the interior of the large condo. Nikki and Corbin were pleased to see their comrade return. Even baby Megan cooed with approval. James and Kara moved into the living room and sat on the feline-patterned cloth couch. Nikki had comfortably nestled herself into a well-worn leather recliner and baby Megan rested on her mother's lap. Corbin stood at the window and looked out. The coast was clear…for now. They had survived yet another attack. *When would their luck run out?*

"How do we know this place even exists?" Kara inquired breaking the momentary silence.

"You mean Mount Hope?" Corbin responded.

"Yeah, seems kind of crazy to run blindly towards this ghost town," Kara replied.

"We don't know anything for sure," James said as he grimaced slightly.

"You're hurt!" Nikki exclaimed, pointing at James' right leg. Like a black light, the moon had highlighted a pool of blood at the old marine's feet that had seeped through his fatigues. Kara dropped to one knee from her seated position and gently removed her brother's boot, lifting his pant leg past his knee. Nikki rested Megan on the now-vacant recliner seat and she moved in for a closer look. A large gash ran lengthwise from the old vet's knee all the way to his ankle. The shin bone was exposed.

"We have to stop that bleeding," Corbin said matter-of-factly. "Need to clean that up so we can see how deep that wound is."

"It's pretty bad," James said surveying the injury in the limited lighting. "When I led those meat bags away from us, I ran about six or eight blocks into the neighborhood next to this one. I got turned around and the fog was way too thick…I couldn't see my own damn hand in front of my face. I lost my footing on some slick carport."

"Jim, I can't believe you risked your life like that. That was a stupid-ass stunt!" Kara exclaimed, interrupting her brother - still angry with James for his recent actions. She knew her brother was a war hero – it was just in his nature…but she couldn't stand the thought of losing her only remaining family member to some random act of heroism. Her brother tilted his head and winked at his younger sibling.

After searching quickly through the two rooms downstairs, Nikki rushed up to the second floor to search for any supplies that could be used to clean and bandage James' wound. Had they been able to bring the cars with them, she could have easily scrounged up the needed medical supplies. Now, she would have to search through the mostly ransacked condo to find anything of use.

Corbin gingerly elevated the old vet's leg onto a nearby footstool; James continued with his zombie encounter. "Yeah, like I was saying – I got confused and couldn't see anything. I ran around in circles trying to confuse those undead shits anyway that I could. I figured if I was lost, then those damn cranium cannibals would be all turned around too." James paused as Nikki came back downstairs with an armful of supplies.

"This is all I could find," Nikki said, laying all the items on the floor. She had procured a bed sheet, some sewing needles, thread, a large bottle of isopropyl alcohol, two leather belts and some pain medication.

James reached down for the pain pills and shook the bottle; the medication rattled around inside. "Nice work! I can't believe those are still here. How did the looters and crack heads miss these drugs?" He popped open the bottle top and downed five of the pills and put the almost-full bottle into his pocket.

"So what did you do to your leg?" Kara inquired as she wiped away the blood from around his knee.

"I jumped over a fence as I was coming back here. I heard a noise and turned around, thinking some undead prick had followed me… I wasn't looking where I was running and I slid full force into a boat trailer hitch. It hurts like a son of a bitch."

Corbin and Nikki cleaned out the wound as much as they could. While the wound was pretty deep, the shin bone was only showing in a three-inch section right below the knee, the rest of the wound was grotesque for sure, but easily stitched up. James grimaced a few times here and there as the couple doctored him up. Nikki tore the sheet into three pieces and made a large bandage, placing it on the wound below the knee. Corbin cinched one of the belts around the midsection of the bandage to hold it in place – it wasn't tight enough to be a tourniquet, but it was enough to hold the thick bandage in place and to slow the bleeding.

James stood up and flexed his knee back and forth. He moved from side to side but was unable to put full pressure on the injured leg. "Thanks…that feels much better."

Exhausted from running around the previous night and combined with the early morning zombie mob encounter, the group made their way to the second floor of the condo for some much needed rest. Two mirror image guest rooms and a common bathroom were on the east end of the floor while a small office on the west side of the condo completed the layout of the upstairs floor. The outside balcony ran lengthwise, parallel to the bedrooms.

Kara and James settled down in the bedroom closer to the top of the stairwell. The room was small with two twin size beds snugly placed against opposite walls. Corbin and Nikki helped guide the old vet into the room. He had already become quite groggy from the pills. Kara rummaged around in the closet and found two old quilts. She covered her brother and thanked her friends for bandaging his wounds. She lay down on her bed and covered herself as well.

Corbin, Nikki and baby Megan took the other room. This room was a bit fancier, having a nice queen size bed, with all the linens. It was kind of weird, the room looked untouched. Nothing was out of order. No furniture broken, like in the rest of the condo. Even the bed was fully made. Corbin and Nikki crawled into the bed under the thick covers. Baby Megan, placed on top of the covers, slept soundly between her loving parents.

"I'm exhausted," Corbin said. "It seems like we've been doing this shit forever."

Nikki rolled over and moved closer to him. She glanced down at her gorgeous baby girl between them. She loved her child so much and would do anything to keep her safe. She looked back at Corbin and softly brushed the hair around his ear.

"It's not going to get any easier," she said. "We need to get out of here early tomorrow and get back on track for finding this Mount Hope place in Maine."

Corbin kissed Megan delicately on the forehead and gently kissed Nikki on the side of the mouth. He stared lovingly at her in the pale moonlight. With the whirlwind of events over the past few months, he had forgotten one very important question and now seemed as good of a time as any to ask.

"Would you marry me?"

"I thought you'd never ask," she replied nodding her head affirmatively.

"I'd get down on my knees and promise you the world," he said, "but it isn't worth shit right now."

"It's the thought that counts."

The young family quickly fell to sleep in the warm clutches of the old bed. Tomorrow would be a new day. Tonight they held onto each other and dreamed the dreams of lovers of an age seemingly long since past...

Chapter 24

- *January 3, 2014: Friday, 5:55 AM – Charleston, West Virginia, a small condo in a retirement community …*

*S*CRITCH!! SCRITCH!!

Kara awoke from a fitful sleep filled with bad dreams. She lay motionless in her bed. Flashbacks of her early childhood darted around in her mind. When she was younger and had become frightened, usually from a scary story James had told her prior to bedtime, she would pull the covers up over her head and wish the *"monster"* away. She doubted that would work now.

SCRITCH!! SCRITCH!!

There it was again, she hadn't dreamt it; there was definitely a scratching sound or something just outside the window. Kara looked over to her brother. James was out cold due to the narcotic effects of the pain pills he had taken earlier. She slowly built up enough courage and silently rolled out of the bed. She crawled to the edge of the window where the sound was the loudest and grasped the edge of the silk curtains.

SCRITCH!! SCRITCH!!

Could the zombies from earlier have climbed up to the second floor balcony? The scratching sound stopped abruptly. Kara strained to hear any movement outside the window. Nothing. *Maybe she had imagined it?* She turned towards her bed hoping for a few more moments of sleep.

SCRITCH!! SCRITCH!!

"What the hell?" She muttered barely above a whisper. She pulled the thick window curtain slightly to the side, expecting the worst. A large tree branch danced with the wind rhythmically tapping on the glass.

She sighed deeply - relieved that it was only a large pine tree tapping on the window pane and nothing more. The dim, early morning sunlight trickled through the pine needles; the warming rays felt wonderful on her face.

CRAAACK!! A deafening sound echoed from the first floor moments later.

Kara knew that the sound from downstairs was definitely not a tree branch. The loud crashing noise was the exact same that the front door had made earlier when she had made her not-so-graceful entrance. She heard light footsteps outside her door moving towards the railing. Kara rushed to the door and peeked out. Corbin stood at the railing looking down.

"Shit! They've found us," he said quietly.

Kara looked over the railing. Ten or so ice and snow covered zombies moved in through the obliterated front door in single file. Soon the first floor filled with zombies. The stench from their rotting flesh wafted quickly up the stairs. It filled Kara's nostrils and she felt the urge to vomit.

Three zombies awkwardly attempted to ascend the stairway. Like a scene from a Three Stooges' movie, the zombies comically bumped into one another and slipped down the stairs. Undeterred, the undead reached out and grasped each of the wooden stairs by hand. The creatures pulled themselves up one step at a time, each clawing handful of stair echoing a terrible grating noise like fingers across a chalkboard.

"They'll figure out a way up here soon," Kara said. "We've got to slow them down."

Corbin darted across the floor from the railing in front of his room to the opening of the staircase where a large armoire stood. He positioned himself behind the antique and lowered his center of gravity trying to force the armoire towards the stairs below. The massive piece of furniture defiantly held its ground - barely budging a few inches.

Kara hurried over and looked down the stairs. Two zombies were upright and had made their way to the middle of the stairs. She stepped behind the armoire and pushed with Corbin. The wooden front feet creaked across the floor inch-by-inch; the dresser lurched past its tipping point and cart-wheeled down the staircase bouncing off the wall and smashing into the interlopers.

"That will only hold them for a few minutes," Corbin said as he looked at the newly created barrier at the base of the stairs.

Nikki burst out of the bedroom holding Megan tightly to her chest. The baby cried loudly and Corbin saw a look of fear dart across his fiancée's face. Corbin had never seen her so startled; she appeared almost ghost like…

"What is it, Nikki?" Corbin asked, rushing over to the mother of his child.

Before she could answer a loud crash echoed out of the room behind her. Corbin had his answer - zombies had infiltrated the second floor. The two-pronged, almost planned assault kept his mind occupied; he was unable to fully rectify how one set of zombies could barely ascend a staircase…while other zombies were able to climb up to the second story of the condo with apparent ease. *Maybe some zombies were smarter than others?*

"I've got to wake James," Kara shouted as she ran into her bedroom.

"Wait!" Corbin yelled.

Kara kicked open the bedroom door. The shy, early morning sunlight slightly illuminated the interior of the room. Four zombies surrounded James' bed. Kara froze, unsure what to do next. A fifth zombie was straddled above the covers on the bed, violently thrashing and ripping deeply into the linens. She was too late. Her brother had survived the earlier zombie encounter, surely he was now dead.

BOOM!!

A shotgun blast from the opposite side of the room deafened Kara. She clutched her ringing ears, dropped down to one knee and glanced over her right shoulder.

BOOM!!

A muzzle flash from the closet gave away her brother's position. Apparently the old vet had been prepared, even with enough narcotics in him to down a small horse. Kara looked over to the closet and she couldn't quite make out her brother's face, but she had a strange feeling that he was winking at her as he pumped more rounds into the zombies.

Two zombies lurched towards the closet. James shoved the barrel of the shotgun into the lead zombie's mouth, busting out the final few rotten teeth of the creature; the vet pulled the trigger.

BOOM!!

Two heads exploded in unison, spraying gory bits of undead flesh all over the opposite wall. The bodies slumped to the ground. The other three zombies moved towards the closet.

"How the hell...did these meat bags get up here?" James asked as he jumped from the closet, grabbing his sister's wrist and pulling her into the hallway. Kara slammed the door behind them as they exited.

"They must have climbed up the back stairs," Kara said.

"I know I lost them…it doesn't make any sense – how did they find us?!" James asked as he looked over the railing at the pool of zombies on the first floor.

James and Kara grouped up with Corbin, Nikki and Megan. Violent scratching and moaning came from the zombies trying to get out of James' and Kara's former room. The zombies from Nikki's bedroom began to emerge and the undead from downstairs had moved to the top of the indoor staircase; the group was completely surrounded by the living dead.

James rapidly pulled the trigger over and over again but the shotgun remained silent. He handed the empty weapon to Kara. She grasped the barrel of the gun and held it like a professional baseball player. Now Corbin and Kara were back-to-back. Nikki and Megan moved away from the zombies and James stood between the undead emerging from the bedrooms and his companions.

"We're surrounded," Corbin said, pointing at the zombies moving up the staircase.

"Bullshit!" James yelled.

The old marine ran towards the zombies at the top of the staircase. He heaved himself into the air like a human spear wrapping his arms around the waists of the zombies tackling the mindless beasts like a linebacker. The zombies moaned and clawed at James as the whole pile flipped end-over-end down the stairs. Kara rushed to the railing and looked down to the first floor.

The cannonball of flesh came to rest at the bottom of the stairs next to the shattered armoire with James underneath two of the zombies. The marine threw uppercuts and elbows from the ground bashing faces and busting jaws with each blow, but the zombies did not concede. The larger, once-female zombie hunched over and bit James on the back of his right shoulder.

"NO!" Kara screamed as she saw blood spew from her brother's wound.

The three lingering zombies from Kara's former room burst through the door and combined forces with the four zombies from Nikki's room. Nikki and Megan were surrounded. The frightened mother instinctively turned her back to the zombies shielding Megan as the undead groped her. Corbin snapped off part of the railing and began swinging wildly.

THUNK!! THUNK!! THUNK!!

The sound of wet, dead flesh being pummeled by the solid oak railing turned into a weapon filled the upstairs. Zombies collapsed like dominoes from the vicious blows.

Nikki dropped into a semi-fetal position to cover her baby. The zombies did not slow down, even with Corbin waylaying them over and over. One fat, gray haired zombie bent down and grabbed a handful of Nikki's hair and pulled violently. Another zombie that appeared to be a young teenager reached down and grabbed Megan's leg. Megan shrieked with fear.

"Help! One of them has Megan's leg!" Nikki cried as she clawed at the zombie's hand.

Corbin began smashing the oak club in a downward motion repeatedly onto the teenage zombie's spine; it shuttered as if having a seizure and fell motionless to the ground. Nikki kicked and flailed against the fat, gray haired zombie but the creature would not let go of her hair. The obese, undead creature smashed her head against the ground multiple times. A flash of light and searing pain filled her head as she blacked out.

Corbin looked over where Kara was standing mere seconds ago, but she was no longer upstairs – she had run down the stairs to aid her brother. Corbin could see her swinging wildly with the empty shotgun trying to save her brother's life. Corbin turned as he heard Nikki's head smash against the ground.

The former firefighter ran full speed, leaping into the air and drop kicked the fat zombie away from his fiancée. The force of the kick catapulted the obese zombie through the closed office door; the rotten faced undead creature crashed violently through the window to the unforgiving earth below. Corbin landed awkwardly on his back, smashing his head on the hard flooring. He rolled onto his right side and looked over to his family – they would surely die if he lost consciousness.

Corbin took a deep breath and pushed himself up to his elbows, his adrenaline pumping full force – keeping his aching muscles firing on all cylinders. As he got onto his knees, he saw the teenage zombie roll over next to Megan. The creature opened its mouth. Corbin pushed off the ground with all his might, but it was as if he was in molasses, time had ceased to function. In a millisecond, which seemed to last an eternity, Corbin lunged for the teenage zombie's throat but it was too late. The teenage zombie bit Megan's tiny left leg. The baby wailed in tremendous pain.

Corbin swung the oak railing like a samurai sword, decapitating the teenage zombie, but the damage was done. Nikki lay unconscious on the floor. Megan whimpered. In a berserker rage, the distraught father massacred the rest of the zombies on the second floor. He collapsed to his knees next to his would-be wife and his tiny daughter. Nikki regained consciousness as Corbin held baby Megan close to his chest. Nikki's motherly instinct kicked in – she knew her baby was injured.

Corbin's eyes filled with tears as he held his baby. He looked down at his wife. "I...couldn't stop them...they bit our baby...I..." Corbin, overcome with grief was unable to speak.

"Oh my God," Nikki cried as she struggled to a seated position. She enveloped Corbin and her baby in a desperate hug, horrible thoughts running through her mind of losing her child.

Downstairs, Kara had cleared away the zombies from her injured brother. James groggily stood up placing his left hand on his shoulder applying pressure to slow the bleeding. He stooped down and grabbed a large piece of the broken armoire. In tandem, brother and sister swung their weapons from side-to-side clearing a path to the front door.

"Get down here now, guys," Kara instructed, "we've cleared a path. We need to get the hell out of here before the other zombies get in!"

Corbin stood up and held baby Megan in his left arm. He bent over and scooped up his injured wife and slung her over his shoulder – the classic fireman carry came in very handy as he sprinted down the stairs. His exhausted body wanting to give in but his mind and heart urged him forward – he had to get his family and friends out of the slaughterhouse.

The battered group stumbled out into the snow covered grass on the front lawn. The fog had retreated from the bright sun. The early morning sun watched silently as the group scrambled away from the condo to find safety.

Chapter 25

- *January 3, 2014: Friday, 6:30 AM – Charleston, West Virginia, an empty street leading towards an old bookstore …*

For almost half an hour, the group ran in a mostly southerly direction away from the condo, led by James; he attempted to lose any zombies that might be following them. He wasn't one hundred percent sure on the direction to the vehicles; this frightened him. Excruciating pain echoed up and down his entire body from the massive shoulder wound, but the old vet pushed forward. It wasn't just the physical pain of the wound. He had definitely had worse. However, he could feel something burning deep inside of him; he knew it was the virus. His whole body ached, like a terrible flu but deep within his very core.

How could he have been so weak – so foolish? Was the transformation already starting? How long did he have? He couldn't dwell on these thoughts right now; he knew the group had to get to safety. They had to put plenty of distance between themselves and the zombies that had just attacked them. James felt compelled to lead his friends to safety even though his GPS-like sense of direction was failing him.

"Slow down, Jim," Kara begged, out of breath and exhausted. "We've been on the run forever. I think we've lost them."

"Just a little bit more, sis – we are almost back to where we left the cars last night when those undead meat sacks first showed up."

A few hundred yards after escaping from the condo, Corbin had put Nikki down on her feet; she had regained enough of her composure to move on her own. Corbin clutched baby Megan close to his chest. Her constant crying tore at his heart…his baby was badly injured and he feared the worst. He could feel her tiny body shivering with fear. Even though he didn't want to think about it… he knew his baby was infected. He had failed his precious baby and his beautiful wife.

What kind of father was he? How could he not protect his family? Terrible thoughts raced through his mind, but he moved forward. James would get them to safety. James always found a way to keep them safe. Always.

The marine prodded the group to move very quickly but to move with extreme caution. Zombies could be anywhere. They could be around any corner. The undead could spring up any time of day or night. They seemed particularly drawn to loud noises, groups of people and the undead were eerily prone to be extremely attracted to the smell of cooked food.

James wasn't sure if the cooking of food lured in the undead because of a connection the zombies had made where cooked food equaled human activity…or maybe, cooked food somehow rekindled latent memories in the back of their minds. *Probably not the latter*, he thought to himself…no, that would give those meat sacks too much humanity.

The group raced down a few empty, pothole-filled streets until they located the parking lot between the old bookstore and the burned out children's clothing store; they had finally worked their way back to where they had abandoned the Impala and the van the previous night. The group still had no fuel for the vehicles but at least they could get to their supplies to help treat their wounds.

Gas had been difficult to come by, even in the early days of the zombie infestation, but now, now it was almost impossible to find. During the past six months, the group had been resourceful in refilling their vehicles. Mostly, they would venture into the automobile graveyards of the interstates and siphon fuel from the long since abandoned vehicles. Even this tactic was becoming less and less reliable.

The friends stood on the sidewalk and peered into the icy parking lot. No signs of any activity. The vehicles rested quietly, like obedient dogs, waiting for their masters to return. A strong breeze between the two buildings tossed around trash and papers like butterflies fluttering aimlessly about in a late summer breeze.

The parking lot appeared empty, but that meant nothing – danger could be lurking anywhere and they knew it. Nowhere was ever safe or secure. Always having to watch over your shoulder – just to make sure you didn't end up in a zombie feeding frenzy. You never really got a peaceful, relaxing sleep since the zombie apocalypse started. If you slept too soundly, well you ended up getting your face eaten. Lack of sleep meant one was always tired – likely to make mental mistakes – often leading to death. Belonging to a close-knit group improved your odds of surviving and lessened the likelihood that one small mistake would get you killed. This group of friends knew that fact all too well. They had battled many zombies, struggled together to find warmth and shelter and procured food and clothing against almost insurmountable odds.

"Kara and I will take a closer look," Nikki said to James. She turned towards Corbin and looked with sad, but loving motherly eyes, at her baby. "Then I want to hold our baby – she needs her momma."

The two women entered the parking lot with weapons drawn. They searched behind and in the trash dumpster. Nothing was hiding, waiting for its next meal. The thick metal exit doors on the children's clothing store were rusted shut. No undead would burst through those doors without making tremendous amounts of noise. The final spots to check were the vehicles. Kara checked in and under the van. All clear. Nikki checked the Impala. Nothing. The area was secure.

The past six months together, on the run, had honed their skills. Meticulous attention to detail, understanding their environment and just the sheer will to survive kept them sharp and on their toes. That was true for the whole group. Even though no one had mentioned it in the short time since the attack at the condo…but all of them had thought about it…whether they would admit it or ever say it out loud. *How did they mess up last night? How did the zombies find them? What had gone wrong?*

The two seasoned women gave the all-clear sign and everyone moved towards the Impala. Exhausted and all-but-defeated, the group collapsed into the comfortable seats of their car. Corbin lovingly handed Megan to her mother. The baby had stopped crying; only minor whimpers and some bleeding from her leg told of her recent encounter with the zombies. Kara had not joined them. She gathered medical supplies from the trunk of the car and the backseat of the van to treat her brother and the baby.

Nikki rocked Megan softly, the baby resting, mostly silently, against her mother's shoulder. Tears welled up in Nikki's eyes slowly at first and then, as if a dam had broken, a deluge of sadness opened up. Corbin put his arm around his wife and baby and the family rocked back and forth in a tear-filled silence.

Kara swung open the passenger side door and slid into the front seat next to her brother. She had filled a backpack full of supplies to treat their injuries. James' eyes were closed and his head was tilted fully forward resting on the steering wheel. Blood from his wound had already stained the driver side seat and was streaming down his limp arm to the floorboard.

"James, take off your shirt," Kara said. "I need to stitch you up."

James turned his head towards his sister. He tried to be strong for her. He could see her fear and concern. "No, help the baby first."

Kara turned towards the backseat. Corbin had moved slightly away to give Kara more room, but Nikki still clutched baby Megan firmly.

"Nikki, I need to doctor up Megan," Kara said in a low, firm tone. "Will you let me do that?"

"Here take my seat," Corbin said as he opened the back door and slid out into the bright morning sunlight.

Kara crawled between the front seats to the back of the car and sat beside Nikki. She watched the young mother rock back and forth. She hadn't heard it earlier while she was up in the front seat, but Nikki was softly singing a lullaby to Megan. Kara couldn't make out the words; the sweet, but melancholy tune brought tears to her eyes.

Nikki kissed her baby gently on the top of the forehead just below her soft, curly auburn hairline. The young mother felt extreme heat coming from Megan's head; her baby had a very high temperature. She knew her baby was badly ill. Nikki turned her baby so that Kara could have easy access to the injured left leg.

Kara pulled up the hem of the dirty blue dress covered in a daffodil motif. The baby's tiny thigh was badly bruised and deep teeth marks could be seen from almost the top of the hip to the knee. The leg had scabbed over some but had already turned a dark blue-black tinge from the deep muscle damage. Baby Megan barely made a sound as Kara stitched up and wrapped the injured limb.

"There we go, Megan – that was a good girl," Kara said softly. "I bet that would have even made mean ol' James cry." She leaned forward and kissed baby Megan lightly on the side of her neck.

Kara then quickly shimmied up into the front seat next to her brother and Corbin resumed his position in the backseat with his family. No one spoke.

Kara skillfully stitched up her brother. She had to take it slowly, even though she had done this many times, this time was different. Her eyes were red and swollen from tears. She could barely see what she was doing, but her hands took care of the rest. As she finished up, she wiped the tears from her eyes to inspect her work. The bleeding had been stopped and the bandages were well secured.

After about fifteen minutes of rest, James opened his eyes and spoke. "We need to get some gas. I doubt we'll find enough for two vehicles." He paused, taking a long breath – the pain was excruciating but he tried not to let on. "Let's consolidate all our stuff into the van. There's more room in there anyway."

"We'll take care of that," Corbin said as he nodded towards Kara. "You three rest."

Kara and Corbin took the next twenty minutes to unload all of their supplies from the Impala to the van. Both were shocked at how much stuff they had accumulated over their journey together - clothes, food, medical supplies and even some toys for baby Megan. All of these things made their lives easier. The last of the items to move were weapons and ammo. These items kept them alive – gave them an upper hand against the undead. The weapons also brought some peace of mind. The items never made the group over confident, but it did help them sleep a bit better each night.

"That's all of it, Kara," Corbin said as he leaned against the side of the van.

"We're in trouble, huh?"

Corbin bowed his head, fighting back tears. "Yeah, I think our luck ran out this morning..." Kara moved over towards her friend and embraced him in a tight hug. He hugged her back. Both cried for a few moments and then returned to the Impala and entered the vehicle.

"Since you two are finished making out," James said with a slight smile, "we really need to go and get some gas for the van. I figure we are about two miles from the interstate. Maybe we'll get lucky and find a few still full of gas..." James tried to get out of the car but had no energy.

"Shit!" James said, clasping the steering wheel tightly for support. "Give me a second and I'll be fine...then one of y'all can come with me and we'll find some fuel."

"I don't think so, old man," Kara said. "You and Nikki move over to the van and stay put. Corbin and I'll find the gas." The old vet and Nikki didn't complain. They moved over to the van with some help. Kara kissed her brother on the cheek and he playfully waved her off. He was in so much pain but didn't want his sister to worry any more than she had to.

Nikki sat in the front passenger seat with baby Megan. Corbin closed the door softly behind his fiancée. He leaned in through the open window and kissed her and then his tiny daughter. As he was pulling away, Nikki pulled him closely to her lips and whispered in his ear.

"Hurry back to me...I'm worried about our baby. She's too sick and I can't do anything for her except hold her."

Corbin nodded unable to speak...his emotions were running high. He didn't want to leave at all, even for a short time, but they needed gas and they needed to get the hell out of this town.

Corbin and Kara armed themselves. Both took small amounts of food and water in their backpacks just in case the trip took longer than anticipated. They also dressed in their heavy winter coats and gloves to fight off the bitter wind chill. The two friends began their journey east towards the interstate on foot.

About twenty minutes into their trip they heard the loud roaring of a V8 engine behind them. They instinctively ran behind the edge of a building for cover. As they peeked around the corner they were shocked to see their old Ford van sitting at the intersection. James slowly motioned them back to the van.

"What the hell?" Corbin inquired after jogging up to the van.

"Where did you find the gas so quickly, James," Kara asked.

"I wasn't thinking…nor had I thought to check when we first 'acquired' this van. As I was trying to get comfortable, I must have nudged the selector switch to the extra tank. I heard the click and looked down…and well, here we are. This van has dual gas tanks and those idiots we met back in Arkansas must have filled it up before we took it from them…"

Corbin and Kara threw their supplies in the back and got in the van. No one spoke as the van sat idling in the intersection. James pulled off to the side of the road, mostly out of habit; it wasn't as if he was holding up traffic. As the van's wheels brushed the curb on the edge of the empty sidewalk, James shut off the engine to conserve precious gas. He took the keys from the ignition and handed them to Kara.

"You drive," he said softly. James slid out of the driver's seat and Kara slid across to take his place.

No one spoke; silence filled every nook and cranny of the van. However, everyone in the van, except baby Megan, contemplated the gravity of their current situation. They all knew the reality. They all knew the truth: Everyone ever bitten since the start of the zombie pandemic turned. Everyone. No exceptions. It was just a matter of time.

How long before their time was up?

Chapter 26

•   *January 3, 2014: Friday, 7:17 AM – Charleston, West Virginia,
    two miles from the interstate, an almost completely abandoned inter-
    section in the middle of a once bustling town…*

Thirty minutes passed as the group silently rested in their old van. The seats were not necessarily the most comfortable, but the passengers had much more room than when they were cramped up in the Impala. What the van lacked in the *"sex appeal"* of an old muscle car, it sure the hell made up for it with roominess and extra storage capacity.

"Waah!" Megan screeched, breaking the deafening silence. Her wailing soon turned into constant crying. Deep painful howls coming from such a tiny baby – with no real way to express her pain other than cries for help. Her young body was quickly succumbing to the ravishing effects of the zombie plague. Megan flailed her tiny arms in desperation. Corbin reached over and held her tiny hands in his, trying to comfort his child.

"She's burning up," Nikki said as she cradled the baby on her shoulder. The heat from the Megan's extreme fever made the side of Nikki's face sweat where the two touched. "I don't know what to do. She's in so much pain…she's been shaking the whole time."

James too had been shivering, but only for the last half hour or so. He could feel the poison, or disease or whatever it was exploding throughout his veins. Only his anger about being weak and getting bitten in the first place kept his mind off the agonizing pain.

"Maybe we could give her a small piece of James' pain pills?" Kara offered. "Maybe those would ease some of her pain?"

Nikki shook her head.

"Maybe that isn't such a bad idea," James added. "Maybe it would be better for her if she took more than a few…"

"Are you out of your fucking mind?" Nikki yelled, clearly understanding the intent behind James' recommendation. "Are you telling me to put my child to sleep permanently? You want me to kill my own baby? What the hell is wrong with you?"

"Calm down, honey," Corbin said. "I don't think James meant that."

"Yes, that is precisely what I meant. We all know what's going to happen. We've all been sitting here for close to an hour now." James paused, fighting off the sudden urge to vomit. The disease coursed through his body. "We all know what is going to happen…"

"We don't know that!" Kara yelled defiantly at her brother, knowing full well that the transformation was an undeniable fact. They had all seen it before. They all knew what would happen… just not when.

"Why don't you gag on your own fucking pills?" Nikki screamed as she angrily waved her middle finger from side-to-side in his face.

James looked at Nikki, seemingly un-phased by her angry outburst. He wasn't surprised with her reaction. Hell he expected it. Actually, he expected worse. Had she not been holding the baby, he fully well expected her to have hit him…repeatedly…for making such a suggestion.

James spoke evenly and calmly without stuttering or blinking: "Oh, believe me, I'd down this whole bottle but pills take too long. I'll know when my time is up. Understand this, I will not become one of those meat sacks." The old vet popped open the pill bottle and downed a small handful of the narcotics to ease some of his pain. He turned back towards the front windshield and sat in silence with his head slightly bowed and his eyes closed.

"Let's all just calm down," Kara pleaded.

Nikki and Corbin both moved from the captain's chairs in the van's second row of seats to the couch-like back seat in the very back of the van. There they could both be close to one another. Corbin rested his back against the side of the van. Nikki squeezed her body in next to him, laying her head on his shoulder; her hands in constant contact with her precious baby.

After everyone appeared to be calm and as comfortable as could be expected, Kara spoke once again: "I'm going to start up the van and we can get back on course for Maine. No need to sit here any longer." She fired up the V8 engine, put it into drive, checked the side mirror and turned on the left blinker to merge into non-existent traffic. Had the situation not been so dire, she would have been able to laugh at the automatic, ingrained driving response she had just exhibited. *Checking the mirrors? What for? And a turn signal?*

The mind did weird things when exposed to extreme stress…

- *January 3, 2014: Friday, 8:57 AM – in the middle of nowhere, outside of the Charleston city limits, an access road running parallel to the interstate …*

Kara skillfully maneuvered the van around charred and forgotten vehicles on the crooked access road. On her left hand side, she could see the wrecked cars and flipped over SUVs blocking all four lanes of the interstate. She could only imagine the fear and confusion that must have taken place as droves upon droves of families tried to escape from the city. She remembered back to the first months after the initial onset of the zombie infestation.

News reporters and emergency officials had begged people to stay home, to stay off the interstates. No one listened. City officials had warned of the imminent highway congestion and the very real possibility of fear induced road rage for those becoming trapped on the freeways. Frightened citizens disregarded the sound advice of emergency workers; millions rushed onto the antiquated thoroughfares.

Back then, just over eight months ago, her immediate reaction, after seeing the first confirmed reports of the outbreak on the news, was to flee the city - just like everyone else. She remembered hastily packing clothes and other important items from her small apartment located on the outskirts of Albuquerque, New Mexico. She had packed up her car and was ready to make a break for the more sparsely populated areas of the New Mexico desert. She would have gone too, had it not been for her older brother.

On that fateful day, almost as if on cue, James had pulled his Jeep Wrangler up behind her tiny foreign car as she was backing out of the apartment complex. He had blocked her way out and convinced her that every other idiot in the city would be doing the exact same thing. That everyone would be racing to the worst traffic jam in human history.

While she didn't care to be lumped in *with all the other idiots,* she knew her brother was right. The interstate would be a deathtrap filled with angry, scared motorists. He painted a horrific picture of the possible carnage that lay in wait for overzealous travelers.

He convinced her that the two of them should find somewhere safe in the city. That's when he told her of the old family bunker that he had renovated a few years ago. They could easily make their way to the bunker without fear of being followed. No one would care about folks staying in the city. Everyone would be trying to leave. No one would even notice them. There in the bunker they could safely wait out the madness.

They transferred her belongings into his Jeep and made their way to the family bunker. Kara remembered that James told her that they had enough supplies for five months...his only mistake, that she recalled, was that he told her this whole mess would be over with in less than two months...

What kind of car did she drive then? Weird, she couldn't remember. It was quite strange how all of the *"necessities"* of the pre-zombie era quickly faded from importance as the world raced headlong to its own demise. She guessed the end of days had a way of making one re-prioritize the important things in life.

"Where are we?" James asked, coughing and clearing his throat, breaking his sister's train of thought.

"I guess about an hour and half outside of the city limits. You've been asleep pretty much since I hit the access road."

"Can we pull over? I need to piss."

"Same here," Corbin said from the backseat. "Plus I really need to stretch my legs." He had been holding Megan since they entered the access road. Nikki was curled up next to him on the third row back seat. Megan had been whimpering softly the entire time. Her fever had acquiesced some, but the baby's condition continued to deteriorate quickly.

Kara eased the van off to the side of the road and parked next to a wide open field. The ground was frozen solid, but clear of snow. In the center of the open field, two large boulders, seemingly out of place, appeared to stand guard over the land.

After both men had relieved themselves, Kara and Nikki exited the vehicle. Nikki kissed Megan on the back of her head and gently handed the child to her father. While the men didn't give a damn about privacy – and pissed where they pleased, the two ladies still held fast to the antiquated idea; both meandered towards the boulders to relieve themselves in private. They returned to the van after a few short moments.

"I never understood that. Why do women always seem to go to the bathroom in pairs?" James said, cracking a small smile. His levity went almost completely unnoticed as the group hastily reentered the van. They closed all of the doors and Kara switched on the heater to force out the chilly winter air.

A few quiet moments passed and then Megan began crying again. She vomited down the back of her father's arm. It seemed the more she cried, the more she vomited. Nikki opened up her arms and Corbin reluctantly handed the child to Nikki after wiping off the baby's tiny mouth.

Then as suddenly as the baby's crying began, it stopped. Nikki held her baby out in front of her. Megan looked as if she was gasping for air, her face and neck began turning red from the sudden lack of oxygen.

"NO!" Nikki screamed. "She's not breathing!" Nikki carefully, but firmly, smacked the child on the back. It's all she could think to do. *Maybe Megan was choking on some fluids or something?* After a moment's hesitation, the tactic magically seemed to work. Baby Megan began whimpering again.

Corbin bowed his head and muttered softly, "Thank, God."

"Is she OK?" Kara inquired, feeling dumb after the words exited her mouth. *Of course the child wasn't OK...what the hell was she thinking? The baby was infected...of course she wasn't OK.* "I mean... umm," Kara stumbled around trying to find the right words.

"She's breathing," Nikki said flatly.

Corbin crawled into the back of the van. He returned with some isopropyl alcohol and a two small pieces of linen. He doused the cloth with alcohol and proceeded to wipe Megan's forehead, neck and chest with the damp cloth. After Corbin had wiped down his daughter, Nikki rested the child on her right shoulder. She wanted to listen to her baby breathe.

"The alcohol will evaporate. It should cool her skin," he said. "Maybe it will help lower the fever." Corbin doused the second cloth and handed it up front to James. James took the cloth, nodded in appreciation and wiped down his own face and neck.

"So what do we do now?" James asked. Corbin glanced up to the front of the van, looking down near the van's center console. He saw Kara's hand firmly holding her brother's shaking left hand. Corbin knew James wasn't scared. He knew the old vet was terribly sick. He caught Kara's eyes in the rearview mirror, just for instant. She looked so afraid, so alone.

Nikki rocked Megan slowly, back and forth. The baby had stopped crying but Nikki could still hear the labored breathing. Then without warning, baby Megan began trembling. Nikki held her firmly and looked confusingly at her husband, expecting him to do something. But there was nothing to be done. Megan seized violently for two minutes and then her whole body relaxed, her tiny body seemed relieved, like the first few moments after one works a bad leg cramp out.

Nikki placed Megan gently on the third row backseat. She wiped down the baby again with the damp cloth. Megan began cooing softly. With tear filled eyes, Nikki lovingly stared directly into Megan's tired eyes. The baby's cooing stopped. Nikki lowered her head towards her daughter's chest.

"Momma," Megan whispered, almost inaudibly, into her mother's ear with her final breath.

"She's not breathing, do something!" Nikki shrieked. "Do mouth-to-mouth, Corbin – for God's sake, help me!!"

"Wait!" James yelled as he moved to the back of the van. "Don't do it, let me. Please. I'm already infected. If you put your mouth onto hers, you run the risk of being infected too!"

"I don't care," Nikki cried. Corbin gently pulled his wife away from their child.

"Give James some room, let him try," the distraught father said.

For ten minutes, the old vet delicately tried to resuscitate the baby, but it was too late. The zombie venom within her blood had done too much damage. The old vet stopped mouth-to-mouth and then stopped chest compressions. She was gone. He moved away from the tiny baby.

"I'm sorry," the old marine said sincerely as he passed by Nikki and Corbin to return to the front of the van.

Kara wept loudly as her brother put his arm around her neck. Corbin held Nikki who in turn clutched baby Megan close to her chest. Kara allowed the van to continue idling; the heat wafted about but no one was thinking about the cold.

Chapter 27

- *January 3, 2014: Friday, 10:22 AM – a small field protected by the watchful gaze of two stone giants...*

The group sat in a tight semi-circle around a small mound of dirt in between the two behemoth boulders. A small makeshift headstone stood at the northern end of the small burial patch. James was covered in dirt and sweat. Almost an hour had passed since he had finished packing the dirt around the grave.

An hour ago, James had offered to dig the grave for the baby and no one objected, not even Nikki. The old marine had dug the grave with a hubcap off the back tire of the old van. The top layer of dirt was frozen solid, but after some considerable effort, the old vet reached softer soil. James took his time as he dug out the gravesite. Each hubcap full of dark earth was placed next to the small opening.

Corbin gently held the small child next to his broken heart. Mother and father kissed Megan's tiny forehead for the final time and Corbin had lowered her into the shallow grave. Both parents turned away from the gravesite; neither of them could watch as the old vet respectfully shoveled handfuls of dirt over the baby. Once her body was mostly covered, he used the hubcap to push the rest of the dirt into the hole.

Nikki sat silently staring at the final resting place of her precious child. She tried to cry but couldn't; her mind and body were in shock. *Did this really just happen? Was her baby girl truly dead?* She knew the answer…she just couldn't accept it.

"I'm sorry, Megan," Corbin said breaking the almost hour long silence. "I couldn't stop…that creature from biting you. I'm so sorry…" The young father burst into a fit of deep sobs. Nikki moved over next to him and put her arm around him. She cried heartily as well.

• *January 3, 2014: Friday, 12:02 PM – a gravesite nestled between two boulders, in a fertile field off a once busy access road …*

"It's time for you guys to get moving," James said as he rested against one of the large boulders. "You should make as much distance as you can while there is plenty of sunshine."

Kara had been lying in the grass, on top of her heavy winter coat, next to the other rock and sat up after hearing her brother speak. She did not care for the tone in his voice. "You make it sound like you are not coming with us," she said.

"I'm not. I can't."

Corbin and Nikki looked over at the old marine, also somewhat shocked by his recent statement. While still in deep mourning over the loss of their child, they still couldn't fathom losing another member of their group so quickly.

"Corbin," James said without looking up." Please take care of Kara. I won't be around to watch her. Promise me that you'll keep her safe. I know she's tough, but it would make this old man happy to know that someone is watching over her in my absence."

Kara began crying and ran over to her brother wrapping her arms around him, sobbing heavily into the nape of his neck. The old vet wrapped his arms around his younger sister and rocked her slightly, back and forth.

"You have to go…now. I don't want you to be here when it happens. I can feel it inside of me trying to get out," James said as he gently unclasped her fingers from around his neck. "Corbin, please – take your wife and my sister and get the hell out of here!"

Corbin and Nikki rose from their seated positions next to Megan's grave and walked towards the old vet. Kara tried to grab hold of her brother's neck again, but he kept her at arm's length. The old vet stood up and Kara dropped even lower to the ground grabbing hold of the old man's legs, like a child throwing a tantrum.

James gently lifted his distraught sister to her feet and walked her to the van. Nikki and Corbin stood solemnly over the freshly dug gravesite one final time as they said one last silent prayer. Corbin bent down, kissed his palm and gently touched the middle of the small mound. "Good bye, baby girl." He rose from his kneeled position and grabbed Nikki's hand. They walked to the van.

"Please James, don't do this," Kara pleaded from the passenger side seat. "Come with us, you don't have to stay here. You'll be all alone!"

"I'm not alone," the old vet said as he nodded in the direction of Megan's grave. "Now, give Corbin the keys so you can get moving." Reluctantly she handed the keys over and Corbin started up the van. Nikki lay on the third row back seat, using some of Megan's stuffed animals as a tiny pillow.

"Go," James instructed Corbin. Corbin reached across to the passenger side window and shook James' hand. Both men nodded with mutual respect. James opened up his rucksack and pulled out the atlas; he knew his days as group navigator were over. "Don't forget this," James said handing over the rumpled collection of maps. "I've highlighted a few different paths for you just in case."

James kissed Kara gently on her forehead and he stepped away from the van. Corbin put the van in gear and sped off towards the access road with tears welling up in his eyes. Kara watched her brother in the rearview mirror. She saw him walk over to the gravesite and sit down. She continued to watch until she could no longer see the giant boulders. She wept, knowing full well what was coming next…she knew she would never see her brother again.

• *January 3, 2014: Friday, 2:45 PM – a freshly dug gravesite in the middle of nowhere …*

James lay next to the tiny grave that he had dug just a few hours earlier. Next to him lay the discarded, empty bottle of narcotic pain killers and his shotgun. Birds chirped over head and the Sun warmed the grass around the motionless old marine.

"What did you say?" the old vet inquired as he slowly rolled over on his side and faced Megan's grave.

"Yeah, I'm still here. No they left a few hours ago." James' dangerously high fever had caused him to hallucinate; he didn't know the difference between what was real or what was imagined. His body had all but given out on him from the deleterious effects of the zombie venom within his veins…his mind followed closely behind.

"No, I think I've got it figured out now. I know how those zombies found us."

James forced himself to sit in an upright position. He picked up the empty bottle of pills, shook some imaginary pills into his outstretched hand and tossed the magic pills into his mouth. He threw the bottle over his shoulder; the plastic container bounced off one of the large rocks behind him and came to rest in a small patch of brown grass.

"No, I already told you. You can't have any of these, your mother said not to let you have any. Besides, they might stunt your growth."

James vomited and his body seized violently on him. For almost three full minutes, his arms and legs shook out of control. He collapsed backwards to the hard ground behind him. His head flopped back and forth, side-to-side. At one point he almost swallowed his tongue but the violent shaking caused him to flip over on his chest, dislodging the muscle from his throat.

A few moments passed and his body relaxed. His face had come to rest in a pool of his own vomit. Blood trickled out of his mouth from a wound on his tongue, inflicted by a severe bite from his out-of-control muscle spasms. He coughed violently and cleared his throat and again returned to an upright seated position next to the dirt mound.

"Like I was saying before I was so rudely interrupted, I've figured out how those zombies found us the other night. It was my fault. I thought I had lost them, but I was wrong. I cut open my leg on that fucking boat trailer."

"What?"

"Oh, yeah, sorry about the language…that boat trailer cut me open badly. Those zombies must have followed the blood trail to the condo."

James reached over and grabbed his shotgun. Through muscle memory alone, he checked the ammunition and pumped the gun. Proof those years of training and experience can automate certain reflexes in times of critical need or emergencies.

"I'm going to tell you a secret," James said as he leaned over close to the grave. "I think I'm losing my mind..." The old marine lay down beside the grave wrapping his arm around the dirt mound, hugging the tiny baby, the fresh soil sliding through his fingers.

"Well that's enough of that emotional bullshit. Yeah, yeah I know...I'll watch the language. You sure are chatty now that nobody's around."

James again forced himself to his knees and crawled over next to the larger of the two boulders. He rested his back against the cool rock and placed the butt of the shotgun between his boots, with the muzzle end pointing towards his face. Three or four large birds had landed on the boulders; they were seemingly transfixed on the scene about to play out below.

"I'm sorry for a lot of things in my life, but two things I want to apologize to you for: one, I'm sorry for never calling you by your rightful name. And two, I'm sorry for getting you killed."

"It's time for me to go now. I can't let those meat sacks have me. Goodbye, Megan." With those final words, the old vet pulled the trigger.

BOOM!!

The old marine's headless body slumped to the ground. The voyeuristic birds that were watching the show from their perched position on the large rocks scattered into the air. The rugged facade of the large boulders facing the baby's grave was painted a slight crimson hue as the sun continued to illuminate the grotesque scene.

Soon, birds began to circle overhead, interested in what had transpired below. After a few moments, the braver birds of the flock returned to the rocks, but none of them dared to go any lower.

However, one adventurous bird hopped down on the freshly dug gravesite and began foraging around for earthworms and grubs.

Without warning, a tiny hand shot through the loosely packed earth and grabbed the bird, pulling it down into the darkness below…

Chapter 28

- *January 4, 2014: Saturday, 10:22 AM – Mount Hope Research Facility, Bangor, Maine …*

"This place is so beautiful," Mandy commented.

She walked hand-in-hand with her husband down the crooked dirt path leading from the research facility to the base of the small hill. The day was strangely warm and the couple took advantage of some free time to enjoy just being outside. Soon their daily walk would come to an end, like it always did, as they reached the fence at the bottom of the hillside. A towering chain link fence ran around the entire complex providing an adequate barrier against unwanted visitors – human or otherwise.

As she looked out into the distance through the fence, she could see the gorgeous rolling hillside lazily crawling up the horizon to meet her. She no longer heard or saw *"them"* standing outside the gated area. A few months of being surrounded by the undead, she had learned to look past their hideous, foul bodies that lined the entirety of the fence.

"I agree," Craig said as they reached the bottom of the tiny trail.

Craig and Amanda now stood mere yards from the fence. While they did their best to avoid seeing or listening to the rotting creatures, their noses were not yet trained to be so dismissive… the zombie's foul, pungent scent permeated the area. Amanda held her hand up to her nose briefly as the smell began to infiltrate her nostrils.

"That's enough for me today," she said.

"Yeah it was good while it lasted. I hate those damn things."

BLAM!! BLAM!!

Two shots rang out overhead; Craig and Mandy barely reacted – Craig glanced over his shoulder as he saw two zombies crumple headless to the ground. All the residents had become accustomed to the deadeye shots of the snipers. Sure, the sturdy chain link fence provided pretty good protection, but the snipers positioned around the facility added more of a human touch for the inhabitants. Each day, the sniper squad would take out a few zombies that had become seemingly cleverer in their attempts to breach the fence. The fence/sniper combo had well served the safety concerns of the tenants living within the complex.

The couple retraced their steps back towards the research facility. Craig thought back, as he often did, to how terrible the first three months of the pandemic had been. The two of them along with Theo had stayed on the run, hiding in various rest stops and abandoned buildings to keep concealed from the authorities. At the end of July, Theo postulated that no one from the Rochester facility had reported anything. In addition, he proposed that the police were considerably more occupied with maintaining order than searching for them in connection with the bloody night that Julie and Alexander had been killed.

The trio cautiously tested the theory and it turned out to be correct. With the coast clear, Craig led the group to Mandy's parent's house hoping against all odds that they were OK. The group arrived at Mandy's childhood home; the house was empty. It had been completely ransacked by looters and rioters. However, there was no sign of her parents at all. The not knowing seemed to bother Mandy the most. She had no idea if her parents were alive or dead.

Mandy, Craig and Theo stayed at the house for about two weeks. They gathered supplies from other houses in the neighborhood that had fared better during the initial and subsequent waves of rioting humans and droves of zombies that had passed through. At the end of the second week, they moved onwards after picking up a static-filled radio broadcast promising safe haven for travelers. They made their way to the Mount Hope Research facility. They had spent the last half of the year living and working at the complex.

"Hey guys!" Destin smiled as he waved at the couple.

Destin Anderson was a tall young man in his early twenties with dark black hair and a friendly smile that put people at ease. He had worked at a nearby church for a few years preparing to go overseas to preach with his Bible group. At the onset of the undead rising, Destin was forced out of his church, not by the zombies, but by so-called religious fanatics that burned his church down. He helped a few members from his congregation escape and they ended up at the Mount Hope facility. He was saddened that he was unable to save his pastor – his mentor who died in the ensuing church fire along with more than half of the congregation. The surviving members had turned to Destin for guidance.

For a few weeks, he struggled realizing his lifelong dream of spreading the word of God to the far reaches of the globe had been cut short before it really even began. The plague made all types of mass travel nearly impossible. In addition, he felt awkward that the congregation looked to him for guidance – he felt that he was too inexperienced, too young to lead anyone. However, he knew and trusted that God worked in mysterious ways; the young man may not have been able to minister to faraway lands, but he was more than capable and willing to share the word with those around him. It had been his idea to set up the repeating radio transmission to guide others to this safe haven.

"Hey, Destin," Mandy replied, hugging the young man.

"Are you guys coming to service tomorrow?"

"We'll be there for sure," Craig replied as he shook the young man's hand.

"What about Theo," Destin inquired. "Do you think he'll come?"

"I would tell you to give up on him," Craig said, "but I know that isn't your style. He told us that religion makes no sense to him. He said something to the effect that religion was some kind of man-made oppression tool or something like that…"

Destin smiled. He had been trying since day one to persuade Theo to come to some of his lessons but had failed to convince the man to even attend one session. If anything, Destin was determined that everyone, now more so than ever in this time of peril, needed to be right with the Lord. Destin was never rude or pushy as he told of his loving God. Many people that had not worshipped prior to the zombie apocalypse had quickly found a need to hear and learn more about God. Destin felt that given a bit more time, with some of his peaceful prodding – that even Theo would find his way to the light.

Destin looked up on the rooftop and saw that Major Pavlik was on sniper detail. The young man waved and the old soldier nodded. "Nice shooting," Destin said. The soldier grunted something inaudibly and backed away from the edge of the building.

The three friends at ground level entered into the building through the south entrance and walked up the stairs to the cafeteria on the second floor. It was close to lunchtime and it was their weekend to set up the dinner tables and chairs. The cafeteria served two purposes: one - it was a place to eat breakfast, lunch and dinner and two - on Wednesday and Sunday, it was set up for church services.

- *January 5, 2014: Sunday, 1:22 AM – ...Mount Hope Research Facility, Bangor, Maine third floor research station room 301...*

Theo poured over the results in defeated frustration. It didn't make any sense to him. Since last week, it appeared that their efforts had been going in reverse. The other scientists were just as baffled. Two weeks ago they felt confident that the path they had chosen had tremendous potential for producing a universal remedy to combat the Z1N1 infected creatures. The lead scientist at Mount Hope - Obadiah Jennings - had excitedly presented the research and data via email to Dr. Ferguson and his team at the Langston Research Facility in St. Louis. The hope was to *"weaponize"* the solution. The scientists of these two locations were confident that there was no way to save the infected after months of failed attempts. The only sure fire way to reclaim the planet for humans was to eradicate the plagued victims.

"I don't understand," Theo said in disgust.

Obadiah looked up from his lab station suppressing an overwhelming urge to cough; he had been sick for the past three days and his throat and chest was sore from all of the coughing. The lead scientist had worked in this facility for twenty five years. The older gentleman was seventy two years old, had a full head of gray hair with matching almost-chest length beard. He wore thick, black rimmed bifocals and a yellowish tan cowboy hat. The older scientist removed his hat, brushed his hands through his hair in frustration and cleared his throat; he put on a good face to keep morale up. Even though his cough had visibly worn him down, he continued to move forward with the agonizing tests – his attention to detail and perseverance energized the younger folks around him. He had become a father figure to the entire community.

"It's just a minor setback, Theo," Obadiah said in a cool, monotone voice. "We must have missed something…something little. Let's go back over the last week worth of tests." The elder scientist entered more data into his always present laptop computer. All of their work, all of the tests and various data regarding samples used on zombies were all stored on the device.

The other scientists in the room groaned but they pushed forward. These eight men and three women knew they were close. If they could finalize their work and mass produce the universal remedy – people of the world could eventually come out of hiding once the creatures were destroyed. Then everyone could focus on rebuilding communities at the local level and then, over time, be able to reinstate the federal government.

"Even if we figure this out," Theo began, "and make this a viable option – how will it be mass delivered?"

"You worry too much young man," Obadiah said. "Our colleagues at Langston assure us they can get the compound airborne and expeditiously delivered onto the infected masses."

The scientists at Mount Hope had been working to create a compound that would destroy the zombies at the cellular level. The role of the Langston facility was twofold: one, procure aircraft to disperse the remedy as quickly as possible throughout the United

States – then when feasible – to the rest of the world and two, communication overseas. Langston had actually been able to send and receive emails from the United Kingdom's Center for Disease Control. These three facilities operated at thirty percent or less of their pre-crises capabilities which impeded progress. In addition, sporadic movement of the functional communication satellites orbiting the Earth hindered the transmission of data to and from each facility; Obadiah believed that this was the limiting factor keeping them from communicating directly with the UK.

"You should get some sleep, Theo. Church comes early you know?"

Theo looked up briefly from the last email he had received from his peers at Langston. "I still don't understand how a man of science like you can even stomach that mumbo-jumbo hocus-pocus tripe."

Obadiah understood where Theo was coming from. The old man had only recently made the journey to Christ. While he didn't fully understand all the nuances and details of his newly found faith, he had seen the light – his young friend, Destin had spent many long nights sharing the Gospel with him and others.

"You know that organized religion is just a way to control the masses, right? Promise the lower- and middle classes that if they are *'good'* here on Earth – then heavenly riches await them on the other side; that single promise keeps the masses from uprising against the wealthy."

"How very Marxist of you... Theo, you are way too young to be this jaded - even with everything going on around us these days. Come to Church with me later this morning. You will see that science and religion can be balanced. I don't think they were ever meant to be separate."

Theo shook his head and returned to his results. He heard Obadiah close up his notebook computer for the evening and the old man walked over to Theo placing a caring, firm hand on the young man's shoulder.

"I'm off to bed now – I hope to see you in church later today."

The old man exited the room and Theo heard him cough one time as he walked down the hallway. Soon the night was quiet and still and Theo began to browse through his notes on previous serums that had failed to meet their needs. Something was missing and he needed to find out what had gone wrong.

• *January 5, 2014: Sunday, 11:22 AM – ...Mount Hope Research Facility, Bangor, Maine- the converted cafeteria for church services...*

Destin stared out into the multitudes taking their seats. He was visibly nervous, not because he hadn't prepared his sermon, but because this morning brought the most attendees he had ever seen since he began teaching many months ago. From a quick glance, at least fifty people sat in the makeshift pews. There were only seventy five people total living in the complex. Destin knew each and every face. He nodded as he made eye contact. As usual, the *"no shows"* like Theo and some of the military folk didn't find the time to attend.

"Good morning everyone," he began.

"Good morning," the crowd cheerfully responded.

"It's good to see my regular faces in the crowd and I'm grateful to see some newer faces as well. Welcome."

Craig and Mandy sat near the front next to Obadiah. The three of them had helped Destin earlier in the day to transform the cafeteria into a reasonably apportioned venue for today's sermon. They had removed all the round lunch tables and stored them in the back closet. Obadiah's cough began acting up, so he had to rest frequently. Mandy and Craig finished the rest of the setup by dividing the sixty stackable chairs into two sections; each section consisted of five rows of six chairs. There were only a few Bibles available but pens and scratch paper was laid beneath each chair should anyone care to take notes.

Destin began today's sermon with a prayer wishing for the well-being of his friends and asked God to end the blight currently ailing the world. As he finished the congregation raised their heads in unison saying "Amen".

"Today I want to talk to you about the Book of Revelation or sometimes referred to as the Apocalypse of John. We've all suffered our own personal losses over the past year. The zombies easily have us outnumbered now. Maybe this plague is some kind of judgment on us? It's easy to give up these days. Why should we continue to fight?"

Destin could sense the crowd's confusion. He could almost read their minds. Many thought to themselves why would the preacher bring up such a downtrodden message today? They all needed a message of hope – not one of vague imagery and despair.

"I know what many of you are thinking. Hear me out. Sure Revelation portends terrible seals and judgments upon mankind. Why would I bring up this message now? Simple. With all the turmoil in our lives, the Spirit of the Lord has moved us all together to worship and pray in his name. In the Book of Revelation, many terrible things are visited upon humans, but the Lord promises his swift return. Maybe our current test brings us one step closer to being with the Lord?"

Destin found his voice for the day and continued for the next twenty minutes non-stop telling everyone of the glories and riches waiting for them in the next life. Obadiah found a bit of irony in the statement considering the last conversation he had with Theo the night before. However, he felt the love and meaning of the words, not the jaded interpretation that the younger scientist rambled off last night.

After the sermon ended, a few parishioners stayed behind and set up the cafeteria for lunchtime. Today's menu, like every Sunday was special. A whole smorgasbord of fresh vegetables from the garden on the east side of the complex was served. Broccoli, cauliflower, cabbage and collard greens littered the buffet table. The garden was the pride and joy of the Mount Hope community.

The garden had been started a few months ago during the middle part of summer. The first month, the garden produced very little. Hopes for fresh produce dwindled. With a bit of patience and caring, the garden began to provide for the community in its second month of existence. As winter approached, fears again began to rise that they would have to go without vegetables, but a creative young woman remembered back to an article that she had read many years ago about growing crops and how to harvest in the winter time.

The woman took some bricks to the edge of the garden. In the center she placed a few bricks one on top of another. Then by stretching a thick plastic sheet from one end of the garden to the next, she created a pseudo-cloche like enclosure that protected the plants from the deadly frost. The ends of the plastic sheet were wrapped around the base of the bricks keeping it in place. The raised center allowed for some air circulation. Today's lunch was proof that her idea worked to perfection.

And just like each Sunday for the past half year, everyone in the complex showed up for *"Vegetable Sunday"* to enjoy their little weekly miracle. Even the kids at the complex had no dislike for any of the vegetables. Children often had a second and sometimes even a third plate. Even the adults piled their plates high with unstable leaning towers of vegetables – there was plenty to go around for everyone.

"Ha! That's funny," Craig said whimsically as he sat down with a plateful of food next to his wife.

"Oh yeah, what's that?" Mandy inquired.

"It only took a zombie apocalypse to get these kids to eat their vegetables without complaining!"

Chapter 29

- *January 9, 2014: Thursday, 4:22 PM – outside a small elementary school, Harrisburg, Pennsylvania …*

A grueling, taciturn week passed as Kara, Corbin and Nikki slowly trudged along inconspicuous access roads heading northeast. The weather had been fairly decent precipitation wise over the past few days, but the cold temperatures were not so accommodating. The ice and thick snow on the roads continued to retard any meaningful forward progression. Anything that did manage to thaw quickly refroze during the frigid nighttime hours.

The van's old heater had done just enough to keep frostbite from setting in during the daylight hours, but they knew it was reckless to let the van idle all night – doing so would quickly drain their finite fuel reserves. Frequent stops along the way yielded only small amounts of gas; fuel had to be conserved whenever possible. At night, the group huddled together in the middle of the van under heavy blankets to generate as much body heat as they could; the aphonic nights were long and silent except for sporadic fits of crying from the bereaved within.

Since leaving West Virginia, Corbin had done most of the driving and navigating; he followed James' directions in the old atlas whenever possible. Focusing on the road and the destination kept his mind off Megan – even if only for the briefest of moments. Kara had offered to navigate but seeing her brother's handwriting and notes inside the old atlas was too much for her to bear. She didn't have to see her brother's final sacrifice back at the two boulders, but she knew him well enough to know that he would not have allowed himself to turn. Nikki slept most of the time never far from Megan's soft pink blanket; the baby's gentle aroma of innocence deeply saturated the wool comforter.

The weather worsened as soon as they had entered Pennsylvania. Corbin continued to drive through the whiteout conditions until visibility outside of the van barely passed the rusted front bumper. He pulled the van to the side of the road between a burned out husk of a bank on the passenger side of the street and an elementary school on the driver's side. He traced with his index finger an alternate route that James had marked. The old marine's notes indicated that from their current position on the map – they would need to travel another six hundred or so miles before reaching Bangor.

Corbin began coughing; he had felt lousy for the better part of the past three days. He knew his fever was quite high from the alternating periods of freezing and sweating his ass off. The long, cold nights stuck in the van plus the strain of the past many months combined with the loss of his beloved daughter was too much. He had not allowed his body to rest and now he was paying for it.

"Are you OK?" Nikki asked from the backseat as Corbin continued to cough.

"I'm not sure," he responded. "I was hoping it was just a cold but I've had a fever for a few days now that I thought would pass… but I guess not."

Nikki sat up and folded the pink blanket into a perfect square laying it securely on the seat before walking to the front of the van. She placed her hand on Corbin's head feeling the intense heat radiating from his body. She turned walking to the storage area in the very back of the van to get some rubbing alcohol and a dishrag like he had done for Megan a few days back…but she began to cry before she reached the backseat as images of Megan overwhelmed her. She stood there hunched over in the center of the van crying, but no tears fell from her swollen eyes; she had long since exhausted those watery reserves. She wondered if survival was worth the effort…

"What are we doing?" she asked to no one in particular.

"I thought we were going to Maine," Kara answered only half paying attention.

The death of her brother had numbed her mind, body and soul. She felt isolated, detached from the world around her; the willowy tendrils of depression had set in. She had scarcely eaten anything in the past week. She rarely slept as haunting dreams of her decaying brother frolicked around in her subconscious mind. She possessed the wherewithal to know she teetered on the edge of madness but wondered silently why she continued the struggle.

"No, I mean why are pushing on? What's the point? It seems like every step we take we lose someone we love…"

Corbin bowed his head resting it on the steering wheel; he too had thought similarly. *What was the point of living in a world like this? The days never got any better. Things from the old world meant nothing now. Who cares if it was your birthday? Who cares about saving money for retirement? Seeing your kids graduate from high school meant nothing now.* He began coughing again and could feel the phlegm stuck in his throat and chest.

"Let me see if I can find you something for that cough," Nikki offered.

"Don't worry about it now," Corbin replied. "We have a few more hours of driving before nightfall. Let's just get back on…"

"What the hell is that?" Kara shrieked as she pointed out the driver's side window. "Did you see that?"

"See what?" Nikki asked. "I'm surprised you can see anything with all of this damn snow that keeps following us around."

"I saw a little girl run inside that school building," Kara said.

"I think you are seeing things," Corbin said as he strained his neck looking towards the school building. "I'm the one with the high fever here – if anyone should be hallucinating it should be me."

"She might be hurt or lost. Please can we help her?" Kara pleaded.

"There's no one out there," Corbin insisted.

Kara pushed open the passenger side door; Corbin instinctively reached out to grab her but she slipped through his fingers. She ran in front of the van and across the street into the alabaster soaked periphery. Corbin and Nikki watched in shocked awe as their companion struggled through the knee-deep snow towards the school.

"Sit down," Corbin yelled but Nikki had already taken a seat. Corbin threw the van into drive and slammed his foot on the accelerator but the van, embedded deep in the snow and ice, refused his heavy-footed prodding. He rammed the column-mounted shifter into reverse and then drive and then reverse again trying to rock the van free from the clutches of its icy prison.

"I don't see her anymore," Nikki cried out.

"Fuck!" Corbin yelled as he shifted into park shutting off the engine. "Grab your coat and gun. We have to go after her." Corbin stepped out of the van adjusting his heavy coat as his feet sank deeply into the fresh snow. He grabbed his backpack and handgun from behind the seat and slammed the door. Nikki exited the passenger side of the van fully decked out in her thick winter coat with Kara's rifle strung over her back; she moved to the front of the van with her husband.

The malevolent breath of Old Man Winter scooped up snow and ice from all directions mercilessly pelting the young couple as they struggled across the road to the erstwhile school building. The gray stone walls that once enclosed bright minds and limitless futures now provided no real service except breaking the monotony of the wintery landscape. A patchwork awning, missing several sections of tin roofing, lazily sheltered a sidewalk winding to the front of the building; the remaining patches of the metal canopy offered no protection from the bone-chilling precipitation.

"There!" Corbin pointed to the ground as he shouted over the blustery wind.

Nikki could barely make them out, but sure enough two sets of footprints, now half filled with snow, led directly into the main doors of the elementary school. The couple followed the gradually evanescing trail into the Cimmerian antechamber. Abandoned text books, precariously perched within tiny metal lockers along the wall, peeked out partially agape doors at the uninvited guests. Sheets of liberated notebook paper and other miscellaneous school materials littered the hallway. While the temperature inside the building mirrored that of the outside, it felt much warmer without the constant bullying of the subzero wind chill beyond the thick stone walls.

Corbin led the way down the first hallway encountering an empty cafeteria on his left. Farther down the hallway, they passed by the teacher's lounge and principal's office on the right. The main hallway branched left at the boy's restroom. Corbin and Nikki hunched down stopping at the corner when they both heard a soft voice almost inaudibly whispering around the corner. Corbin began to inch his way to the edge of the corner but Nikki grabbed his arm pulling him back towards her. He stared deeply into her fear-stricken eyes knowing full well that his eyes too betrayed his bravado. They recognized the voice even though they had no idea what she was murmuring on about…Kara was around the corner.

The couple concurrently rounded the corner. In the middle of the hallway, approximately twenty feet from them, Kara was kneeling, her arms wrapped around an unseen child – the child's arms wrapped around Kara's neck. The curly, dark brown hair draped over Kara's shoulder clashed with the woman's straight blonde hair. Kara rocked back and forth humming an unknown melody.

"Kara?" Nikki spoke her friend's name softly.

"I told you I saw someone," Kara said flatly.

"Looks like you were right, Kara," Corbin answered. "Are you OK?"

"You shouldn't be out here without a hall pass," Kara replied.

"Kara," Nikki said – a bit unsure of her friend's off-the-wall statement, "that doesn't make any sense. Why don't you come back here where we are?"

Kara released her protective embrace and stood up sluggishly turning towards her friends, her hand now locked tightly around the young girl's hand. As Kara faced them, the couple could see a small girl, in her dirty blue school outfit with a ragged hall monitor's sash draped over one shoulder. The girl languidly raised her head; her brown hair fell away exposing her dead rotting face and sinister hematic eyes.

"Move Kara!" Corbin yelled as he pointed his gun towards the undead child.

Kara staggered and fell to one knee as she continued to hold the zombie girl's hand. She turned her head towards the child exposing two child-sized bite marks on her neck and face. "It's fine," Kara whispered to the undead girl. "They are the friends I told you about…" Dark viscous blood crept down the left side of Kara's neck; her life slowly draining away with each erratic pump of her heart. The zombie juvenile stared blankly towards Corbin and Nikki.

"No!" Nikki screamed as she advanced towards Kara. Corbin restrained his distraught wife by her shoulders; she didn't fight him – she knew there was nothing she or anyone else could do to save Kara.

Loud crashing from a room on the left side of the hallway that sounded like desks being knocked over snapped Corbin back to attention. The scuffling of feet sliding across the tiled floor made the hair on Nikki's neck stand up. The couple stared at the slightly opened entryway leading into the classroom. The flimsy door violently swung outwards, almost detaching itself from the hinges, as a colony of undead children in matching blue school uniforms poured into the hallway. Angry, feral growls and moans erupted from their bloated desecrated faces.

"Run, Nikki!" Corbin screamed.

The duo glanced briefly in the direction of Kara for one final time as they turned running around the corner heading for the exit. Nikki slipped on some of the loose-leaf paper strewn on the floors crashing to the ground sliding head first into the wall between the principal's office and the teacher's lounge. The gaggle of undead school children descended upon Nikki's outstretched body. Two of the children grabbed her ankles but she furiously kicked them away.

Corbin stopped, spun around and fired off his entire clip of ammunition. Four of the ten rounds found a home wedged deep into the craniums and necks of the soulless terrors. He sprinted back to his wife and helped her to her feet. The smell of stinking zombie flesh crowded the hallway; the nauseating stench was unbearable. Both covered their mouths as they reached the doors leading outside to the van – the zombie gang mere seconds behind them.

The couple, barely slowed by the fathomless snow, quickly reached the van. Corbin swung open the driver's side door and Nikki dove through to the passenger seat; Corbin leapt into the seat bashing his head against the low roofline. Momentarily dazed, he fumbled with the keys trying to insert them into the ignition; Nikki steadied his hand and they both started the van. The van danced back and forth as Corbin again tried to free the behemoth from the icy ruts.

The undead school children surrounded the van scratching and clawing on the sheet metal and windows. One of the larger zombie pre-teens climbed onto the hood of the van and began ramming his fists and head into the windshield trying to touch the human flesh within. Nikki watched in horror as the young dead boy's decaying flesh splattered across the windshield with each successive blow. She saw more children coming from the school building. *No!* She thought to herself. *Those were not children; they were zombies – undead corpses undeserving the label of children.*

The van's futile struggle for traction finally paid off as tiny zombie bodies fell underneath the tires; the massive wheels gripped the rotting child flesh underneath propelling the van from its icy confinement to the middle of the street. Corbin struggled briefly with the steering wheel but regained control of the vehicle. The large zombie boy held onto the windshield wipers; his thick grayish-yellow saliva dripping from his mouth and freezing onto the windshield. Corbin swerved from side-to-side finally discarding the unwanted passenger; the airborne undead boy crashed sideways into a drooping street sign – the force of the impact eviscerating the tiny monster.

And then there were two…

• *January 14, 2014: Tuesday, 3:22 AM – a parking lot outside a small Methodist Church, Danbury, Connecticut …*

"Where are we?" Corbin asked as he pushed aside a blanket covering his face.

"Connecticut," Nikki replied.

Corbin had taken a turn for the worse after their hasty exit from Pennsylvania. Nikki had taken over driving duties before departing the Keystone State. Corbin had tried to navigate for her from the passenger seat, but he was exhausted and couldn't focus. They passed quietly through New Jersey and New York while he slept on the couch-like back seat. Nikki had taken frequent breaks to hydrate her husband and feed him soup whenever he was conscious.

This evening, like the past few nights -Nikki had been unable to sleep. The traumatic, unnecessary death of Kara coupled with the ailing health of her husband kept her from any significant amounts of rest. He lay next to her shivering the entire night even though he was thoroughly wrapped in winter clothing and blankets. His fever had ebbed and flowed the past three days, but still whatever his immune system was fighting kept him delirious and strung out.

"Go back to sleep, babe," Nikki said as she draped her arm over his chest. "We'll be back on the road in a few hours." She rubbed his soft graying beard; it had taken her a good bit of time to get used to seeing him with the facial hair – she could barely remember what his clean-shaven face looked like.

Corbin nodded off into a dreamless sleep.

- *January 18, 2014: Saturday, 10:52 AM – parked behind an abandoned service station off of Interstate-95, Portsmouth, New Hampshire …*

Corbin sat up; his back ached from the lumpy backseat. Something had stirred him from his fitful rest. *What was that noise?* The van was not moving and strangely silent. He drank deeply from the canteen that had been placed by his feet. He glanced quickly around the van but his wife was not inside.

"Nikki? Nikki!" Corbin yelled as he stood up. His legs complained from lack of use over the past week; needles of pain shot up and down his legs as the blood and muscles struggled to react as commanded. He hobbled to the side door balancing himself on the middle row seats; he slid open the bay door stepping out into the cold morning air.

"I'm over here," Nikki replied just loud enough for him to hear from her position at the front of the van. She motioned for Corbin to get lower to the ground as he approached her. She pointed towards a small cadre of men in camouflaged uniforms holed up underneath an overpass.

"What's going on?"

"The van was overheating so I pulled over to refill the radiator," she replied. "You should be resting – not out here in the cold."

"What's going on down there?"

Corbin counted twelve men dressed similarly in tattered camouflage fatigues. They were hooting and hollering as they taunted a man, a woman and a slender teenage girl that huddled behind one of the giant columns supporting the overpass. Corbin couldn't make out what was being said but he knew the man on his knees was pleading for the lives of his wife and daughter.

Two of the soldiers separated from the group moving towards the mother. She and her daughter dashed around the column just out of arm's reach of the men. The father stood up from his kneeling position as he slugged one of the soldiers. The other soldier swung the butt of his gun smashing it into the back of the man's head… he fell to the ground in a semi-conscious fetal position. Three more soldiers began jumping around laughing and taunting the family. The father reached out towards his wife and daughter but watched helplessly as the soldiers grabbed the mother and daughter dragging them across the rough pavement to the other side of the opposite support column.

"Let's go," Nikki said as she turned away from the disgusting scene playing out below. "We can't do anything for them."

• *January 20, 2014: Monday, 1:47 PM – Bicentennial Park, Augusta, Maine …*

The persnickety van continued its relentless protest as Nikki maneuvered through the empty streets of Maine's capital city. Continued pit stops along the way to baby the radiator impeded their headway to Mount Hope. The van had been pushed well past its breaking point and through sheer happenstance the duo was able to glean a few more precious miles out of the antiquated vehicle.

However, Fate had apparently decided that the old van's final resting place would be this local state park just off the main thoroughfare.

"That's it," Nikki announced. She threw her hands into the air as the idle van coasted slowly to a complete stop next to a medium-sized stone statue of one of the city's founding fathers.

"There are no other markings on the map," Corbin replied from the passenger side seat. He had been feeling a bit better but his weakened body ached constantly. "I guess James must have figured that once we made it this far, we would just follow the street signs."

"Let's grab all the supplies we can carry," Nikki remarked. "We'll get out and move towards Bangor on foot. Maybe we'll find another car or something…" She didn't want to overtax her husband's enfeebled body but she knew it wasn't safe to stay out in the open either. "We'll rest whenever you need to."

They layered many levels of clothing and stuffed other items such as food, water and ammunition into duffle bags and backpacks. They piled all of their bounty on the ground on the passenger side of the van. While they tried to take only needed items, when they inspected the massive load of supplies – they knew there was no way to take all of the items with them.

"You know we can't take all of this stuff," Corbin said.

"I've got an idea," Nikki smiled wryly. "Get the tool box from the back of the van and meet me up front. See if we have any twine or rope back there as well."

Corbin fished around in the back of the van until he found the old toolbox and some rope. He walked to the front of the van where Nikki had already popped open the hood. He placed the toolbox and twine on the ground and watched his wife. She ferreted out a hefty sized wrench and went to work loosening the bolts holding the hood in place. After thirty grueling minutes of wrestling with the rusted bolts, the thin metal hood lay on the ground.

She attached a rope to each end of the bolt arms that once held the hood into place. Nikki dragged the makeshift sled to the pile of goods and loaded it up with Corbin's help. The hood slid effortlessly across the packed snow as the duo headed northeast towards Mount Hope.

Chapter 30

- *January 22, 2014: Wednesday, 1:14 AM – Mount Hope Research Facility, Bangor, Maine third floor research station room 301…*

Obadiah and Theo again worked through the evening into the early hours of the following day. They had stumbled upon a new variation of an old version of their serum that had promising initial results. The rest of the scientists would venture into the lab about six hours from now to assist in developing the *"cure"* should it pan out. An extensive set of testing needed to be performed; the new formula had to be put through rigorous complicated trials to determine its potential for destroying the infected masses of the outside world. Additional tests meant bringing in the undead from beyond the fence – an always dangerous course of action.

It had been proposed, almost mandated by some of the community, that the testing should take place outside the facility to reduce the risk to the inhabitants. Many of the more vocal inhabitants, largely the overly zealous of Destin's congregation, felt that the risks of such experimentation severely outweighed the potential rewards. The scientists had argued that the request to move the operation bordered on impossible since the testing had to be done in a controlled environment. Such a venue was currently only provided for by using the lab of the main facility. A compromise was reached that a new building would be constructed and all science equipment would be moved thereto.

The new building, referred to as the *"Annex"*, had been planned to be built outside the fenced in area, but after further considerations, the Annex would be built within the fence in the southeast corner– a good distance from the main facility. The foundation of the new structure had been poured earlier at the start of the week, but it would take another six to eight weeks before the medium-sized construc- tion would be fully functional. In the post-zombie world, complex architectural designs were impossible to duplicate without the CAD programs used by architects of the past. Thus, the building would be fairly straightforward but construction would be slow going.

With a community of old folks and children, the sparse labor pool could provide only minimal time each week for building the Annex. Compounding the build time was the fact that supplies such as wood, nails, concrete and tools had to be scavenged from outside the complex. These excursions were dangerous; braving the *"outer lands"* ran the risk of people being infected or even alerting hordes of the undead to the existence of the complex. Each successive trip over the course of the past many months had exhausted close by resources forcing each subsequent trip farther and farther out from the safe zone.

The door behind Obadiah opened but the old man focused on the specimen underneath the powerful microscope. He had carved a piece of flesh from one of the zombies late last night. He adeptly injected a tiny amount of the new formula into the skin cells to watch the results. Soon the fleshy cells were drawn to the serum like moths to a flame. As the old scientist watched, the cells began to rupture and dissolve. The old man was pleased.

Craig walked through the door rubbing his eyes. As he passed by Obadiah, he gently patted the elder man on his back but continued on to his workstation next to Theo. Theo had looked up briefly when Craig first entered the room. Their friendship had bettered over the past few months, but Theo felt as if Craig still hated him for the night that Julie died. Theo knew, even though Craig had dismissed his earlier suppositions, that Craig still harbored great anger at him.

"You're in early today," Theo noted.

"Yeah, I couldn't sleep. I guess I'm excited to see if the new serum plays out like we think it will."

Obadiah entered his findings into his small laptop computer. Over thirty different serums had been developed since the science group had started down the path to eradicate the zombies. It became readily apparent after the first few rounds of testing that it would be easier to destroy the infected instead of trying to find a vaccine for the remaining humans. Just over six months of data and tests had led the group to where they were today. Many serums never panned out past the initial theory stage. As the application crunched numbers in the background, the old man minimized the program exposing his well-organized desktop. He clicked a folder named "Citizens of Mount Hope" and a small document opened up.

The document outlined a three page list of everyone that had arrived and/or died at the complex over the past nine months. Some had died in the early months before the fence was erected and others were scientists that had died during the initial zombie trials. Obadiah had been here since the beginning and had welcomed all the new comers and shed tears for all of those that had died. He felt as if it was his duty to maintain some sort of records of the events and people that passed through this makeshift community. The old man, lost briefly in the past, failed to hear Craig calling out his name.

"How're you doing over there, Obadiah?" Craig inquired louder and for a third time.

"I want the two of you to take over the Friday status reports for me," the old man said without answering or acknowledging the previously posed question.

"Is everything OK?" Theo asked.

Both he and Craig were worried about the old man's health. Obadiah had continued to work in the lab even though he fought through one major cold after another. The inexperienced onsite doctors had advised Obadiah to rest but he had waved them off. He was eventually convinced to take some medication that helped to reduce the violent coughs so that he could continue his work. Obadiah felt the medicine was wasted on him and should be saved for real emergencies.

The old man took out his handkerchief and coughed into it. He wiped his mouth noting the now ever present minute amounts of blood. He quickly wiped the corner of his mouth and stuffed the cloth into his back pocket. He cleared his throat and addressed the two younger men.

"I'm fine. Stop worrying about me. I just need a little more rest here and there." The old man stood up and stretched his aching back. "I'm going to lie down. Wake me if anything develops." Obadiah picked up his laptop and walked over to Craig handing him the device. "I think you'll be pleased at what you see. We can discuss the results after my nap." The old man turned and exited the room.

- *January 22, 2014: Wednesday, 9:01 AM – Mount Hope Research Facility, Bangor, Maine – the roof of the main complex…*

Major Pavlik walked along his normal route while on sniper patrol methodically going from one corner of the roof to the next until he had made the full rotation. At each corner he would spend a few minutes inspecting the area around the fence to get a quick count of zombies. If too many of them had piled up, they would need to be cleared out. So far it appeared that only the east section had any considerable pile up; the west and south sections were clear. Many of the undead paraded about the hillside but only a handful ever ventured close to the fence. *Maybe they recognized the danger of being too close?*

The north section of the fence was built into the hillside that continued upwards into the sky another five to six hundred feet above the base; the total height of the large hill measured about eight hundred feet. The wooded area above the main complex at the summit had been cleared out more than half a year ago. Very rarely had any undead climbed the other side of the hill to work their way down to the facility, but it had happened before. Major Pavlik constantly reminded his young troops to monitor the north section of the fence.

The south section of the fence served as the main entry point into Mount Hope. Two colossal steel double gates, barred from the inside, stood as silent sentries guarding the research facility. On the inward side of the fence, in the southwest corner, a small brick structure stood alone. This mediocre edifice was used as a staging area to house new visitors.

Through a series of unfortunate circumstances, early in the post-zombie age, the founding members of Mount Hope had unknowingly allowed a group of infected humans directly into the complex. During that long ago evening, two of the visitors that had survived a zombie attack prior to their arrival hid their wounds when they entered Mount Hope. Their wounds dire, the pair succumbed to the zombie infection and died. The undead duo arose in the pre-dawn hours attacking some of the residents while they slept; the two newcomers were killed along with seven of their victims.

Going forward from that incident, new arrivals were sequestered into the *"Box"* for upwards of a week as tests were run against them. Every group of new arrivals serving a tour in the Box vehemently opposed the unlawful incarceration. However, they were soon convinced of the merits of the procedure and the good faith of the community. Those being held were extended as many creature comforts as possible to make their stay in the Box livable. Once given the all clear by the scientists and doctors, the new arrivals would be allowed inside the main facility with free reign of the property and all the privileges of the established tenants.

Major Pavlik crouched down on the rooftop as he probed the landscape – something in the distance had caught his attention. He raised his rifle peering through the powerful scope. Approaching from the south, a man and woman arduously trekked towards the hillside community. The dark haired man in the distant landscape, sporting a thick gray streaked beard, carried an overstuffed backpack slung over his shoulders; he pulled a rusty sled behind him packed with full duffle bags. His companion, a woman, carried a duffle bag at her side – its dingy white strap draped across her chest; her shoulder length red hair flowed in the cold morning breeze from beneath a dark blue knitted cap. Major Pavlik could see what appeared to be a pink blanket protruding slightly from one of the woman's bags. Of more importance, the sniper could see that both were armed, the man toted a rifle attached to his backpack and the woman a large caliber handgun at her side.

Major Pavlik walked over to the metal staircase leading down to the ground. Patchy ice had made the stairs quite slick but he traversed them with ease; the rubberized soles of his boots gripped each stair confidently. As he descended the final stair, he walked around the corner to a group of five soldiers huddled together for warmth around a fire burning within an old oil barrel. He tapped a young soldier on her shoulder nodding for her to take his place on the roof. She saluted and moved up the stairs.

Major Pavlik addressed the four remaining soldiers doling out orders to each individual. "We have visitors on the horizon. Private Robinson - you go inside and inform Obadiah. Atkins – prepare the Box. Jimenez and McCree – you two come with me."

• *January 22, 2014: Wednesday, 9:35 AM – a field on the outskirts of the Mount Hope Research Facility, Bangor, Maine …*

"I need to rest," Corbin said as he rubbed his hands together for warmth.

"We are so close," Nikki responded as she pointed towards the fenced off area in the distance. "Look over there. I'm sure they've seen us by now. It's just a little bit farther, baby." Nikki feared that if they didn't make contact with Mount Hope soon, that she would lose the last person in the world that she loved.

Corbin knew they were close, but he still sat down on the small sled using the duffle bags to cushion his exhausted body. They had been on foot for nearly two days since the van broke down. Sure they were a few hundred yards from their destination, but his body needed to rest and he didn't have the energy to push forward without a brief respite – the building would still be there after he caught his breath.

BLAM!! BLAM!! BRRAPPT!! BRAPPT!! BRAPPT!!

Nikki and Corbin both ducked down behind the overloaded sled. They recognized the small arms fire coming from the building nestled against the hillside. The couple piled the duffle bags and the baggage they carried up into a large mound on the sled and crouched behind. Corbin pulled back the bolt action on his rifle ensuring the bullet was chambered. Nikki spun the silver chamber of the revolver around checking her ammunition.

BLAM!! BLAM!! BRRAPPT!! BRAPPT!! BRAPPT!!

Corbin leaned his back against the duffle bag barrier covering his mouth with the back of his hand as he coughed. A look of concern crossed his face. *Had they come this far only to be killed before reaching their final destination?* They were sitting ducks out in the open field – nowhere to run. He glanced at Nikki as she peeked around the edges of the sled towards the facility. She saw a group of three men that had exited the gated area…she also saw that the men had not been shooting at them but clearing a path through some huddled up zombies at the entrance. She watched as the men decapitated the downed zombies with their machetes.

"Listen, Nikki – I don't have the energy to run. I can give you enough time to make a decent getaway but you have to go now." Corbin looked at the beautiful woman crouched next to him thinking of how their life could have been so different if it wasn't for the fucking zombies.

"They weren't shooting at us," she began. "They were clearing away some of the undead from their gates." She peeked back around the barrier and the military men were less than one hundred yards from them. She was a bit hesitant based on their recent exposure to the other military outfits that they had run across as they plodded through the New England states.

"Just be ready for anything," he replied.

The couple lay waiting in silence. They knew the trio of soldiers were close, they could hear their feet on the crunchy snow covered ground; the footsteps stopped. A symphony of silence permeated the small patch of land as both groups tried to anticipate the next actions of the opposing group. If they were actors in an old western movie depicting a cowboy showdown, tumbleweeds might have pirouetted through, but alas – this was no movie; both sides clutched their weapons at the ready.

"My husband is sick," Nikki yelled breaking the silence. "He needs help. We mean you no harm."

"My name is Martin Pavlik – we mean you no harm. We are lowering our weapons and ask you to do likewise."

Both groups, reluctantly but honestly, brought low their weapons. Nikki stood up and assisted Corbin to his feet. Introductions were made; the two groups advanced towards the complex. Private McCree tugged the overloaded sled behind him. Within moments, they arrived to the southern gate. No zombies obstructed their paths; the remaining onsite soldiers had cleared away the jetsam of the undead. An old bearded man wearing a cowboy hat along with four others waited outside the gated area anticipating the arrival of the new guests.

"I'm Obadiah," the old man said stepping forward. "These are my friends: Craig, Mandy, Theo and Destin."

"I'm Nikki and this is my husband, Corbin. He's not well. We need your help and have traveled a long way to this place…this is Mount Hope, isn't it?"

"It is, my dear," Obadiah spoke. "You are safe here."

Chapter 31

- *January 22, 2014: Wednesday, 10:02 AM – Mount Hope Research Facility, Bangor, Maine …*

M ajor Pavlik gave the signal and two of his soldiers within the gates grabbed each of the massive chain link doors. The soldiers pulled opposite each other and the doors opened wide allowing the new visitors to enter inside the community. Obadiah and the other four residents followed closely behind the new arrivals. Two of the three onsite doctors waited with their limited supplies to treat the guests if need be.

"Hi, I'm Mandy and this is my husband Craig and our friend Theo." Both men nodded as their names were called out.

"I'm Obadiah and this young man over here is our pastor – Destin."

"Welcome," Destin said. "I'm glad the Lord has led you to our humble community."

"You've already met Major Pavlik," Obadiah continued. "He's head of security and I'm sure in due time you will meet his security detail and the rest of our extended family."

"You are most kind," Nikki replied. "As I mentioned outside the gates, we've come a long way and my husband is quite ill."

BLAM!! BLAM!!

Two shots rang out from the opposite side of the main facility. Corbin grabbed Nikki and pulled her lower to the ground. He reached for the handgun at his wife's side, but the clasp kept the weapon in place.

"It's OK," Mandy said reassuringly. "You'll get used to that. Our on duty snipers clear out the zombies on the outside of the fence when they get too clumped up."

Obadiah motioned for the two young doctors to move forward. Both approached the new guests and they introduced themselves; the young man was Winston Jeffries and the woman was named Ashley Cooper. Winston put down his satchel of medicines and tonics as he inspected Corbin. Ashley began to examine Nikki but Nikki stepped back slightly.

"I'm fine, please treat my husband first," she said.

"It's our way…our procedure to thoroughly check out all new arrivals to our facility," Theo stated matter-of-factly. "Then you will spend three days in the Box undergoing various tests and checkups."

"What?" Corbin and Nikki apprehensively questioned in unison.

BLAM!! BLAM!!

"Damn it, Theo," Craig said angrily. "You could be a bit more tactful, don't you think?"

Theo just shrugged his shoulders. He hadn't misstated anything. In fact, he felt as if he presented the standard routine quite clearly. New arrivals spent time in the Box. While in the Box you'd be taken care of but with the understanding that certain tests had to be run like blood tests. He spent his time in the Box without complaints. The system was logical. Why new arrivals objected to the routine baffled him.

"Come, follow me," Obadiah said soothingly. "Let me show you what our residents lovingly refer to as the 'Box'."

Obadiah walked slowly over the uneven ground; his advancing age clearly evident. Corbin held Nikki's hand as they followed the old man. Major Pavlik dismissed his soldiers to return to their duties and he walked towards the Box. Craig and Mandy followed behind the military man. Theo stood contemplating his remaining tasks for the day. Destin felt an opportunity to minister might be at hand.

"Hello, Theo," Destin said cheerfully. "Will we see you at tonight's service?"

"No."

"You're a very stubborn man, Theo. I like the challenge."

"There's no challenge here, preacher. I have been abundantly clear over the passing months, haven't I? I'm not interested in your fairy tales nor do I believe in your God or any god for that matter."

"He believes in you, Theo."

Theo turned and walked away from Destin. The young scientist had an annoying habit (at least that is what others had told him) where he would callously disengage from conversations that he no longer had interest in - like someone had just flipped a switch from *ON* to *OFF*. In regards to this persistent conversation with Destin - he had more important things to worry about than his eternal soul. It seemed pretty evident to him that if all the God hoopla existed then by logical deduction – the folks stuck here with the flesh-eating zombies must already be in Hell.

- *January 22, 2014: Wednesday, 11:11 AM – The Box, Bangor, Maine …*

Corbin and Nikki cautiously inspected the inside of the Box. There were two small rooms joined by a common area. A bathroom and shower occupied the east side of the building. A small, black freestanding fireplace sat on a stone hearth in the center of the common room. The four windows, one in each bedroom and two on either side of the main door were barred with thick wrought iron rods. Obadiah carefully watched his new wards and felt their concern as they eyed the bars.

"It's not a prison, my friends," the old patriarch commented. "It's for our protection. You must understand that."

"What about the tests?" Nikki asked.

"Mostly observational in nature," Ashley answered. "There will be a few blood tests over the next three days. Once you are cleared - meaning no zombie infection found - then you will no longer be required to live in the Box."

"She's correct," Winston chimed in. "You'll be a full-fledged member of our society with all the rights and freedom of movement as everyone else."

"Again, welcome to our humble home," Obadiah said. "Our doctors here will treat you for your flu-like symptoms and will monitor you for the next three days. I must leave now and return to my work in the lab."

Mandy and Craig said their goodbyes and left the small enclosure. Ashley provided some medication to Corbin for his cough and slight fever and something to break up the mucus and phlegm deep within his chest. Winston took blood samples from the couple and labeled them *"Day 1, Test 1"* before he too departed the Box.

Ashley left after writing some notes for Corbin to follow regarding the pills she left for him. Major Pavlik was the last one standing at the entrance.

"There will be at least one guard posted here twenty four hours a day," the Major stated as he closed the door behind him bolting the door from the outside.

The couple had traveled through many states and lost friends and family but they had finally made it. Mount Hope. Both of them sat on the edge of the bed in the first small room. Nikki wiped sweat from her husband's brow as he drank cool water that had been left on the table for them. He felt much better than he had in weeks. Both were a bit hesitant at the new arrangement but trusted the old man and his kind words. In three days they would be officially part of the hillside community.

"We did it," Corbin said after a few moments. "We made it."

"Yes we did. They seem like nice people. Let's get these socks and shoes off of you so you can lie down. I'll see about building us a fire."

• *January 23, 2014: Thursday, 10:45 AM – The Box, Bangor, Maine …*

"I miss her so very much," Nikki said. "I miss all of them."

"I do too," Corbin said as he sat down on the bed next to his wife. He laid his arm across her shoulders and pulled her close to his body.

"Our baby girl is gone. Kara is gone. James is gone. It's not fair…"

Corbin couldn't respond. He rocked gently back and forth with his beautiful wife. They both felt guilty for being alive. Each of them was unable to reconcile why they had made it this far. They were grateful to be alive even with the world spiraling quickly out of control around them. A deep emptiness welled up within them – they knew full well that the hollow feeling would be with them until their dying day. One doesn't lose that many loved ones without paying a hefty toll.

A knock at the door caused both to jump slightly. *Was it time for the second day's tests already?* Nikki inched away from her husband. As she stood wiping her eyes, she bent over and kissed him gently on the forehead. He grabbed her hands and pressed them against his lips. He knew they would make it – no matter what.

Another knock echoed throughout the tiny structure and Nikki walked to the door. She stood by the door until the bolt on the other side was slid out of place. A key jiggled in the lock and soon the door opened. A soldier stepped back to the side of the entryway and Nikki recognized the three people standing in front of her…she didn't remember their names but they had greeted them yesterday.

"Hi," Nikki said cautiously.

"Do you mind if we come in?" Mandy asked. She could tell Nikki had forgotten their names but that was OK – it was easy to remember the names of the newcomers, not so easy for them to remember everyone else's name – that took a while. "I'm Mandy, by the way. This is my husband Craig and our friend Theo."

"Come in," Corbin said from his seated position.

"We wanted to talk with you guys," Craig began. "We want to share our experiences here with you. Let you know how we got used to the place and the people."

For the rest of the day, except when Winston and Ashley showed up to take blood tests, the two groups discussed how they got to Mount Hope, the losses they encountered and the feelings of guilt as survivors.

Even Theo opened up some to discuss his take on everything that had happened since the first zombie appearance. Craig, Mandy and Theo left late that evening after having dinner with their new friends.

Friday, the same scene played out sans Theo. Theo had some work to finish in the lab and couldn't rejoin the group. Plus he had already shared his thoughts and feelings – he didn't want things to get out of hand and turn into an after school special. He had important tests to focus on with Obadiah and asked that Craig apologize for him to Corbin and Nikki.

- *January 25, 2014: Saturday, 5:31 PM – Destin's study, first floor of the main complex Bangor, Maine …*

"It's not safe, Destin. It never has been."

Todd Cooper and four other members of Destin's congregation had interrupted the young pastor as he finished up his final notes for the upcoming Sunday service. The men had complained previously about the zombie trials taking place within the fenced in area - backhanded comments and snide remarks mostly at least until this evening. The men had surrounded Destin hoping to get his backing for their complaints. With his buy-in, they could approach the community and force the scientists to take their testing outside of Mount Hope – away from their families.

"Todd, I understand your concerns," Destin replied. "I believe that those men and women researching an end to this undead plague have no intention to endanger our lives."

"We will not help them build the Annex," Todd continued. "There are others of us that feel the same way but they are too afraid to speak up."

"Why are they afraid to make themselves known?" Destin looked confused. "We've never stifled anyone's right to speak their mind. Obadiah has done his utmost to ensure the safety of their tests. Do you honestly think he would needlessly endanger his friends and family?"

The men that had entered the small study with Todd mumbled amongst themselves; Todd stood with his arms crossed. Private Jake Robinson stood silently at the back of the group watching the young preacher. The man had his rifle strapped to his back since he was going on sniper duty in less than an hour. Destin didn't care for the guns but realized that the community needed this type of firepower to keep them safe from the zombies; the young pastor did feel slightly offended that the soldier brought his gun inside the study.

Destin closed his notes and stood up walking over to the concerned man standing on the other side of his desk. The preacher calmly placed his hand on Todd's shoulder trying to appease the agitated spokesman of the group. Todd brushed off Destin's hand and stepped back a few paces; the man was quite upset that he couldn't get through to Destin – couldn't make him see how dangerous the scientist's tests had become.

"Destin – people are afraid. They're scared. Only a very small part of the community, namely those Godless scientists, supports these tests. The vast majority of your congregation and the community at large do not understand these tests or why our lives have to be risked each and every time a zombie is brought inside the safe zone."

"I understand your concerns, Todd, but I think that you are overreacting."

Todd shook his head and walked out; the rest of the men followed behind. Private Robinson looked back at the preacher; Destin felt emptiness in the man's brief gaze. The preacher felt that if Todd was in control of the group, that he could be reasoned with. Destin had always felt uncomfortable around Jake; with the unpredictable private intermixed with the group – Destin feared for the worst...

• *January 26, 2014: Sunday, 9:45 AM – The Box, Mount Hope ...*

A loud knocking at the door startled Nikki and Corbin. They had just finished breakfast and were sitting close to the fireplace to warm up. The previous night had been exceptionally cold and they had let the fire go out. Once again, a loud knock echoed through the small structure. Nikki stood up and went to the door. As she looked out, Obadiah, Ashley, Winston and at least half of the Mount Hope community waited outside.

"Yes?" she asked timidly.

"Your test results are completely clean except for a few nasty, but normal, germs in Corbin's system," Ashley stated.

"Welcome to your new home, my friends," Obadiah said as he hugged Nikki. The old man also hugged Corbin who was standing just behind his wife.

"All of your supplies that you came here with, plus some additional items are in the dormitory portion of the main complex," Winston said. "Someone will show you around and help you familiarize yourself with the general layout."

"Today, the Mount Hope community becomes two members stronger," Obadiah said proudly.

Chapter 32

- *March 6, 2014: Thursday, 3:53 PM – the Annex - Mount Hope Research Facility, Bangor, Maine …*

The month of February sped by quicker than the time it takes to turn the page of a familiar novel. March arrived in full force promising the return of spring. After being cleared by the doctors, Corbin had spent the last two weeks of February working in the garden; it was slow, easy work that allowed him to contribute at his own pace. Nikki poured blood, sweat and tears into helping the limited labor force build the Annex. She felt liberated; she had never really made anything with her hands before now. She felt wonderful that through her hard work she was able to give back in a meaningful way to the community that had taken them in.

Today, the last bit of touch-up work would mark the end of the long project. Somehow, the team had completed the Annex by the end of the first week of March - ahead of original estimates. The shortened timeframe resulted mostly from the fact that the final dimension of the building was approximately sixty percent of the original design. The scientists - with help from some members of the community - transferred computers, printers and other equipment to the Annex. Running and maintaining a consistent power supply to the building proved to be the most difficult task in finally establishing a working environment for the scientists.

The holding facility of the Annex was tested immediately to assuage the fears of the community. The back part of the building was built directly into the southeast corner of the fence; a sliding door on a pulley system could be opened from inside the building to allow movement to and from. This allowed the undead to be ushered in from outside the safe zone, through the opening of the fence directly into the holding cell without ever stepping one rotten foot into the safe zone.

Five zombies – the max that the containment area had been designed to safely hold – were enticed to enter the confinement area. Once the beasts entered the room, the sliding door dropped behind them. The undead specimens raked and clawed their deformed hands and teeth against the thick walls. The monsters relentlessly bashed their bodies against the substantial plastic viewing window. Like off rhythm drummers, the creatures beat their fists against the metal door that they had been forced through. The zombie dungeon functioned as anticipated; the designers had taken special precautions to ensure that nothing could break out of the enclosure.

- *March 9, 2014: Sunday, 2:30 AM – the rooftop of the Main Complex - Mount Hope Research Facility, Bangor, Maine …*

"It's just going to be enough to scare them," Todd Cooper said softly. "I'll only let out a few of those creatures."

"What?" Winston Jeffries gasped loudly. He had grudgingly followed Todd to the top of the roof, but what he had just heard blew his mind. While he hated the fact that the scientist continually endangered the community – he had no idea of the true devious intentions of the two men standing beside him in the cold, dark hours of morning.

"Don't act so shocked," Private Jake Robinson chimed in. "We've tried over the past few months to reason with these people. Have you seen them respond to our concerns?"

"Yes," Winston answered. "They built the new Annex away from the main facility."

"That's bullshit, Winston and you know it," Jake said through clenched teeth. "That new building is still inside the fence."

"I won't be a part of this," Winston said calmly, belying his immense fear of repercussion from the two men. He began backing slowly towards the metal staircase leading to the ground level.

"You're in this with us till the end," Todd said as he grabbed the man by his shoulders.

"Get your hands off of me!" Winston yelled.

Jake moved behind the young doctor and cupped his hands over Winston's mouth to keep the frightened man from alerting others. The private pulled a stiletto from his belt and rammed the short dagger deep into Winston's left kidney. Winston struggled but the soldier was much too strong. Todd looked around nervously; this was not part of his plan, but he knew better than to cross Jake. The soldier jabbed the sharp knife deep into Winston's right kidney. Sticky, warm blood gushed out the man's back; the steamy life force escaped quickly barely visible in the starless night sky. Winston dropped to one knee and Jake ended the man's life with a quick, forceful twist of his neck; a morbid, dull snapping sound preceded the young doctor's limp body thudding to the ground.

"What the fuck, Jake?" Todd said as he looked around. "That was not part of the plan. We are so fucked…"

"Shut up!" Jake said as he backhanded Todd across the mouth. "You get your skinny ass down there and do your part."

Todd stepped over Winston's dead body and moved down the old metal staircase. He considered running and alerting everyone but knew Jake would gun him down. Things were not going as planned; he began to panic. *At no time during the past two weeks of planning did anyone ever mention anything about killing. Jake had overreacted. Winston could have been convinced to do his part but now it was too late.*

Todd crept along the poorly lit grounds of the safe zone and moved towards the southeast corner of the fence. His part of the plan was to open the confinement area of the Annex and allow a few straggler zombies into the courtyard of the main facility. Jake had guaranteed his complete control over the situation; he would easily be able to keep the zombies in check from his sniper position on the roof.

At the midway point to the Annex, Todd froze like a deer in headlights when he heard a loud whistle behind him. He turned back and saw Jake a few yards behind him. The soldier carried Winston's limp body slung callously over his right shoulder. Todd began to freak out, panicked sweat beaded up on his neck and fore-head as the soldier approached him.

"What are you doing?" Todd asked unable to look directly at Winston's lifeless body.

"I didn't tell you about this part of the plan," Jake said as he dropped the corpse to the ground like a sack of potatoes. "I knew you wouldn't go along with it."

"What do you mean?"

"We needed a volunteer casualty," Jake said with a sickening smile on his face. "So I volunteered old Winston here…"

"I'm not following you. I don't understand."

Jake shook his head and explained to Todd as he would to a five year old. "When you let the zombies out, they will need a victim. They will tear into Winston's body covering up the knife wounds. I will shoot the zombies dead. The gunfire will wake up everyone and they'll find that their secured *"zombie jail"* isn't so safe."

Jake picked up the body as he led the way to the westward facing outer wall of the Annex. No one patrolled the south gates at this time of the morning – Jake was intimately familiar with the schedules and routines of his fellow soldiers. No one was in the Box either. The shadowy courtyard hid their movements as if ashamed of what currently transpired within its enclosure. Jake propped Winston's dead body against the cold brick wall next to the fence. There was light coming from inside the Annex.

"I thought you said it would be empty," Todd's voice cracked as his nerves got the better of him.

"It is empty. Stop being such a bitch. I saw Obadiah and the last two scientists leave just before you and Winston climbed up to the rooftop."

Jake told the truth. He had done his due diligence in preparation for this moment. Over the past two weeks he watched the scientists leave the Annex between midnight and 2:00 AM on Sunday mornings. The building was empty. The two men had free reign of the facility to put their plan into motion. By the time the morning sunshine arrived, the deed would be done and the residents would fully recognize the danger of allowing the zombie filth to enter the safe zone.

The two men entered the Annex and worked their way back to the containment area. A large, thick window of Plexiglas that started waist high and continued upwards till almost touching the ceiling was nestled snuggly on the farthest wall. The men could not see anything past the plastic window – the lights were off. Todd found the light switch on the far left side of the window next to the cranking mechanism used to lift the outer garage-like door. The young man hesitated to flip the switch. Jake shoved the man sideways and flipped the switch upwards.

Three zombies lurched forward from the once dark room and pounded their heads and fists against the thick plastic. Jake stumbled backwards but caught himself before falling. The beasts screamed and babbled incoherently as they groped the slick window trying to reach the humans on the opposite side. Todd backed away beginning to hyperventilate; he was petrified – he had never really seen the monsters up close and personal like this. Their gray skin clung strangely to their faces and bodies, their eyes red and inflamed – Todd watched as the creatures broke off remaining rotten teeth as they chomped down fiercely on the window.

"Let's do this," Jake said as he began to crank open the garage door. Slowly the heavy door raised up inch by inch.

The undead continued to squeal and pound on the window. Todd stood frozen in fear. He watched as the door lifted; he could see a few more grotesque legs of zombies from the outside. Some without legs began to crawl under the half raised door. Jake struggled with the less-than-stellar mechanism but continued to raise the door – now three-fourths of the way fully raised.

"What the hell are you guys doing?"

Todd and Jake both turned towards the direction of the unanticipated voice. It was Obadiah standing just a few feet from them. The old scientist stood confused trying to piece together the scene playing out in front of him. Jake stopped cranking the door lever and pulled his pistol from his side holster pointing it at the old man.

"Woah!" Todd yelled as he stepped away from the soldier.

"What are you doing back here, old man?" Jake questioned.

"I forgot my laptop," the old man replied as he held up the slim black computer. "I think the appropriate question is what are you two doing in here?"

"Don't point that at Obadiah," Todd pleaded but was quickly rewarded with a pistol whipping blow to his mouth; he dropped to one knee as blood gushed from his split lip.

"Get over here, old man," Jake yelled as he motioned with his gun for Obadiah to line up next to the window.

Obadiah did as instructed. Jake pressed the cold steel barrel against the patriarch's wrinkled forehead; the old man closed his eyes as thoughts of how his name and contributions would look in his "Citizens of Mount Hope" document.

Todd had seen enough; the plan had veered way off course. He leapt from his crouched position grabbing Jake's pistol arm. The two men struggled fiercely. Todd punched and clawed the face of his partner in crime with his free hand; his other hand firmly clenching Jake's wrist keeping the pistol pointed away from him and Obadiah. Jake squeezed the trigger multiple times – the rounds fractured the Plexiglas – the zombies pounded against the aperture. Jake spun Todd around slamming him into the archaic garage door mechanism; the crank snapped off – the gaping mouth to the outside world slid open to its fullest extent.

Todd fell to his knees as blood poured from the gash in his side caused by the sharp metal handle. Obadiah moved forward to help Todd but Jake violently backhanded the septuagenarian to the cold hard floor. The soldier turned his attention to Todd and pointed his pistol at the man.

"Now, Todd – you are my second volunteer casualty…"

The window exploded behind Jake as filthy, rotten arms shot through the fissured plastic. He tried to break free but the beasts pulled him through to their side. Loud, almost cheering screams reverberated off the thick brick walls. More and more zombies poured in through the opening from the outside. They converged upon the human feast in front of them ripping his face off and gnawing on his fingers and legs. A deluge of undead poured through the window devouring the two other men in the tiny space as they crammed themselves like sardines into the small confines of the Annex. The mass of hungry creatures bullied their way through the doors and windows of the Annex and into the safe zone.

• *March 9, 2014: Sunday, 3:18 AM – the dormitory of the Main Complex - Mount Hope Research Facility, Bangor, Maine …*

"Wake up, Nikki," Corbin said forcefully as he gently shook his wife.

She barely opened her eyes. Corbin stood above her with a panicked look on his face; he was holding her winter clothes and shoes. Theo, Craig and Mandy stood behind him close to the door. All of them were fully dressed but their disheveled appearances told of their hasty preparations. Screams from the hallway coupled with gunfire from outside told Nikki all she needed to know before she even asked her first question.

"What's going on?" she asked groggily.

"We have to go now," Theo said as he looked out into the hallway.

Nikki sat up in bed as she tried to hold onto the last vestiges of the first peaceful dream that she had dreamt in almost a year. She felt around for her gun forgetting that she had tucked the weapon safely into the desk drawer across the room. Nikki dressed quickly with the aid of her husband. She walked to the lonely desk in the corner and grabbed her gun from the bottom drawer; the weapon slid perfectly into her waistband.

The group rushed through the hallway out of the main complex and into the frigid, uncaring morning air. Gunfire echoed from the rooftop behind them. The Annex engulfed completely in hot orange flames highlighted the horrifying scene. At least forty bodies of community members that Nikki would never get to meet lay in distorted, broken throws of death. The living dead roamed about the safe zone feasting on residents that were trying to escape. Dozens of stinking undead corpses that had been gunned down by snipers paved the way towards the south gates. The trampled vegetable garden faded into the bleak horizon…

Epilogue

- *March 15, 2014: Saturday, 8:32 AM – Room #2307, Langston Research Facility – St. Louis, Missouri …*

"There's still no response, sir."

"Keep trying, Andrea."

Andrea MacArthur and Dr. Clancy Ferguson sat staring at the empty inbox. No new messages from their *"sister"* facility in the northeast had them worried. There had been a few times before, over the past year, that communications had broken down between the two facilities - never more than two, maybe three days tops. It had now been just shy of a full week since their last interaction with Obadiah and his scientists.

"We don't even know if they're still alive…"

"Don't say that!" Dr. Ferguson snapped.

Andrea recoiled slightly, but that was the first thought that had come to her mind; she absently blurted it out. The rest of the small team had come to the same dire conclusion. Even Dr. Ferguson assumed the worst…whether or not he would ever admit it.

"I'm sorry, Andrea. I didn't mean to yell."

"It's OK."

"It's probably nothing. Maybe their computers are down? Maybe the satellite is out of synch? It could be anything." Dr. Ferguson's hollow words failed to convince Andrea (or even himself) that *"technical difficulties"* were to blame for the communication blackout. He didn't want to consider the very real possibility that his peers in Maine had suffered at the insatiable hands of the undead.

BING!!

The computer dinged loudly indicating a new message had arrived. Without his reading glasses, Dr. Ferguson had to lean forward to read the screen. To their surprise, the email message was not from Mount Hope. A high-priority message from the United Kingdom blinked in the inbox; the timestamp of the message indicated that it had been sent two days ago.

Andrea double clicked the message.

*** URGENT ***

March 13, 2014
11:45 PM

From: United Kingdom - Center for Disease Control
To: Langston Research Facility

RE: Z1N1 transmission

We now know that the first cases of the Z1N1 mutation resulted from a specific combination of the H1N1 vaccine, the actual H1N1 antibodies and the increased gamma radiation during the period from December 2012 thru February 2013.

This mutation took as long as two months to manifest itself, while in some cases, as little as two weeks. Patients suffered with severe flu-like symptoms until death occurred. Then the transformation to the *"post-trauma"* or *"zombie"* state happened within hours.

After the initial onset period, the Z1N1 pandemic spread by subcutaneous injuries. Most new cases resulting from bites or ingestion or exposure to copious amounts of infected fluids. The newly infected adults would die within an eight-to-ten hour window, depending on body mass and health. Children and teenagers took even less time.

Another shocking development, reported but not fully verified, is that the mutation can and has spread to non-human life. Additional research was in progress until our experts in the field confirmed a most heinous turn of events...

According to our research and calculations, the Z1N1 transmission has mutated once again, no longer requiring direct contact. Our working theory is that someone with tuberculosis or other respiratory disease must have been turned. Our worst fears have now been realized.

Z1N1 is now airborne...

Breinigsville, PA USA
18 November 2010
249536BV00003B/1/P